Best Stories and Humour of Herman Charles Bosman

Other works by and about Herman Charles Bosman

Mafeking Road and Other Stories: Anniversary Edition (1998)
Willemsdorp: Anniversary Edition (1998)
Cold Stone Jug: Anniversary Edition (1999)
Idle Talk: Voorkamer Stories: Anniversary Edition (1999)
Jacaranda in the Night: Anniversary Edition (2000)
Old Transvaal Stories: Anniversary Edition (2000)
The Rooinek and other Boer War stories (2000)
Verborge Skatte: Anniversary Edition (2001)
Seed-time and Harvest and Other Stories: Anniversary Edition (2001)
A Cask of Jerepigo: Anniversary Edition (2002)
Unto Dust and Other Stories: Anniversary Edition (2002)
My Life and Opinions: Anniversary Edition (2003)
Young Bosman: Anniversary Edition (2003)
Wild Seed: Anniversary Edition (2004)
Homecoming: Voorkamer Stories II: Anniversary Edition (2005)
Life Sentence: A biography of Herman Charles Bosman,
by Stephen Gray (2005)
The Complete Oom Schalk Lourens Stories (2006)
A Bosman Companion: from Abjaterskop to Zwingli,
by Craig MacKenzie & Tim Sandham (2011)
The Complete Voorkamer Stories (2011)

Best stories and Humour of Herman Charles Bosman

Chosen by
Craig MacKenzie
and
Stephen Gray

Human & Rousseau

First edition published as a set of two books,
Starlight on the Veld and *Recognising Blues*
with the overall title *Best of Bosman*, in 2001

Second edition published in this form in 2013
by Human & Rousseau
an imprint of NB Publishers
a division of Media24 Boeke (Pty) Ltd
Cover design by Mike Cruywagen
Set in 11.5 on 15 pt Times New Roman PS by Etienne van Duyker, Cape Town
Printed and bound by Paarl Media Paarl,
15 Jan van Riebeeck Drive, Paarl, South Africa

ISBN 978-0-7981-6370-5
ISBN 978-0-7981-6371-2 (epub)
ISBN 978-0-7981-6372-9 (mobi)

HERMAN CHARLES BOSMAN WAS BORN at Kuils River near Cape Town in 1905. In 1916 the family moved to the Transvaal, settling first in Potchefstroom and then, in 1918, in Johannesburg. After studying at the University of the Witwatersrand and Normal College, Bosman was posted as a young teacher to a farm school near Zwingli in the Marico District of what was then the Western Transvaal. It was there that he encountered a community rich in storytellers – raconteurs who could spin marvellous tales about the Boer War and other memorable events. He would later immortalise these figures in his own Oom Schalk Lourens character.

His stay in the Marico was abruptly terminated after he was arrested and convicted for the murder of his step-brother during a vacation at the family home in Johannesburg. Initially he was condemned to hang, but his sentence was commuted and he served four years in Pretoria Central Prison.

Upon his release in 1930 he embarked on a career as a journalist and began writing short stories. Among his earliest works were Oom Schalk Lourens tales, which he wrote steadily between 1930 and 1951, the year of his death. In 1950 he began the 'Voorkamer' sequence, and wrote some eighty of these pieces in all. He also sporadically wrote stories in which he spoke in his own voice as author; these have recently been collected as *Old Transvaal Stories* (2000). All three story modes are represented here.

Bosman died suddenly of heart failure in October, 1951. He saw only three of his works into print in his lifetime: *Jacaranda in the Night* (1947), *Mafeking Road* (1947) and *Cold Stone Jug* (1949), his prison memoir.

Starlight on the Veld

CONTENTS

PREFACE

THIS VOLUME HAS THE SIMPLE AIM of gathering the best of Bosman's stories – the most striking, the most moving, the most memorable. He wrote some 170 in all – around sixty Oom Schalks and eighty Voorkamer pieces, with another thirty miscellaneous stories written alongside these two main sequences. So when it came to gathering his best, there was never any question of making weight; on the contrary, the hardest part was deciding what to leave out.

An essay by Bosman (written in late 1944) on a return visit to the Marico heads the sequence, and this provides the reader with all of the contextual detail required to place the stories that follow. Unsurprisingly, the rest of the selection is dominated by Oom Schalk Lourens stories – fourteen in all, arranged in order of publication from 1930 to 1951 (which is also the span of Bosman's writing life). Four 'Voorkamer' pieces follow, and the volume closes with a further four stories in which Bosman uses an authorial narrator.

This roughly chronological sequence reveals that Bosman's story oeuvre is not characterised by tentative, rough beginnings, proceeding steadily towards ever-greater sophistication and technical accomplishment. While we may discern a degree of over-writing in "The Rooinek", for example, it is true to say that Bosman found his voice (or, perhaps more accurately, found a narrative voice in Oom Schalk) from the outset. Among his earliest ventures into fiction are "Makapan's Caves" (1930) and "The Rooinek" (1931) – both of them fine, strong stories with compelling narrative lines.

There is a long and venerable literary ancestry to the kind of 'oral-style' story Bosman adopted, stretching from Boccaccio and Chaucer in the fourteenth century to Irving, Twain, Harte and other American humorists more recently. South Africa itself has a tradition of yarn-spinning that can be traced back as far as the mid-nineteenth century and that takes in writers like W. C. Scully, J. Percy FitzPatrick, Perceval Gibbon and Pauline Smith. Through Oom Schalk, Bosman placed himself indisputably at the pinnacle of this style of storytelling in South Africa.

Although he continued to write Oom Schalks throughout his life, Bosman turned in his later years to the more technically challenging genre of the multi-voiced 'conversation' piece represented by his Voorkamer sequence. Bosman wrote these pieces in serialised form for the Johannesburg news weekly, *The Forum*. The series appeared under the rubric 'In die Voorkamer', and was clearly intended to provide a comic counterpoint to the more sober 'forum' of political commentary and opinion-pieces that constituted the staple of this liberal-left periodical. Bosman's stamina was remarkable: he wrote all of the eighty Voorkamer pieces in what would be the last eighteen months of his life, never once missing his weekly deadline.

The pieces take the form of conversations among the Marico farmers who gather in Jurie Steyn's voorkamer, which doubles as the local post office. Maintaining momentum and narrative thrust in the resultant mêlée of competing voices was more demanding than stage-managing Oom Schalk, and Bosman clearly relished the challenge. Although they are best read in sequence, where the unfolding larger story emerges from amidst the detail of each individual episode, some of the Voorkamer pieces can also be read to advantage as independent items. I have selected four such here.

Where Oom Schalk is situated in the early decades of the twentieth century (with recollections stretching as far back as the 1850s), the farmers who foregather in Jurie Steyn's voorkamer are contemporaneous with the date of publication of the stories (i.e. the 1950s), and, indeed, they frequently comment on current events – the Korean War, the escalation of the Cold War, and the development of modern technology. The most striking example in this respect is "Birth Certificate", which, notwithstanding its extremely funny moments, comments obliquely but scathingly on the passage of the infamous Population Registration Act through Parliament at the time.

The third category of Bosman's story oeuvre is represented by the last four stories in this selection. In these Bosman speaks in his own voice as a writer, and reflects humorously and self-ironically on the art of storytelling. One of the fascinations of Bosman's writing is his skill at smuggling artful, sophisticated commentary on the writing process itself into the apparently artless, homely form of the fireside tale. "The Affair at Ysterspruit" and "A Boer Rip van Winkel" return to the familiar Bosman subject matter of the Boer War, this time incorporating observations on the way he as a writer turns anecdote and folk history into moving fictional narrative.

"The Ox-riem" is not as well known as the other stories included here. It occurs as a tale within the novel fragment "Louis Wassenaar", and was not published until it appeared in Stephen Gray's compilation, *Bosman's Johannesburg* (1986). Bosman returned to the theme in "The Clay-pit", which also only appeared posthumously (in *Unto Dust*, Lionel Abrahams's 1963 edition of Bosman's tales). I have included the original version here as I think it deserves to be better known for its taut narrative structure and deep psychological exploration of thwarted desire.

The selection ends with the famous "Old Transvaal Story" (1948), a late Bosman story that, in its amusing reflections on the source of most of his stories (oral lore), loops back to the prefatory "Marico Revisited." The story is redolent of old, rural South African life: it is a distillation in many ways of hundreds of years of oral culture, of tales doing the rounds by word of mouth from tribal kraal to farm stoep to village bar. In the way it treats its rustic material, however, it is quintessentially modern, and it therefore stands on the cusp of the present era.

This last group of stories brings to the fore the metafictional tendency in much of Bosman's work. The preoccupation with how to tell a story (in evidence as far back as 1935 with "Mafeking Road"), the intertextual reference to other writers, and the mixing of modes (discursive, fictional) all illustrate Bosman's life-long fascination with the techniques of storytelling.

"Old Transvaal Story" is also interesting for its portentous qualities: by 1948 not only was the old Marico as Bosman knew it in 1925 fast disappearing, but the election victory of the National Party, which was to be followed by the banning of political parties, the introduction of racist legislation and the suppression of freedom of expression, would begin to erode the basis for the humanistic and romantic vision of Oom Schalk Lourens.

The stories gathered here startlingly reveal Bosman's temporal and thematic range. Thanks to Oom Schalk's incredible memory, Bosman was able to reflect ironically on the events of a century of South African history. In the years between the 1850s (when Oom Schalk first went on commando – see "Makapan's Caves") and the 1950s (when the later generation of farmers gather in Jurie Steyn's voorkamer), numerous wars between Dutch settlers and African tribesmen had taken place; two Anglo–Boer Wars had been fought; South Africa had achieved Union and had participated in the Great War; and the Depression and the war following it had been experienced.

Bosman's stories take in this entire sweep of history. His absorption in his backveld setting is thus cunningly deceptive: his characters may be rustics, but their backwoods canniness and their creator's ability to imbue them with timeless qualities mean that the stories they tell hold true for us today. Bosman's enduring popularity for over half a century is eloquent testimony to this. May this selection of his best help to sustain his popularity in the years to come.

Craig MacKenzie
Johannesburg, 2001

Marico Revisited

A month ago I revisited the Marico Bushveld, a district in the Transvaal to which I was sent, a long time ago, as a school-teacher, and about which part of the country I have written, in the years that followed, a number of simple stories which I believe, in all modesty, are not without a certain degree of literary merit.

There were features about the Marico Bushveld that were almost too gaudy. That part of the country had been practically derelict since the rinderpest and the Boer War. Many of the farms north of the Dwarsberge had been occupied little more than ten years before by farmers who had trekked into the Marico from the Northern Cape and the Western Transvaal. The farmers there were real Boers. I am told that I have a deep insight into the character of the Afrikaner who lives his life on the platteland. I acquired this knowledge in the Marico, where I was sent when my mind was most open to impressions.

Then there was the bush. Thorn-trees. Withaaks and kameeldorings. The kremetart-boom. Swarthaak and blinkblaar and wag 'n bietjie. Moepels and maroelas. The sunbaked vlakte and the thorn-tree and South Africa. Trees are more than vegetation and more than symbols and more than pallid sentimentality of the order of "Woodman, spare that tree" or "Poems are made by fools like me." Nevertheless, what the oak and the ash and the cypress are to Europe, the thorn-tree is to South Africa. And if laurel and myrtle and bay are for chaplet and wreath, thorns are for a crown.

The bush was populated with kudus and cows and duikers and steenbokkies and oxen and gemsbok and donkeys and occasional leopards. There were also ribbokke in the krantzes and green and brown mambas, of which hair-raising stories were told, and mules that were used to pull carts because it was an unhealthy area for horses. Mules were also used for telling hair-raising stories about.

And the sunsets in the Marico Bushveld are incredible things, heavily striped like prison bars and flamboyant like their kaffir blankets.

Then there were boreholes, hundreds of feet deep, from which water had to be pumped by hand into the cattle troughs in times of drought. And there was a Bechuana chief who had once been to London, where he had been received in audience by His Majesty, George V, a former English king: and when, on departing from Buckingham Palace, he had been questioned by the High Commissioner as to what form the conversation had taken, he had replied, very simply, this Bechuana chief, "We kings know what to discuss."

There were occasional visits from the Dutch Reformed Church predikants. And a few meetings of the Dwarsberg Debatsvereniging. And there were several local feuds. For I was to find that while the bush was of infinite extent, and the farms very many miles apart, the paths through the thorn-trees were narrow.

It was to this part of the country, the northern section of the Marico Bushveld, where the Transvaal ends and the Bechuanaland Protectorate begins, that I returned for a brief visit after an absence of many years. And I found, what I should have known all along, of course, that it was the present that was haunted, and that the past was not full of ghosts. The phantoms are what you carry around with you, in your head, like you carry dreams under your arm.

And when you revisit old scenes it is yourself, as you were in the past, that you encounter, and if you are in love with yourself – as everybody should be in love with himself, since it is only in that way, as Christ pointed out, that a man can love his neighbour – then there is a sweet sadness in a meeting of this description. There is the gentle melancholy of the twilight, dark eyes in faces upturned in a trancelike pallor. And fragrances. And thoughts like soft rain falling on old tombstones.

And on the train that night, on my way back to the Bushveld, I came across a soldier who said to me, "As soon as I am out of this uniform I am going back to cattle-smuggling."

These words thrilled me. A number of my stories have dealt with the time-honoured Marico custom of smuggling cattle across the frontier of the Bechuanaland Protectorate. So I asked whether cattle-smuggling still went on. "More than ever," the soldier informed me. He looked out of the train window into the dark. "And I'll tell you that at this moment, as I am sitting here talking to you, there is somebody bringing in cattle through the wire."

I was very glad to hear this. I was glad to find that the only part of my stories that could have dated had not done so. It is only things indirectly connected with economics that can change. Drought and human nature don't.

Next morning we were in Mafeking. Mafeking is outside the Transvaal. It is about twenty miles inside the borders of the Northern Cape. And to proceed to Ramoutsa, a native village in the Bechuanaland Protectorate which is the nearest point on the railway line to the part of the Groot Marico to which we wanted to go, we had first to get a permit from the immigration official in Mafeking. All this seemed very confusing, somehow. We merely wanted to travel from Johannesburg to an area in the North-west Transvaal, and in order to get there it turned out that we had first to cross into the Cape Province, and that from the Cape we had to travel through the Bechuanaland Protectorate, which is a Crown Colony, and which you can't enter until an immigration official has first telephoned Pretoria about it.

We reached Ramoutsa late in the afternoon.

From there we travelled to the Marico by car. Within the hour we had again crossed the border into the Transvaal. We were once more on the Transvaal soil, for which we were, naturally, homesick, having been exiles in foreign parts from since early morning. So the moment we crossed the barbed-wire fence separating the Bechuanaland Protectorate from the Marico we stopped the car and got out on to the veld. We said it was fine to set foot on Transvaal soil once more. And we also said that while it was a good thing to travel through foreign countries, which we had been doing since six o'clock that morning, and that foreign travel had a broadening effect on the mind, we were glad that our heads had not been turned by these experiences, and that we had not permitted ourselves to be influenced by alien modes of life and thought.

We travelled on through the bush over stony paths that were little more than tracks going in between the trees and underneath their branches, the thorns tearing at the windscreen and the hood of the car in the same way as they had done years ago, when I had first visited the Marico. I was glad to find that nothing had changed.

Dusk found us in the shadow of the Dwarsberge, not far from our destination, and we had come across a spot on the veld that I recognised. It was one of the stations at which the bi-weekly Government lorry from Zeerust stopped on its way up towards the Limpopo. How the lorry drivers knew that this place was a station, years ago, was through the presence of a large ant-hill, into the crest of which a pair of kudu antlers had been thrust. That spot had not changed. The ant-hill was still surmounted by what looked like that same pair of kudu horns. The station had not grown perceptibly in the intervening years. The only sign of progress was that, in addition to the horns on its summit, the ant-hill was further decorated with a rusty milk-can from which the bottom had been knocked out.

And so I arrived back in that part of the country to which the Transvaal Education Department in its wisdom had sent me years before. There is no other place I know that is so heavy with atmosphere, so strangely and darkly impregnated with that stuff of life that bears the authentic stamp of South Africa.

When I first went to the Marico it was in that season when the moepels were nearly ripening. And when I returned, years later, it was to find that the moepels in the Marico were beginning to ripen again.

MAKAPAN'S CAVES

KAFFIRS? (SAID OOM SCHALK LOURENS). Yes, I know them. And they're all the same. I fear the Almighty, and I respect His works, but I could never understand why He made the kaffir and the rinderpest. The Hottentot is a little better. The Hottentot will only steal the biltong hanging out on the line to dry. He won't steal the line as well. That is where the kaffir is different.

Still, sometimes you come across a good kaffir, who is faithful and upright and a true Christian and doesn't let the wild-dogs catch the sheep. I always think that it isn't right to kill that kind of kaffir.

I remember about one kaffir we had, by the name of Nongaas. How we got him was after this fashion. It was in the year of the big drought, when there was no grass, and the water in the pan had dried up. Our cattle died like flies. It was terrible. Every day ten or twelve or twenty died. So my father said we must pack everything on the wagons and trek up to the Dwarsberge, where he heard there had been good rains. I was six years old, then, the youngest in the family. Most of the time I sat in the back of the wagon, with my mother and my two sisters. My brother Hendrik was seventeen, and he helped my father and the kaffirs to drive on our cattle. That was how we trekked. Many more of our cattle died along the way, but after about two months we got into the Lowveld and my father said that God had been good to us. For the grass was green along the Dwarsberge.

One morning we came to some kaffir huts, where my father bartered two sacks of mealies for a roll of tobacco. A piccanin of about my own age was standing in front of a hut, and he looked at us all the time and grinned. But mostly he looked at my brother Hendrik. And that was not a wonder, either. Even in those days my brother Hendrik was careful about his appearance, and he always tried to be fashionably dressed. On

Sundays he even wore socks. When we had loaded up the mealies, my father cut off a plug of Boer tobacco and gave it to the piccanin, who grinned still more, so that we saw every one of his teeth, which were very white. He put the plug in his mouth and bit it. Then we all laughed. The piccanin looked just like a puppy that has swallowed a piece of meat, and turns his head sideways, to see how it tastes.

That was in the morning. We went right on until the afternoon, for my father wanted to reach Tweekoppiesfontein, where we were going to stand with our cattle for some time. It was late in the afternoon when we got there, and we started to outspan. Just as I was getting off the wagon, I looked round and saw something jumping quickly behind a bush. It looked like some animal, so I was afraid, and told my brother Hendrik, who took up his gun and walked slowly towards the bush. We saw, directly afterwards, that it was the piccanin whom we had seen that morning in front of the hut. He must have been following behind our wagons for about ten miles. He looked dirty and tired, but when my brother went up to him he began to grin again, and seemed very happy. We didn't know what to do with him, so Hendrik shouted to him to go home, and started throwing stones at him. But my father was a merciful man, and after he had heard Nongaas's story – for that was the name of the piccanin – he said he could stay with us, but he must be good, and not tell lies and steal, like the other kaffirs. Nongaas told us in the Sechuana language, which my father understood, that his father and mother had been killed by the lions, and that he was living with his uncle, whom he didn't like, but that he liked my brother Hendrik, and that was why he had followed our wagons.

Nongaas remained with us for many years. He grew up with us. He was a very good kaffir, and as time went by he became much attached to all of us. But he worshipped my brother Hendrik. As he grew older, my father sometimes spoke to Nongaas about his soul, and explained to him about God. But although he told my father that he understood, I could see that whenever Nongaas thought of God, he was really only thinking of Hendrik.

It was just after my twenty-first birthday that we got news that Hermanus Potgieter and his whole family had been killed by a kaffir tribe under Makapan. They also said that, after killing him, the kaffirs stripped off old Potgieter's skin and made wallets out of it in which to carry their dagga. It was very wicked of the kaffirs to have done that, especially as dagga makes you mad and it is a sin to smoke it. A commando was called up from our district to go and attack the tribe and teach them to have respect for the white man's laws – and above all, to have more respect for the white man's skin. My mother and sisters baked a great deal of harde beskuit, which we packed up, together with mealie-meal and biltong. We also took out the lead mould and melted bullets. The next morning my brother and I set out on horseback for Makapan's kraal. We were accompanied by Nongaas, whom we took along with us to look after the horses and light the fires. My father stayed at home. He said that he was too old to go on commando, unless it was to fight the redcoats, if there were still any left.

But he gave us some good advice.

"Don't forget to read your Bible, my sons," he called out as we rode away. "Pray the Lord to help you, and when you shoot always aim for the stomach." These remarks were typical of my father's deeply religious nature, and he also knew that it was easier to hit a man in the stomach than in the head: and it is just as good, because no man can live long after his intestines have been shot away.

Well, we rode on, my brother and I, with Nongaas following a few yards behind us on the pack-horse. Now and again we fell in with other burghers, many of whom brought their wagons with them, until, on the third day, we reached Makapan's kraal, where the big commando had already gone into camp. We got there in the evening, and everywhere as far as we could see there were fires burning in a big circle. There were over two hundred wagons, and on their tents the fires shone red and yellow. We reported ourselves to the veldkornet, who showed us a place where we could camp, next to the four Van

Rensburg brothers. Nongaas had just made the fire and boiled the coffee when one of the Van Rensburgs came up and invited us over to their wagon. They had shot a rietbok and were roasting pieces of it on the coals.

We all shook hands and said it was good weather for the mealies if only the ruspes didn't eat them, and that it was time we had another president, and that rietbok tasted very fine when roasted on the coals. Then they told us what had happened about the kaffirs. Makapan and his followers had seen the commandos coming from a distance, and after firing a few shots at them had all fled into the caves in the krantz. These caves stretched away underground very far and with many turnings. So, as the Boers could not storm the kaffirs without losing heavily, the kommandant gave instructions that the ridge was to be surrounded and the kaffirs starved out. They were all inside the caves, the whole tribe, men, women and children. They had already been there six days, and as they couldn't have much food left, and as there was only a small dam with brackish water, we were hopeful of being able to kill off most of the kaffirs without wasting ammunition.

Already, when the wind blew towards us from the mouth of the caves, the stink was terrible. We would have pitched our camp further back, only that we were afraid some of the kaffirs would escape between the fires.

The following morning I saw for the first time why we couldn't drive the kaffirs from their lairs, even though our commando was four hundred strong. All over, through the rocks and bushes, I could see black openings in the krantz, that led right into the deep parts of the earth. Here and there we could see dead bodies lying. But there were still left a lot of kaffirs that were not dead, and them we could not see. But they had guns, which they had bought from the illicit traders and the missionaries, and they shot at us whenever we came within range. And all the time there was that stench of decaying bodies.

For another week the siege went on. Then we heard that our leaders, Marthinus Wessels Pretorius and Paul Kruger, had quarrelled.

Kruger wanted to attack the kaffirs immediately and finish the affair, but Pretorius said it was too dangerous and he didn't want any more burghers killed. He said that already the hand of the Lord lay heavy upon Makapan, and in another few weeks the kaffirs would all be dead of starvation. But Paul Kruger said that it would even be better if the hand of the Lord lay still heavier upon the kaffirs. Eventually Paul Kruger obtained permission to take fifty volunteers and storm the caves from one side, while Kommandant Piet Potgieter was to advance from the other side with two hundred men, to distract the attention of the kaffirs. Kruger was popular with all of us, and nearly everyone volunteered to go with him. So he picked fifty men, among whom were the Van Rensburgs and my brother. Therefore, as I did not want to stay behind and guard the camp, I had to join Piet Potgieter's commando.

All the preparations were made, and the following morning we got ready to attack. My brother Hendrik was very proud and happy at having been chosen for the more dangerous part. He oiled his gun very carefully and polished up his veldskoens.

Then Nongaas came up and I noticed that he looked very miserable.

"My baas," he said to my brother Hendrik, "you mustn't go and fight. They'll shoot you dead."

My brother shook his head.

"Then let me go with you, baas," Nongaas said; "I will go in front and look after you."

Hendrik only laughed.

"Look here, Nongaas," he said, "you can stay behind and cook the dinner. I will get back in time to eat it."

The whole commando came together and we all knelt down and prayed. Then Marthinus Wessels Pretorius said we must sing Hymn Number 23, "Rest my soul, thy God is king." Furthermore, we sang another hymn and also a psalm. Most people would have thought that one hymn would be enough. But not so Pretorius. He always made quite sure of everything he did. Then we moved off to the attack.

We fought bravely, but the kaffirs were many, and they lay in the darkness of the caves, and shot at us without our being able to see them. While the fighting lasted it was worse than the lyddite bombs at Paardeberg. And the stench was terrible. We tied handkerchiefs round the lower part of our face, but that did not help. Also, since we were not Englishmen, many of us had no handkerchiefs. Still we fought on, shooting at an enemy we could not see. We rushed right up to the mouth of one of the caves, and even got some distance into it, when our leader, Kommandant Piet Potgieter, flung up his hands and fell backwards, shot through the breast. We carried him out, but he was quite dead. So we lost heart and retired.

When we returned from the fight we found that the other attacking party had also been defeated. They had shot many kaffirs, but there were still hundreds of them left, who fought all the more fiercely with hunger gnawing at their bellies.

I went back to our camp. There was only Nongaas, sitting forward on a stone, with his face on his arms. An awful fear clutched me as I asked him what was wrong.

"Baas Hendrik," he replied, and as he looked at me in his eyes there was much sorrow, "Baas Hendrik did not come back."

I went out immediately and made enquiries, but nobody could tell me anything for sure. They remembered quite well seeing my brother Hendrik when they stormed the cave. He was right in amongst the foremost of the attackers. When I heard that, I felt a great pride in my brother, although I also knew that nothing else could be expected of the son of my father. But no man could tell me what had happened to him. All they knew was that when they got back he was not amongst them.

I spoke to Marthinus Wessels Pretorius and asked him to send out another party to seek for my brother. But Pretorius was angry.

"I will not allow one more man," he replied. "It was all Kruger's doing. I was against it from the start. Now Kommandant Potgieter has been killed, who was a better man than Kruger and all his Dopper clique put together. If any man goes back to the caves I shall discharge him from the commando."

But I don't think it was right of Pretorius. Because Paul Kruger was only trying to do his duty, and afterwards, when he was nominated for president, I voted for him.

It was eleven o'clock when I again reached our part of the laager. Nongaas was still sitting on the flat stone, and I saw that he had carried out my brother Hendrik's instructions, and that the pot was boiling on the fire. The dinner was ready, but my brother was not there. That sight was too much for me, and I went and lay down alone under the Van Rensburgs' wagon.

I looked up again, about half an hour later, and I saw Nongaas walking away with a water-bottle and a small sack strapped to his back. He said nothing to me, but I knew he was going to look for my brother Hendrik. Nongaas knew that if his baas was still alive he would need him. So he went to him. That was all. For a long while I watched Nongaas as he crept along through the rocks and bushes. I supposed it was his intention to lie in wait near one of the caves and then crawl inside when the night came. That was a very brave thing to do. If Makapan's kaffirs saw him they would be sure to kill him, because he was helping the Boers against them, and also because he was a Bechuana.

The evening came, but neither my brother Hendrik nor Nongaas. All that night I sat with my face to the caves and never slept. Then in the morning I got up and loaded my gun. I said to myself that if Nongaas had been killed in the attempt there was only one thing left for me to do. I myself must go to my brother.

I walked out first into the veld, in case one of the officers saw me and made me come back. Then I walked along the ridge and got under cover of the bushes. From there I crawled along, hiding in the long grass and behind the stones, so that I came to one part of Makapan's stronghold where things were more quiet. I got to within about two hundred yards of a cave. There I lay very still, behind a big rock, to find out if there were any kaffirs watching from that side. Occasionally I heard the sound of a shot being fired, but that was far away. Afterwards I fell asleep, for I was very weary with the anxiety and through not having slept the night before.

When I woke up the sun was right overhead. It was hot and there were no clouds in the sky. Only there were a few aasvoëls, which flew round and round very slowly, without ever seeming to flap their wings. Now and again one of them would fly down and settle on the ground, and it was very horrible. I thought of my brother Hendrik and shivered. I looked towards the cave. Inside it seemed as though there was something moving. A minute later I saw that it was a kaffir coming stealthily towards the entrance. He appeared to be looking in my direction, and for fear that he should see me and call the other kaffirs, I jumped up quickly and shot at him, aiming at the stomach. He fell over like a sack of potatoes and I was thankful for my father's advice. But I had to act quickly. If the other kaffirs had heard the shot they would all come running up at once. And I didn't want that to happen. I didn't like the look of those aasvoëls. So I decided to take a great risk. Accordingly I ran as fast as I could towards the cave and rushed right into it, so that, even if the kaffirs did come, they wouldn't see me amongst the shadows. For a long time I lay down and waited. But as no more kaffirs came, I got up and walked slowly down a dark passage, looking round every time to see that nobody followed me, and to make sure that I would find my way back. For there were many twists and turnings, and the whole krantz seemed to be hollowed out.

I knew that my search would be very difficult. But there was something that seemed to tell me that my brother was nearby. So I was strong in my faith, and I knew that the Lord would lead me aright. And I found my brother Hendrik, and he was alive. It was with a feeling of great joy that I came across him. I saw him in the dim light that came through a big split in the roof. He was lying against a boulder, holding his leg and groaning. I saw afterwards that his leg was sprained and much swollen, but that was all that was wrong. So great was my brother Hendrik's surprise at seeing me that at first he could not talk. He just held my hand and laughed softly, and when I touched his forehead I knew he was feverish. I gave him some brandy out of my flask, and in a few words he told me all that had happened. When they stormed the cave he was right in front and as the kaffirs retreated he followed them up. But they all ran in different ways, until my brother found himself alone. He tried to get back, but lost his way and fell down a dip. In that way he sprained his ankle so severely that he had been in agony all the time. He crawled into a far corner and remained there, with the danger and the darkness and his pain. But the worst of all was the stink of the rotting bodies.

"Then Nongaas came," my brother Hendrik said.

"Nongaas?" I asked him.

"Yes," he replied. "He found me and gave me food and water, and carried me on his back. Then the water gave out and I was very thirsty. So Nongaas took the bottle to go and fill it at the pan. But it is very dangerous to get there, and I am so frightened they may kill him."

"They will not kill him," I said. "Nongaas will come back." I said that, but in my heart I was afraid. For the caves were many and dark, and the kaffirs were blood-mad. It would not do to wait. So I lifted Hendrik on my shoulder and carried him towards the entrance. He was in much pain.

"You know," he whispered, "Nongaas was crying when he found me. He thought I was dead. He has been very good to me – so very good. Do you remember that day when he followed behind our wagons? He looked so very trustful and so little, and yet I – I threw stones at him. I wish I did not do that. I only hope that he comes back safe. He was crying and stroking my hair."

As I said, my brother Hendrik was feverish.

"Of course he will come back," I answered him. But this time I knew that I lied. For as I came through the mouth of the cave I kicked against the kaffir I had shot there. The body sagged over to one side and I saw the face.

The Rooinek

Rooineks, said Oom Schalk Lourens, are queer. For instance, there was that day when my nephew Hannes and I had dealings with a couple of Englishmen near Dewetsdorp. It was shortly after Sanna's Post, and Hannes and I were lying behind a rock watching the road. Hannes spent odd moments like that in what he called a useful way. He would file the points of his Mauser cartridges on a piece of flat stone until the lead showed through the steel, in that way making them into dum-dum bullets.

I often spoke to my nephew Hannes about that.

"Hannes," I used to say. "That is a sin. The Lord is looking at you."

"That's all right," Hannes replied. "The Lord knows that this is the Boer War, and in war-time he will always forgive a little foolishness like this, especially as the English are so many."

Anyway, as we lay behind that rock we saw, far down the road, two horsemen come galloping up. We remained perfectly still and let them approach to within four hundred paces. They were English officers. They were mounted on first-rate horses and their uniforms looked very fine and smart. They were the most stylish-looking men I had seen for some time, and I felt quite ashamed of my own ragged trousers and veldskoens. I was glad that I was behind a rock and they couldn't see me. Especially as my jacket was also torn all the way down the back, as a result of my having had, three days before, to get through a barbed-wire fence rather quickly. I just got through in time, too. The veldkornet, who was a fat man and couldn't run so fast, was about twenty yards behind me. And he remained on the wire with a bullet through him. All through the Boer War I was pleased that I was thin and never troubled with corns.

Hannes and I fired just about the same time. One of the officers fell off his horse. He struck the road with his shoulders and rolled over twice, kicking up the red dust as he turned. Then the other soldier did a queer thing. He drew up his horse and got off. He gave just one look in our direction. Then he led his horse up to where the other man was twisting and struggling on the ground. It took him a little while to lift him on to his horse, for it is no easy matter to pick up a man like that when he is helpless. And he did all this slowly and calmly, as though he was not concerned about the fact that the men who had shot his friend were lying only a few hundred yards away. He managed in some way to support the wounded man across the saddle, and walked on beside the horse. After going a few yards he stopped and seemed to remember something. He turned round and waved at the spot where he imagined we were hiding, as though inviting us to shoot. During all that time I had simply lain watching him, astonished at his coolness.

But when he waved his hand I thrust another cartridge into the breach of my Martini and aimed. At that distance I couldn't miss. I aimed very carefully and was just on the point of pulling the trigger when Hannes put his hand on the barrel and pushed up my rifle.

"Don't shoot, Oom Schalk," he said. "That's a brave man."

I looked at Hannes in surprise. His face was very white. I said nothing, and allowed my rifle to sink down on to the grass, but I couldn't understand what had come over my nephew. It seemed that not only was that Englishman queer, but that Hannes was also queer. That's all nonsense not killing a man just because he's brave. If he's a brave man and he's fighting on the wrong side, that's all the more reason to shoot him.

I was with my nephew Hannes for another few months after that. Then one day, in a skirmish near the Vaal River, Hannes with a few dozen other burghers was cut off from the commando and had to surrender. That was the last I ever saw of him. I heard later on that, after taking him prisoner, the English searched Hannes and found dum-dum bullets in his possession. They shot him for that. I was very much grieved when I heard of Hannes's death. He had always been full of life and high spirits. Perhaps Hannes was right in saying that the Lord didn't mind about a little foolishness like dum-dum bullets. But the mistake he made was in forgetting that the English did mind.

I was in the veld until they made peace. Then we laid down our rifles and went home. What I knew my farm by was the hole under the koppie where I quarried slate-stones for the threshing-floor. That was about all that remained as I left it. Everything else was gone. My home was burnt down. My lands were laid waste. My cattle and sheep were slaughtered. Even the stones I had piled for the kraals were pulled down. My wife came out of the concentration camp, and we went together to look at our old farm. My wife had gone into the concentration camp with our two children, but she came out alone. And when I saw her again and noticed the way she had changed, I knew that I, who had been through all the fighting, had not seen the Boer War.

Neither Sannie nor I had the heart to go on farming again on that same place. It would be different without the children playing about the house and getting into mischief. We got paid out some money by the new Government for part of our losses. So I bought a wagon and oxen and left the Free State, which was not even the Free State any longer. It was now called the Orange River Colony.

We trekked right through the Transvaal into the northern part of the Marico Bushveld. Years ago, as a boy, I had trekked through that same country with my parents. Now that I went there again I felt that it was still a good country. It was on the far side of the Dwarsberge, near Derdepoort, that we got a Government farm. Afterwards other farmers trekked in there as well. One or two of them had also come from the Free State, and I knew them. There were also a few Cape rebels whom I had seen on commando. All of us had lost relatives in the war. Some had died in the concentration camps or on the battlefield. Others had been shot for going into rebellion. So, taken all in all, we who had trekked into that part of the Marico that lay nearest the Bechuanaland border were very bitter against the English.

Then it was that the rooinek came.

It was in the first year of our having settled around Derdepoort. We heard that an Englishman had bought a farm next to Gerhardus Grobbelaar. This was when we were sitting in the voorkamer of Willem Odendaal's house, which was used as a post office. Once a week the post-cart came up with letters from Zeerust, and we came together at Willem Odendaal's house and talked and smoked and drank coffee. Very few of us ever got letters, and then it was mostly demands to pay for the boreholes that had been drilled on our farms or for cement and fencing materials. But every week regularly we went for the post. Sometimes the post-cart didn't come, because the Groen River was in flood, and we would most of us have gone home without noticing it, if somebody didn't speak about it.

When Koos Steyn heard that an Englishman was coming to live amongst us he got up from the riempies-bank.

"No, kêrels," he said. "Always when the Englishman comes, it means that a little later the Boer has got to shift. I'll pack up my wagon and make coffee, and just trek first thing tomorrow morning."

Most of us laughed then. Koos Steyn often said funny things like that. But some didn't laugh. Somehow, there seemed to be too much truth in Koos Steyn's words.

We discussed the matter and decided that if we Boers in the Marico could help it the rooinek would not stay amongst us too long. About half an hour later one of Willem Odendaal's children came in and said that there was a strange wagon coming along the big road. We went to the door and looked out. As the wagon came nearer we saw that it was piled up with all kinds of furniture and also sheets of iron and farming implements. There was so much stuff on the wagon that the tent had to be taken off to get everything on.

The wagon rolled along and came to a stop in front of the house. With the wagon there were one white man and two kaffirs. The white man shouted something to the kaffirs and threw down the whip. Then he walked up to where we were standing. He was dressed just as we were, in shirt and trousers and veldskoens, and he had dust all over him. But when he stepped over a thorn-bush we saw that he had got socks on. Therefore we knew that he was an Englishman.

Koos Steyn was standing in front of the door.

The Englishman went up to him and held out his hand.

"Good afternoon," he said in Afrikaans. "My name is Webber."

Koos shook hands with him.

"My name is Prince Lord Alfred Milner," Koos Steyn said.

That was when Lord Milner was Governor of the Transvaal, and we all laughed. The rooinek also laughed.

"Well, Lord Prince," he said, "I can speak your language a little, and I hope that later on I'll be able to speak it better. I'm coming to live here, and I hope that we'll all be friends."

He then came round to all of us, but the others turned away and refused to shake hands with him. He came up to me last of all; I felt sorry for him, and although his nation had dealt unjustly with my nation, and I had lost both my children in the concentration camp, still it was not so much the fault of this Englishman. It was the fault of the English Government, who wanted our gold mines. And it was also the fault of Queen Victoria, who didn't like Oom Paul Kruger, because they say that when he went over to London Oom Paul spoke to her only once for a few minutes. Oom Paul Kruger said that he was a married man and he was afraid of widows.

When the Englishman Webber went back to his wagon Koos Steyn and I walked with him. He told us that he had bought the farm next to Gerhardus Grobbelaar and that he didn't know much about sheep and cattle and mealies, but he had bought a few books on farming, and he was going to learn all he could out of them. When he said that I looked away towards the poort. I didn't want him to see that I was laughing. But with Koos Steyn it was otherwise.

"Man," he said, "let me see those books."

Webber opened the box at the bottom of the wagon and took out about six big books with green covers.

“These are very good books,” Koos Steyn said. “Yes, they are very good for the white ants. The white ants will eat them all in two nights.”

As I have told you, Koos Steyn was a funny fellow, and no man could help laughing at the things he said.

Those were bad times. There was drought, and we could not sow mealies. The dams dried up, and there was only last year’s grass on the veld. We had to pump water out of the borehole for weeks at a time. Then the rains came and for a while things were better.

Now and again I saw Webber. From what I heard about him it seemed that he was working hard. But of course no rooinek can make a living out of farming, unless they send him money every month from England. And we found out that almost all the money Webber had was what he had paid on the farm. He was always reading in those green books what he had to do. It’s lucky that those books are written in English, and that the Boers can’t read them. Otherwise many more farmers would be ruined every year. When his cattle had the heart-water, or his sheep had the blue-tongue, or there were cut-worms or stalk-borers in his mealies, Webber would look it all up in his books. I suppose that when the kaffirs stole his sheep he would look that up too.

Still, Koos Steyn helped Webber quite a lot and taught him a number of things, so that matters did not go as badly with him as they would have if he had only acted according to the lies that were printed in those green books. Webber and Koos Steyn became very friendly. Koos Steyn’s wife had had a baby just a few weeks before Webber came. It was the first child they had after being married seven years, and they were very proud of it. It was a girl. Koos Steyn said that he would sooner it had been a boy; but that, even so, it was better than nothing. Right from the first Webber had taken a liking to that child, who was christened Jemima after her mother. Often when I passed Koos Steyn’s house I saw the Englishman sitting on the front stoep with the child on his knees.

In the meantime the other farmers around there became annoyed on account of Koos Steyn's friendship with the rooinek. They said that Koos was a hendsopper and a traitor to his country. He was intimate with a man who had helped to bring about the downfall of the Afrikaner nation. Yet it was not fair to call Koos a hendsopper. Koos had lived in the Graaff-Reinet District when the war broke out, so that he was a Cape Boer and need not have fought. Nevertheless, he joined up with a Free State commando and remained until peace was made, and if at any time the English had caught him they would have shot him as a rebel, in the same way that they shot Scheepers and many others.

Gerhardus Grobbelaar spoke about this once when we were in Willem Odendaal's post office.

"You are not doing right," Gerhardus said; "Boer and Englishman have been enemies since before Slagtersnek. We've lost this war, but some day we'll win. It's the duty we owe to our children's children to stand against the rooineks. Remember the concentration camps."

There seemed to me to be truth in what Gerhardus said.

"But the English are here now, and we've got to live with them," Koos answered. "When we get to understand one another perhaps we won't need to fight any more. This Englishman Webber is learning Afrikaans very well, and some day he might almost be one of us. The only thing I can't understand about him is that he has a bath every morning. But if he stops that and if he doesn't brush his teeth any more you will hardly be able to tell him from a Boer."

Although he made a joke about it, I felt that in what Koos Steyn said there was also truth.

Then, the year after the drought, the miltsiek broke out. The miltsiek seemed to be in the grass of the veld, and in the water of the dams, and even in the air the cattle breathed. All over the place I would find cows and oxen lying dead. We all became very discouraged. Nearly all of us in that part of the Marico had started farming again on what the Government had given us. Now that the stock died we had nothing. First the drought had put us back to where we were when we started.

Now with the miltsiek we couldn't hope to do anything. We couldn't even sow mealies, because, at the rate at which the cattle were dying, in a short while we would have no oxen left to pull the plough. People talked of selling what they had and going to look for work on the gold mines. We sent a petition to the Government, but that did no good.

It was then that somebody got hold of the idea of trekking. In a few days we were talking of nothing else. But the question was where we could trek to. They would not allow us into Rhodesia for fear we might spread the miltsiek there as well. And it was useless going to any other part of the Transvaal. Somebody mentioned German West Africa. We had none of us been there before, and I suppose that really was the reason why, in the end, we decided to go there.

"The blight of the English is over South Africa," Gerhardus Grobbelaar said. "We'll remain here only to die. We must go away somewhere where there is not the Englishman's flag."

In a few weeks' time we arranged everything. We were going to trek across the Kalahari into German territory. Everything we had we loaded up. We drove the cattle ahead and followed behind on our wagons. There were five families: the Steyns, the Grobbelaars, the Odendaals, the Ferreiras and Sannie and I. Webber also came with us. I think it was not so much that he was anxious to leave as that he and Koos Steyn had become very much attached to one another, and the Englishman did not wish to remain alone behind.

The youngest person in our trek was Koos Steyn's daughter Jemima, who was then about eighteen months old. Being the baby, she was a favourite with all of us.

Webber sold his wagon and went with Koos Steyn's trek.

When at the end of the first day we outspanned several miles inside the Bechuanaland Protectorate, we were very pleased that we were done with the Transvaal, where we had had so much misfortune. Of course, the Protectorate was also British territory, but all the same we felt happier there than we had done in our country. We saw Webber every day now, and although he was a foreigner with strange ways, and would remain an Uitlander until he died, yet we disliked him less than before for being a rooinek.

It was on the first Sunday that we reached Malopolole. For the first part of our way the country remained Bushveld. There were the same kind of thorn-trees that grew in the Marico, except that they became fewer the deeper into the Kalahari that we went. Also, the ground became more and more sandy, until even before we came to Malopolole it was all desert. But scattered thorn-bushes remained all the way. That Sunday we held a religious service. Gerhardus Grobbelaar read a chapter out of the Bible and offered up a prayer. We sang a number of psalms, after which Gerhardus prayed again. I shall always remember that Sunday and the way we sat on the ground beside one of the wagons, listening to Gerhardus. That was the last Sunday that we were all together.

The Englishman sat next to Koos Steyn and the baby Jemima lay down in front of him. She played with Webber's fingers and tried to bite them. It was funny to watch her. Several times Webber looked down at her and smiled. I thought then that although Webber was not one of us, yet Jemima certainly did not know it. Maybe in a thing like that the child was wiser than we were. To her it made no difference that the man whose fingers she bit was born in another country and did not speak the same language that she did.

There are many things that I remember about that trek into the Kalahari. But one thing that now seems strange to me is the way in which, right from the first day, we took Gerhardus Grobbelaar for our leader. Whatever he said we just seemed to do without talking very much about it. We all felt that it was right simply because Gerhardus wished it. That was a strange thing about our trek. It was not simply that we knew Gerhardus had got the Lord with him – for we did know that – but it was rather that we believed in Gerhardus as well as in the Lord. I think that even if Gerhardus Grobbelaar had been an ungodly man we would still have followed him in exactly the same way. For when you are in the desert and there is no water and the way back is long, then you feel that it is better to have with you a strong man who does not read the Book very much, than a man who is good and religious, and yet does not seem sure how far to trek each day and where to outspan.

But Gerhardus Grobbelaar was a man of God. At the same time there was something about him that made you feel that it was only by acting as he advised that you could succeed. There was only one other man I have ever known who found it so easy to get people to do as he wanted. And that was Paul Kruger. He was very much like Gerhardus Grobbelaar, except that Gerhardus was less quarrelsome. But of the two Paul Kruger was the bigger man.

Only once do I remember Gerhardus losing his temper. And that was with the Nagmaal at Elandsberg. It was on a Sunday, and we were camped out beside the Crocodile River. Gerhardus went round early in the morning from wagon to wagon and told us that he wanted everybody to come over to where his wagon stood. The Lord had been good to us at that time, so that we had had much rain and our cattle were fat. Gerhardus explained that he wanted to hold a service, to thank the Lord for all His good works, but more especially for what He had done for the farmers of the northern part of the Groot Marico District. This was a good plan, and we all came together with our Bibles and hymn-books. But one man, Karel Pieterse, remained behind at his wagon. Twice Gerhardus went to call him, but Karel Pieterse lay down on the grass and would not get up to come to the service. He said it was all right thanking the Lord now that there had been rains, but what about all those seasons when there had been drought and the cattle had died of thirst. Gerhardus Grobbelaar shook his head sadly, and said there was nothing he could do then, as it was Sunday. But he prayed that the Lord would soften Brother Pieterse's heart, and he finished off his prayer by saying that in any case, in the morning, he would help to soften the brother's heart himself.

The following morning Gerhardus walked over with a sjambok and an ox-riem to where Karel Pieterse sat before his fire, watching the kaffir making coffee. They were both of them men who were big in the body. But Gerhardus got the better of the struggle. In the end he won. He fastened Karel to the wheel of his own wagon with the ox-riem. Then he thrashed him with the sjambok while Karel's wife and children were looking on.

That had happened years before. But nobody had forgotten. And now, in the Kalahari, when Gerhardus summoned us to a service, it was noticed that no man stayed away.

Just outside Malopolole is a muddy stream that is dry part of the year and part of the year has a foot or so of brackish water. We were lucky in being there just at the time when it had water. Early the following morning we filled up the water-barrels that we had put on our wagons before leaving the Marico. We were going right into the desert, and we did not know where we would get water again. Even the Bakwena kaffirs could not tell us for sure.

"The Great Dorstland Trek," Koos Steyn shouted as we got ready to move off. "Anyway, we won't fare as badly as the Dorstland Trekkers. We'll lose less cattle than they did because we've got less to lose. And seeing that we are only five families, not more than about a dozen of us will die of thirst."

I thought it was bad luck for Koos Steyn to make jokes like that about the Dorstland Trek, and I think that others felt the same way about it. We trekked right through that day, and it was all desert. By sunset we had not come across a sign of water anywhere. Abraham Ferreira said towards evening that perhaps it would be better if we went back to Malopolole and tried to find out for sure which was the best way of getting through the Kalahari. But the rest said that there was no need to do that, since we would be sure to come across water the next day. And, anyway, we were Doppers and, having once set out, we were not going to turn back. But after we had given the cattle water our barrels did not have too much left in them.

By the middle of the following day all our water had given out except a little that we kept for the children. But still we pushed on.

Now that we had gone so far we were afraid to go back because of the long way that we would have to go without water to get back to Malopolole. In the evening we were very anxious. We all knelt down in the sand and prayed. Gerhardus Grobbelaar's voice sounded very deep and earnest when he besought God to have mercy on us, especially for the sakes of the little ones. He mentioned the baby Jemima by name. The Englishman knelt down beside me, and I noticed that he shivered when Gerhardus mentioned Koos Steyn's child.

It was moonlight. All around us was the desert. Our wagons seemed very small and lonely; there was something about them that looked very mournful. The women and children put their arms round one another and wept a long while. Our kaffirs stood some distance away and watched us. My wife Sannie put her hand in mine, and I thought of the concentration camp. Poor woman, she had suffered much. And I knew that her thoughts were the same as my own: that after all it was perhaps better that our children should have died then than now.

We had got so far into the desert that we began telling one another that we must be near the end. Although we knew that German West was far away, and that in the way we had been travelling we had got little more than into the beginning of the Kalahari, yet we tried to tell one another lies about how near water was likely to be. But, of course, we told those lies only to one another. Each man in his own heart knew what the real truth was. And later on we even stopped telling one another lies about what a good chance we had of getting out alive. You can understand how badly things had gone with us when you know that we no longer troubled about hiding our position from the women and children. They wept, some of them. But that made no difference then. Nobody tried to comfort the women and children who cried. We knew that tears were useless, and yet somehow at that hour we felt that the weeping of the women was not less useless than the courage of the men. After a while there was no more weeping in our camp. Some of the women who lived through the dreadful things of the days that came after, and got safely back to the Transvaal, never again wept.

What they had seen appeared to have hardened them. In this respect they had become as men. I think that is the saddest thing that ever happens in this world, when women pass through great suffering that makes them become as men.

That night we hardly slept. Early the next morning the men went out to look for water. An hour after sun-up Ferreira came back and told us that he had found a muddy pool a few miles away. We all went there, but there wasn't much water. Still, we got a little, and that made us feel better. It was only when it came to driving our cattle towards the mudhole that we found our kaffirs had deserted us during the night. After we had gonc to sleep they had stolen away. Some of the weaker cattle couldn't get up to go to the pool. So we left them. Some were trampled to death or got choked in the mud, and we had to pull them out to let the rest get to the hole. It was pitiful.

Just before we left one of Ferreira's daughters died. We scooped a hole in the sand and buried her.

So we decided to trek back.

After his daughter was dead Abraham Ferreira went up to Gerhardus and told him that if we had taken his advice earlier on and gone back, his daughter would not have died.

"Your daughter is dead now, Abraham," Gerhardus said. "It is no use talking about her any longer. We all have to die some day. I refused to go back earlier. I have decided to go back now."

Abraham Ferreira looked Gerhardus in the eyes and laughed. I shall always remember how that laughter sounded in the desert. In Abraham's voice there was the hoarseness of the sand and thirst. His voice was cracked with what the desert had done to him; his face was lined and his lips were blackened. But there was nothing about him that spoke of grief for his daughter's death.

"Your daughter is still alive, Oom Gerhardus," Abraham Ferreira said, pointing to the wagon wherein lay Gerhardus's wife, who was weak, and the child to whom she had given birth only a few months before. "Yes, she is still alive. . . so far."

Ferreira turned away laughing, and we heard him a little later explaining to his wife in cracked tones about the joke he had made.

Gerhardus Grobbelaar merely watched the other man walk away without saying anything. So far we had followed Gerhardus through all things, and our faith in him had been great. But now that we had decided to trek back we lost our belief in him. We lost it suddenly, too. We knew that it was best to turn back, and that to continue would mean that we would all die in the Kalahari. And yet, if Gerhardus had said we must still go on we would have done so. We would have gone through with him right to the end. But now that he as much as said he was beaten by the desert we had no more faith in Gerhardus. That is why I have said that Paul Kruger was a greater man than Gerhardus. Because Paul Kruger was that kind of man whom we still worshipped even when he decided to retreat. If it had been Paul Kruger who told us that we had to go back we would have returned with strong hearts. We would have retained exactly the same love for our leader, even if we knew that he was beaten. But from the moment that Gerhardus said we must go back we all knew that he was no longer our leader. Gerhardus knew that also.

We knew what lay between us and Malopolole and there was grave doubt in our hearts when we turned our wagons round. Our cattle were very weak, and we had to inspan all that could walk. We hadn't enough yokes, and therefore we cut poles from the scattered bushes and tied them to the trek-chains. As we were also without skeis we had to fasten the necks of the oxen straight on to the yokes with strops, and several of the oxen got strangled.

Then we saw that Koos Steyn had become mad. For he refused to return. He inspanned his oxen and got ready to trek on. His wife sat silent in the wagon with the baby; wherever her husband went she would go, too. That was only right, of course. Some women kissed her goodbye, and cried. But Koos Steyn's wife did not cry. We reasoned with Koos about it, but he said that he had made up his mind to cross the Kalahari, and he was not going to turn back just for nonsense.

"But, man," Gerhardus Grobbelaar said to him, "you've got no water to drink."

"I'll drink coffee then," Koos Steyn answered, laughing as always, and took up the whip and walked away beside the wagon. And Webber went off with him, just because Koos Steyn had been good to him, I suppose. That's why I have said that Englishmen are queer. Webber must have known that if Koos Steyn had not actually gone wrong in the head, still what he was doing now was madness, and yet he stayed with him.

We separated. Our wagons went slowly back to Malopolole. Koos Steyn's wagon went deeper into the desert. My wagon went last. I looked back at the Steyns. At that moment Webber also looked round. He saw me and waved his hand. It reminded me of that day in the Boer War when that other Englishman, whose companion we had shot, also turned round and waved.

Eventually we got back to Malopolole with two wagons and a handful of cattle. We abandoned the other wagons. Awful things happened on that desert. A number of children died. Gerhardus Grobbelaar's wagon was in front of me. Once I saw a bundle being dropped through the side of the wagon-tent. I knew what it was. Gerhardus would not trouble to bury his dead child, and his wife lay in the tent too weak to move. So I got off the wagon and scraped a small heap of sand over the body. All I remember of the rest of the journey to Malopolole is the sun and the sand. And the thirst. Although at one time we thought that we had lost our way, yet that did not matter much to us. We were past feeling. We could neither pray nor curse, our parched tongues cleaving to the roofs of our mouths.

Until today I am not sure how many days we were on our way back, unless I sit down and work it all out, and then I suppose I get it wrong. We got back to Malopolole and water. We said we would never go away from there again. I don't think that even those parents who had lost children grieved about them then. They were stunned with what they had gone through. But I knew that later on it would all come back again. Then they would remember things about shallow graves in the sand, and Gerhardus Grobbelaar and his wife would think of a little bundle lying out in the Kalahari. And I knew how they would feel.

Afterwards we fitted out a wagon with fresh oxen; we took an abundant supply of water and went back into the desert to look for the Steyn family. With the help of the Sechuana kaffirs, who could see tracks that we could not see, we found the wagon. The oxen had been outspanned; a few lay dead beside the wagon. The kaffirs pointed out to us footprints on the sand, which showed which way those two men and that woman had gone.

In the end we found them.

Koos Steyn and his wife lay side by side in the sand; the woman's head rested on the man's shoulder; her long hair had become loosened, and blew about softly in the wind. A great deal of fine sand had drifted over their bodies. Near them the Englishman lay, face downwards. We never found the baby Jemima. She must have died somewhere along the way and Koos Steyn must have buried her. But we agreed that the Englishman Webber must have passed through terrible things; he could not even have had any understanding left as to what the Steyns had done with their baby. He probably thought, up to the moment when he died, that he was carrying the child. For, when we lifted his body, we found, still clasped in his dead and rigid arms, a few old rags and a child's clothes.

It seemed to us that the wind that always stirs in the Kalahari blew very quietly and softly that morning.

Yes, the wind blew very gently.

Veld Maiden

I KNOW WHAT IT IS – Oom Schalk Lourens said – when you talk that way about the veld. I have known people who sit like you do and dream about the veld, and talk strange things, and start believing in what they call the soul of the veld, until in the end the veld means a different thing to them from what it does to me.

I only know that the veld can be used for growing mealies on, and it isn't very good for that, either. Also, it means very hard work for me, growing mealies. There is the ploughing, for instance. I used to get aches in my back and shoulders from sitting on a stone all day long on the edge of the lands, watching the kaffirs and the oxen and the plough going up and down, making furrows. Hans Coetzee, who was a Boer War prisoner at St. Helena, told me how he got sick at sea from watching the ship going up and down, up and down, all the time.

And it's the same with ploughing. The only real cure for this ploughing sickness is to sit quietly on a riempies bench on the stoep, with one's legs raised slightly, drinking coffee until the ploughing season is over. Most of the farmers in the Marico Bushveld have adopted this remedy, as you have no doubt observed by this time.

But there the veld is. And it is not good to think too much about it. For then it can lead you in strange ways. And sometimes – sometimes when the veld has led you very far – there comes into your eyes a look that God did not put there.

It was in the early summer, shortly after the rains, that I first came across John de Swardt. He was sitting next to a tent that he had pitched behind the maroelas at the far end of my farm, where it adjoins Frans Welman's lands. He had been there several days and I had not known about it, because I sat much on my stoep then, on account of what I have already explained to you about the ploughing.

He was a young fellow with long black hair. When I got nearer I saw what he was doing. He had a piece of white bucksail on a stand in front of him and he was painting my farm. He seemed to have picked out all the useless bits for his picture – a krantz and a few stones and some clumps of kakiebos.

"Young man," I said to him, after we had introduced ourselves, "when people in Johannesburg see that picture they will laugh and say that Schalk Lourens lives on a barren piece of rock, like a lizard does. Why don't you rather paint the fertile parts? Look at that vlei there, and the dam. And put in that new cattle-dip that I have just built up with reinforced concrete. Then, if Piet Grobler or General Kemp sees this picture, he will know at once that Schalk Lourens has been making improvements on the farm."

The young painter shook his head.

"No," he said, "I want to paint only the veld. I hate the idea of painting boreholes and cattle-dips and houses and concrete – especially concrete. I want only the veld. Its loneliness. Its mystery. When this picture is finished I'll be proud to put my name to it."

"Oh, well, that is different," I replied, "as long as you don't put my name to it. Better still," I said, "put Frans Welman's name to it. Write underneath that this is Frans Welman's farm."

I said that because I still remembered that Frans Welman had voted against me at the last election of the Drogekop School Committee.

John de Swardt then took me into his tent and showed me some other pictures he had painted at different places along the Dwarsberge. They were all the same sort of picture, barren and stony. I thought it would be a good idea if the Government put up a lot of pictures like that on the Kalahari border for the locusts to see. Because that would keep the locusts out of the Marico.

Then John de Swardt showed me another picture he had painted and when I saw that I got a different opinion about this thing that he said was Art. I looked from De Swardt to the picture and then back again to De Swardt.

"I'd never have thought it of you," I said, "and you look such a quiet sort, too."

"I call it the 'Veld Maiden'," John de Swardt said.

"If the predikant saw it he'd call it by other names," I replied. "But I am a broad-minded man. I have been once in the bar in Zeerust and twice in the bioscope when I should have been attending Nagmaal. So I don't hold it against a young man for having ideas like this. But you mustn't let anybody here see this Veld Maiden unless you paint a few more clothes on her."

"I couldn't," De Swardt answered, "that's just how I see her. That's just how I dream about her. For many years now she has come to me so in my dreams."

"With her arms stretched out like that?" I asked.

"Yes."

"And with – "

"Yes, yes, just like that," De Swardt said very quickly. Then he blushed and I could see how very young he was. It seemed a pity that a nice young fellow like that should be so mad.

"Anyway, if ever you want a painting job," I said when I left, "you can come and whitewash the back of my sheep-kraal."

I often say funny things like that to people.

I saw a good deal of John de Swardt after that, and I grew to like him. I was satisfied – in spite of his wasting his time in painting bare stones and weeds – that there was no real evil in him. I was sure that he only talked silly things about visions and the spirit of the veld because of what they had done to him at the school in Johannesburg where they taught him all that nonsense about art, and I felt sorry for him. Afterwards I wondered for a little while if I shouldn't rather have felt sorry for the art school. But when I had thought it all out carefully I knew that John de Swardt was only very young and innocent, and that what happened to him later on was the sort of thing that does happen to those who are simple of heart.

On several Sundays in succession I took De Swardt over the rant to the house of Frans Welman. I hadn't a very high regard for Frans's judgment since the time he voted for the wrong man at the School Committee. But I had no other neighbour within walking distance, and I had to go somewhere on a Sunday.

We talked of all sorts of things. Frans's wife Sannie was young and pretty, but very shy. She wasn't naturally like that. It was only that she was afraid to talk in case she said something of which her husband might disapprove. So most of the time Sannie sat silent in the corner, getting up now and again to make more coffee for us.

Frans Welman was in some respects what people might call a hard man. For instance, it was something of a mild scandal the way he treated his wife and the kaffirs on his farm. But then, on the other hand, he looked very well after his cattle and pigs. And I have always believed that this is more important in a farmer than that he should be kind to his wife and the kaffirs.

Well, we talked about the mealies and the drought of the year before last and the subsidies, and I could see that in a short while the conversation would come round to the Volksraad, and as I wasn't anxious to hear how Frans was going to vote at the General Election – believing that so irresponsible a person should not be allowed to vote at all – I quickly asked John de Swardt to tell us about his paintings.

Immediately he started off about his Veld Maiden.

"Not that one," I said, kicking his shin, "I meant your other paintings. The kind that frighten the locusts."

I felt that this Veld Maiden thing was not a fit subject to talk about, especially with a woman present. Moreover, it was Sunday.

Nevertheless, that kick came too late. De Swardt rubbed his shin a few times and started on his subject, and although Frans and I cleared our throats awkwardly at different parts, and Sannie looked on the floor with her pretty cheeks very red, the young painter explained everything about that picture and what it meant to him.

"It's a dream I have had for a long time, now," he said at the end, "and always she comes to me, and when I put out my arms to clasp her to me she vanishes, and I am left with only her memory in my heart. But when she comes the whole world is clothed in a terrible beauty."

"That's more than she is clothed in, anyway," Frans said, "judging from what you have told us about her."

"She's a spirit. She's the spirit of the veld," De Swardt murmured, "she whispers strange and enchanting things. Her coming is like the whisper of the wind. She's not of the earth at all."

"Oh, well," Frans said shortly, "you can keep these Uitlander ghost-women of yours. A Boer girl is good enough for ordinary fellows like me and Schalk Lourens."

So the days passed.

John de Swardt finished a few more bits of rock and drought-stricken kakiebos, and I had got so far as to persuade him to label the worst-looking one "Frans Welman's Farm."

Then one morning he came to me in great excitement.

"I saw her again, Oom Schalk," he said, "I saw her last night. In a surpassing loveliness. Just at midnight. She came softly across the veld towards my tent. The night was warm and lovely, and the stars were mad and singing. And there was low music where her white feet touched the grass. And sometimes her mouth seemed to be laughing, and sometimes it was sad. And her lips were very red, Oom Schalk. And when I reached out with my arms she went away. She disappeared in the maroelas, like the whispering of the wind. And there was a ringing in my ears. And in my heart there was a green fragrance, and I thought of the pale asphodel that grows in the fields of paradise."

"I don't know about paradise," I said, "but if a thing like that grew in my mealie-lands I would see to it at once that the kaffirs pulled it up. I don't like this spook nonsense."

I then gave him some good advice. I told him to beware of the moon, which was almost full at the time. Because the moon can do strange things to you in the Bushveld, especially if you live in a tent and the full moon is overhead and there are weird shadows amongst the maroelas.

But I knew he wouldn't take any notice of what I told him.

Several times after that he came with the same story about the Veld Maiden. I started getting tired of it.

Then, one morning when he came again, I knew everything by the look he had in his eyes. I have already told you about that look.

"Oom Schalk," he began.

"John de Swardt," I said to him, "don't tell me anything. All I ask of you is to pack up your things and leave my farm at once."

"I'll leave tonight," he said. "I promise you that by tomorrow morning I will be gone. Only let me stay here one more day and night."

His voice trembled when he spoke, and his knees were very unsteady. But it was not for these reasons or for his sake that I relented. I spoke to him civilly for the sake of the look he had in his eyes.

"Very well, then," I said, "but you must go straight back to Johannesburg. If you walk down the road you will be able to catch the Government lorry to Zeerust."

He thanked me and left. I never saw him again.

Next day his tent was still there behind the maroelas, but John de Swardt was gone, and he had taken with him all his pictures. All, that is, except the Veld Maiden one. I suppose he had no more need for it.

And, in any case, the white ants had already started on it. So that's why I can hang the remains of it openly on the wall in my voorhuis, and the predikant does not raise any objection to it. For the white ants have eaten away practically all of it except the face.

As for Frans Welman, it was quite a long time before he gave up searching the Marico for his young wife, Sannie.

The Music Maker

Of course, I know about history – Oom Schalk Lourens said – it's the stuff children learn in school. Only the other day, at Thys Lemmer's post office, Thys's little son Stoffel started reading out of his history book about a man called Vasco da Gama, who visited the Cape. At once Dirk Snyman started telling young Stoffel about the time when he himself visited the Cape, but young Stoffel didn't take much notice of him. So Dirk Snyman said that that showed you.

Anyway, Dirk Snyman said that what he wanted to tell young Stoffel was that the last time he went down to the Cape a kaffir came and sat down right next to him in a tram. What was more, Dirk Snyman said, was that people seemed to think nothing of it.

Yes, it's a queer thing about wanting to get into history.

Take the case of Manie Kruger, for instance.

Manie Kruger was one of the best farmers in the Marico. He knew just how much peach brandy to pour out for the tax-collector to make sure that he would nod dreamily at everything Manie said. And at a time of drought Manie Kruger could run to the Government for help much quicker than any man I ever knew.

Then one day Manie Kruger read an article in the *Kerkbode* about a musician who said that he knew more about music than Napoleon did. After that –having first read another article to find out who Napoleon was – Manie Kruger was a changed man. He could talk of nothing but his place in history and of his musical career.

Of course, everybody knew that no man in the Marico could be counted in the same class with Manie Kruger when it came to playing the concertina.

No Bushveld dance was complete without Manie Kruger's concertina. When he played a vastrap you couldn't keep your feet still. But after he had decided to become the sort of musician that gets into history books, it was strange the way that Manie Kruger altered. For one thing, he said he would never again play at a dance. We all felt sad about that. It was not easy to think of the Bushveld dances of the future. There would be the peach brandy in the kitchen; in the voorkamer the feet of the dancers would go through the steps of the schottische and the polka and the waltz and the mazurka, but on the riempies bench in the corner, where the musicians sat, there would be no Manie Kruger. And they would play "Die Vaal Hare en die Blou Oge" and "Vat Jou Goed en Trek, Ferreira," but it would be another's fingers that swept over the concertina keys. And when, with the dancing and the peach brandy, the young men called out "Dagbreek toe!" it would not be Manie Kruger's head that bowed down to the applause.

It was sad to think about all this.

For so long, at the Bushveld dances, Manie Kruger had been the chief musician.

And of all those who mourned this change that had come over Manie, we could see that there was no one more grieved than Letta Steyn.

And Manie said such queer things at times. Once he said that what he had to do to get into history was to die of consumption in the arms of a princess, like another musician he had read about. Only it was hard to get consumption in the Marico, because the climate was so healthy.

Although Manie stopped playing his concertina at dances, he played a great deal in another way. He started giving what he called recitals. I went to several of them. They were very impressive.

At the first recital I went to, I found that the front part of Manie's voorkamer was taken up by rows of benches and chairs that he had borrowed from those of his neighbours who didn't mind having to eat their meals on candle-boxes and upturned buckets. At the far end of the voorkamer a wide green curtain was hung on a piece of string.

When I came in the place was full. I managed to squeeze in on a bench between Jan Terreblanche and a young woman in a blue kappie. Jan Terreblanche had been trying to hold this young woman's hand.

Manie Kruger was sitting behind the green curtain. He was already there when I came in. I knew it was Manie by his veldskoens, which were sticking out from underneath the curtain. Letta Steyn sat in front of me. Now and again, when she turned round, I saw that there was a flush on her face and a look of dark excitement in her eyes.

At last everything was ready, and Joel, the farm kaffir to whom Manie had given this job, slowly drew the green curtain aside. A few of the younger men called out "Middag, ou Manie," and Jan Terreblanche asked if it wasn't very close and suffocating, sitting there like that behind that piece of green curtain.

Then he started to play.

And we all knew that it was the most wonderful concertina music we had ever listened to. It was Manie Kruger at his best. He had practised a long time for that recital; his fingers flew over the keys; the notes of the concertina swept into our hearts; the music of Manie Kruger lifted us right out of that voorkamer into a strange and rich and dazzling world.

It was fine.

The applause right through was terrific. At the end of each piece the kaffir closed the curtains in front of Manie, and we sat waiting for a few minutes until the curtains were drawn aside again. But after that first time there was no more laughter about this procedure. The recital lasted for about an hour and a half, and the applause at the end was even greater than at the start. And during those ninety minutes Manie left his seat only once. That was when there was some trouble with the curtain and he got up to kick the kaffir.

At the end of the recital Manie did not come forward and shake hands with us, as we had expected. Instead, he slipped through behind the green curtain into the kitchen, and sent word that we could come and see him round the back. At first we thought this a bit queer, but

Letta Steyn said it was all right. She explained that in other countries the great musicians and stage performers all received their admirers at the back. Jan Terreblanche said that if these actors used their kitchens for entertaining their visitors in, he wondered where they did their cooking.

Nevertheless, most of us went round to the kitchen, and we had a good time congratulating Manie Kruger and shaking hands with him; and Manie spoke much of his musical future, and of the triumphs that would come to him in the great cities of the world, when he would stand before the curtain and bow to the applause.

Manie gave a number of other recitals after that. They were all equally fine. Only, as he had to practise all day, he couldn't pay much attention to his farming. The result was that his farm went to pieces and he got into debt. The court messengers came and attached half his cattle while he was busy practising for his fourth recital. And he was practising for his seventh recital when they took away his ox-wagon and mule-cart.

Eventually, when Manie Kruger's musical career reached that stage when they took away his plough and the last of his oxen, he sold up what remained of his possessions and left the Bushveld, on his way to those great cities that he had so often talked about. It was very grand, the send-off that the Marico gave him. The predikant and the Volksraad member both made speeches about how proud the Transvaal was of her great son. Then Manie replied. Instead of thanking his audience, however, he started abusing us left and right, calling us a mob of hooligans and soulless Philistines, and saying how much he despised us.

Naturally, we were very much surprised at this outburst, as we had always been kind to Manie Kruger and had encouraged him all we could. But Letta Steyn explained that Manie didn't really mean the things he said. She said it was just that every great artist was expected to talk in that way about the place he came from.

So we knew it was all right, and the more offensive the things were that Manie said about us, the louder we shouted "Hoor, hoor vir Manie." There was a particularly enthusiastic round of applause when he said that we knew as much about art as a boomslang. His language was hotter than anything I had ever heard – except once. And that was when De Wet said what he thought of Cronjé's surrender to the English at Paardeberg. We could feel that Manie's speech was the real thing. We cheered ourselves hoarse, that day.

And so Manie Kruger went. We received one letter to say that he had reached Pretoria. But after that we heard no more from him.

Yet always, when Letta Steyn spoke of Manie, it was as a child speaks of a dream, half wistfully, and always, with the voice of a wistful child, she would tell me how one day, one day he would return. And often, when it was dusk, I would see her sitting on the stoep, gazing out across the veld into the evening, down the dusty road that led between the thorn-trees and beyond the Dwarsberg, waiting for the lover who would come to her no more.

It was a long time before I again saw Manie Kruger. And then it was in Pretoria. I had gone there to interview the Volksraad member about an election promise. It was quite by accident that I saw Manie. And he was playing the concertina – playing as well as ever, I thought. I went away quickly. But what affected me very strangely was just that one glimpse I had of the green curtain of the bar in front of which Manie Kruger played.

Mafeking Road

When people ask me – as they often do – how it is that I can tell the best stories of anybody in the Transvaal (Oom Schalk Lourens said, modestly), then I explain to them that I just learn through observing the way that the world has with men and women. When I say this they nod their heads wisely, and say that they understand, and I nod my head wisely also, and that seems to satisfy them. But the thing I say to them is a lie, of course.

For it is not the story that counts. What matters is the way you tell it. The important thing is to know just at what moment you must knock out your pipe on your veldskoen, and at what stage of the story you must start talking about the School Committee at Drogevlei. Another necessary thing is to know what part of the story to leave out.

And you can never learn these things.

Look at Floris, the last of the Van Barnevelts. There is no doubt that he had a good story, and he should have been able to get people to listen to it. And yet nobody took any notice of him or of the things he had to say. Just because he couldn't tell the story properly.

Accordingly, it made me sad whenever I listened to him talk. For I could tell just where he went wrong. He never knew the moment at which to knock the ash out of his pipe. He always mentioned his opinion of the Drogevlei School Committee in the wrong place. And, what was still worse, he didn't know what part of the story to leave out.

And it was no use my trying to teach him, because as I have said, this is the thing that you can never learn. And so, each time he had told his story, I would see him turn away from me, with a look of doom on his face, and walk slowly down the road, stoop-shouldered, the last of the Van Barnevelts.

On the wall of Floris's voorkamer is a long family tree of the Van Barnevelts. You can see it there for yourself. It goes back for over two hundred years, to the Van Barnevelts of Amsterdam. At one time it went even further back, but that was before the white ants started on the top part of it and ate away quite a lot of Van Barnevelts. Nevertheless, if you look at this list, you will notice that at the bottom, under Floris's own name, there is the last entry, "Stephanus." And behind the name, "Stephanus," between two bent strokes, you will read the words: "Obiit Mafeking."

At the outbreak of the Second Boer War Floris van Barnevelt was a widower, with one son, Stephanus, who was aged seventeen. The commando from our part of the Transvaal set off very cheerfully. We made a fine show, with our horses and our wide hats and our bandoliers, and with the sun shining on the barrels of our Mausers.

Young Stephanus van Barnevelt was the gayest of us all. But he said there was one thing he didn't like about the war, and that was that, in the end, we would have to go over the sea. He said that, after we had invaded the whole of the Cape, our commando would have to go on a ship and invade England also.

But we didn't go overseas, just then. Instead, our veldkornet told us that the burghers from our part had been ordered to join the big commando that was lying at Mafeking. We had to go and shoot a man there called Baden-Powell.

We rode steadily on into the west. After a while we noticed that our veldkornet frequently got off his horse and engaged in conversation with passing kaffirs, leading them some distance from the roadside and speaking earnestly to them. Of course, it was right that our veldkornet should explain to the kaffirs that it was war-time, now, and that the Republic expected every kaffir to stop smoking so much dagga and to think seriously about what was going on. But we noticed that each time at the end of the conversation the kaffir would point towards something, and that our veldkornet would take much pains to follow the direction of the kaffir's finger.

Of course, we understood, then, what it was all about. Our veldkornet was a young fellow, and he was shy to let us see that he didn't know the way to Mafeking.

Somehow, after that, we did not have so much confidence in our veldkornet.

After a few days we got to Mafeking. We stayed there a long while, until the English troops came up and relieved the place. We left, then. We left quickly. The English troops had brought a lot of artillery with them. And if we had difficulty in finding the road to Mafeking, we had no difficulty in finding the road away from Mafeking. And this time our veldkornet did not need kaffirs, either, to point with their fingers where we had to go. Even though we did a lot of travelling in the night.

Long afterwards I spoke to an Englishman about this. He said it gave him a queer feeling to hear about the other side of the story of Mafeking. He said there had been very great rejoicings in England when Mafeking was relieved, and it was strange to think of the other aspect of it – of a defeated country and of broken columns blundering through the dark.

I remember many things that happened on the way back from Mafeking. There was no moon. And the stars shone down fitfully on the road that was full of guns and frightened horses and desperate men. The veld throbbed with the hoof-beats of baffled commandos. The stars looked down on scenes that told sombrely of a nation's ruin; they looked on the muzzles of the Mausers that had failed the Transvaal for the first time.

Of course, as a burgher of the Republic, I knew what my duty was. And that was to get as far away as I could from the place where, in the sunset, I had last seen English artillery. The other burghers knew their duty also. Our kommandants and veldkornets had to give very few orders. Nevertheless, though I rode very fast, there was one young man who rode still faster. He kept ahead of me all the time.

He rode, as a burgher should ride when there may be stray bullets flying, with his head well down and with his arms almost round the horse's neck.

He was Stephanus, the young son of Floris van Barnevelt.

There was much grumbling and dissatisfaction, some time afterwards, when our leaders started making an effort to get the commandos in order again. In the end they managed to get us to halt. But most of us felt that this was a foolish thing to do. Especially as there was still a lot of firing going on, all over the place, in haphazard fashion, and we couldn't tell how far the English had followed us in the dark. Furthermore, the commandos had scattered in so many different directions that it seemed hopeless to try and get them together again until after the war. Stephanus and I dismounted and stood by our horses. Soon there was a large body of men around us. Their figures looked strange and shadowy in the starlight. Some of them stood by their horses. Others sat on the grass by the roadside. "Vas staan, burghers, vas staan," came the commands of our officers. And all the time we could still hear what sounded a lot like lyddite. It seemed foolish to be waiting there.

"The next they'll want," Stephanus van Barnevelt said, "is for us to go back to Mafeking. Perhaps our kommandant has left his tobacco pouch behind, there."

Some of us laughed at this remark, but Floris, who had not dismounted, said that Stephanus ought to be ashamed of himself for talking like that. From what we could see of Floris in the gloom, he looked quite impressive, sitting very straight in the saddle, with the stars shining on his beard and rifle.

"If the veldkornet told me to go back to Mafeking," Floris said, "I would go back."

"That's how a burgher should talk," the veldkornet said, feeling flattered. For he had had little authority since the time we found out what he was talking to the kaffirs for.

"I wouldn't go back to Mafeking for anybody," Stephanus replied, "unless, maybe, it's to hand myself over to the English."

"We can shoot you for doing that," the veldkornet said. "It's contrary to military law."

"I wish I knew something about military law," Stephanus answered. "Then I would draw up a peace treaty between Stephanus van Barnevelt and England."

Some of the men laughed again. But Floris shook his head sadly. He said the Van Barnevelts had fought bravely against Spain in a war that lasted eighty years.

Suddenly, out of the darkness there came a sharp rattle of musketry, and our men started getting uneasy again. But the sound of the firing decided Stephanus. He jumped on his horse quickly.

"I am turning back," he said, "I am going to hands-up to the English."

"No, don't go," the veldkornet called to him lamely, "or at least, wait until the morning. They may shoot you in the dark by mistake." As I have said, the veldkornet had very little authority.

Two days passed before we again saw Floris van Barnevelt. He was in a very worn and troubled state, and he said that it had been very hard for him to find his way back to us.

"You should have asked the kaffirs," one of our number said with a laugh. "All the kaffirs know our veldkornet."

But Floris did not speak about what happened that night, when we saw him riding out under the starlight, following after his son and shouting to him to be a man and to fight for his country. Also, Floris did not mention Stephanus again, his son who was not worthy to be a Van Barnevelt.

After that we got separated. Our veldkornet was the first to be taken prisoner. And I often felt that he must feel very lonely on St. Helena. Because there were no kaffirs from whom he could ask the way out of the barbed-wire camp.

Then, at last our leaders came together at Vereeniging, and peace was made. And we returned to our farms, relieved that the war was over, but with heavy hearts at the thought that it had all been for nothing and that over the Transvaal the Vierkleur would not wave again.

And Floris van Barnevelt put back in its place, on the wall of the voorkamer, the copy of his family tree that had been carried with him in his knapsack throughout the war. Then a new schoolmaster came to this part of the Marico, and after a long talk with Floris, the schoolmaster wrote behind Stephanus's name, between two curved lines, the two words that you can still read there: "Obiit Mafeking."

Consequently, if you ask any person hereabouts what "obiit" means, he is able to tell you, right away, that it is a foreign word, and that it means to ride up to the English, holding your Mauser in the air, with a white flag tied to it, near the muzzle.

But it was long afterwards that Floris van Barnevelt started telling his story.

And then they took no notice of him. And they wouldn't allow him to be nominated for the Drogevlei School Committee on the grounds that a man must be wrong in the head to talk in such an irresponsible fashion.

But I knew that Floris had a good story, and that its only fault was that he told it badly. He mentioned the Drogevlei School Committee too soon. And he knocked the ash out of his pipe in the wrong place. And he always insisted on telling that part of the story that he should have left out.

Starlight on the Veld

It was a cold night (Oom Schalk Lourens said), the stars shone with that frosty sort of light that you see on the wet grass some mornings, when you forget that it is winter, and you get up early, by mistake. The wind was like a girl sobbing out her story of betrayal to the stars.

Jan Ockerse and I had been to Derdepoort by donkey-cart. We came back in the evening. And Jan Ockerse told me of a road round the foot of a koppie that would be a short cut back to Drogevlei. Thus it was that we were sitting on the veld, close to the fire, waiting for the morning. We would then be able to ask a kaffir to tell us a short cut back to the foot of that koppie.

"But I know that it was the right road," Jan Ockerse insisted, flinging another armful of wood on the fire.

"Then it must have been the wrong koppie," I answered, "or the wrong donkey-cart. Unless you also want me to believe that I am at this moment sitting at home, in my voorkamer."

The light from the flames danced frostily on the spokes of a cartwheel, and I was glad to think that Jan Ockerse must be feeling as cold as I was.

"It is a funny sort of night," Jan Ockerse said, "and I am very miserable and hungry."

I was glad of that, too. I had begun to fear that he was enjoying himself.

"Do you know how high up the stars are?" Jan asked me next.

"No, not from here," I said, "but I worked it all out once, when I had a pencil. That was on the Highveld, though. But from where we are now, in the Lowveld, the stars are further away. You can see that they look smaller, too."

"Yes, I expect so," Jan Ockerse answered, "but a school-teacher told me a different thing in the bar at Zeerust. He said that the stargazers work out how far away a star is by the number of years that it takes them to find it in their telescopes. This school-teacher dipped his finger in the brandy and drew a lot of pictures and things on the bar counter, to show me how it was done. But one part of his drawings always dried up on the counter before he had finished doing the other part with his finger. He said that was the worst of that dry sort of brandy. Yet he didn't finish his explanations, because the barmaid came and wiped it all off with a rag. Then the school-teacher told me to come with him and he would use the blackboard in the other classroom. But the barmaid wouldn't allow us to take our glasses into the private bar, and the school-teacher fell down just about then, too."

"He seems to be one of that new kind of school-teacher," I said, "the kind that teaches the children that the earth turns round the sun. I am surprised they didn't sack him."

"Yes," Jan Ockerse answered, "they did."

I was glad to hear that also.

It seemed that there was a waterhole near where we were outspanned. For a couple of jackals started howling mournfully. Jan Ockerse jumped up and piled more wood on the fire.

"I don't like those wild animal noises," he said.

"They are only jackals, Jan," I said.

"I know," he answered, "but I was thinking of our donkeys. I don't want our donkeys to get frightened."

Suddenly a deep growl came to us from out of the dark bush. And it didn't sound a particularly mournful growl, either. Jan Ockerse worked very fast then with the wood.

"Perhaps it will be even better if we make two fires, and lie down between them," Jan Ockerse said, "our donkeys will feel less frightened if they see that you and I are safe. You know how a donkey's mind works."

The light of the fire shone dimly on the skeletons of the tall trees that the white ants had eaten, and we soon had two fires going. By the time that the second deep roar from the bush reached us, I had made an even bigger fire than Jan Ockerse, for the sake of the donkeys.

Afterwards it got quiet again. There was only the stirring of the wind in the thorn branches, and the rustling movement of things that you hear in the Bushveld at night.

Jan Ockerse lay on his back and put his hands under his head, and once more looked up at the stars.

"I have heard that these stars are worlds, just like ours," he said, "and that they have got people living on them, even."

"I don't think they would be good for growing mealies on, though," I answered, "they look too high up. Like the rante of the Sneeuberge, in the Cape. But I suppose they would make quite a good horse and cattle country. That's the trouble with these low-lying districts, like the Marico and the Waterberg: there is too much horse-sickness and tsetse-fly here."

"And butterflies," Jan Ockerse said sleepily, "with gold wings."

I also fell asleep shortly afterwards. And when I woke up again the fires were almost dead. I got up and fetched more wood. It took me quite a while to wake Jan Ockerse, though. Because the veldskoens I was wearing were the wrong kind, and had soft toes. Eventually he sat up and rubbed his eyes; and he said, of course, that he had been lying awake all night. What made him so certain that he had not been asleep, he said, was that he was imagining all the time that he was chasing bluebottles amongst the stars.

"And I would have caught up with them, too," he added, "only a queer sort of thing happened to me, while I was jumping from one star to another. It was almost as though somebody was kicking me."

Jan Ockerse looked at me in a suspicious kind of way.

So I told him that it was easy to see that he had been dreaming.

When the fires were piled high with wood, Jan Ockerse again said that it was a funny night, and once more started talking about the stars.

"What do you think sailors do at sea, Schalk," he said, "if they don't know the way and there aren't any other ships around from whom they can ask?"

"They have got it all written down on a piece of paper with a lot of red and blue on it," I answered, "and there are black lines that show you the way from Cape Town to St. Helena. And figures to tell you how many miles down the ship will go if it sinks. I went to St. Helena during the Boer War. You can live in a ship just like an ox-wagon. Only, a ship isn't so comfortable, of course. And it is further between outspans."

"I heard, somewhere, that sailors find their way by the stars," Jan Ockerse said. "I wonder what people want to tell me things like that for."

He lay silent for a while, looking up at the stars and thinking.

"I remember one night when I stood on Annie Steyn's stoep and spoke to her about the stars," Jan Ockerse said, later. "I was going to trek with the cattle to the Limpopo because of the drought. I told Annie that I would be away until the rains came, and I told her that every night, when I was gone, she had to look at a certain star and think of me. I showed her which star. Those three stars there, that are close together in a straight line. She had to remember me by the middle one, I said. But Annie explained that Willem Mostert, who had trekked to the Limpopo about a week before, had already picked that middle star for her to remember him by. So I said, all right, the top star would do. But Annie said that one already belonged to Stoffel Brink. In the end I agreed that she could remember me by the bottom star, and Annie was still saying that she would look at the lower one of those three stars every night and think of me, when her father, who seemed to have been listening behind the door, came on to the stoep and said: 'What about cloudy nights?' in what he supposed was a clever sort of way."

"What happened then?" I asked Jan Ockerse.

"Annie was very annoyed," he replied, "she told her father that he was always spoiling things. She told him that he wasn't a bit funny, really, especially as I was the third young man to whom he had said the same thing. She said that no matter how foolish a young man might be, her father had no right to make jokes like that in front of him. It was good to hear the way that Annie stood up for me. Anyway, what followed was a long story. I came across Willem Mostert and Stoffel Brink by the Limpopo. And we remained together there for several months. And it must have been an unusual sight for a stranger to see three young men sitting round the camp-fire, every night, looking up at the stars. We got friendly, after a while, and when the rains came the three of us trekked back to the Marico. And I found, then, that Annie's father had been right. About the cloudy nights, I mean. For I understood that it was on just such a sort of night that Annie had run off to Johannesburg with a bywoner who was going to look for work on the mines."

Jan Ockerse sighed and returned to his thinking.

But with all the time that we had spent in talking and sleeping, most of the night had slipped away. We kept only one fire going now, and Jan Ockerse and I took turns in putting on the wood. It gets very cold just before dawn, and we were both shivering.

"Anyway," Jan Ockerse said after a while, "now you know why I am interested in stars. I was a young man when this happened. And I have told very few people about it. About seventeen people, I should say. The others wouldn't listen. But always, on a clear night, when I see those three bright stars in a row, I look for a long time at that lowest star, and there seems to be something very friendly about the way it shines. It seems to be my star, and its light is different from the light of the other stars. . . and you know, Schalk, Annie Steyn had such red lips. And such long, soft hair, Schalk. And there was that smile of hers."

Afterwards the stars grew pale and we started rounding up the donkeys and got ready to go. And I wondered what Annie Steyn would have thought of it, if she had known that during all those years there was this man, looking up at the stars on nights when the sky was clear, and dreaming about her lips and her hair and her smile. But as soon as I reflected about it, I knew what the answer was, also. Of course, Annie Steyn would think nothing of Jan Ockerse. Nothing at all.

And, no doubt, Annie Steyn was right.

But it was strange to think that we had passed a whole night in talking about the stars. And I did not know, until then, that it was all on account of a love story of long ago.

We climbed on to the cart and set off to look for the way home.

"I know that school-teacher in the Zeerust bar was all wrong," Jan Ockerse said, finally, "when he tried to explain how far away the stars are. The lower one of those three stars – ah, it has just faded – is very near to me. Yes, it is very near."

SPLENDOURS FROM RAMOUTSA

NO – OOM SCHALK LOURENS SAID – no, I don't know why it is that people always ask me to tell them stories. Even though they all know that I can tell better stories than anybody else. Much better. What I mean is, I wonder why people listen to stories. Of course, it is easy to understand why a man should ask me to tell him a story when there is drought in the Marico. Because then he can sit on the stoep and smoke his pipe and drink coffee, while I am talking, so that my story keeps him from having to go to the borehole, in the hot sun, to pump water for his cattle.

By the earnest manner in which the farmers of the Marico ask me for stories at certain periods, I am always able to tell that there is no breeze to drive the windmill, and the pump-handle is heavy, and the water is very far down. And at such times I have often observed the look of sorrow that comes into a man's eyes, when he knows that I am near the end of my story and that he will shortly have to reach for his hat.

And when I have finished the story he says, "Yes, Oom Schalk. That is the way of the world. Yes, that story is very deep."

But I know that all the time he is really thinking of how deep the water is in the borehole.

As I have said, it is when people have other reasons for asking me to tell them a story that I start wondering as I do now. When they ask me at those times when there is no ploughing to be done and there are no barbed-wire fences to be put up in the heat of the day. And I think that these reasons are deeper than any stories and deeper than the water in the boreholes when there is drought.

There was young Krisjan Geel, for instance. He once listened to a story. It was foolish of him to have listened, of course, especially as I hadn't told it to him. He had heard it from the Indian behind the counter of the shop in Ramoutsa. Krisjan Geel related this story to me, and I told him straight out that I didn't think much of it. I said anybody could guess, right from the start, why the princess was sitting beside the well. Anybody could see that she hadn't come there just because she was thirsty. I also said that the story was too long, and that even if I was thinking of something else I would still have told it in such a way that people would have wanted to hear it to the end. I pointed out lots of other details like that.

Krisjan Geel said he had no doubt that I was right, but that the man who told him the story was only an Indian, after all, and that for an Indian, perhaps, it wasn't too bad. He also said that there were quite a number of customers in the place, and that made it more difficult for the Indian to tell the story properly, because he had to stand at such an awkward angle, all the time, weighing out things with his foot on the scale.

By his tone it sounded as though Krisjan Geel was quite sorry for the Indian.

So I spoke to him very firmly.

"The Indian in the store at Ramoutsa," I said, "has told me much better stories than that before today. He once told me that there were no burnt mealies mixed with the coffee-beans he sold me. Another one that was almost as good was when he said – "

"And to think that the princess went and waited by the well," Krisjan Geel interrupted me, "just because once she had seen the young man there."

" – Another good one," I insisted, "was when he said that there was no Kalahari sand in the sack of yellow sugar I bought from him."

"And she had only seen him once," Krisjan Geel went on, "and she was a princess."

" – And I had to give most of that sugar to the pigs," I said, "it didn't melt or sweeten the coffee. It just stayed like mud at the bottom of the cup."

"She waited by the well because she was in love with him," Krisjan Geel ended up, lamely.

" – I just mixed it in with the pigs' mealie-meal," I said, "they ate it very fast. It's funny how fast a pig eats."

Krisjan Geel didn't say any more after that one. No doubt he realised that I wasn't going to allow him to impress me with a story told by an Indian; and not very well told either. I could see what the Indian's idea was. Just because I had stopped buying from his shop after that unpleasantness about the coffee-beans and the sugar – which were only burnt mealies and Kalahari sand, as I explained to a number of my neighbours – he had hit on this uncalled-for way of paying me back. He was setting up as my rival. He was also going to tell stories.

And on account of the long start I had on him he was using all sorts of unfair methods. Like putting princesses in his stories. And palaces. And elephants that were all dressed up with yellow and red hangings and that were trained to trample on the king's enemies at the word of command. Whereas the only kind of elephants I could talk about were those that didn't wear red hangings or gold bangles and that didn't worry about whether or not you were the king's enemy: they just trampled on you first, anyhow, and without any sort of training either.

At first I felt it was very unfair of the Indian to come along with stories like that. I couldn't compete. And I began to think that there was much reason in what some of the speakers said at election meetings about the Indian problem.

But when I had thought it over carefully, I knew it didn't matter. The Indian could tell all the stories he wanted to about a princess riding around on an elephant. For there was one thing that I knew I could always do better than the Indian. Just in a few words, and without even talking about the princess, I would be able to let people know, subtly, what was in her heart. And this was more important than the palaces and the temples and the elephants with gold ornaments on their feet.

Perhaps the Indian realised the truth of what I am saying now. At all events, after a while he stopped wasting the time of his customers with stories of emperors. In between telling them that the price of sheep-dip and axle-grease had gone up. Or perhaps his customers got tired of listening to him.

But before that happened several of the farmers had hinted to me, in what they thought was a pleasantly amusing manner, that I would have to start putting more excitement into my stories if I wanted to keep in the fashion. They said I would have to bring in at least a king and a couple of princes, somehow, and also a string of elephants with Namaqualand diamonds in their ears.

I said they were talking very foolishly. I pointed out that there was no sense in my trying to tell people about kings and princes and trained elephants, and so on, when I didn't know anything about them or what they were supposed to do even.

"They don't need to do anything," Frik Snyman explained, "you can just mention that there was a procession like that nearby when whatever you are talking about happened. You can just mention them quickly, Oom Schalk, and you needn't say anything about them until you are in the middle of your next story. You can explain that the people in the procession had nothing to do with the story, because they were only passing through to some other place."

Of course, I said that that was nonsense. I said that if I had to keep on using that same procession over and over again, the people in it would be very travel-stained after they had passed through a number of stories. It would be a ragged and dust-laden procession.

"And the next time you tell us about a girl going to Nagmaal in Zeerust, Oom Schalk," Frik Snyman went on, "you can say that two men held up a red umbrella for her and that she had jewels in her hair, and she was doing a snake-dance."

I knew that Frik Snyman was only speaking like that, thoughtlessly, because of things he had seen in the bioscope that had gone to his head.

Nevertheless, I had to listen to many unreasonable remarks of this description before the Indian at Ramoutsa gave up trying to entertain his customers with empty discourse.

The days passed, and the drought came, and the farmers of the Marico put in much of their time at the boreholes, pushing the heavy pump-handles up and down. So that the Indian's brief period of story-telling was almost forgotten. Even Krisjan Geel came to admit that there was such a thing as overdoing these stories of magnificence.

"All these things he says about temples, and so on," Krisjan Geel said, "with white floors and shining red stones in them. And rajahs. Do you know what a rajah is, Oom Schalk? No, I don't know, either. You can have too much of that. It was only that one story of his that was any good. That one about the princess. She had rich stones in her hair, and pearls sewn on to her dress. And so the young man never guessed why she had come there. He didn't guess that she loved him. But perhaps I didn't tell you the story properly the first time, Oom Schalk. Perhaps I should just tell it to you again. I have already told it to many people."

But I declined his offer hurriedly. I replied that there was no need for him to go over all that again. I said that I remembered the story very well and that if it was all the same to him I should prefer not to hear it a second time. He might just spoil it in telling it again.

But it was only because he was young and inexperienced, I said, that he had allowed the Indian's story to carry him away like that. I told him about other young men whom I had known at various times, in the Marico, who had formed wrong judgments about things and who had afterwards come along and told me so.

"Why you are so interested in that story," I said, "is because you like to imagine yourself as that young man."

Krisjan Geel agreed with me that this was the reason why the Indian's story had appealed to him so much. And he went on to say that a young man had no chance, really, in the Marico. What with the droughts, and the cattle getting the miltsiek, and the mosquitoes buzzing around so that you couldn't sleep at night.

And when Krisjan Geel left me I could see, very clearly, how much he envied the young man in the Indian's story.

As I have said before, there are some strange things about stories and about people who listen to them. I thought so particularly on a hot afternoon, a few weeks later, when I saw Lettie Viljoen. The sun shone on her upturned face and on her bright yellow hair. She sat with one hand pressed in the dry grass of last summer, and I thought of what a graceful figure she was, and of how slender her wrists were.

And because Lettie Viljoen hadn't come there riding on an elephant with orange trappings and gold bangles, and because she wasn't wearing a string of red stones at her throat, Krisjan Geel knew, of course, that she wasn't a princess.

And I suppose that this was the reason why, during all the time in which he was talking to her, telling her that story about the princess at the well, Krisjan Geel never guessed about Lettie Viljoen, and what it was that had brought her there, in the heat of the sun, to the borehole.

THE PROPHET

NO, I NEVER CAME ACROSS THE Prophet van Rensburg, the man who told General Kemp that it was the right time to rebel against the English. As you know, General Kemp followed his advice and they say that General Kemp still believed in Van Rensburg's prophecies, even after the two of them were locked up in the Pretoria Gaol.

But I knew another prophet. His name was Erasmus. Stephanus Erasmus. Van Rensburg could only foretell that so and so was going to happen, and then he was wrong, sometimes. But with Stephanus Erasmus it was different. Erasmus used to make things come true just by prophesying them.

You can see what that means. And yet, in the end I wondered about Stephanus Erasmus.

There are lots of people like Van Rensburg who can just foretell the future, but when a man comes along who can actually make the future, then you feel that you can't make jokes about him. All the farmers in Drogedal talked about Stephanus Erasmus with respect. Even when he wasn't present to hear what was being said about him. Because there would always be somebody to go along and tell him if you happened to make some slighting remark about him.

I know, because once in Piet Fourie's house I said that if I was a great prophet like Stephanus Erasmus I would try and prophesy myself a new pair of veldskoens, seeing that his were all broken on top and you could see two corns and part of an ingrowing toenail. After that things went all wrong on my farm for six months. So I knew that Piet Fourie had told the prophet what I had said. Amongst other things six of my best trek-oxen died of the miltsiekte.

After that, whenever I wanted to think anything unflattering about Stephanus Erasmus I went right out into the veld and did it all there.

You can imagine that round that time I went into the veld alone very often. It wasn't easy to forget about the six trek-oxen.

More than once I hoped that Stephanus Erasmus would also take it into his head to tell General Kemp that it was the right time to go into rebellion. But Erasmus was too wise for that. I remember once when we were all together just before a meeting of the Dwarsberg School Committee I asked Stephanus about this.

"What do you think of this new wheel-tax, Oom Stephanus?" I said. "Don't you think the people should go along with their rifles and hoist the Vierkleur over the magistrate's court at Zeerust?"

Erasmus looked at me and I lowered my eyes. I felt sorry in a way that I had spoken. His eyes seemed to look right through me. I felt that to him I looked like a springbok that has been shot and cut open, and you can see his heart and his ribs and his liver and his stomach and all the rest of his inside. It was not very pleasant to be sitting talking to a man who regards you as nothing more than a cut-open springbok.

But Stephanus Erasmus went on looking at me. I became frightened. If he had said to me then, "You know you are just a cut-open springbok," I would have said, "Yes, Oom Stephanus, I know." I could see then that he had a great power. He was just an ordinary sort of farmer on the outside, with a black beard and dark eyes and a pair of old shoes that were broken on top. But inside he was terrible. I began to be afraid for my remaining trek-oxen.

Then he spoke, slowly and with wisdom.

"There are also magistrates' courts at Mafeking and Zwartruggens and Rysmierbult," he said. "In fact there is a magistrates' court in every town I have been in along the railway line. And all these magistrates' courts collect wheel-tax," Oom Stephanus said.

I could see then that he not only had great power inside him, but that he was also very cunning. He never went in for any wild guessing, like saying to a stranger, "You are a married man with five children and in your inside jacket-pocket is a letter from the Kerkraad asking you to become an ouderling." I have seen some so-called fortune-tellers say that to a man they had never seen in their lives before in the hope that they might be right.

You know, it is a wonderful thing this, about being a prophet. I have thought much about it, and what I know about it I can't explain. But I know it has got something to do with death. This is one of the things I have learnt in the Marico, and I don't think you could learn it anywhere else. It is only when you have had a great deal of time in which to do nothing but think and look at the veld and at the sky where there have been no rain-clouds for many months, that you grow to an understanding of these things.

Then you know that being a prophet and having power is very simple. But it is also something very terrible. And you know then that there are men and women who are unearthly, and it is this that makes them greater than kings. For a king can lose his power when people take it away from him, but a prophet can never lose his power – if he is a real prophet.

It was the schoolchildren who first began talking about this. I have noticed how often things like this start with the stories of kaffirs and children.

Anyway, a very old kaffir had come to live at the outspan on the road to Ramoutsa. Nobody knew where he had come from, except that when questioned he would lift up his arm very slowly and point towards the west. There is nothing in the west. There is only the Kalahari Desert. And from his looks you could easily believe that this old kaffir had lived in the desert all his life. There was something about his withered body that reminded you of the Great Drought.

We found out that this kaffir's name was Mosiko. He had made himself a rough shelter of thorn-bushes and old mealie bags. And there he lived alone. The kaffirs round about brought him mealies and beer, and from what they told us it appeared that he was not very grateful for these gifts, and when the beer was weak he swore vilely at the persons who brought it.

As I have said, it was the kaffirs who first took notice of him. They said he was a great witch-doctor. But later on white people also started taking him presents. And they asked him questions about what was going to happen. Sometimes Mosiko told them what they wanted to know. At other times he was impudent and told them to go and ask Baas Stephanus Erasmus.

You can imagine what a stir this created.

"Yes," Frans Steyn said to us one afternoon, "and when I asked this kaffir whether my daughter Anna should get married to Gert right away or whether she should go to High School to learn English, Mosiko said that I had to ask Baas Stephanus. 'Ask him,' he said, 'that one is too easy for me'."

Then the people said that this Mosiko was an impertinent kaffir, and that the only thing Stephanus could do was not to take any notice of him.

I watched closely to see what Erasmus was going to do about it. I could see that the kaffir's impudence was making him mad. And when people said to him, "Do not take any notice of Mosiko, Oom Stephanus, he is a lazy old kaffir," anyone could see that this annoyed him more than anything else. He suspected that they said this out of politeness. And there is nothing that angers you more than when those who used to fear you start being polite to you.

The upshot of the business was that Stephanus Erasmus went to the outspan where Mosiko lived. He said he was going to boot him back into the Kalahari, where he came from. Now, it was a mistake for Stephanus to have gone out to see Mosiko. For Mosiko looked really important to have the prophet coming to visit him. The right thing always is for the servant to visit the master.

All of us went along with Stephanus.

On the way down he said, "I'll kick him all the way out of Zeerust. It is bad enough when kaffirs wear collars and ties in Johannesburg and walk on the pavements reading newspapers. But we can't allow this sort of thing in the Marico."

But I could see that for some reason Stephanus was growing angry as we tried to pretend that we were determined to have Mosiko shown up. And this was not the truth. It was only Erasmus's quarrel. It was not our affair at all.

We got to the outspan.

Mosiko had hardly any clothes on. He sat up against a bush with his back bent and his head forward near his knees. He had many wrinkles. Hundreds of them. He looked to be the oldest man in the world. And yet there was a kind of strength about the curve of his back and I knew the meaning of it. It seemed to me that with his back curved in that way, and the sun shining on him and his head bent forward, Mosiko could be much greater and do more things just by sitting down than other men could do by working hard and using cunning. I felt that Mosiko could sit down and do nothing and yet be more powerful than the Kommandant-General.

He seemed to have nothing but what the sun and the sand and the grass had given him, and yet that was more than what all the men in the world could give him.

I was glad that I was there that day, at the meeting of the wizards.

Stephanus Erasmus knew who Mosiko was, of course. But I wasn't sure if Mosiko knew Stephanus. So I introduced them. On another day people would have laughed at the way I did it. But at that moment it didn't seem so funny, somehow.

"Mosiko," I said, "this is Baas Prophet Stephanus Erasmus."

"And, Oom Stephanus," I said, "this is Witch-doctor Mosiko."

Mosiko raised his eyes slightly and glanced at Erasmus. Erasmus looked straight back at Mosiko and tried to stare him out of countenance. I knew the power with which Stephanus Erasmus could look at you. So I wondered what was going to happen. But Mosiko looked down again, and kept his eyes down on the sand.

Now, I remembered how I felt that day when Stephanus Erasmus had looked at me and I was ready to believe that I was a cut-open springbok. So I was not surprised at Mosiko's turning away his eyes. But in the same moment I realised that Mosiko looked down in the way that seemed to mean that he didn't think that Stephanus was a man of enough importance for him to want to stare out of countenance. It was as though he thought there were other things for him to do but look at Stephanus.

Then Mosiko spoke.

"Tell me what you want to know, Baas Stephanus," he said, "and I'll prophesy for you."

I saw the grass and the veld and the stones. I saw a long splash of sunlight on Mosiko's naked back. But for a little while I neither saw nor heard anything else. For it was a deadly thing that the kaffir had said to the white man. And I knew that the others also felt it was a deadly thing. We stood there, waiting. I was not sure whether to be glad or sorry that I had come. The time seemed so very long in passing.

"Kaffir," Stephanus said at last, "you have no right to be here on a white man's outspan. We have come to throw you off it. I am going to kick you, kaffir. Right now I am going to kick you. You'll see what a white man's boot is like."

Mosiko did not move. It did not seem as though he had heard anything Stephanus had said to him. He appeared to be thinking of something else – something very old and very far away.

Then Stephanus took a step forward. He paused for a moment. We all looked down.

Frans Steyn was the first to laugh. It was strange and unnatural at first to hear Frans Steyn's laughter. Everything up till then had been so tense and even frightening. But immediately afterwards we all burst out laughing together. We laughed loudly and uproariously. You could have heard us right at the other side of the bult.

I have told you about Stephanus Erasmus's veldskoens, and that they were broken on top. Well, now, in walking to the outspan, the last riem had burst loose, and Stephanus Erasmus stood there with his right foot raised from the ground and a broken shoe dangling from his instep.

Stephanus never kicked Mosiko. When we had finished laughing we got him to come back home. Stephanus walked slowly, carrying the broken shoe in his hand and picking the soft places to walk on, where the burnt grass wouldn't stick into his bare foot.

Stephanus Erasmus had lost his power.

But I knew that even if his shoe hadn't broken, Stephanus would never have kicked Mosiko. I could see by that look in his eyes that, when he took the step forward and Mosiko didn't move, Stephanus had been beaten for always.

Seed-time and Harvest

At the time of the big drought (Oom Schalk Lourens said) Jurie Steyn trekked with what was left of his cattle to the Schweizer-Reneke District. His wife, Martha, remained behind on the farm. After a while an ouderling from near Vleisfontein started visiting Jurie Steyn's farm to comfort Martha. And as time went on everybody in the Marico began talking about the ouderling's visits, and they said that the ouderling must be neglecting his own affairs quite a lot, coming to Jurie Steyn's farm so often, especially since Vleisfontein was so far away. Other people, again, said that Vleisfontein couldn't be far enough away for the ouderling: not when Jurie Steyn got back, they said.

The ouderling was a peculiar sort of man, too. When some neighbour called at Jurie Steyn's farm, and Martha was there alone with the ouderling, and the neighbour would drop a hint about the drought breaking some time, meaning that Jurie Steyn would then be coming back to the Marico from the Schweizer-Reneke District with his cattle, then the ouderling would just look very solemn, and he would say that it must be the Lord's will that this drought had descended on the Marico, and that he himself had been as badly stricken by the hand of the Lord as anybody and that the windmill pumped hardly enough water even for his prize Large Whites, and that in spite of what people might think he would be as pleased as anybody else when the rains came again.

That was a long drought. It was a very bitter period. But a good while before the drought broke the ouderling's visits to Martha Steyn had ceased. And the grass was already turning green in the heavy rains that followed on the great drought when Jurie Steyn got back to his farmhouse with his wagon and his red Afrikaner cattle. And by that time the ouderling's visits to Martha were hardly even a memory any longer.

But a while later, when Martha Steyn had a child, again, there was once more a lot of talk, especially among the women. But there was no way of telling how much Jurie Steyn knew or guessed about what was being said about himself and Martha and the ouderling, and about his youngest child, whom they had christened Kobus.

It only seemed that for a good while thereafter Jurie Steyn seemed to be like a man lost in thought. And it would appear that he had grown absent-minded in a way that we hadn't noticed about him before. And it would seem, also, that his absent-mindedness was of a sort that did not make him very reliable in his dealings with his neighbours. It was almost as though what had been happening between the ouderling and Martha Steyn – whatever had been happening – had served to undermine not Martha's moral character but Jurie Steyn's.

This change that had taken place in Jurie Steyn was brought home to me most forcibly some years later in connection with some fence-poles that he had gone to fetch for me from Ramoutsa station. There was a time when I had regarded Jurie Steyn as somebody strong and upright, like a withaak tree, but it seemed that his character had gradually grown flat and twisted along the ground, like the tendrils of a pumpkin that has been planted in the cool side of a manure-pile at the back of the house. And that is a queer thing, too, that I have noticed about pumpkins. They thrive better if you plant them at the back of the house than in the front. Something like that seemed to be the case with Jurie Steyn, too, somehow.

Anyway, it was when the child Kobus was about nine years old, and Jurie Steyn's mind seemed to have grown all curved like a green mamba asleep in the sun, that the incident of the fence-poles occurred.

But I must first tell you about the school-teacher that we had at Drogevlei then. This school-teacher started doing a lot of farming in his spare time. Then he began taking his pupils round to his farm, some afternoons, and he showed them how to plant mealies as part of their school subjects. We all said that that was nonsense, because there was nothing that we couldn't teach the children ourselves, when it came to matters like growing mealies. But the teacher said, no, the children had to learn the theory of what nature did to the seeds, and it was part of natural science studies, and he said our methods of farming were all out of date, anyway.

We didn't know whether our methods of farming were out of date, but we certainly thought that there were things about the teacher's methods of education that were altogether different from anything we had come across so far. Because the school hours got shorter and shorter as the months went by, and the children spent more and more time on the teacher's farm, on their hands and knees, learning how to put things into the ground to make them grow. And when the mealies were about a foot high the teacher made the whole school learn how to pull up the weeds that grew between the mealies. This lesson took about a week: the teacher had planted so large an area. The children would get home from school very tired and stained from their lessons on the red, clayey sort of soil that was on that part of the teacher's farm.

And near the end of the school term, when the dams were drying up, the children were given an examination in pumping water out of the borehole for the teacher's cattle.

But afterwards, when the teacher showed the children how to make a door for his pigsty out of the school blackboard, and how to wrap up his eggs for the Zeerust market in the pages torn from their exercise books, we began wondering whether the more old-fashioned kind of school-teacher was not perhaps better – the kind of schoolmaster who only taught the children to read and write and to do sums, and left the nature-science job of cooking the mangolds for the pigs' supper to the kaffirs.

And then there came that afternoon when I went to see Jurie Steyn about some fence-poles that he had gone to fetch for me from Ramoutsa station, and I found that Jurie was too concerned about something that the teacher had said to be able to pay much attention to my questions. I have mentioned how the deterioration in his moral character took the form of making him absent-minded, at times, in a funny sort of way.

"You can have the next lot I fetch," Jurie said. "I have been so worried about what the school-teacher said that I have already planted all your fence-poles – look, along there – by mistake. I planted them without thinking. I was so concerned about the schoolmaster's impudence that I had got the kaffirs to dig the holes and plant in the poles before I realised what I was doing. But I'll pay you for them, some time – when I get my cheque from the creamery, maybe. And while we are about it, I may as well use up the roll of barbed wire that is also lying at Ramoutsa station, consigned to you. You won't need that barbed wire, now."

"No," I said, looking at my fence-poles planted in a long line. "No, Jurie, I won't need that barbed wire now. And another thing, if you stand here, just to the left of this ant-hill, and you look all along the tops of the poles, you will see that they are not planted in a straight line. You can see the line bends in two places."

But Jurie said, no, he was satisfied with the way he had planted in my fence-poles. The line was straight enough for him, he said. And I felt that this was quite true, and that anything would be straight enough for him – even if it was something as twisted as a raw ox-hide thong that you brei with a stick and a heavy stone slung from a tree.

"What did the school-teacher say about you?" I asked Jurie eventually, doing my best not to let him see how eager I was to hear if what had been said about him was really low enough.

"He said I was dishonest," Jurie answered. "He said. . . "

"How does he know?" I interrupted him quickly. "He's so busy on his farm there, with the harvesting, I didn't think he would have time to hear what is going on among us farmers. Did he make any mention of my fence-poles at all?"

"He didn't mean it that way," Jurie answered, standing to the side of the ant-hill and gazing into the distance with one eye shut. "No,

I think those poles are planted in all right. When the schoolmaster told me I was dishonest he meant it in a different sense. But what he said was bad enough. He said that my youngest son, Kobus, was dishonest, and that he feared that in that respect Kobus took after me."

I thought this was very singular. Did not the school-teacher know the story of the ouderling's visits to Jurie Steyn's wife, Martha, in the time of the big drought? Had Jurie Steyn no suspicions, either, about the boy, Kobus, not being his own child? But I did not let on to Jurie Steyn, of course, what my real thoughts were.

"So he said Kobus is dishonest?" I continued, trying to make my voice sound disarming. "Why, did Kobus go along to Ramoutsa station with you, for my poles?"

"No," Jurie Steyn answered. "The schoolmaster won't allow Kobus to stay away from school for a day – not until the harvesting is over. But I am sending Kobus and a kaffir to Ramoutsa on Saturday, by donkey-cart. I am sending him for that roll of barbed wire. And, oh, by the way, Schalk, while Kobus is in Ramoutsa, is there anything you would like him to get for you?"

I thanked Jurie and said, no, there was nothing for me at Ramoutsa that had not already been fetched. Then I asked him another question.

"Did the schoolmaster perhaps say that you and Kobus were a couple of aardvarks?" I asked. "I daresay he used pretty rough language. Snakes, too, he must have said. I mean to say. . . "

"You are quite right," Jurie interrupted me. "That fourth pole from the end must come out. It's not in line."

"The whole lot must come out," I said, "and be planted on my farm. That's what I ordered those poles for."

"That fourth pole of yours, Oom Schalk," Jurie repeated, "must be taken out and planted further to the left – I planted it in crooked because I was so upset by the schoolmaster. It was only when I got home that I realised the cheek of the whole thing. I have got a good mind to report the schoolmaster to the Education Department for writing private letters with school ink. I'd like to see him get out of that one."

If the Education Department did not take any action after the schoolmaster had used the front part of the school building to store his sweet-potatoes in, I did not think they would worry much about this complaint of Jurie Steyn's. By way of explanation the school-teacher told the parents that why he had to store the sweet-potatoes in that part of the school building for a while was because the prices on the Johannesburg market were so low, it was sheer robbery. He also complained that the Johannesburg produce agents had no sense of responsibility in regard to the interests of the farmers.

"If I had so little sense of responsibility about my duties as a school-teacher," he said, "the Education Department would have sacked me long ago."

When the schoolmaster made this remark several of the parents looked at him with a good deal of amazement.

These were the things that were passing through my mind while Jurie Steyn was telling me about the way the school-teacher had insulted him. I was anxious to learn more about it. I tried another way of getting Jurie to talk. I wanted to find out how much the schoolmaster knew, and how much Jurie himself suspected, of the facts of Kobus's paternity. I felt almost as inquisitive as a woman, then.

"I once heard the schoolmaster using very strong expressions, Jurie," I said, "and that was when he spoke to a Pondo kaffir whom he had caught stealing one of the back wheels of his ox-wagon. I have never been able to understand how that kaffir got the wheel off so quickly, because he didn't have a jack, as far as I know, and they say that the wagon had not been outspanned for more than two hours. But that was only a Pondo kaffir without much understanding of the white man's language of abuse. No doubt what the school-teacher said about you and your son Kobus was. . ."

"It's possible to get a back wheel off an ox-wagon even if you haven't got a jack, so long as the wagon isn't too heavily loaded," Jurie said, without giving me a chance to finish, "and as long as you have got two other men to help you. Still, it would be interesting to know how the Pondo did it. Was it dark at the time, do you know?"

I couldn't tell him. But it was getting dark on Jurie Steyn's farm. The deep shadows of the evening lay heavy across the thorn-bushes, and the furthest of my fence-poles had grown blurred against the sky. It seemed a strange thought to me that my fence-poles were that night for the first time standing upright and in silence, like the trees, awaiting the arrival of the first stars.

Jurie Steyn and I started walking towards the farmhouse, in front of which I had left my mule-cart. The boy Kobus came out to meet us, and I could see from the reddish clay on his knees that he had studied hard at school that day.

"You look tired, Kobus," Jurie Steyn said. And his voice suddenly sounded very soft when he spoke.

And in the dusk I saw the way that Kobus's eyes lit up when he took Jurie Steyn's hand. A singular variety of ideas passed through my mind, then, and I found that I no longer bore Jurie Steyn that same measure of resentment on account of his thoughtless way of acting with my fence-poles. I somehow felt that there were more important things in life than the question of what happened to my roll of barbed wire at Ramoutsa. And more important things than what had happened about the ouderling from near Vleisfontein.

Cometh Comet

Hans Engelbrecht was the first farmer in the Schweizer-Reneke District to trek (Oom Schalk Lourens said). With his wife and daughter and what was left of his cattle, he moved away to the northern slopes of the Dwarsberge, where the drought was less severe. Afterwards he was joined by other farmers from the same area. I can still remember how untidy the veld looked in those days, with rotting carcasses and sun-bleached bones lying about everywhere. Day after day we had stood at the boreholes, pumping an ever-decreasing trickle of brackish water into the cattle troughs. We watched in vain for a sign of a cloud. And it seemed that if anything did fall out of that sky, it wouldn't do us much good: it would be a shower of brimstone, most likely.

Still, it was a fine time for the aasvoëls and the crows. That was at the beginning, of course. Afterwards, when all the carcasses had been picked bare, and the Boers had trekked, most of the birds of prey flew away, also.

We trekked away in different directions. Four or five families eventually came to a halt at the foot of the Dwarsberge, near the place where Hans Engelbrecht was outspanned. In the vast area of the Schweizer-Reneke District only one man had chosen to stay behind. He was Ocker Gieljan, a young bywoner who had worked for Hans Engelbrecht since his boyhood. Ocker Gieljan spoke rarely, and then his words did not always seem to us to make sense.

Hans Engelbrecht was only partly surprised when, on the morning that the ox-wagon was loaded and the long line of oxen that were skin and bone started stumbling along the road to the north, Ocker Gieljan made it clear that he was not leaving the farm. The native voorloper had already gone to the head of the span and Hans Engelbrecht's wife and his eighteen-year-old daughter, Maria, were seated on the wagon, under the tent-sail, when Ocker Gieljan suddenly declared that he had decided to stay behind on the farm "to look after things here."

This was another instance of Ocker Gieljan's saying something that did not make sense. There could be nothing for him to look after, there, since in the whole district hardly a lizard was left alive.

Hans Engelbrecht was in no mood to waste time in arguing with a daft bywoner. Accordingly, he got the kaffirs to unload half a sack of mealie-meal and a quantity of biltong in front of Ocker Gieljan's mud-walled room.

During the past few years it had not rained much in the Marico Bushveld, either. But there was at least water in the Molopo, and the grazing was fair. Several months passed. Every day, from our camp by the Molopo, we studied the skies, which were of an intense blue. There was no longer that yellow tinge in the air that we had got used to in the Schweizer-Reneke District. But there was never a rain-cloud.

The time came, also, when Hans Engelbrecht was brought to understand that the Lord had visited still more trouble on himself and his family. A little while before we had trekked away from our farms, a young insurance agent had left the district suddenly for Cape Town. That was a long distance to run away, especially when you think of how bad the roads were in those days. And in some strange fashion it seemed to me as though that young insurance agent was actually our leader. For he stood, after all, with his light hat and short jacket, at the head of our flight out of the Schweizer-Reneke area.

It became a commonplace, after a while, for Maria Engelbrecht to be seen seated in the grass beside her father's wagon, weeping. Few pitied her. She must have sat in the grass too often, with that insurance agent with the pointed, polished shoes, Lettie Grobler said to some of the women – forgetting that there had been no grass left in the Schweizer-Reneke veld at the time when Hans Engelbrecht's daughter was being courted.

It was easy for Maria to wipe the tears from her face, another woman said. Easier than to wipe away her shame, the woman meant.

Now and again, from some traveller who had passed through Schweizer-Reneke, we who had trekked out of that stricken region would hear a few useless things about it. We learnt nothing that we did not already know. Ocker Gieljan was still on the Engelbrecht farm, we heard. And the only other living creature in the whole district was a solitary crow. A passing traveller had seen Ocker Gieljan at the borehole. He was pumping water into a trough for the crow, the traveller said.

"When his mealie-meal gives out, Ocker will find his way here, right enough," Hans Engelbrecht growled impatiently.

Then the night came when, from our encampment beside the Molopo, we first saw the comet, in the place above the Dwarsberg rante where the sun had gone down. We all began to wonder what that new star with the long tail meant. Would it bring rain? We didn't know. We could see, of course, that the star was an omen. Even an uneducated kaffir would know that. But we did not know what sort of omen it was.

If the bark of the maroelas turned black before the polgras was in seed, we would know that it would be a long winter. And if a wind sprang up suddenly in the evening, blowing away from the sunset, we would next morning send the cattle out later to graze. We knew many things about the veld and the sky and the seasons. But even the oldest Free State farmer among us didn't know what effect a comet had on a mealie-crop.

Hans Engelbrecht said that we should send for Rev. Losper, the missionary who ministered to the Bechuanas at Ramoutsa. But the rest of us ignored his suggestion.

During the following nights the comet became more clearly visible. A young policeman on patrol in these parts called on us one evening. When we spoke to him about the star, he said that he could do nothing about it, himself. It was a matter for the higher authorities, he said, laughing.

Nevertheless, he had made a few calculations, the policeman explained, and he had sent a report to Pretoria. He estimated that the star was twenty-seven and a half miles in length, and that it was travelling faster than a railway train. He would not be surprised if the star reached Pretoria before his report got there. That would spoil his chances of promotion, he added.

We did not take much notice of the policeman's remarks, however. For one thing, he was young. And, for another, we did not have much respect for the police.

"If a policeman doesn't even know how to get on to the spoor of a couple of kaffir oxen that I smuggle across the Bechuanaland border," Thys Bekker said, "how does he expect to be able to follow the footprints of a star across the sky? That is big man's work."

The appearance of the comet caused consternation among the Bechuanas in the village of Ramoutsa, where the mission station was. It did not take long for some of their stories about the star to reach our encampment on the other side of the Molopo. And although, at first, most of us professed to laugh at what we said were just ignorant kaffir superstitions, yet in the end we also began to share something of the Bechuana's fears.

"Have you heard what the kaffirs say about the new star?" Arnoldus Grobler, husband of Lettie Grobler, asked of Thys Bekker. "They say that it is a red beast with a fat belly like a very great chief, and it is going to come to eat up every blade of grass and every living thing."

"In that case, I hope he lands in Schweizer-Reneke," Thys Bekker said. "If that red beast comes down on my farm, all that will happen is that in a short while there will be a whole lot more bones lying around to get white in the sun."

Some of us felt that it was wrong of Thys Bekker to treat the matter so lightly. Moreover, this story only emanated from Ramoutsa, where there were a mission station and a post office. But a number of other stories, that were in every way much better, started soon afterwards to come out of the wilder parts of the Bushveld, travelling on foot. It seemed that the further a tribe of kaffirs lived away from civilisation, the more detailed and dependable was the information they had about the comet.

I know that I began to feel that Hans Engelbrecht had made the right suggestion in the first place, when he had said that we should send for the missionary. And I sensed that a number of others in our camp shared my feelings. But not one of us wanted to make this admission openly.

In the end it was Hans Engelbrecht himself who sent to Ramoutsa for Rev. Losper. By that time the comet was – each night in its rising – higher in the heavens, and it soon got round that the new star portended the end of the world. Lettie Grobler went so far as to declare that she had seen the good Lord Himself riding in the tail of the comet. What convinced us that she had, indeed, seen the Lord, was when she said that He had on a hat of the same shape as the predikant in Zwartruggens wore.

Lettie Grobler also said that the Lord was coming down to punish all of us for the sins of Maria Engelbrecht. This thought disturbed us greatly. We began to resent Maria's presence in our midst.

It was then that Hans Engelbrecht had sent for the missionary.

Meanwhile, Rev. Losper had his hands full with the Bechuanas at Ramoutsa, who seemed on the point of panicking in earnest. The latest story about the comet had just reached them, and because it had come from somewhere out of the deepest part of Africa, where the natives wore arrows tipped with leopard fangs stuck through their nostrils, like moustaches, it was easily the most terrifying story of all. The story had come to the village, thumped out on the tom-toms.

The Bechuana chief at Ramoutsa – so Rev. Losper told us afterwards – fell into such a terror at the message brought by the speaking drums, that he thrust a handful of earth into his mouth, without thinking. He would have swallowed it, too, the missionary said, if one of his indunas hadn't restrained him in time, pointing out to the chief that perhaps the drum-men had got the message wrong. For, since the post office had come to Ramoutsa, the kaffirs whose work in the village it was to receive and send out messages on their tom-toms had got somewhat out of practice.

Consequently, because of the tumult at Ramoutsa, it happened that Ocker Gieljan arrived at the encampment before Rev. Losper got there.

Ocker Gieljan looked very tired and dusty on that afternoon when he walked up to Hans Engelbrecht's wagon. He took off his hat and, smiling somewhat vacantly, sat down without speaking in the shade of the veld-tent, inside which Maria Engelbrecht lay on a mattress. Neither Hans Engelbrecht nor his wife asked Ocker Gieljan any questions about his journey from the Schweizer-Reneke farm. They knew that he could have nothing to tell.

Shortly afterwards, Ocker Gieljan made a communication to Hans Engelbrecht, speaking diffidently. Thereupon Hans Engelbrecht went into the tent and spoke to his wife and daughter. A few minutes later he came out, looking pleased with himself.

"Sit down here on this riempiestoel, Ocker," Hans Engelbrecht said to his prospective son-in-law, "and tell me how you came to leave the farm."

"I got lonely," Ocker Gieljan answered, thoughtfully. "You see, the crow flew away. I was alone, after that. The crow was then already weak. He didn't fly straight, like crows do. His wings wobbled."

When he told me about this, years later, Hans Engelbrecht said that something in Ocker Gieljan's tone brought him a sudden vision of the way his daughter, Maria, had also left the Schweizer-Reneke District. With broken wings.

I thought that Rev. Losper looked relieved to find, on his arrival at the camp, some time later, that all that was required of him, now, was the performance of a marriage ceremony.

On the next night but one, Maria Engelbrecht's child was born. All the adults in our little trekker community came in the night and the rain – which had been falling steadily for many hours – with gifts for Maria and her child.

And when I saw the star again, during the temporary break in the rain-clouds, it seemed to me that it was not such a new star, at all: that it was, indeed, a mighty old star.

Graven Image

Yes, I know those wood-carvings that the kaffirs used to make long ago (Oom Schalk Lourens said). They were very silly things, of course, and I had a good laugh at them myself, more than once. Several of my neighbours, including Karel Nienaber, had a good laugh at them, also, at various times. In fact, when you come to think of it, the one particular thing about those figures that the kaffirs used to carve out of soft wood like kremetart or 'ndubu was that you could always get a good laugh out of them.

And it is singular how into these mirthful incidents there got tangled part of the darker being of Louisa Wessels, a girl who did not laugh. And she seems almost as reluctant now to enter the story as she was then about becoming Karel Nienaber's bride. I can picture Louisa Wessels yet, shy but firm in her withdrawing, and as still as blue water.

It was all right, of course, as long as those wood-carvers stuck to chiselling certain kinds of animals that they knew well. The way they could carve a giraffe, for instance: his long neck, cut out of a piece of mesetla wood with a blunt knife, and the whole of him covered in black spots burnt with a red-hot iron, and his pointed head turned to one side, half upwards – why, you could *see* that giraffe. It was almost as though you could see the leaves of the tree, too, that he was pulling down and eating for his breakfast.

Although we knew that the whole thing was cut out of a piece of Bushveld wood by a lazy Bechuana, who would have been better employed in chopping up that wood and bringing a bundle of it into a farmer's kitchen, nevertheless, we could see that, for all his ignorance, the Bechuana kaffir knew how to carve a giraffe so that it looked really life-like. Because we Marico farmers knew a giraffe when we saw one. And when one of those wood-carvers brought along a model of a giraffe, we would smile to think that that kaffir was so uneducated, but we would also know that the thing he had carved was exactly like a giraffe. Sometimes we could even tell, from the way that the giraffe was standing, as to what particular kind of tree he was eating his breakfast from. Just from the way his head was turned, and the position in which his hind legs were placed, and the manner in which he would droop his shoulders to miss the thorns.

And the wood-carvers would also cut out, joined together on a piece of stick, three wild ducks swimming one behind the other. That was one of their favourite pieces of carving. The way that the ducks sat on the water was very true to life, the front duck swimming with his head high up, since he was naturally proud to be the leader. The only thing that was wrong was that those three wild ducks were held together by a piece of stick. That used to give us a very good laugh. I mean, we had often seen three ducks swimming in a row in that particular way. But they had never been tied together on a piece of stick.

It was when an old Bechuana wood-carver named Radipalong, in Ramoutsa, began carving what he said were the images of various white men living in the Marico, that we really started laughing.

I suppose you know that a kaffir wood-carver will never cut a figure of another kaffir. He's not allowed to. Because, if that kaffir finds out about it, there will be a lot of trouble in the kraal. The kaffirs believe that if you have got an enemy that you want to get rid of, then what you have to do is to make an image of him: it doesn't matter if it is a good likeness or not, as long as you yourself know what is meant by it: and then you hammer something, a strip of brass or an iron nail, into that part of your enemy that you want to get stricken. And the kaffirs say that it always works, when you do that. They say that that is the reason, for instance, why many an unpopular chief has been known to die prematurely, going to his death with a sudden pain in his belly, for which there has been no explanation. And then, later on, in the hut of some enemy of the chief, there has been found a little wooden image with an iron nail driven through its stomach. And how they knew that it was the chief was because something that belonged to him, like a piece of his kaross, was attached to the wooden image. . . And, also, of course, because the chief had died. . .

For this reason a kaffir is not very happy when a wood-carver comes along to him with a piece of wood fashioned in the likeness of a human being, and informs him, "This is you." Even when the image hasn't got a piece of brass driven into its belly, the ordinary ignorant kaffir, confronted with his own likeness cut out of wood, will bid the wood-carver tarry a little while in front of the hut – while he goes round to the back to look for his axe.

All of this brings me to that wood-carver in Ramoutsa, Radipalong, who, because the kaffirs would not allow him to carve likenesses of themselves, took it into his head to cut what he thought were images of white people.

There is no doubt about it that when Radipalong, who was very old and emaciated-looking, confined himself to cutting the figures of animals from soft wood – the softer, the better, because you had merely to look at him to see that he did not like exerting himself too much – then what he carved was quite all right. He could carve a hippopotamus, or a rhinoceros, or an elephant, or a yellow-bellied hyena – the more low sort of hyena – in such a way that you *knew* that animal exactly, through your having seen it grazing under a tree, or drinking at a waterhole, or just leaning against an ant-hill without doing anything in particular.

But it was when Radipalong started carving what he imagined, in his kaffir ignorance, to be the likenesses of Boer farmers in this part of the Marico, that we commenced laughing differently from the way we laughed at his wild ducks. Our laughter now seemed to have more meaning in it.

For instance, Radipalong carved what he said was the image of the Dutch Reformed Church missionary at Ramoutsa, Rev. Kriel. That was one of the first good laughs we had, Rev. Kriel joining in loudly – although I thought that his laughter came from rather too deep down.

"See how silly that kaffir, Radipalong, makes me look," Rev. Kriel said to us, one day, after he had conducted a service in Jurie Bekker's farmhouse. "I brought along this carving that he made of me. I brought it along just for fun. I gave him one shilling and ninepence for it, also just for fun. Look how foolishly he makes my collar stand up, right under my ears. And my eyes – so close together. Have you ever seen such a dishonest-looking pair of eyes before? And the way he makes my chin slope backwards from my bottom teeth. . . You should have heard how my wife laughed when I showed her this carving. In fact, every time she sees me now, she laughs. I suppose she feels how incredible it is that, in these times, you can still find as benighted a heathen as that old Radipalong is. And the funny part of it is that he seems to take his ridiculous wood-carving seriously. As though he is carving out a career for himself, I said to my wife. Ha, ha."

We all laughed at that. Ha, ha, we said.

After that, Radipalong made an image of Karel Nienaber. Once more we laughed a good deal. That was in the Nienaber voorhuis, where we were drinking coffee. Old Piet Nienaber's son, Karel, was engaged to be married to Louisa Wessels, and Louisa and her parents, who stayed at Abjaterskop, were on a visit that afternoon to the Nienaber family. A few neighbours had dropped in as well, and, as I have said, there was much laughter when young Karel produced Radipalong's latest piece of wood-carving. The wood that the image was made of was so soft that it was more like cork. Almost like a piece of sponge, I thought. It seemed that Radipalong was getting lazier than ever.

"Just see how low he makes my forehead," Karel Nienaber said, and we all laughed again, at the idea that that kaffir, who could carve a leopard exactly like it was, should be so ignorant when it came to making the image of a white man.

"And look at my ears," Karel added, "the way they stick out. They look as though they have been made for a person twice my size."

Again we all guffawed. All of us, that is, except Louisa Wessels. I noticed that she was not laughing at all. Naturally, this circumstance did not at first appear singular to me. It was only right, I felt, that a young girl should not laugh at seeing her lover made to look ridiculous – even though that kaffir wood-carver did not mean to poke fun at Karel, of course. Radipalong just didn't know any better.

Nevertheless, there was something in Louisa's manner that disturbed me. She seemed too quiet. And when Karel Nienaber said, "Just look at my ears," she had not looked at the wooden likeness that he was holding in his hand. Instead, her dark eyes went actually to her lover's face. For a few moments she appeared to be studying Karel's ears, which did, somehow, in that instant, seem to be somewhat too large for the rest of him.

"And what do you think of the way he has done the rest of me?" Karel Nienaber asked again, and by this time he could hardly talk, he was laughing so much at the kaffir's absurd misrepresentation of his figure. "Why, he makes my body look all clumsy, like a sort of pumpkin. To move, I would have to go on wheels."

Once again I noticed that Louisa Wessels looked at Karel Nienaber and not at the carving. And this time, too, she did not laugh. And so I remembered that young man who had been courting Louisa in the past, and to whom her parents had objected, because they wanted their daughter to marry Karel Nienaber. And I wondered what thoughts were going on behind Louisa's expressionless features, when Karel came up to her and laughingly placed the image in her lap.

"You can look after this for us," Karel said. "I gave Radipalong a piece of roll-tobacco for it, just for fun. I asked him why he used such a white piece of wood to carve my image out of, and what do you think he said? He said, 'Well, but you are a white man, baas Karel.' And I said, well of course, I was white but I wasn't sick. And then I asked him why he had made me out of such soft wood. And – you know what? – he just didn't answer me at all."

Louisa sat with her eyes lowered. And, as I am talking to you, I can sense how unwillingly she comes into this story, even now.

Anyway, the stupidity of that wood-carver caused a good deal of merriment in the Marico Bushveld for a while. When Radipalong brought me a carving of myself, with a jaw like an aardvark and big, flat feet, I laughed so much that I just pulled the thing away from him roughly, without paying him anything – not even for fun. And when Radipalong gave Hendrik Pretorius his likeness, Hendrik was so amused that Radipalong had a lump behind his ear from where Hendrik Pretorius hit him with a piece of wood that was harder than the wood out of which he made the carving.

Shortly afterwards, Radipalong went out of the business of carving images of white men.

The white men laughed too much.

It was some time later that the engagement between Louisa Wessels and Karel Nienaber got broken off. Although nobody knew all the details surrounding the circumstances under which those two young people parted, we had a pretty good general sort of idea. And we were not surprised when, shortly afterwards, Karel Nienaber left the Marico Bushveld to go and work for a blacksmith in Zeerust. He said he felt it wasn't healthy living in the Bushveld, among all those dark trees.

But what we never understood clearly was how Karel Nienaber had come to open the tamboetie kist in which Louisa Wessels was collecting her trousseau. We did know, however, that Karel found, lying on top of the bridal silks and ribbons, the wooden image that Radipalong had carved of him. And, driven into the place where the heart was, were several rusty nails.

Unto Dust

I HAVE NOTICED THAT WHEN a young man or woman dies, people get the feeling that there is something beautiful and touching in the event, and that it is different from the death of an old person. In the thought, say, of a girl of twenty sinking into an untimely grave, there is a sweet wistfulness that makes people talk all kinds of romantic words. She died, they say, young, she that was so full of life and so fair. She was a flower that withered before it bloomed, they say, and it all seems so fitting and beautiful that there is a good deal of resentment, at the funeral, over the crude questions that a couple of men in plain clothes from the landdrost's office are asking about cattle-dip.

But when you have grown old, nobody is very much interested in the manner of your dying. Nobody except you yourself, that is. And I think that your past life has got a lot to do with the way you feel when you get near the end of your days. I remember how, when he was lying on his death-bed, Andries Wessels kept on telling us that it was because of the blameless path he had trodden from his earliest years that he could compose himself in peace to lay down his burdens. And I certainly never saw a man breathe his last more tranquilly, seeing that right up to the end he kept on murmuring to us how happy he was, with heavenly hosts and invisible choirs of angels all around him.

Just before he died, he told us that the angels had even become visible. They were medium-sized angels, he said, and they had cloven hoofs and carried forks. It was obvious that Andries Wessels's ideas were getting a bit confused by then, but all the same I never saw a man die in a more hallowed sort of calm.

Once, during the malaria season in the Eastern Transvaal, it seemed to me, when I was in a high fever and like to die, that the whole world was a big burial-ground. I thought it was the earth itself that was a graveyard, and not just those little fenced-in bits of land dotted with tombstones, in the shade of a Western Province oak-tree or by the side of a Transvaal koppie. This was a nightmare that worried me a great deal, and so I was very glad, when I recovered from the fever, to think that we Boers had properly marked-out places on our farms for white people to be laid to rest in, in a civilised Christian way, instead of having to be buried just anyhow, along with a dead wild-cat, maybe, or a Bushman with a clay pot, and things.

When I mentioned this to my friend, Stoffel Oosthuizen, who was in the Low Country with me at the time, he agreed with me wholeheartedly. There were people who talked in a high-flown way of death as a great leveller, he said, and those high-flown people also declared that everyone was made kin by death. He would still like to see those things proved, Stoffel Oosthuizen said. After all, that was one of the reasons why the Boers had trekked into the Transvaal and the Free State, he said, because the British Government wanted to give the vote to any Cape Coloured person walking about with a kroes head and big cracks in his feet.

The first time he heard that sort of talk about death coming to all of us alike, and making us all equal, Stoffel Oosthuizen's suspicions were aroused. It sounded like out of a speech made by one of those liberal Cape politicians, he explained.

I found something comforting in Stoffel Oosthuizen's words.

Then, to illustrate his contention, Stoffel Oosthuizen told me a story of an incident that took place in a bygone Transvaal kaffir war. I don't know whether he told the story incorrectly, or whether it was just that kind of a story, but, by the time he had finished, all my uncertainties had, I discovered, come back to me.

"You can go and look at Hans Welman's tombstone any time you are at Nietverdiend," Stoffel Oosthuizen said. "The slab of red sandstone is weathered by now, of course, seeing how long ago it all happened.

But the inscription is still legible. I was with Hans Welman on that morning when he fell. Our commando had been ambushed by the kaffirs and was retreating. I could do nothing for Hans Welman. Once, when I looked round, I saw a tall kaffir bending over him and plunging an assegai into him. Shortly afterwards I saw the kaffir stripping the clothes off Hans Welman. A yellow kaffir dog was yelping excitedly around his black master. Although I was in grave danger myself, with several dozen kaffirs making straight for me on foot through the bush, the fury I felt at the sight of what that tall kaffir was doing made me hazard a last shot. Reining in my horse, and taking what aim I could under the circumstances, I pressed the trigger. My luck was in. I saw the kaffir fall forward beside the naked body of Hans Welman. Then I set spurs to my horse and galloped off at full speed, with the foremost of my pursuers already almost upon me. The last I saw was that yellow dog bounding up to his master – whom I had wounded mortally, as we were to discover later.

"As you know, that kaffir war dragged on for a long time. There were few pitched battles. Mainly, what took place were bush skirmishes, like the one in which Hans Welman lost his life.

"After about six months, quiet of a sort was restored to the Marico and Zoutpansberg Districts. Then the day came when I went out, in company of a handful of other burghers, to fetch in the remains of Hans Welman, at his widow's request, for burial in the little cemetery plot on the farm. We took a coffin with us on a Cape-cart.

"We located the scene of the skirmish without difficulty. Indeed, Hans Welman had been killed not very far from his own farm, which had been temporarily abandoned, together with the other farms in that part, during the time that the trouble with the kaffirs had lasted. We drove up to the spot where I remembered having seen Hans Welman lying dead on the ground, with the tall kaffir next to him. From a distance I again saw that yellow dog. He slipped away into the bush at our approach. I could not help feeling that there was something rather stirring about that beast's fidelity, even though it was bestowed on a dead kaffir.

"We were now confronted with a queer situation. We found that what was left of Hans Welman and the kaffir consisted of little more than pieces of sun-dried flesh and the dismembered fragments of bleached skeletons. The sun and wild animals and birds of prey had done their work. There was a heap of human bones, with here and there leathery strips of blackened flesh. But we could not tell which was the white man and which the kaffir. To make it still more confusing, a lot of bones were missing altogether, having no doubt been dragged away by the wild animals into their lairs in the bush. Another thing was that Hans Welman and that kaffir had been just about the same size."

Stoffel Oosthuizen paused in his narrative, and I let my imagination dwell for a moment on that situation. And I realised just how those Boers must have felt about it: about the thought of bringing the remains of a Transvaal burgher home to his widow for Christian burial, and perhaps having a lot of kaffir bones mixed up with the burgher – lying with him in the same tomb on which the mauve petals from the oleander overhead would fall.

"I remember one of our party saying that that was the worst of these kaffir wars," Stoffel Oosthuizen continued. "If it had been a war against the English, and part of a dead Englishman had got lifted into that coffin by mistake, it wouldn't have mattered so much, he said."

There seemed to me in this story to be something as strange as the African veld.

Stoffel Oosthuizen said that the little party of Boers spent almost a whole afternoon with the remains in order to try to get the white man sorted out from the kaffir. By the evening they had laid all they could find of what seemed like Hans Welman's bones in the coffin in the Cape-cart. The rest of the bones and flesh they buried on the spot.

Stoffel Oosthuizen added that, no matter what the difference in the colour of their skin had been, it was impossible to say that the kaffir's bones were less white than Hans Welman's. Nor was it possible to say that the kaffir's sun-dried flesh was any blacker than the white man's.

Alive, you couldn't go wrong in distinguishing between a white man and a kaffir. Dead, you had great difficulty in telling them apart.

"Naturally, we burghers felt very bitter about this whole affair," Stoffel Oosthuizen said, "and our resentment was something that we couldn't explain, quite. Afterwards, several other men who were there that day told me that they had the same feelings of suppressed anger that I did. They wanted somebody – just once – to make a remark such as 'in death they were not divided.' Then you would have seen an outburst, all right. Nobody did say anything like that, however. We all knew better. Two days later a funeral service was conducted in the little cemetery on the Welman farm, and shortly afterwards the sandstone memorial was erected that you can still see there."

That was the story Stoffel Oosthuizen told me after I had recovered from the fever. It was a story that, as I have said, had in it features as strange as the African veld. But it brought me no peace in my broodings after that attack of malaria. Especially when Christoffel Oosthuizen spoke of how he had occasion, one clear night when the stars shone, to pass that quiet graveyard on the Welman farm. Something leapt up from the mound beside the sandstone slab. It gave him quite a turn, Stoffel Oosthuizen said, for the third time – and in that way – to come across that yellow kaffir dog.

FUNERAL EARTH

WE HAD A DIFFICULT TASK, THAT TIME (Oom Schalk Lourens said), teaching Sijefu's tribe of Mtosas to become civilised. But they did not show any appreciation. Even after we had set fire to their huts in a long row round the slopes of Abjaterskop, so that you could see the smoke almost as far as Nietverdiend, the Mtosas remained just about as unenlightened as ever. They would retreat into the mountains, where it was almost impossible for our commando to follow them on horseback. They remained hidden in the thick bush.

"I can sense these kaffirs all around us," Veldkornet Andries Joubert said to our seksie of about a dozen burghers when we had come to a halt in a clearing amid the tall withaaks. "I have been in so many kaffir wars that I can almost *smell* when there are kaffirs lying in wait for us with assegais. And yet all day long you never see a single Mtosa that you can put a lead bullet through."

He also said that if this war went on much longer we would forget altogether how to handle a gun. And what would we do then, when we again had to fight England?

Young Fanie Louw, who liked saying funny things, threw back his head and pretended to be sniffing the air with discrimination. "I can smell a whole row of assegais with broad blades and short handles," Fanie Louw said. "The stabbing assegai has got more of a selon's rose sort of smell about it than a throwing spear. The selon's rose that you come across in graveyards."

The veldkornet did not think Fanie Louw's remark very funny, however. And he said we all knew that this was the first time Fanie Louw had ever been on commando. He also said that if a crowd of Mtosas were to leap out of the bush on to us suddenly, then you wouldn't be able to smell Fanie Louw for dust. The veldkornet also said another thing that was even better.

Our group of burghers laughed heartily. Maybe Veldkornet Joubert could not think out a lot of nonsense to say just on the spur of the moment, in the way that Fanie Louw could, but give our veldkornet a chance to reflect, first, and he would come out with the kind of remark that you just had to admire.

Indeed, from the very next thing Veldkornet Joubert said, you could see how deep was his insight. And he did not have to think much, either, then.

"Let us get out of here as quick as hell, men," he said, speaking very distinctly. "Perhaps the kaffirs are hiding out in the open turf lands, where there are no trees. And none of this long tamboekie grass, either."

When we emerged from that stretch of bush we were glad to discover that our veldkornet had been right, like always.

For another group of Transvaal burghers had hit on the same strategy.

"We were in the middle of the bush," their leader, Combrinck, said to us, after we had exchanged greetings. "A very thick part of the bush, with withaaks standing up like skeletons. And we suddenly thought the Mtosas might have gone into hiding out here in the open."

You could see that Veldkornet Joubert was pleased to think that he had, on his own, worked out the same tactics as Combrinck, who was known as a skilful kaffir-fighter. All the same, it seemed as though this was going to be a long war.

It was then that, again speaking out of his turn, Fanie Louw said that all we needed now was for the kommandant himself to arrive there in the middle of the turf lands with the main body of burghers. "Maybe we should even go back to Pretoria to see if the Mtosas aren't perhaps hiding in the Volksraad," he said. "Passing laws and things. You know how cheeky a Mtosa is."

"It can't be worse than some of the laws that the Volksraad is already passing now," Combrinck said, gruffly. From that we could see that why he had not himself been appointed kommandant was because he had voted against the President in the last elections.

By that time the sun was sitting not more than about two Cape feet above a tall koppie on the horizon. Accordingly, we started looking about for a place to camp. It was muddy in the turf lands, and there was no firewood there, but we all said that we did not mind. We would not pamper ourselves by going to sleep in the thick bush, we told one another. It was war-time, and we were on commando, and the mud of the turf lands was good enough for us, we said.

It was then that an unusual thing happened.

For we suddenly did see Mtosas. We saw them from a long way off. They came out of the bush and marched right out into the open. They made no attempt to hide. We saw in amazement that they were coming straight in our direction, advancing in single file. And we observed, even from that distance, that they were unarmed. Instead of assegais and shields they carried burdens on their heads. And almost at the same moment we realised, from the heavy look of those burdens, that the carriers must be women.

For that reason we took our guns in our hands and stood waiting. Since it was women, we were naturally prepared for the lowest form of treachery.

As the column drew nearer we saw that at the head of it was Ndambe, an old native whom we knew well. For years he had been Sijefu's chief counsellor. Ndambe held up his hand. The line of women halted. Ndambe spoke. He declared that we white men were kings among kings and elephants among elephants. He also said that we were rinkhals snakes more poisonous and generally disgusting than any rinkhals snake in the country.

We knew, of course, that Ndambe was only paying us compliments in his ignorant Mtosa fashion. And so we naturally felt highly gratified. I can still remember the way Jurie Bekker nudged me in the ribs and said, "Did you hear that?"

When Ndambe went on, however, to say that we were filthier than the spittle of the green tree-toad, several burghers grew restive. They felt that there was perhaps such a thing as carrying these tribal courtesies a bit too far.

It was then that Veldkornet Joubert, slipping his finger inside the trigger guard of his gun, requested Ndambe to come to the point. By the expression on our veldkornet's face, you could see that he had had enough of compliments for one day.

They had come to offer peace, Ndambe told us then.

What the women carried on their heads were presents.

At a sign from Ndambe the column knelt in the mud of the turf land. They brought lion and zebra skins and elephant tusks, and beads and brass bangles and, on a long grass mat, the whole haunch of a red Afrikaner ox, hide and hoof and all. And several pigs cut in half. And clay pots filled to the brim with white beer, and also – and this we prized most – witch-doctor medicines that protected you against goël spirits at night and the evil eye.

Ndambe gave another signal. A woman with a clay pot on her head rose up from the kneeling column and advanced towards us. We saw then that what she had in the pot was black earth. It was wet and almost like turf soil. We couldn't understand what they wanted to bring us that for. As though we didn't have enough of it, right there where we were standing, and sticking to our veldskoens, and all. And yet Ndambe acted as though that was the most precious part of the peace offerings that his chief, Sijefu, had sent us.

It was when Ndambe spoke again that we saw how ignorant he and his chief and the whole Mtosa tribe were, really.

He took a handful of soil out of the pot and pressed it together between his fingers. Then he told us how honoured the Mtosa tribe was because we were waging war against them. In the past they had only had flat-faced Mshangaans with spiked knobkerries to fight against, he said, but now it was different. Our veldkornet took half a step forward, then, in case Ndambe was going to start flattering us again. So Ndambe said, simply, that the Mtosas would be glad if we came and made war against them later on, when the harvests had been gathered in. But in the meantime the tribe did not wish to continue fighting.

It was the time for sowing.

Ndambe let the soil run through his fingers, to show us how good it was. He also invited us to taste it. We declined.

We accepted the presents and peace was made. And I can still remember how Veldkornet Joubert shook his head and said, "Can you beat the Mtosas for ignorance?"

And I can still remember what Jurie Bekker said, also. That was when something made him examine the haunch of beef more closely, and he found his own brand mark on it.

It was not long afterwards that the war came against England.

By the end of the second year of the war the Boer forces were in a very bad way. But we would not make peace. Veldkornet Joubert was now promoted to kommandant. Combrinck fell in the battle before Dalmanutha. Jurie Bekker was still with us. And so was Fanie Louw. And it was strange how attached we had grown to Fanie Louw during the years of hardship that we went through together in the field. But up to the end we had to admit that, while we had got used to his jokes, and we knew there was no harm in them, we would have preferred it that he should stop making them.

He did stop, and for ever, in a skirmish near a blockhouse. We buried him in the shade of a thorn-tree. We got ready to fill in his grave, after which the kommandant would say a few words and we would bare our heads and sing a psalm. As you know, it was customary at a funeral for each mourner to take up a handful of earth and fling it in the grave.

When Kommandant Joubert stooped down and picked up his handful of earth, a strange thing happened. And I remembered that other war, against the Mtosas. And we knew – although we would not say it – what was now that longing in the hearts of each of us.

For Kommandant Joubert did not straightway drop the soil into Fanie Louw's grave. Instead, he kneaded the damp ground between his fingers. It was as though he had forgotten that it was funeral earth. He seemed to be thinking not of death, then, but of life.

We patterned after him, picking up handfuls of soil and pressing it together. We felt the deep loam in it, and saw how springy it was, and we let it trickle through our fingers. And we could remember only that it was the time for sowing.

I understood then how, in an earlier war, the Mtosas had felt, they who were also farmers.

Peaches Ripening in the Sun

The way Ben Myburg lost his memory (Oom Schalk Lourens said) made a deep impression on all of us. We reasoned that that was the sort of thing that a sudden shock could do to you. There were those in our small section of General du Toit's commando who could recall similar stories of how people in a moment could forget everything about the past, just because of a single dreadful happening.

A shock like that can have the same effect on you even if you are prepared for it. Maybe it can be worse, even. And in this connection I often think of what it says in the Good Book, about that which you most feared having now at last caught up with you.

Our commando went as far as the border by train. And when the engine came to a stop on a piece of open veld, and it wasn't for water, this time, and the engine-driver and fireman didn't step down with a spanner and use bad language, then we understood that the train stopping there was the beginning of the Second Boer War.

We were wearing new clothes and we had new equipment, and the sun was shining on the barrels of our Mausers. Our new clothes had been requisitioned for us by our veldkornet at stores along the way. All the veldkornet had to do was to sign his name on a piece of paper for whatever his men purchased.

In most cases, after we had patronised a store in that manner, the shopkeeper would put up his shutters for the day. And three years would pass and the Boer War would be over before the shopkeeper would display any sort of inclination to take the shutters down again.

Maybe he should have put them up before we came.

Only one seksie of General du Toit's commando entered Natal looking considerably dilapidated. This seksie looked as though it was already the end of the Boer War, and not just the beginning. Afterwards we found out that their veldkornet had never learnt to write his name. We were glad that in the first big battle these men kept well to the rear, apparently conscious of how sinful they looked. For, to make matters worse, a regiment of Indian troops was fighting on that front, and we were not anxious that an Eastern race should see white men at such a disadvantage.

"You don't seem to remember me, Schalk," a young fellow came up and said to me. I admitted that I didn't recognise him, straight away, as Ben Myburg. He did look different in those smart light-green riding pants and that new hat with the ostrich feather stuck in it. You could see that he had patronised some mine concession store before the owner got his shutters down.

"But I would know you anywhere, Schalk," Ben Myburg went on. "Just from the quick way you hid that soap under your saddle a couple of minutes ago. I remembered where I had last seen something so quick. It was two years ago, at the Nagmaal in Nylstroom."

I told Ben Myburg that if it was that jar of brandy he meant, then he must realise that there had also been a good deal of misunderstanding about it. Moreover, it was not even a full jar, I said.

But I congratulated him on his powers of memory, which I said I was sure would yet stand the Republic in good stead.

And I was right. For afterwards, when the war of the big commandos was over, and we were in constant retreat, it would be Ben Myburg who, next day, would lead us back to the donga in which we had hidden some mealie-meal and a tin of cooking fat. And if the tin of cooking fat was empty, he would be able to tell us right away if it was kaffirs or baboons. A kaffir had a different way of eating cooking fat out of a tin from what a baboon had, Ben Myburg said.

Ben Myburg had been recently married to Mimi van Blerk, who came from Schweizer-Reneke, a district that was known as far as the Limpopo for its attractive girls. I remembered Mimi van Blerk well. She had full red lips and thick yellow hair. Ben Myburg always looked forward very eagerly to getting letters from his pretty young wife. He would also read out to us extracts from her letters, in which she encouraged us to drive the English into the blue grass – which was the name we gave to the sea in those days. For the English we had other names.

One of Mimi's letters was accompanied by a wooden candle-box filled with dried peaches. Ben Myburg was most proud to share out the dried fruit among our company, for he had several times spoken of the orchard of yellow cling peaches that he had laid out at the side of his house.

"We've already got dried peaches," Jurie Bekker said. Then he added, making free with our projected invasion of Natal: "In a few weeks' time we will be picking bananas."

It was in this spirit, as I have said, that we set out to meet the enemy. But nobody knew better than ourselves how much of this fine talk was to hide what we really felt. And I know, speaking for myself, that when we got the command "Opsaal", and we were crossing the border between the Transvaal and Natal, I was less happy at the thought that my horse was such a mettlesome animal. For it seemed to me that my horse was far more anxious to invade Natal than I was. I had to rein him in a good deal on the way to Spioenkop and Colenso. And I told myself that it was because I did not want him to go too fast downhill.

Eighteen months later saw the armed forces of the Republic in a worse case than I should imagine any army has ever been in, and that army still fighting. We were spread all over the country in small groups. We were in rags.

Many burghers had been taken prisoner. Others had yielded themselves up to British magistrates, holding not their rifles in their hands but their hats. There were a number of Boers, also, who had gone and joined the English.

For the Transvaal Republic it was near the end of a tale that you tell, sitting around the kitchen fire on a cold night. The story of the Transvaal Republic was at that place where you clear your throat before saying which of the two men the girl finally married. Or whether it was the cattle smuggler or the Sunday school superintendent who stole the money. Or whether it was a real ghost or just her uncle with a sheet round him that Lettie van Zyl saw at the drift.

One night, when we were camped just outside Nietverdiend, and it was Ben Myburg's and my turn to go on guard, he told me that he knew that part well.

"You see that rant there, Schalk?" he asked. "Well, I have often stood on the other side of it, under the stars, just like now. You know, I've got a lot of peach-trees on my farm. Well, I have stood there, under the ripening peaches, just after dark, with Mimi at my side. There is no smell like the smell of young peach-trees in the evening, Schalk, when the fruit is ripening. I can almost imagine I am back there now. And it is just the time for it, too."

I tried to explain to Ben Myburg, in a roundabout way, that although everything might be exactly the same on this side of the rant, he would have to be prepared for certain changes on the other side, seeing that it was war.

Ben Myburg agreed that I was probably right. Nevertheless, he began to talk to me at length about his courtship days. He spoke of Mimi with her full red lips and her yellow hair.

"I can still remember the evening when Mimi promised that she would marry me, Schalk," Ben Myburg said. "It was in Zeerust. We were there for the Nagmaal. When I walked back to my tent on the kerkplein I was so happy that I just kicked the first three kaffirs I saw."

I could see that, talking to me while we stood on guard, Ben Myburg was living through that time all over again. I was glad, for their sakes, that no kaffirs came past at that moment. For Ben Myburg was again very happy.

I was pleased, too, for Ben Myburg's own sake, that he did at least have that hour of deep joy in which he could recall the past so vividly. For it was after that that his memory went.

By the following evening we had crossed the rant and had arrived at Ben Myburg's farm. We camped among the smoke-blackened walls of his former homestead, erecting a rough shelter with some sheets of corrugated iron that we could still use. And although he must have known only too well what to expect, yet what Ben Myburg saw there came as so much of a shock to his senses that from that moment all he could remember from the past vanished for ever.

It was pitiful to see the change that had come over him. If his farm had been laid to ruins, the devastation that had taken place in Ben Myburg's mind was no less dreadful.

Perhaps it was that, in truth, there was nothing more left in the past to remember.

We noticed, also, that in singular ways, certain fragments of the bygone would come into Ben Myburg's mind; and that he would almost – but not quite – succeed in fitting these pieces together.

We observed that almost immediately. For instance, we remained camped on his farm for several days. And one morning, when the fire for our mealie-pap was crackling under one of the few remaining fruit-trees that had once been an orchard, Ben Myburg reached up and picked a peach that was, in advance of its season, ripe and yellow.

"It's funny," Ben Myburg said, "but I seem to remember, from long ago, reaching up and picking a yellow peach, just like this one. I don't quite remember where."

We did not tell him that he was picking one of his own peaches.

Some time later our seksie was captured in a night attack.

For us the Boer War was over. We were going to St. Helena. We were driven to Nylstroom, the nearest railhead, in a mule-wagon. It was a strange experience for us to be driving along the main road, in broad daylight, for all the world to see us. From years of war-time habit, our eyes still went to the horizon. A bitter thing about our captivity was that among our guards were men of our own people.

Outside Nylstroom we alighted from the mule-wagon and the English sergeant in charge of our escort got us to form fours by the roadside. It was queer – our having to learn to be soldiers at the end of a war instead of at the beginning.

Eventually we got into some sort of formation, the veldkornet, Jurie Bekker, Ben Myburg and I making up the first four. It was already evening. From a distance we could see the lights in the town. The way to the main street of Nylstroom led by the cemetery. Although it was dark, we could yet distinguish several rows of newly made mounds. We did not need to be told that they were concentration camp graves. We took off our battered hats and tramped on in great silence.

Soon we were in the main street. We saw, then, what those lights were. There was a dance at the hotel. Paraffin lamps were hanging under the hotel's low, wide veranda. There was much laughter. We saw girls and English officers. In our unaccustomed fours we slouched past in the dark.

Several of the girls went inside, then. But a few of the womenfolk remained on the veranda, not looking in our direction. Among them I noticed particularly a girl leaning on an English officer's shoulder. She looked very pretty, with the light from a paraffin lamp shining on her full lips and yellow hair.

When we had turned the corner, and the darkness was wrapping us round again, I heard Ben Myburg speak.

"It's funny," I heard Ben Myburg say, "but I seem to remember, from long ago, a girl with yellow hair, just like that one. I don't quite remember where."

And this time, too, we did not tell him.

THE BUDGET

WE WERE SITTING IN JURIE STEYN'S voorkamer at Drogevlei, waiting for the Government lorry from Bekkersdal, that brought us our letters and empty milk-cans. Jurie Steyn's voorkamer had served as the Drogevlei post office for some years, and Jurie Steyn was postmaster. His complaint was that the post office didn't pay. It didn't pay him, he said, to be called away from his lands every time somebody came in for a penny stamp. What was more, Gysbert van Tonder could walk right into his voorkamer whenever he liked, and without knocking. Gysbert was Jurie Steyn's neighbour, and Jurie had naturally not been on friendly terms with him since the time Gysbert van Tonder got a justice of the peace and a land-surveyor and a policeman riding a skimmel horse to explain to Jurie Steyn on what side of the vlei the boundary fence ran.

What gave Jurie Steyn some measure of satisfaction, he said, was the fact that his post office couldn't pay the Government, either.

"Maybe it will pay better now," At Naudé said. "Now that you can charge more for the stamps, I mean."

At Naudé had a wireless, and was therefore always first with the news. Moreover, At Naudé made that remark with a slight sneer.

Now, Jurie Steyn is funny in that way. He doesn't mind what he himself says about his post office. But he doesn't care much for the ill-informed kind of comment that he sometimes gets from people who don't know how exacting a postmaster's duties are. I can still remember some of the things Jurie Steyn said to a stranger who dropped in one day for a half-crown postal order, when Jurie had been busy with the cream separator. The stranger spoke of the buttermilk smudges on the postal order, which made the ink run in a blue blotch when he tried to fill it in. It was then that Jurie Steyn asked the stranger if he thought Marico buttermilk wasn't good enough for him, and what he thought he could get for half a crown. Jurie Steyn also started coming from behind the counter, so that he could explain better to the stranger what a man could get in the Bushveld for considerably less than half a crown. Unfortunately, the stranger couldn't wait to hear. He said that he had left his engine running when he came into the post office.

From that it would appear that he was not such a complete stranger to the ways of the Groot Marico.

With regard to At Naudé's remark now, however, we could see that Jurie Steyn would have preferred to let it pass. He took out a thick book with black covers and started ticking off lists with a pencil in an important sort of a way. But all the time we could sense the bitterness against At Naudé that was welling up inside him. When the pencil-point broke, Jurie Steyn couldn't stand it any more.

"Anyway, At," he said, "even twopence a half-ounce is cheaper than getting a Mchopi runner to carry a letter in a long stick with a cleft in the end. But, of course, you wouldn't understand about things like progress."

Jurie Steyn shouldn't have said that. Immediately three or four of us wanted to start talking at the same time.

"Cheaper, maybe," Johnny Coen said, "but not better, or quicker – or – or – *cleaner* – " Johnny Coen almost choked with laughter. He thought he was being very clever.

Meanwhile, Chris Welman was trying to tell a story we had heard from him often before about a letter that was posted at Christmas time in Volksrust and arrived at its destination, Magoeba's Kloof, twenty-eight years later, and on Dingaan's Day.

"If a native runner took twenty-eight years to get from Volksrust to Magoeba's Kloof," Chris Welman said, "we would have known that he didn't run much. He must at least have stopped once or twice at huts along the way for kaffir beer."

Meanwhile, Oupa Sarel Bekker, who was one of the oldest inhabitants of the Marico and had known Bekkersdal before it was even a properly measured-out farm, started taking part in the conversation. But because Oupa Bekker was slightly deaf, and a bit queer in the head through advancing years, he thought we were saying that Jurie Steyn had been running along the main road, carrying a letter in a cleft stick. Accordingly, Oupa Bekker warned Jurie Steyn to be careful of mambas. The kloof was full of brown mambas at that time of year, Oupa Bekker said.

"All the same, in the days of the Republics you would not get a white man doing a thing like that," Oupa Bekker went on, shaking his head. "Not even in the Republic of Goosen. And not even after the Republic of Goosen's Minister of Finance had lost all the State revenues in an unfortunate game of poker that he had been invited to take part in at the Mafeking Hotel. And there was quite a big surplus, too, that year, which the Minister of Finance kept tucked away in an inside pocket right through the poker game, and which he could still remember having had on him when he went into the bar. Although he could never remember what happened to that surplus afterwards. The Minister of Finance never went back to Goosen, of course. He stayed on in Mafeking. When I saw him again he was offering to help carry people's luggage from the Zeederberg coach station to the hotel."

Oupa Bekker was getting ready to say a lot more, when Jurie Steyn interrupted him, demanding to know what all that had got to do with his post office.

"I said that even when things were very bad in the old days, you would still never see a white postmaster running in the sun with a letter in a cleft stick," Oupa Bekker explained, adding, "like a Mchopi."

Jurie Steyn's wife did not want any unpleasantness. So she came and sat on the riempies bench next to Oupa Bekker and made it clear to him, in a friendly sort of way, what the discussion was all about.

"You see, Oupa," Jurie Steyn's wife said finally, after a pause for breath, "that's just what we have been *saying*. We've been saying that in the old days, before they had proper post offices, people used to send letters with Mchopi runners."

"But that's what I've been saying also," Oupa Bekker persisted. "I say, why doesn't Jurie rather go in his mule-cart?"

Jurie Steyn's wife gave it up after that. Especially when Jurie Steyn himself walked over to where Oupa Bekker was sitting.

"You know, Oupa," Jurie said, talking very quietly, "you have been an ouderling for many years, and we all respect you in the Groot Marico. We also respect your grey hairs. But you must not lose that respect through – through talking about things that you don't understand."

Oupa Bekker tightened his grip on his tamboetie-wood walking-stick.

"Now if you had spoken to me like that in the Republican days, Jurie Steyn," the old man said, in a cracked voice. "In the Republic of Stellaland, for instance – "

"You and your republics, Oupa," Jurie Steyn said, giving up the argument and turning back to the counter. "Goosen, Stellaland, Lydenburg – I suppose you were also in the Ohrigstad Republic?"

Oupa Bekker sat up very stiffly on the riempies bench, then.

"In the Ohrigstad Republic," he declared, and in his eyes there gleamed for a moment a light as from a great past, "in the Republic of Ohrigstad I had the honour to be the Minister of Finance."

"Honour," Jurie Steyn repeated, sarcastically, but yet not speaking loud enough for Oupa Bekker to hear. "I wonder how *he* lost the money in the State's skatkis. Playing snakes and ladders, I suppose."

All the same, there were those of us who were much interested in Oupa Bekker's statement. Johnny Coen moved his chair closer to Oupa Bekker, then. Even though Ohrigstad had been only a small republic, and hadn't lasted very long, still there was something about the sound of the words "Minister of Finance" that could not but awaken in us a sense of awe.

"I hope you deposited the State revenues in the Reserve Bank, in a proper manner," At Naudé said, winking at us, but impressed all the same.

"There was no Reserve Bank in those days," Oupa Bekker said, "or any other kind of banks either, in the Republic of Ohrigstad. No, I just kept the national treasury in a stocking under my mattress. It was the safest place, of course."

Johnny Coen put the next question.

"What was the most difficult part of being Finance Minister, Oupa?" he asked. "I suppose it was making the budget balance?"

"Money was the hardest thing," Oupa Bekker said, sighing.

"It still is," Chris Welman interjected. "You don't need to have been a Finance Minister, either, to know that."

"But, of course, it wasn't as bad as today," Oupa Bekker went on. "Being Minister of Finance, I mean. For instance, we didn't need to worry about finding money for education, because there just wasn't any, of course."

Jurie Steyn coughed in a significant kind of way, then, but Oupa Bekker ignored him.

"I don't think," he went on, "that we would have stood for education in the Ohrigstad Republic. We knew we were better off without it. And then there was no need to spend money on railways and harbours, because there weren't any, either. Or hospitals. We lived a healthy life in those days, except maybe for lions. And if you died from a lion, there wasn't much of you left over that could be *taken* to a hospital. Of course, we had to spend a good bit of money on defence, in those days. Gunpowder and lead, and oil to make the springs of our Ou-Sannas work more smoothly. You see, we were expecting trouble any day from Paul Kruger and the Doppers. But it was hard for me to know how to work out a popular budget, especially as there were only seventeen income-tax payers in the whole of the Republic. I thought of imposing a tax on the President's state coach, even. I found that that suggestion was very popular with the income-tax paying group. But you have no idea how much it annoyed the President.

"I imposed all sorts of taxes afterwards, which nobody would have to pay. These taxes didn't bring in much in the way of money, of course. But they were very popular, all the same. And I can still remember how popular my budget was, the year I put a very heavy tax on opium. I had heard somewhere about an opium tax. Naturally, of course, I did not expect this tax to bring in a penny. But I knew how glad the burghers of the Ohrigstad Republic would be, each one of them, to think that there was a tax that they escaped. In the end I had to repeal the tax on opium, however. That was when one of our seventeen income-tax payers threatened to emigrate to the Cape. This income-tax payer had a yellowish complexion and sloping eyes, and ran the only laundry in the Ohrigstad Republic."

Oupa Bekker was still talking about the measures he introduced to counteract inflation in the early days of the Republic of Ohrigstad, when the lorry from Bekkersdal arrived in a cloud of dust. The next few minutes were taken up with a hurried sorting of letters and packages, all of which proceeded to the background noises of clanking milk-cans. Oupa Bekker left when the lorry arrived, since he was expecting neither correspondence nor a milk-can. The lorry-driver and his assistant seated themselves on the riempies bench which the old man had vacated. Jurie Steyn's wife brought them in coffee.

"You know," Jurie Steyn said to Chris Welman, in between putting sealing wax on a letter he was getting ready for the mailbag. "I often wonder what is going to happen to Oupa Bekker – such an old man and all, and still such a liar. All that Finance Minister rubbish of his. How they ever appointed him an ouderling in the church, I don't know. For one thing, I mean, he couldn't have been *born*, at the time of the Ohrigstad Republic." Jurie reflected for a few moments. "Or could he?"

"I don't know," Chris Welman answered truthfully.

A little later the lorry-driver and his assistant departed. We heard them putting water in the radiator. Some time afterwards we heard them starting up the engine, noisily, the driver swearing quite a lot to himself.

It was when the lorry had already started to move off that Jurie Steyn remembered about the registered letter on which he had put the seals. He grabbed up the letter and was over the counter in a single bound.

Chris Welman and I followed him to the door. We watched Jurie Steyn for a considerable distance, streaking along in the sun behind the lorry and shouting and waving the letter in front of him, and jumping over thorn-bushes.

"Just like a Mchopi runner," I heard Chris Welman say.

News Story

"The way the world is today," At Naudé said, shaking his head, "I don't know what is going to happen."

From that it was clear that At Naudé had been hearing news over the wireless again that made him fear for the future of the country. We did not exactly sit up, then. We in the Dwarsberge knew that it was the wireless that made At Naudé that way. And he could tremble as much as he liked for the country's future or his own. There was never any change, either, in the kind of news he would bring us. Every time it was about stone-throwings in Johannesburg locations and about how many new kinds of bombs the Russians had got, and about how many people had gone to gaol for telling the Russians about still other kinds of bombs they could make. Although it did not look as though the Russians needed to be educated much in that line.

And we could never really understand why At Naudé listened at all. We hardly ever listened to *him*, for that matter. We would rather hear from Gysbert van Tonder if it was true that the ouderling at Pilanesberg really forgot himself in the way that Jurie Steyn's wife had heard about from a kraal Mtosa at the kitchen door. The Mtosa had come by to buy half-penny stamps to stick on his forehead for the yearly Ndlolo dance. Now, there was news for you. About the ouderling, I mean. And even to hear that the Ndlolo dance was being held soon again was at least something. And if it should turn out that what was being said about the Pilanesberg ouderling was not true, well, then, the same thing applied to a lot of what At Naudé heard over the wireless also.

"I don't know what is going to happen," At Naudé repeated, "the way the world is today. I just heard over the wireless – "

"That's how the news we got in the old days was better," Oupa

Bekker said. "I mean in the real old days, when there was no wireless, and there was not the telegraph, either. The news you got then you could do something with. And you didn't have to go to the post office and get it from the newspaper. The post office is the curse of the Transvaal. . . "

Jurie Steyn said that Oupa Bekker was quite right, there. He himself would never have taken on the job of postmaster at Drogevlei if he had as much as guessed that there were four separate forms that he would have to fill in, each of them different, just for a simple five-shilling money order. It was so much brainier and neater, Jurie Steyn said, for people who wanted to send five shillings somewhere, if they would just wrap up a couple of half-crowns in a thick wad of brown paper and then post them in the ordinary way, like a letter. That was what the new red pillar-box in front of his door was *for*, Jurie Steyn explained. The authorities had gone to the expense of that red pillar-box in order to help the public. And yet you still found people coming in for postal orders and money orders. The other day a man even came in and asked could he telegraph some money, somewhere.

"I gave that man a piece of brown paper and showed him the pillar-box," Jurie Steyn said. "It seemed, until then, that he did not know what kind of progress we had been making here. I therefore asked him if I could show him some more ways in regard to how advanced the Groot Marico was getting. But he said, no, the indications I had already given him were plenty."

Jurie Steyn said that he thought it was handsome of the man to have spoken up for the Marico like that, seeing that he was quite a newcomer to these parts.

Because we never knew how long Jurie Steyn would be when once he got on the subject of his work, we were glad when Johnny Coen asked Oupa Bekker to explain some more to us about how they got news in the old days. We were all pleased, that is, except At Naudé, who had again tried to get in a remark but had got no further than to say that if we knew something we would all shiver in our veldskoens.

"How did we get news?" Oupa Bekker said, replying to another question of Johnny Coen's. "Well, you would be standing in the lands, say, and then one of the Bechuanas would point to a small cloud of dust in the poort, and you would walk across to the big tree by the dam, where the road bends, and the traveller would come past there, with two vos horses in front of his Cape-cart, and he would get off from the cart and shake hands and say he was Du Plessis. And you would say you were Bekker, and he would say, afterwards, that he couldn't stay the night on your farm, because he had to get to Tsalala's Kop. Well, there was *news*. You could talk about it for days. For weeks even. You have got no idea how often my wife and I discussed it. And we knew everything that there was to know about the man. We knew his name was Du Plessis."

At Naudé said, then, that he did not think much of that sort of news. People must have been a bit *simpel* in the head, in those old times that Oupa Bekker was talking about, if they thought anything about that sort of news. Why, if you compared it with what the radio announcer said, only yesterday. . .

Jurie Steyn's wife came in from the kitchen at that moment. There was a light of excitement in her eyes. And when she spoke it was to none of us in particular.

"It has just occurred to me," Jurie Steyn's wife said, "that is, if it's *true* what they are saying about the Pilanesberg ouderling, of course. Well, it has just struck me that, when he forgot himself in the way they say – provided that he *did* forget himself like that, mind you – well, perhaps the ouderling didn't know that anybody was looking."

That was a possibility that had not so far occurred to us, and we discussed it at some length. In between our talk At Naudé was blurting out something about the rays from a still newer kind of bomb that would kill you right in the middle of the veld and through fifty feet of concrete. So we said, of course, that the best thing to do would be to keep a pretty safe distance away from concrete, with those sort of rays about, if concrete was as dangerous as all that.

We were in no mood for foolishness. Oupa Bekker took this as an encouragement for him to go on.

"Or another day," Oupa Bekker continued, "you would again be standing in your lands, say, or sitting, even, if there was a long day of ploughing ahead, and you did not want to tire yourself out unnecessarily. You would be sitting on a stone in the shade of a tree, say, and you would think to yourself how lazy those Bechuanas look, going backwards and forwards, backwards and forwards, with the plough and the oxen, and you would get quite sleepy, say, thinking to yourself how lazy those Bechuanas are. If it wasn't for the oxen to keep them going, they wouldn't do any work at all, you might perhaps think.

"And then, without your in the least expecting it, you would again have news. And the news would find a stone for himself and come along and sit down right next to you. It would be the new veldkornet, say. And why nobody saw any dust in the poort, that time, was because the veldkornet didn't come along the road. And you would make a joke with him and say: 'I suppose that's why they call you a *veld*kornet, because you don't travel along the road, but you come by the *veld*langes.' And the veldkornet would laugh and ask you a few questions, and he would tell you that they had good rains at Derdepoort. . . Well, there was something that I could tell my wife over and over again, for weeks. It was news. For weeks I had that to think about. The visit of the veldkornet. In the old days it was real news."

We could see, from the way At Naudé was fidgeting in his chair, that he guessed we were just egging the old man on to talk in order to scoff at all the important European news that At Naudé regularly retailed to us, and that we were getting tired of.

After a while At Naudé could no longer contain himself.

"This second-childhood drivel that Oupa Bekker is talking," At Naudé announced, not looking at anybody in particular, but saying it to all of us, in the way Jurie Steyn's wife had spoken when she came out of the kitchen. "Well, I would actually sooner listen to scandal about the Pilanesberg ouderling. There is at least some sort of meaning to it.

I am not being unfriendly to Oupa Bekker, of course. I know it's just that he's old. But it's also quite clear to me that he doesn't know what news is, at all."

Jurie Steyn said that it was at least as sensible as a man lying on the veld under fifty feet of concrete because of some rays. If a man were to lie under fifty feet of concrete he wouldn't be able to breathe, leave alone anything else.

In the meantime, Johnny Coen had been asking Oupa Bekker to tell us some more.

"On another day, say," Oupa Bekker went on, "you would not be in your lands at all, but you would be sitting on your front stoep, drinking coffee, say. And the Cape-cart with the two vos horses in front would be coming down the road again, but in the opposite direction, going *towards* the poort, this time. And you would not see much of Du Plessis's face, because his hat would be pulled over his eyes. And the veldkornet would be sitting on the Cape-cart next to him, say."

Oupa Bekker paused. He paused for quite a while, too, holding a lighted match cupped over his pipe as though he was out on the veld where there was wind, and puffing vigorously.

"And my wife and I would go on talking about it for years afterwards, say," Oupa Bekker went on. "For years after Du Plessis was hanged, I mean."

School Concert

THE PREPARATIONS FOR THE ANNUAL school concert were in full swing.

In the Marico these school concerts were held in the second part of June, when the nights were pleasantly cool. It was too hot, in December, for recitations and singing and reading the Joernaal that carried playful references to the activities and idiosyncrasies of individual members of the Dwarsberg population. On a midsummer's night, in a little school building crowded to the doors with children and adults and with more adults leaning in through the windows and keeping out the air, the songs and the recitations sounded limp, somehow. Moreover, the personal references in the Joernaal did not sound quite as playful, then, as they were intended to be.

The institution of the Joernaal dated back to the time of the first Hollander schoolmaster in the Groot Marico. The Joernaal was a very popular feature of school concerts in Limburg, where he came from, the Hollander schoolmaster explained. For weeks beforehand the schoolmaster, assisted by some of the pupils in the upper class, would write down, in the funniest way they knew, odds and ends of things about people living in the neighbourhood. Why, they just about killed themselves laughing, while they were writing those things down in a classroom in old Limburg, the Hollander schoolmaster said, and then, at the concert, one of the pupils would read it all out. Oh, it was a real scream. You wouldn't mention people's names, of course, the Hollander schoolmaster went on to say. They would just *hint* at who they were. It was all done in a subtle sort of way, naturally, but it was also clear enough so that you couldn't possibly miss the allusion. And you knew straight away who was *meant*.

That was what the first Hollander schoolmaster in the Marico explained, oh, long ago, before the reading, at a school concert, of the first Joernaal.

Today, in the Dwarsberge, they still talk about that concert.

It would appear, somehow, that in drawing up the Joernaal, the Hollander schoolmaster had not been quite subtle enough. Or, maybe, what they would split their sides laughing at in Limburg would raise quite different sorts of emotions north of the railway line to Ottoshoop. That's the way it is with humour, of course. Anyway, while the head pupil was reading out the Joernaal – stuttering a bit now and again because he could sense what that silence on the part of a Bushveld audience meant – the Hollander schoolmaster had tears streaming down his cheeks, the way his laughter was convulsing him. Seated on the platform next to the pupil who was reading, the schoolmaster would reach into his pocket every so often for his handkerchief to wipe his eyes with. That made the audience freeze into a yet greater stillness.

A farmer's wife said afterwards that she felt she could just choke, then.

"If what was in that Joernaal were *jokes*, now," Koos Kirstein – who had been a prominent cattle-smuggler in his day – said, "well, I can laugh at a joke with the best of them. I read the page of jokes at the back of the *Kerkbode* regularly every month. But can anybody see anything to titter at in asking where I got the money from to buy that harmonium that my daughter plays hymns on? That came in the Joernaal."

Koos Kirstein asked that question of a church elder a few days after the school concert, and the elder said, no, there was nothing funny in it. Everybody in the Marico *knew* where Koos Kirstein got his money from, the elder said.

"And saying I am so well in with the police," Koos Kirstein continued. "Saying in the Joernaal that a policeman on border patrol went and hid behind my harmonium when a special plain-clothes inspector from Pretoria walked into my voorkamer unexpectedly.

Why, the schoolmaster just about doubled up laughing, when that bit was being read out."

Anyway, the reading of that first Joernaal at a Marico school concert never reached a proper end. When the proceedings terminated the head pupil still had a considerable number of unread foolscap sheets in his hand. And he was stuttering more than ever. For he had just finished the part about the Indian store at Ramoutsa refusing to give Giel Oosthuizen any more credit until he paid off something on last year's account.

Before that he had read out something about a crateful of muscovy ducks at the Zeerust market that Faans Lemmer had loaded on to his own wagon by mistake, and that he afterwards, still making the same error, unloaded into his own chicken pen – not noticing at the time the difference between the muscovy ducks and his own Australorps, as he afterwards explained to the market master.

The head pupil had also read out something about why Frikkie Snyman's grandfather had to stay behind in the tent on the kerkplein when the rest of the family went to the Nagmaal. It wasn't the rheumatics that kept Frikkie Snyman's grandfather away from the Communion service, the Joernaal said, but he stayed behind in the tent because he didn't have an extra pair of laced-up shop boots. It was when Frikkie Snyman's wife, Hanna, knelt in church at the end of a pew and her long skirt that had all flowers on came up over one ankle – the Joernaal said – that you realised how Frikkie Snyman's grandfather was sitting barefooted in the tent on the kerkplein.

That was about as far as the head pupil got with the reading of the Joernaal. . . And to this day they can still show you, in an old Marico schoolroom, the burnt corner of a blackboard from where the lamp fell on it when the audience turned the platform upside down on the Hollander schoolmaster. Nothing happened to the head pupil, however. He sensed what was coming and got away, in time, into the rafters. Unlike most head pupils, he had a quick mind.

All that happened very long ago, of course, as we were saying to each other in Jurie Steyn's post office. Today, the Marico was very different, we said to one another. Those old farmers didn't have the advantages that we enjoyed today, we said. There was no Afrikaner Cattle Breeders' Society in those days, or even the Dwarsberge Hog Breeders' Society, and you would never see a front garden with irises in it – or a front garden at all, for that matter. And you couldn't order clothes from Johannesburg, just filling in your measurements, so that all your wife had to do was. . .

But it was when Jurie Steyn's wife explained what she had to do to the last serge suit that Jurie Steyn ordered by post, just giving his size, that we saw that this example that we mentioned did not perhaps reflect progress in the Marico in its best light.

From the way Jurie Steyn's wife spoke, it would seem that the easiest part of the alterations she had to make was cutting off the trouser turn-ups and inserting the material in the neck part of the jacket. "And then the suit still hung on Jurie like a sack," she concluded.

But Gysbert van Tonder said that she must not blame the Johannesburg store for it too much. There was something about the way Jurie Steyn was *built*, Gysbert van Tonder said. And we could not help noticing a certain nasty undertone in his voice, then, when he said that.

Johnny Coen smoothed the matter over very quickly, however. He had also had difficulties, ordering suits by post, he said. But he found it helped the Johannesburg store a lot if you sent a full-length photograph of yourself along with the order. They always returned the photograph. No, Johnny Coen said in reply to a question from At Naudé, he didn't know *why* that Johannesburg store sent the photographs back so promptly, under registered cover and all. And then, when he saw that At Naudé was laughing, Johnny Coen said that that firm could, perhaps, if it wanted to, keep all those photographs and frame them. But, all the same, he added, it would help the shop a lot if, next time Jurie Steyn ordered a suit by post, he also put in a full-length photograph of himself.

But all this talk was getting us away from what we had been saying about how more broad-minded the Groot Marico had become since the old days, due to progress. It was then that Koos Nienaber brought us back to what we were discussing.

"Where our forefathers in the Marico were different from the way we are today," Koos Nienaber said, "is because they hadn't learnt to laugh at themselves, yet. They took themselves much too seriously. Although they had to, I suppose, since it was all going to be put into history books. Or at least as much of it as could be put into history books. But we today are different. We wouldn't carry on in an undignified manner if, at the next concert, there should be something in the Joernaal to show up our little human weaknesses. We would laugh, I mean. Take Jurie Steyn and his serge suit, now. Well, we've got a sense of humour, today. I mean, Jurie Steyn would be the first to laugh at how funny he looks in that serge suit – "

"How do you mean I look funny in my new suit?" Jurie Steyn demanded.

At Naudé came in between the two of them, then, and made it clear to Jurie Steyn that Koos Nienaber had been saying those things merely by way of argument, and to prove his point. Koos Nienaber didn't mean that Jurie Steyn actually looked funny in his new suit, At Naudé explained.

"If he doesn't mean it, what does he want to say it for?" Jurie Steyn said, sounding only half convinced. "And, anyway, Koos Nienaber needn't talk. When he came round with the collection plate at the last Nagmaal, and he was wearing his new manel, I thought Koos Nienaber was an ourang-outan."

Nevertheless, we all acknowledged at the end that we were looking forward to the school concert. And there should be quite a lot of fun in having the Joernaal, we said. Seeing how today we had a sense of humour.

It was not only schoolchildren and their parents that came to attend the concert in that little school building of which the middle partition had been taken away to make it into one hall. For instance, there was Hendrik Prinsloo, who had come all the way from Vleispoort by Cape-cart, and had not meant to attend the concert at all, since he was on his way to Zeerust and was just passing that way, when some of the parents persuaded him, for the sake of his horses, to outspan under the thorn-trees on the school grounds by the side of the Government Road.

It was observed that Hendrik Prinsloo had a red face and that he mistook one of the swingle-bars for the step when he alighted from the Cape-cart. So – after they had looked to see what was under the seat of the Cape-cart – several of the farmers present counselled Hendrik Prinsloo to rest awhile by the roadside, seeing it was already getting on towards evening. They also sent a native over to At Naudé's house for glasses, instructing him to be as quick as he liked. And if At Naudé didn't have glasses, cups would do, one of the farmers added, thoughtfully. By the look of things it was going to be a good children's concert, they said.

Meanwhile the schoolroom was filling up quite nicely. There had been some talk, during the past few days, that a scientist from the Agricultural Research Institute, who was known to be in the neighbourhood, would distribute the school prizes at the concert and also give a little lecture on his favourite subject, which was correct winter grazing. Even that rumour did not keep people away, however. They had the good sense to guess that it was only a rumour, anyhow. Afterwards it was found out that it had been started by Chris Welman, because the schoolmaster had turned down Chris Welman's offer to sing "Boereseun," with actions, at the concert.

There was loud applause when young Vermaak, the schoolmaster, came on to the platform. His black hair was neatly parted in the middle and his city suit of blue serge looked very smart in the lamplight. You could hardly notice those darker patches on the jacket to which Jurie Steyn's wife drew attention, when she said that you could see where Alida van Niekerk had again been trying to clean the schoolmaster's suit with paraffin. Vermaak was boarding at the Van Niekerk's, and Alida was their eldest daughter.

The schoolmaster said he was glad to see that there was such a considerable crowd there, tonight, including quite a number of fathers, whom he knew personally, who were looking in at the windows. There were still a few vacant seats for them inside, he said, if they would care to come in. But Gysbert van Tonder, speaking on behalf of those fathers, said no, they did not mind being self-sacrificing in that way. It was not right that the schoolroom should be cluttered up with a lot of fat, healthy men, over whose heads the smaller children would not be able to see properly. There was also a neighbour of theirs, from Vleispoort, Hendrik Prinsloo, who was resting a little. And they wanted to keep an eye on his Cape-cart, which was standing there all by itself in the dark. If the schoolmaster looked out of that nearest window he would be able to see that lonely Cape-cart, Gysbert van Tonder said.

Young Vermaak, who didn't know what was going on, seemed touched at this display of solicitude for a neighbour by just simple-hearted Bushveld farmers. Several of the wives of those farmers sniffed, however.

Three little boys carrying little riding whips and wearing little red jackets came on to the platform and the schoolmaster explained that they would sing a hunting song called "Jan Pohl," which had been translated from English by the great Afrikaans poet, Van Blerk Willemse. Everybody agreed that the translation was a far superior cultural work to the original, the schoolmaster said. In fact you wouldn't recognise that it was the same song, even, if it wasn't for the tune. But that would also be put right shortly, the schoolmaster added. The celebrated Afrikaans composer, Frik Dinkelman, was going to get to work on it.

At Naudé said to the other fathers standing at the window that that man in the song, Jan Pohl, must be a bit queer in the head. "Wearing a red jacket and with a riding whip and a bugle to go and shoot a ribbok in the rante," At Naudé said.

Another father pointed out that Jan Pohl didn't even have such a thing as a native walking along in front, through the tamboekie grass, where there was always a likelihood of mambas.

The next item on the programme was a group of boys and girls, in pairs, pirouetting about the platform to the music of "Pollie, Ons Gaan Pêrel Toe." Since many of the parents were Doppers, the schoolmaster took the trouble first to explain that what the children were doing wasn't really *dancing* at all. They were stepping about, quickly, sort of, in couples, kind of, to the measure of a polka in a manner of speaking. It was Volkspele, and had the approval of the Synod, the schoolmaster said. All the same, a few of the more earnest members of the audience kept their eyes down on the floor, while that was going on. They also refrained, in a quite stern manner, from beating time to the music with their feet.

For that reason it came as something of a relief when, at the end of the Volkspele, a number of children with wide blue collars trooped on to the stage. They were going to sing "Die Vaal se Bootman." It was really a Russian song, the schoolmaster explained. But the way the great Afrikaans poet Van Blerk Willemse had handled it, you wouldn't think it, at all. Maybe why it was such an outstanding translation, the schoolmaster said, was because Van Blerk Willemse didn't know any Russian, and didn't want to, either.

The song was a great success. The audience was still humming "Yo–ho–yo" to themselves a good way into the next item on the programme.

Meanwhile, the fathers outside the school building had deserted their places by the windows and had drifted in the direction of the Cape-cart to make sure that everything was still in order there. And they sat down on the ground as close as they could get to the Cape-cart, to make sure that things stayed in order. One of the fathers, still singing "Yo-ho-yo" even went and sat right on top of Hendrik Prinsloo's face, without noticing anything wrong. Hendrik Prinsloo didn't notice anything, either, at first, but when he did he made such a fuss, shouting "Elephants" and such-like, that At Naudé, who had remained at the schoolroom window, came running up to the Cape-cart, fearing the worst.

"Is that all?" At Naudé asked, when it was explained to him what had happened. "From the way Hendrik Prinsloo was carrying on, I thought some clumsy —" he used a strong word, "some clumsy — had kicked over the jar."

In the meantime Hendrik Prinsloo had risen to a half-sitting posture, with his hand up to his face. "Feel here, kêrels," he said. "The middle part of my face has suddenly gone all flat, and my jaw is all sideways. Just feel here."

The farmers around the Cape-cart were fortunately able – in between singing "Yo–ho–yo" – to set Hendrik Prinsloo's mind at rest. He was worrying about nothing at all, they assured him. His face had always been that way

Nevertheless, Hendrik Prinsloo did not appear to be as grateful as he should have been for that explanation. He said quite a lot of things that we felt did not fit in with a school concert.

"The schoolmaster says the Joernaal is going to be read out shortly," At Naudé announced. "Well, I hope there is going to be nothing in it like the sort of things Hendrik Prinsloo is saying now. All the same, I wonder what there is going to be in the Joernaal – you know what I mean – funny stories about people we all know."

Gysbert van Tonder started telling us about a Joernaal he had once heard read out at a Nagelspruit school concert. A deputation of farmers saw the schoolmaster on to the Government lorry immediately afterwards, Gysbert van Tonder said. The schoolmaster's clothes and books they sent after him, carriage forward, next day.

"I wonder, though," At Naudé said, "will young Vermaak mention in the Joernaal about himself and – and – you know who I mean – that will be a laugh."

As it turned out, however, there was no mention of that in the Joernaal. Nor was there any reference, direct or indirect, to anybody else in the Marico, either. In compiling the Joernaal, all that the schoolmaster had done was to cut a whole lot of jokes out of back numbers of magazines and to include also some funny stories that had been popular in the Marico for many years, and for generations, even. And because there was nothing that you enjoy as much as hearing an old joke for the hundredth time, the Joernaal got the audience into a state of uproarious good humour.

It was all so *jolly* that Jurie Steyn's wife did not even say anything sarcastic when Alida van Niekerk went and picked up the schoolmaster's programme, that had dropped on to the floor, for him.

The concert in the schoolroom went on until quite late, and everybody said how successful it was. The concert at the Cape-cart, which nearly all the fathers joined in, afterwards, was perhaps even more successful, and lasted a good deal longer. And Chris Welman did get his chance, there, to sing "Boereseun," with actions.

And when Hendrik Prinsloo drove off eventually, in his Cape-cart, into the night, there was handshaking all round, and they cheered him, and everybody asked him to be sure and come round again to the next school concert, also.

Next day there was only the locked door of the old school building to show that it was the end of term.

And at the side of a footpath that a solitary child walked along to and from school lay fragments of a torn-up quarterly report.

Birth Certificate

It was when At Naudé told us what he had read in the newspaper about a man who had thought all his life that he was white, and had then discovered that he was coloured, that the story of Flippus Biljon was called to mind. I mean, we all knew the story of Flippus Biljon. But because it was still early afternoon we did not immediately make mention of Flippus. Instead, we discussed, at considerable length, other instances that were within our knowledge of people who had grown up as one sort of person and had discovered in later life that they were in actual fact quite a different sort of person.

Many of these stories that we recalled in Jurie Steyn's voorkamer as the shadows of the thorn-trees lengthened were based only on hearsay. It was the kind of story that you had heard, as a child, at your grandmother's knee. But your grandmother would never admit, of course, that she had heard that story at *her* grandmother's knee. Oh, no. She could remember very clearly how it all happened, just like it was yesterday. And she could tell you the name of the farm. And the name of the landdrost who was summoned to take note of the extraordinary occurrence, when it had to do with a more unusual sort of changeling, that is. And she would recall the solemn manner in which the landdrost took off his hat when he said that there were many things that were beyond human understanding.

Similarly now, in the voorkamer, when we recalled stories of white children that had been carried off by a Bushman or a baboon or a werewolf, even, and had been brought up in the wilds and without any proper religious instruction, then we also did not think it necessary to explain where we had first heard those stories. We spoke as though we had been actually present at some stage of the affair – more usually at the last scene, where the child, now grown to manhood and needing trousers and a pair of braces and a hat, gets restored to his parents and the magistrate after studying the birth certificate says that there are things in this world that baffle the human mind.

And while the shadows under the thorn-trees grew longer, the stories we told in Jurie Steyn's voorkamer grew, if not longer, then, at least, taller.

"But this isn't the point of what I have been trying to explain," At Naudé interrupted a story of Gysbert van Tonder's that was getting a bit confused in parts, through Gysbert van Tonder not being quite clear as to what a werewolf was. "When I read that bit in the newspaper I started wondering how must a man *feel*, after he has grown up with adopted parents and he discovers, quite late in life, through seeing his birth certificate for the first time, that he isn't white, after all. That is what I am trying to get at. Supposing Gysbert were to find out suddenly – "

At Naudé pulled himself up short. Maybe there were one or two things about a werewolf that Gysbert van Tonder wasn't too sure about, and he would allow himself to be corrected by Oupa Bekker on such points. But there were certain things he wouldn't stand for.

"All right," At Naudé said hastily, "I don't mean Gysbert van Tonder, specially. What I am trying to get at is, how would any one of us feel? How would any white man feel, if he has passed as white all his life, and he sees for the first time, from his birth certificate, that his grandfather was coloured? I mean, how would he *feel*? Think of that awful moment when he looks at the palms of his hands and he sees – "

"He can have that awful moment," Gysbert van Tonder said. "I've looked at the palm of my hand. It's a white man's palm. And my fingernails have also got proper half-moons."

At Naudé said he had never doubted that. No, there was no need for Gysbert van Tonder to come any closer and show him. He could see quite well enough just from where he was sitting. After Chris Welman had pulled Gysbert van Tonder back on to the rusbank by his jacket, counselling him not to do anything foolish, since At Naudé did not mean *him*, Oupa Bekker started talking about a white child in Schweizer-Reneke that had been stolen out of its cradle by a family of baboons.

"I haven't seen that cradle myself," Oupa Bekker acknowledged, modestly. "But I met many people who have. After the child had been stolen, neighbours from as far as the Orange River came to look at that cradle. And when they looked at it they admired the particular way that Heilart Nortjé – that was the child's father – had set about making his household furniture, with glued klinkpenne in the joints, and all. But the real interest about the cradle was that it was empty, proving that the child had been stolen by baboons. I remember how one neighbour, who was not on very good terms with Heilart Nortjé, went about the district saying that it could only have *been* baboons.

"But it was many years before Heilart Nortjé and his wife saw their child again. By *saw*, I mean getting near enough to be able to talk to him and ask him how he was getting on. For he was always too quick, from the way the baboons had brought him up. At intervals Heilart Nortjé and his wife would see the tribe of baboons sitting on a rant, and their son, young Heilart, would be in the company of the baboons. And once, through his field-glasses, Heilart had been able to observe his son for quite a few moments. His son was then engaged in picking up a stone and laying hold of a scorpion that was underneath it. The speed with which his son pulled off the scorpion's sting and proceeded to eat up the rest of the scorpion whole filled the father's heart of Heilart Nortjé with a deep sense of pride.

"I remember how Heilart talked about it. 'Real intelligence,' Heilart announced with his chest stuck out. 'A real baboon couldn't have done it quicker or better. I called my wife, but she was a bit too late. All she could see was him looking as pleased as anything and scratching himself. And my wife and I held hands and we smiled at each other and we asked each other, where does he get it from?' "

But then there were times again when that tribe of baboons would leave the Schweizer-Reneke area and go deep into the Kalahari, and

Heilart Nortjé and his wife would know nothing about what was happening to their son, except through reports from farmers near whose homesteads the baboons had passed. Those farmers had a lot to say about what happened to some of their sheep, not to talk of their mealies and watermelons. And Heilart would be very bitter about those farmers. Begrudging his son a few prickly-pears, he said.

"And it wasn't as though he hadn't made every effort to get his son back, Heilart said, so that he could go to catechism classes, since he was almost of age to be confirmed. He had set all sorts of traps for his son, Heilart said, and he had also thought of shooting the baboons, so that it would be easier, after that, to get his son back. But there was always the danger, firing into a pack like that, of his shooting his own son.

"The neighbour that I have spoken of before," Oupa Bekker continued, "who was not very well-disposed towards Heilart Nortjé, said that the real reason Heilart didn't shoot was because he didn't always know – actually *know* – which was his son and which was one of the more flat-headed kees-baboons."

It seemed that this was going to be a very long story. Several of us started getting restive. . . So Johnny Coen asked Oupa Bekker, in a polite sort of way, to tell us how it all ended.

"Well, Heilart Nortjé caught his son, afterwards," Oupa Bekker said. "But I am not sure if Heilart was altogether pleased about it. His son was so hard to tame. And then the way he caught him. It was the simplest sort of baboon trap of all. . . Yes, *that* one. A calabash with a hole in it just big enough for you to put your hand in, empty, but that you can't get your hand out of again when you're clutching a fistful of mealies that was put at the bottom of the calabash. Heilart Nortjé never got over that, really. He felt it was a very shameful thing that had happened to him. The thought that his son, in whom he had taken so much pride, should have allowed himself to be caught in the simplest form of monkey-trap."

When Oupa Bekker paused, Jurie Steyn said that it was indeed a sad story, and was, no doubt, perfectly true. There was just a certain tone in Jurie Steyn's voice that made Oupa Bekker continue.

"True in every particular," Oupa Bekker declared, nodding his head a good number of times. "The landdrost came over to see about it, too. They sent for the landdrost so that he could make a report about it. I was there, that afternoon, in Heilart Nortjé's voorkamer, when the landdrost came. And there were a good number of other people, also. And Heilart Nortjé's son, half-tamed in some ways but still baboon-wild in others, was there also. The landdrost studied the birth certificate very carefully. Then the landdrost said that what he had just been present at surpassed ordinary human understanding. And the landdrost took off his hat in a very solemn fashion.

"We all felt very embarrassed when Heilart Nortjé's son grabbed the hat out of the landdrost's hand and started biting pieces out of the crown.'

When Oupa Bekker said those words it seemed to us like the end of a story. Consequently, we were disappointed when At Naudé started making further mention of that piece of news he had read in the daily paper. So there was nothing else for it but that we had to talk about Flippus Biljon. For Flippus Biljon's case was just the opposite of the case of the man that At Naudé's newspaper wrote about.

Because he had been adopted by a coloured family, Flippus Biljon had always regarded himself as a coloured man. And then one day, quite by accident, Flippus Biljon saw his birth certificate. And from that birth certificate it was clear that Flippus Biljon was as white as you or I. You can imagine how Flippus Biljon must have felt about it. Especially after he had gone to see the magistrate at Bekkersdal, and the magistrate, after studying the birth certificate, confirmed the fact that Flippus Biljon was a white man.

"Thank you, baas," Flippus Biljon said. "Thank you very much, *my basie*."

THE AFFAIR AT YSTERSPRUIT

IT WAS IN THE SECOND BOER WAR, at the skirmish of Ysterspruit, near Klerksdorp, in February, 1902, that Johannes Engelbrecht, eldest son of Ouma Engelbrecht, widow, received a considerable number of bullet wounds, from which he subsequently died. And when she spoke about the death of her son in battle, Ouma Engelbrecht dwelt heavily on the fact that Johannes had fought bravely. She would enumerate his wounds, and, if you were interested, she would trace in detail the direction that each bullet took through the body of her son.

If you liked stories of the past, and led her on, Ouma Engelbrecht would also mention, after a while, that she had a photograph of Johannes in her bedroom. It was with great difficulty that a stranger could get her to bring out that photograph. But she usually showed it, in the end. And then she would talk very fast about people not being able to understand the feelings that went on in a mother's heart.

"People put the photograph away from them," she would say, "and they turn it face downwards on the rusbank. And all the time I say to them, no, Johannes died bravely. I say to them that they don't know how a mother feels. One bullet came in from in front, just to the right of his heart, and it went through his gall bladder and then struck a bone in his spine and passed out through his hip. And another bullet. . . "

So she would go on while the stranger studied the photograph of her son Johannes, who died of wounds received in the skirmish at Ysterspruit.

When the talk came round to the old days, leading up to and including the Second Boer War, I was always interested when they had a photograph that I could examine, at some farmhouse in that part of the

Groot Marico District that faces towards the Kalahari. And when they showed me, hanging framed against a wall of the voorkamer – or having brought it from an adjoining room – a photograph of a burgher of the South African Republic, father or son or husband or lover, then it was always with a thrill of pride in my land and my people that I looked on a likeness of a hero of the Boer War.

I would be equally interested whether it were the portrait of a bearded kommandant or of a youngster of fifteen. Or of a newly appointed veldkornet, looking important, seated on a riempiestoel with his Mauser held upright so that it would come into the photograph, but also turned slightly to the side, for fear that the muzzle should cover up part of the veldkornet's face, or a piece of his manly chest. And I would think that that veldkornet never sat so stiffly on his horse – certainly not on the morning when the commando set out for the Natal border. And he would have looked less important, although perhaps more solemn, on a night when the empty bully-beef tins rattled against the barbed wire in front of a blockhouse, and the English Lee-Metfords spat flame.

I was a school-teacher, many years ago, at a little school in the Marico Bushveld, near the border of the Bechuanaland Protectorate. The Transvaal Education Department expected me to visit the parents of the schoolchildren in the area at intervals. But even if this huisbesoek were not part of my after-school duties, I would have gone and visited the parents in any case. And when I discovered, after one or two casual calls, that the older parents were a fund of first-class story material, that they could hold the listener enthralled with tales of the past, with embroidered reminiscences of Transvaal life in the old days, then I became very conscientious about huisbesoek.

"What happened after that, Oom?" I would say, calling on a parent for about the third week in succession, "when you were trekking through the kloof that night, I mean, and you had muzzled both the black calf with the dappled belly and your daughter, so that Mojaja's men would not be able to hear anything?"

And then the oom would knock out the ash from his pipe on to his veldskoen and he would proceed to relate – his words a slow and steady rumble and with the red dust of the road in their sound, almost – a tale of terror or of high romance or of soft laughter.

It was quite by accident that I came across Ouma Engelbrecht in a two-roomed, mud-walled dwelling some little distance off the Government Road and a few hundred yards away from the homestead of her son-in-law, Stoffel Brink, on whom I had called earlier in the afternoon. I had not been in the Marico very long, then, and my interview with Stoffel Brink had been, on the whole, unsatisfactory. I wanted to know how deep the Boer trenches were dug into the foot of the koppies at Magersfontein, where Stoffel Brink had fought. Stoffel Brink, on the other hand, was anxious to learn whether, in regard to what I taught the children, I would follow the guidance of the local school committee, of which he was chairman, or whether I was one of that new kind of school-teacher who went by a little printed book of subjects supplied by the Education Department. He added that this latter class of schoolmaster was causing a lot of unpleasantness in the Bushveld through teaching the children that the earth moved round the sun, and through broaching similar questions of a political nature.

I replied evasively, with the result that Stoffel Brink launched forth for almost an hour on the merits of the old-fashioned Hollander schoolmaster, who could teach the children all he knew himself in eighteen months, because he taught them only facts.

"If a child stays at school longer than that," Stoffel Brink added, "then the rest of the time he can only learn lies."

I left about then, and on my way back, a little distance from the road and half concealed by tall bush, I found the two-roomed dwelling of Ouma Engelbrecht.

It was good, there.

I could see that Ouma Engelbrecht did not have much time for her son-in-law, Stoffel Brink. For when I mentioned his references to education, when I had merely sought to learn some details about the Boer trenches at Magersfontein, she said that maybe he could learn all there was to know in eighteen months, but he had not learnt how to be ordinarily courteous to a stranger who came to his door – a stranger, moreover, who was a schoolmaster asking information about the Boer War.

Then, of course, she spoke about her son, Johannes, who didn't have to hide in a Magersfontein trench, but who was sitting straight up on his horse when all those bullets went through him at Ysterspruit, and who died of his wounds some time later. Johannes had always been such a well-behaved boy, Ouma Engelbrecht told me, and he was gentle and kind-hearted.

She told me many stories of his childhood and early youth. She spoke about a time when the span of red Afrikaner oxen got stuck with the wagon in the drift, and her husband and the labourers, with long whip and short sjambok, could not move them – and then Johannes had come along and he had spoken softly to the red Afrikaner oxen, and he had called on each of them by name, and the team had made one last mighty effort, and had pulled the wagon through to the other side.

"And yet they never understood him in these parts," Ouma Engelbrecht continued. "They say things about him, and I hardly ever talk of him any more. And when I show them his portrait, they hardly even look at it, and they put the picture away from them, and when they are sitting on that rusbank where you are sitting now, they place the portrait of Johannes face downwards beside them."

I told Ouma Engelbrecht, laughing reassuringly the while, that I stood above the pettiness of local intrigue. I told her that I had already noticed that there were all kinds of queer undercurrents below the placid surface of life in the Groot Marico. There was the example of what had happened that very afternoon, when her son-in-law, Stoffel Brink, had conceived a nameless prejudice against me, simply because I was not prepared to teach the schoolchildren that the earth was flat.

I told her that it was ridiculous to imagine that a man in my position, a man of education and wide tolerance, should allow himself to be influenced by local Dwarsberge gossip.

Ouma Engelbrecht spoke freely, then, and the fight at Ysterspruit lived for me again – Kemp and De la Rey and the captured English convoy, the ambush and the booty of a million rounds of ammunition. It was almost as though the affair at Ysterspruit was being related to me, not by a lonely woman whose son received his death wounds on the vlaktes near Klerksdorp, but by a burgher who had taken a prominent part in the battle.

And so, naturally, I wanted to see the photograph of her son, Johannes Engelbrecht.

When it came to the Boer War (although I did not say that to Ouma Engelbrecht), I didn't care if a Boer commander was not very competent or very cunning in his strategy, or if a burgher was not particularly brave. It was enough for me that he had fought. And to me General Snyman, for instance, in spite of the history books' somewhat unflattering assessment of his military qualities, was a hero, none the less. I had seen General Snyman's photograph, somewhere: that face that was like Transvaal blouklip; those eyes that had no fire in them, but a stubborn and elemental strength. You still see Boers in the backveld with that look today.

In my mind I had contrasted the portraits of General Snyman and Comte de Villebois Mareuil, the Frenchman who had come all the way from Europe to shoulder a Mauser for the Transvaal Republic. De Villebois, poet and romantic, last-ditch champion of the forlorn hope and the heroic cause. . . Oh, they were very different, these two men, De Villebois Mareuil, the French nobleman, and Snyman, the Boer. But I had an equal admiration for them both.

Anyway, it was well on towards evening when Ouma Engelbrecht, yielding at last to my cajoleries and entreaties, got up slowly from her chair and went into the adjoining room. She returned with a photograph enclosed in a heavy black frame. I waited, tense with curiosity, to see the portrait of that son of hers who had died of wounds at Ysterspruit, and whose reputation the loose prattle of the neighbourhood had invested with a dishonour as dark as the frame about his photograph.

Flicking a few specks of dust from the portrait, Ouma Engelbrecht handed over the picture to me.

And she was still talking about the things that went on in a mother's heart, things of pride and sorrow that the world did not understand, when, in an unconscious reaction, hardly aware of what I was doing, I placed beside me on the rusbank, face downwards, the photograph of a young man whose hat brim was cocked on the right side, jauntily, and whose jacket with narrow lapels was buttoned up high. With a queer jumble of inarticulate feelings I realised that, in the affair at Ysterspruit, they were all Mauser bullets that had passed through the youthful body of Johannes Engelbrecht, National Scout.

A Boer Rip van Winkel

Every writer has got, lying around somewhere in a suitcase or a trunk, various parts of a story that he has worked on from time to time and that he has never finished, because he hasn't been able to find out how the theme should be handled. Such a story – that I have had lying in a suitcase for many years – centres around the things that happened to Herklaas van Wyk.

The plot of a story has no particular appeal for me. I feel that to sit down and work out a plot does not call for the highest form of literary inspiration. Rather does that form of activity recall the skill of the inventor.

My own stories that I like best are those that have just grown. Some mood, conjured up in half a dozen words, has set me going, and it has often happened to me that only when I have got to very near the end in the writing of it, has the shape of the story suddenly dawned on me. And more than once I have been surprised to find what a very old tale it was that has kept me from the chimney corner. Agreeably surprised, that is, for I have a preference for old tales.

But my inability to finish writing the story of Herklaas van Wyk is not due to the denouement not having taken some recognisable form in my mind within the last few hundred words. It hasn't been that kind of writer's problem: I didn't put my hand in the hat and a story came out that wouldn't unfold. On the contrary, this story told itself quite all right, in all its main essentials. What is more, within the first few paragraphs I realised very clearly to what general class of story it belonged. But there were so many hiatuses between the time when Herklaas van Wyk was last seen with the remnants of the Losberg commando, towards the end of the Boer War, in 1902, and the time when he was captured with General Kemp outside Upington in the rebellion of 1914.

If I could fill in that interval of a dozen years satisfactorily, I would still be able to write the story of Herklaas van Wyk. Yet the very fascination of this story is intimately bound up with the *nature* of that lacuna. It is no new thing to have a story of which the end is a mystery – something that the reader must work out for himself with or without a clue supplied by the author. But when the middle part of a story – which gives the atmosphere to the whole sequence of real and imaginary events – is missing, then I feel that I am confronted with an artistic problem of an order that I am not sure it is wise for a writer to tackle.

I don't mind writing a story in which the plot is vague. But when the atmosphere isn't there – the background and the psychology and the interplay of situation and character – then what is left isn't my idea of a story.

The events with which Herklaas van Wyk was connected in the early part of 1902 were commonplace enough. There are still a number of Boers alive today who were on commando with him. Kritzinger's invasion of the Cape Colony is an episode that has passed into history. And a considerable body of Boers, members of commandos that kept being split up into ever-smaller groups, succeeded in penetrating to the Atlantic Ocean and in remaining in the field, deep inside the Cape Colony, long after the main commando had retreated beyond the Vaal.

It was in 1902 that Herklaas van Wyk, then promoted to the rank of veldkornet, caught sight, in the blue distance, of the unquiet Atlantic. The small body of men pushed on to the beach. They had come a long way, from the Transvaal and the Free State, and also from the Karoo, where a number of Cape rebels had joined the fighting forces of the Republics. It was a mixed group of burghers that came to a halt on the white sand of the beach south of Okiep.

Herklaas van Wyk rode his horse along the shore for a considerable distance. The burghers galloped on behind their veldkornet, the hooves of their horses kicking up a spray of damp sea-sand. For they rode along that strip of beach from which the waves had withdrawn in the ebbing of the Atlantic.

Eventually Herklaas van Wyk reined in his horse. His hand shielding his eyes, he gazed for a long while at the place where the sea and sky met on the horizon. He had known two years before that the Boer War was lost for the Transvaal and the Free State. One last hope had returned to him, early that morning, when he had caught sight of the ocean. That hope, too, had vanished now. He realised that he would not be able, with the handful of burghers under his command, to invade England.

Facing out to the sea, Herklaas van Wyk slowly took off his hat.

"It's no good, kêrels," he called out above the roar of the waves and the wind, "we'll have to go back again. There's no drift around here where we'll be able to get our horses through."

About Herklaas van Wyk there was a certain measure of grandeur even in defeat.

And his story, up to that time when the sea-wind was whistling through his black beard, was straightforward enough. In fact, you can read about him in any history book dealing with that period. But it is on his way back to the Transvaal, when he and his men had to elude flying English columns and had to cross barbed-wire fences with blockhouses threaded on to them, that Herklaas van Wyk quits the pages of printed history, complete with dates and place-names, and enters the realm of legend.

It is generally accepted that he was still in the field when the Boer War ended in May, 1902. His own story is that he crept into a deserted rondavel at the foot of a koppie in the Upington District, and that he fell asleep there, with his Mauser beside him, and his horse tethered to a thorn-tree.

Another story – subscribed to on doubtful authority by fellow members of the rebel commando that surrendered with Herklaas van Wyk in 1915, after General Kemp had failed to take Upington – seeks to account for that interval of a dozen years in a different fashion. In terms of this latter attempt at reconstructing the facts, all that happened to Herklaas van Wyk between 1902, the end of the Boer War, and 1914, the year of the outbreak of the rebellion, was that he lived on some farm in the Upington District as a bywoner. It is readily conceivable, protagonists of this standpoint declare, that he slept quite a lot during that period, especially on hot afternoons when his employer had sent him out to look for strayed cattle. Who has not heard – this school of the doubters asks – of a bywoner lying asleep in his rondavel when he should be at the borehole pumping water?

I can only reply that this theory which represents him as a decadent bywoner does not fit in with my conception of Herklaas van Wyk as a person.

A third school of theorists, drawing attention to the scar of an old bullet wound that Herklaas van Wyk still carried above his left temple when he rode with Kemp in 1915, offers another explanation of that interim period. Quite likely that bullet, searing the flesh at the side of his head, caused loss of memory, they say. Quite likely Herklaas van Wyk did become a bywoner when the Boer War ended. And then, in 1914, when he again heard the hoof-beats of commandos coming out of the veld, and the rattling of musketry, the past was suddenly brought back to him, and he was once more in the saddle, with his Mauser and bandolier. The Boer War came back to him in a single rush. Only, the bywoner period now sank into oblivion. Memory does play tricks like that.

Well, I must confess that I don't care particularly for this latter theory, either.

I still prefer Herklaas van Wyk's own story, which he told to anybody who would listen, after he had been captured by Botha's Government forces. For one thing, if we accept Herklaas van Wyk's account of his long sleep in the abandoned rondavel at the foot of a koppie in the Upington District, we have the material for a South African legend as stirring as the one that Washington Irving chronicled. Van Wyk and Van Winkel. This is surely no idle coincidence. Above all, there is a Gothic quality in Herklaas van Wyk's own story – a gloomy magnificence that is never absent from the interior of a rondavel at the foot of a koppie, if that koppie is composed of ironstone.

Herklaas van Wyk asleep in a dark corner, waiting, a backveld Barbarossa, for his far-off awakening, in an hour filled with the thunder of horse-hooves and the noise of battle.

The old man with the white beard and the rusty Mauser and the walking skeleton of a horse had been with Kemp's rebel commando for the best part of a week of dispirited running away from the Government forces. It now began to dawn on the little band of 1914 rebels that Oom Herklaas van Wyk was (as they interpreted it) in his second childhood. It was clear that he thought the year was 1902; it was obvious that he did not know that he was a rebel who had taken the field against the Union troops; instead, he spoke of himself as a Transvaal burgher, and he referred to Cronjé's surrender at Paardeberg, scornfully, as though it had taken place yesterday.

He was very puzzled, also, when he learnt for the first time that the rebel commando was being pursued by a column of Botha-men.

"But if Botha is chasing us," Herklaas van Wyk demanded, "who is fighting Kitchener?"

Thus it came about, one evening when the rebels were encamped in a bluegum plantation on the road to Upington, that a lot of explanations were made.

"I remember the day you joined us, Oom Herklaas," Jan Gouws, a young rebel, said after Herklaas van Wyk had told his story and they had persuaded him that the year was, indeed, 1915, and that he was not now fighting in the Boer War. "Your white beard was blowing in the wind, Oom Herklaas, and several of us laughed at the awkward way your old horse cantered, throwing his legs all to one side. So you really say you slept for twelve years?"

"I believe now – now that you've told me," Herklaas van Wyk replied, "that I must have lain asleep on the floor of that rondavel all those years. That must have been just at the end of the Boer War.

And it's funny that I didn't wake up before my nation again needed me."

The rebels received the old man's last remark in silence. They were beginning to doubt the wisdom of their armed rising. They had been driven from pillar to post for many days. Incessant rain had damped their ardour.

"Did you remember to wind your watch before you went to sleep in that rondavel, Oom Herklaas?" Jan Gouws asked, trying to change the subject.

The others did not laugh at this sally. For one thing, the rain had started coming down again. . .

Some of the rebels seemed half-inclined to believe Herklaas van Wyk's story. And there seemed to be something inexplicably solemn in the thought of a burgher of the Transvaal Republic going to sleep in the corner of a deserted rondavel, with his Mauser at his side – and only waking up again a dozen years later, when men were once more riding with rifles slung across their shoulders.

"Did you dream at all during that time, Oom Herklaas?" another man asked, in a half-serious tone.

The old man thought for a little while.

"I remember dreaming about a mossie settling on a kaffir-boom that was full of red flowers," Herklaas van Wyk answered slowly, "but I think I dreamt of it a long time back – after I had been asleep only four years, or so."

Jan Gouws shivered. The red flowers on that kaffir-boom must be pretty well faded by now, he thought. And it gave him a queer feeling to think of that mossie, that an old man saw in a dream, flitting about in the sunshine of long ago. It made Jan Gouws feel uncomfortable, for a reason that he could not explain.

"My Mauser is very rusty," Herklaas van Wyk continued. "I've tried oiling it, but that doesn't help. I'll have to hands-up or shoot one of the enemy, and take his Lee-Metford off him, like we used to do. How long will it take us to win this war, do you think?"

The rebels did not answer. They knew that their cause was already shot to pieces. In spite of the old man's senility, there seemed to emanate from his spirit a strange kind of assurance, a form of steadfastness in the face of adversity and defeat that they themselves did not possess. It seemed that there was something inside the entrails of this burgher of the Transvaal Republic that they didn't have. Something firm and constant that they had lost. And they felt, sensing the difference between the previous generation and their own, and without being able to express their feelings in words, that in that difference lay their defeat.

"What happened about your horse, Oom Herklaas?" a young rebel asked eventually.

Outwardly dilapidated, Herklaas van Wyk still seemed to represent, somehow, the gloom and grandeur of a greater day.

"I had tethered my horse to a thorn-tree," Herklaas van Wyk said, "and he, too, must have fallen asleep. And I am sure that the hoof-beats of a commando at full gallop must have awakened him, also. For when I got to the thorn-tree – which hadn't grown much during that time: you know how slowly a thorn-tree grows – my old war-horse was sniffing the wind and pawing the ground. And his neck was arched."

THE OX-RIEM

IT WAS IN THOSE DAYS, when there was no such thing as a Society for the Prevention of Cruelty to Children in the Pilanesberg area – any more than there is today, of course – and the only redress a child had when it was being subjected to inhuman treatment at home was to go and lie in a donga and weep – that the farmers on the other side of the Dwarsberge began to comment, in a somewhat adverse fashion, on the treatment that was being meted out to the young girl, Marie van Zyl, by her guardian, Stefanus Aucamp, the owner of the farm Maanfontein.

Stefanus Aucamp was a man in his early forties. He lived alone on his farm Maanfontein, in a house that had whitewashed walls and a thatched roof and that was built at the foot of a koppie, in a place where the tall withaaks had already given way to thorny scrub.

Stefanus Aucamp had never married. For twenty years a kaffir woman called Blouta and her husband, Kees, had looked after Baas Aucamp's house with the whitewashed walls, cooking the master's meals for him, growing vegetables in the garden between the kitchen and the dam, repairing the thatch when the roof leaked, applying a new coat of whitewash when the walls became discoloured.

It seemed to be only the outside of the house that Stefanus Aucamp cared about at all. What there was of furniture was mostly of tamboekie wood and handmade. A long unpolished table in the voorkamer, a number of chairs and a crudely constructed bench with riempies for the mat, two huge chests in which dried seeds and articles of clothing were packed away almost indiscriminately. The cutlery was worn. The crockery was chipped. It was only on rare occasions, at intervals of several years, sometimes, that Stefanus Aucamp would think of spending a few minutes in that hardware shop, when he was in Zeerust for the Nagmaal, in order to purchase a couple of soup-plates, or half a dozen cups and saucers, to replace those pieces which Blouta and her husband Kees had broken in the kitchen.

There were three bedrooms, one facing on to the front stoep with its slate floor, the other two at the back of the house. Stefanus Aucamp slept in the front room, on a double bed made out of thick bushveld timbers and a mat of plaited thongs to serve as springs. A couple of reebok skins lay on the stone floor. For the rest, there was a wash-stand with a cracked enamel basin and a table and a chair. A piece of curtaining was fastened crosswise in one corner. Behind this hung the store suit that Stefanus Aucamp had worn for the past ten years on each of his visits to the town of Zeerust at Nagmaal.

On a wall was a religious print, the surface considerably damaged by time and damp and the attentions of the white ants.

The furnishing in the other two rooms – one of which was today occupied by the girl-child, Marie van Zyl – was not substantially different from the room in which Stefanus Aucamp slept.

Stefanus Aucamp had had big ideas, at one time, people said. He had had large-scale plans for extending the house and getting the most modern kind of furniture, a chesterfield suite and wardrobes with mirrors and a dressing-table and a piano – all to be railed up from Johannesburg. He had spent a lot of time studying catalogues from furniture dealers. And the catalogues were very much discoloured from the grease on his broad, flat fingers, by the time that he decided that he was going to take no trouble with the interior decoration and furnishing of his house at all.

That was after a young woman in the Schweizer-Reneke District had written to say that she had decided, on thinking the matter over carefully, that she would not marry him. They say that Stefanus Aucamp changed a good deal, after he had received that letter, and that he had ceased taking any further interest in the furnishing of his house, and that he began, from then onwards, to devote all his time to the three thousand morgen of bush country that constituted his farm.

He cut down the trees and shrubbery on a stretch of level ground that was far removed from his homestead, and on this ground he began to sow corn, which was an unknown crop in that part of the country. He did a number of other unusual things as well, all of which were frowned upon by the farmers, at the beginning. But always, when a season or two had elapsed, it was noticed that most of the farmers followed in the footsteps of Stefanus Aucamp.

The only farmer who would not allow himself to be influenced by the innovations which he saw Stefanus Aucamp introducing was a near neighbour, Gawie Steyn.

They were much alike, Gawie Steyn and Stefanus Aucamp. That was after Stefanus Aucamp had got the letter from the girl in Schweizer-Reneke, and he had grown taciturn, almost overnight. And deep lines became suddenly cut in the corners of his mouth. And he would stand for long periods and stare in front of him, in silence, even when he was at a meeting of the Farmers' Association, and there were people present who spoke to him. Stefanus Aucamp and Gawie Steyn were much alike, after that. They were both long, sinewy men, for all the world like the shapes of men fashioned out of dried leather. They spoke little. Most of the time their thoughts seemed to be far away, where their eyes were. It was easy to understand why Stefanus Aucamp should have become like that. Brooding and morose, and speaking but few words. But it was a different thing with Gawie Steyn, who had a young wife, and several children, who would play around his knee in the evening, when the day's work on the farm was done, and he would sit on a riempies chair, in the gathering dusk, and the wind of the early evening would blow though the tall withaaks and the sound of children's voices would be in his ears. And yet Gawie Steyn would sit on his front stoep, smoking away at his pipe, and it would almost be as though he did not notice that his children were there. And he did not speak.

For a while there was a certain measure of life in the farmhouse at Maanfontein. That was when a bywoner and his wife and their daughter, who was then an infant, lived with Stefanus Aucamp in his house with the thatched roof and the whitewashed walls. They remained there for several years, the bywoner, Gert van Zyl, and his wife and their small daughter, Marie. But it did not appear to make much difference to Stefanus Aucamp's disposition, this circumstance of a family coming to live in his house. That air of moody silence never seemed to leave him. Nor did he appear to take much more interest in the domestic arrangements of the place. It was also said that the only time he had been known to quarrel with the bywoner family was on one occasion when Mrs Van Zyl had taken it on herself to order a quantity of household utensils from the store in Zeerust, in order to introduce a measure of rude comfort into the lives of the farmer of Maanfontein and his employee and family.

Then, one day, when the girl-child Marie, then aged about six years, had been left in the house, in the charge of the kaffir woman Blouta, and her parents had set off for Zeerust by mule-cart, to transact certain business for Stefanus Aucamp, there occurred a simple tragedy of the veld that resulted in the child, Marie, becoming an orphan, and in Stefanus Aucamp assuming the office of guardian of a girl of six whose nearest relatives, as far as was known, were a trekboer family who had more children than they could support.

What had happened was simply that Gert van Zyl and his wife, on their return from Zeerust, tried to cross the Molopo River when it was in flood (Gert van Zyl having apparently been drunk at the time), and that the mule-cart was swept downstream and the occupants drowned.

With the kaffir woman, Blouta, to look after her, Marie van Zyl went on staying on the farm Maanfontein. The education she received was sketchy. She attended a farm school eight miles away from Maanfontein for a number of years. She got to the school and back by mule-wagon, which passed near Maanfontein daily to convey the children from the neighbourhood to school. Afterwards, when the school wagon ceased passing near Maanfontein, because of the decline in the number of children in that area who attended school, Stefanus Aucamp kept Marie van Zyl at home. He said that he was not going to provide transport to enable a bywoner's child to get educated above her station.

It was about this time, too, that people began to comment on certain aspects of Stefanus Aucamp's treatment of the orphan girl, saying that the discipline he maintained erred grievously on the side of over-sternness. That Stefanus Aucamps knew what was being said about him by the neighbours was not doubted. There was much talk about his conduct. People also hinted to him openly, and to his face, about the things that went on in their minds in regard to this matter.

This had no effect on Stefanus Aucamp. His manner of using the orphaned Marie van Zyl grew steadily more inhumane.

Long and tough and like dried leather, Stefanus Aucamp spent more and more time on the lands. The barbed wire that fenced in his farm and that divided it into a number of camps was tightly drawn. He experimented with a mixture of Stockholm tar and the powder of cattle-dip and other ingredients which he smeared on the lower parts of his fencing-poles to keep the white ants away. The other farmers at first ridiculed his experiments. Afterwards they came and asked him for the recipe. Sullenly, without any human warmth, but also without resentment, he would impart to them such information as they sought. Afterwards his neighbours would also consult him on other matters, such as his views on how long the keelvel of an Afrikaner bull ought to be. And although they affected to despise his opinions, they themselves being fully versed in such matters, which they had studied almost unconsciously from childhood, the raw things of the soil forming an intimate part of their very breath and being – nevertheless, Stefanus Aucamp's neighbours liked to hear his views, even if it was only in order that they might reject them.

They came and spoke to Stefanus Aucamp, even though he was a difficult man to talk to. He never conversed. He would wait a long time before he replied to a question. It was as though the question and his answer would go round and round in his brain, for a long time, and that what he had to say came out of much darkness, and so when he finally replied it was often in a single word. And there were many occasions when, no matter what was said to him, he did not reply at all.

The only man who did not consult Stefanus Aucamp on any matter was his nearest neighbour, Gawie Steyn, a man who was also taciturn, and long and leathery, and who would sit for long periods in the evening, on his front stoep, gazing out beyond the shadows that were suspended between the koppies, and who did not seem to hear the voices of his children playing about his knee.

What people thought was particularly unnatural in the way Stefanus Aucamp was beginning to treat the child Marie was the fact that from morning to night she was seen working in the fields. She would be sent out to search for strayed cattle, like a boy. She would work on the lands with a hoe, like a kaffir woman. When Stefanus Aucamp planted a large area with potatoes – or a crop which, for once, turned out a failure: the farmers had said that you couldn't grow potatoes in that soil, and Stefanus Aucamp had lost a considerable measure of prestige when the crop came to nothing – then Marie van Zyl worked on the land for day after day with the planting, following behind the plough with a basket of seed potatoes, helping to take turns, with the kaffirs, in thrusting the potatoes into the earth and covering up the furrows again.

By that time Marie van Zyl was about fourteen. Her hands were rough from working in the fields. She had had small opportunity of acquiring knowledge of the softer things of life, or the more womanly side of domesticity. And what people felt most bitter about, people who had children of their own and who knew that a child should not be spoilt, were the things that came to their ears of the merciless fashion in which Stefanus Aucamp thrashed the fourteen-year-old child, Marie van Zyl.

There was a riem of ox-leather hanging on the wall in the kitchen. With this riem Stefanus Aucamp was in the habit of thrashing the child for the most trivial of offences, or even for no reason at all.

Sometimes Marie van Zyl would cower away in the corner, suffering Stefanus Aucamp's blows mutely. At other times she would scream and rush out of the door, and Stefanus Aucamp would go after her, thrashing her across her back with the riem as she ran.

Stefanus Aucamp would thrash this child like you would thrash a kaffir, people said. Like you would thrash a dog.

It was right that children should be properly brought up, that they should be trained in the ways of the Lord from their earliest years. The Bible said so. If you weren't disciplined in your childhood you grew up into a godless person. That much everyone knew. For that reason a child had to be chastised, to be instructed in godliness through the sternness of love.

But what went on there, on the farm Maanfontein, with Stefanus Aucamp running after the child Marie van Zyl and flaying her back open with that ox-riem was a different thing. It was very dreadful. And there was nothing that could be done about it.

When she was fifteen, getting to that age when she began to take an interest in herself and her appearance, Marie van Zyl came out of the kitchen door one Saturday, when it was almost noon, and she carried a soiled cotton frock under her arm.

Stefanus Aucamp was entering the kitchen door at that moment.

"Where are you going?" he demanded, looking sternly at the girl.

Marie van Zyl avoided his gaze.

"To the dam, Oom Stefanus," she answered. "I go to wash my frock for this evening. The Bekkers are fetching me to the debating society meeting in Dwarsvlei."

"Debating society!" Stefanus Aucamp thundered. "Next it will be a dance. Next they will want to make a harlot out of you. Throw drown that frock and start carrying manure to the lands."

Marie van Zyl hesitated for a few moments. The next thing she knew was that Stefanus Aucamp had walked into the kitchen and had returned with the length of ox-riem.

His face looked dreadful in that it was so totally expressionless.

She felt his tall leanness rising up over her. Like the in-heat rearing up of an animal. His breathing, also, was like that of an animal.

The ox-riem bit into her flesh and she ran in the direction of the dam, Stefanus Aucamp following at her heels and striking at her fleeing body, for some distance, until his fury had abated.

Marie van Zyl spent that afternoon, the whole of it, carrying sacks of manure from the kraal to the lands. She winced often, when the weight of the sack was not properly adjusted and a hard lump of manure pressed through the hessian against a place on her back or shoulder where her skin was raw from the impact of the ox-riem.

Stefanus Aucamp spoke to the girl Marie van Zyl but rarely. And what he had to say he conveyed in as few words as possible. And in his voice there was always the undertone of a bitterness that could not be slaked. But in those times when he thrashed the child with the length of ox-hide he did not speak at all. It was like a silent ritual of the earth, those motions gone through in the unbleached monotony of stripes laid on young flesh. And always after he had laid the ox-riem to Marie van Zyl's body Stefanus Aucamp would stride out into the veld, walking for a long while in silence, his footsteps solid on the brown ground, and heavy, as though part of the dry glebe-land and the dusty clods to which Stefanus Aucamp belonged.

But there was another side, also, to the life that surges out of the ploughed field, and to this side of that life Stefanus Aucamp did not belong.

There was again a Saturday on which Stefanus Aucamp encountered Marie van Zyl at the kitchen door. She was once more on her way to the dam, with a cotton dress under her arm. And again Stefanus Aucamp had gone into the kitchen for the ox-riem, and he had driven her out on the mealie-lands, where there was work to be done. But this time, after Stefanus Aucamp had left her, his fury sated, and he had gone back into the kitchen, to restore the ox-riem to its place on the wall, Marie van Zyl had not stopped running. She ran through the mealie-fields and through the clearing beyond, and it was when she was clambering through the barbed-wire fence that separated Gawie Steyn's farm from Maanfontein, that Stefanus Aucamp guessed what was happening.

Stefanus Aucamp went to the stables and saddled his horse with the speed of frenzy. He whipped the animal into a furious gallop. Horse and rider tore through hedge and thorn-bush and cleared barbed-wire fences and grazed past enormous ant-hills.

But Marie van Zyl had had too much of a start. She rushed in at Gawie Steyn's front door a few moments before Stefanus Aucamp came galloping up the path to the farmhouse. He had by this time whipped the horse into a condition of near-madness. The animal was foam-flecked from a three-mile gallop. His barrel-shaped chest heaved in quick pants that seemed like a death agony. His eyes rolled as though in the last pains of torture.

It was at that moment that Gawie Steyn came to his front door. Marie van Zyl had already dashed into the voorkamer. Stefanus Aucamp was getting ready to dismount before his horse had come to a stop in front of the veranda.

Gawie Steyn stepped forward, his arms folded lightly across his chest. He looked Stefanus Aucamp straight in the eyes. With one foot already out of the stirrup, Stefanus Aucamp paused. He understood, then. Neither man spoke. In Gawie Steyn Stefanus Aucamp had found a man as taciturn as himself.

Stefanus Aucamp swung himself back into the saddle. He did not look back again. A moment later horse and rider were careering madly back in the direction from which they had come.

Marie van Zyl did not remain long on Gawie Steyn's farm. Perhaps it was that Gawie Steyn's wife did not welcome the presence in their home of a girl of fifteen, who was near grown to womanhood. Perhaps there were other reasons. At all events, the time came, and soon, when Marie van Zyl set off, on her own, to the city of Johannesburg, and nothing more was heard of her.

It was not unlikely that in the city Marie van Zyl found that her body, lithely rounded in youth, was worth more than it was on the farm. And that her golden hair could be displayed to better advantage against the background of a hotel lounge than it could be, in the old days, in close proximity to a sack of manure.

But the person one should be sorry for, of course, was Stefanus Aucamp, who had once before been disappointed in love, and who had seen a girl-child grow before his eyes into young womanhood, and who knew that he was too old for her, too slow of speech and long and leathery, like the ox-riem. He knew that she could never be his, that she would never look at him as a woman looks at a man.

And there were many nights, in the years that came after, when Stefanus Aucamp would be seated alone in the kitchen, before the big open grate, and nobody could guess what his thoughts were about. And the length of ox-riem would be hanging idle on the wall of the kitchen – the riem that had often curved in a salt caress about the thighs of the young girl, Marie van Zyl.

Old Transvaal Story

As Scully, I think, knew – have you ever chanced upon his "Ukushwama"? – the Transvaal seems to have had only one ghost story. It is a story that I have heard very often, told over and over again in voorkamer and by camp-fire, with the essential features always the same, and with only the details, in respect of characters and locale, differing with the mood and the personality – and the memory, perhaps – of each person that tells it.

The story of the Transvaal's only ghost goes something like this.

A solitary traveller on horseback enquires his way at a farmhouse after dark.

"That means you'll be going through the poort" (or the kloof or the drift, as the case may be) "at full moon," the farmer says to the traveller. "Well, no man has ever been able to ride his horse through that poort at night when the moon is full."

Actually, there is no need to tell the story any further than that. In those few words the farmer has said everything. . . A certain place along the road is haunted, and even if the traveller should not happen to notice the ghost – because he is thinking of something else, likely – the horse certainly *will* see the ghost, and will rear up on his hind legs. After that, neither whip nor spur, nor calling him by his first name, coaxingly, will get the horse past that spot where the spectre lurks.

Accordingly, the traveller turns back along the road he has come, riding quite fast, this time. And he arrives once more at that farmhouse where he received the unearthly warning in the first instance. The wise old farmer has known all along that the traveller would be back, of course, and after having persuaded him, without much difficulty, to spend the night there, proceeds to acquaint him in leisurely fashion over a jar of peach brandy with the circumstances that led to the poort becoming haunted.

This is a good story. I have heard it told – nearly always in the first person – by dozens of different people, always with only slight variations, and these of a strictly local character.

Indeed, I have heard this story so often, in different parts of the Transvaal, that it doesn't make my hair stand on end, any more. If the truth must be known, I've got somewhat blasé about the Transvaal's only ghost.

The result is that, nowadays, when a man says – lowering his voice and trying to make his tones sound sepulchral – "And so Oom Hannes Blignaut said to me that I would not be able to ride my horse through that poort in the full moon," I short-circuit him by asking, "But why didn't you go on a push-bike, instead?"

I have not, to date, found an answer to that one.

Similarly, as far as I have been able to discover, the Transvaal has got only one murder story – this, likewise, an amazingly good one. Only, through constant repetition, the gloss has for me been worn off this stirring old tale as well. I first heard it as a child; since then it has been related to me many times, as I am sure it has been to every South African who has spent some portion of his life on the Transvaal platteland. I suppose the story is based on historical fact: its salient features seem to relate to some murder that actually was committed long ago.

This story, I should like to add in parenthesis, has never been told to me in the first person. No man has ever said to me, "And so after I hit my wife with the chopper I buried her under the mud floor of the voorkamer and later on the police came."

For that, in rough outline, is the Transvaal's only murder story. It sounds bald, somehow, conveyed in those words. Put that way, it sounds more like a murder than like a murder story. But this old tale has a twist to it arising out of what happened in a certain period of time between the committing of the murder and the arrival of the police. The man has murdered his wife. . . Good. . . He has buried her under the floor of the voorkamer. . . Right. . . He proceeds to smooth over the broken portion of the floor with clay and moist cow-dung. . . Yes, excellent. All that seems straightforward enough.

But it is at this very point that the totally unexpected happens. This is the sensational development in the plot that distinguishes the Transvaal's only murder story from almost any other murder story I have ever lighted upon. For it is not two plain-clothes policemen that come walking into the voorkamer, in the early evening, when the murderer is down on his hands and knees putting the final touches to the restoration of the damaged floor. The time for the landdrost's men to arrive is not yet. But a couple of men do enter: only, they carry in bottles. They are followed by a number of girls who carry in the fragrance of romance with red veld-flowers in their hair. Then more men come in with bottles. And then a man with a concertina. And there is much laughter. And more girls. Girls with names like Drieka and Tossie and Francina. It is a surprise party.

Of all things. . . Yes, of all the nights in the year, this man's neighbours had to choose just that particular night for throwing a surprise party in his house.

As I have said, this is the Transvaal's oldest – and, as far as I know, only – murder story. I heard it first as a child. Since then I have heard it many times. So have you, too, I suppose.

Like the one about the ghost in the poort, this is also a very good tale, and where it is particularly admirable, from the narrator's point of view, is that it lends itself to the introduction of an infinite variety of graceful and delicate touches in the psychological unfolding of the later scenes. Here great play can be made of the murderer's character. If he is somebody without much refinement and just says straight out, "I've buried my wife under the floor, there. This is no time for foolishness like dancing" – then the story has got to end right there, of course.

If he says, on the other hand, "I'm sorry, my wife went unexpectedly to Potchefstroom," and then allows the party to go on, trying to be as natural as possible, so as not to awaken unnecessary suspicions, then the subsequent developments offer charming possibilities.

To take, just at random, a single courthouse scene.

"And so you danced," the prosecutor would say to Kittie de Bruyn, one of the girls who was at that party. "Did it not come as a shock to you afterwards to think that you danced all night on the head of a dead woman?"

"But I danced lightly," Kittie de Bruyn would answer, "oh – lightly."

It is a situation providing lots of blossomy openings for fragile irony and high drama.

Incidentally, I, too, have told that story before of the woman interred under the floor of the voorkamer. And I have always known that I would have to dig her up again, some time. She was too useful a character to be left lying there, buried under four lines of prose.

The lack of imagination – or, perhaps, meagreness of event – that has bestowed upon the Transvaal only one ghost story and one murder story, does not apply in respect of love stories. The Transvaal has got hundreds of love stories, all opulently different. Woven on the common pattern of boy-meets-girl, one love story, in respect of its external shape, seems very much the same as another. And it is always at the very moment when you fancy that you have recognised the type of love story, when you have pigeon-holed it in your mind as belonging to such-and-such a category – it is at that very moment that you are betrayed; for, lo, there is sudden witchery, and a wand is waved, and it is as though a line of black dancers comes running in suddenly, and you find that a whole lot of people are laughing at you from behind the feathers and painted wood of their Congo masks.

One must be careful about classifying a love story, tabulating and cataloguing it as belonging to a certain sub-section of a particular group – indexing it and labelling it as conforming, in respect of characters and plot and incident, to a well-known and clearly recognised pattern.

Take the love story of Gideon Welman and Alie du Plessis, for instance. Superficially, it seems to conform to a pretty clearly defined type. A rustic idyll. The course of true love not running entirely smoothly. A vague suggestion of complications arising from the oldest geometrical symbol used in romance – the triangle, which is also the shape of the human heart. On the face of it, this is a simple kind of tale that you would be able to classify very easily. And yet, until almost the very end, Gideon Welman himself did not know what the pattern was into which his own love story fitted.

Gideon Welman and Alie du Plessis were seated under an ox-wagon. It was evening. A number of Boer families were trekking back to the Bushveld from the Nagmaal at Zeerust. Next time Gideon Welman and Alie du Plessis would be on that road they would be travelling down to Zeerust to get married. In a few months' time they would be spending their honeymoon on that same road, inside the ox-wagon under which they were at that moment seated. Alie du Plessis was now half-reclining against Gideon Welman, whose arms were about her. Her fingers were plucking at a tuft of smooth, strong grass. The light of the camp-fire flickered on their young faces. They were oblivious of the people around the fire, who were roasting mealies and telling stories. They were not, however, oblivious of the Bushveld night.

And it had to happen at that moment, while they were seated under the wagon, that Alie said something about Rooi Jan Venter.

"There you go again," Gideon Welman exclaimed. "Why have you got to keep on mentioning his name, anyway?"

The point is that Alie du Plessis cared for Gideon Welman, her bridegroom to be, deeply enough. It was not her fault that her feelings for him were not on a plane of ecstasy – were not in the nature of a romantic passion. She did not get a wild thrill at the name "Welman" – no relation of Gideon's – on the signboard of a butcher-shop in Zeerust. She did not flush tremulously when she saw, outspanned on the kerkplein, a mule-cart whose infirm wheels proclaimed it to be Gideon's.

Not that Alie du Plessis did not have a very genuine affection for Gideon Welman, of course. But there you were. . .

Gideon's face was very white and tense in the flickering gleams of the camp-fire.

So Gideon Welman and Alie du Plessis were married in Zeerust. For a while – as far as the outside world was concerned, at least – they lived together happily in their little house in the Bushveld, with the newly whitewashed walls and the roof thatched with what was still last year's grass. And then events slid into that afternoon on which Gideon Welman was working very fast, and in a half-daze. He had the queer feeling that he was living in another life, going through a thing that had happened before, to somebody else, long ago. It was quite dark by the time a knock came at the door.

And when he got up from the floor quickly, dusting his knees, Gideon Welman knew what that old Transvaal story was, into whose pattern his own story had now fitted, also. For the door of the voorkamer opened. And out of the night came the laughter of girls. And Rooi Jan Venter and another young man entered the voorkamer, carrying bottles.

Recognising Blues

Born in the Cape in 1905, Herman Charles Bosman lived most of his life in the Transvaal. As a high-school boy in Johannesburg he began contributing sketches to *The Sunday Times* – "The Dilettante" and "The Deserter" of 1922 are examples. After teaching in the Marico Bushveld district, he was imprisoned for the murder of his step-brother and spent fours years in Pretoria Central Prison – "The Bluecoat's Story" and "Tex Fraser's Story" are excerpted from *Cold Stone Jug* of 1949, his account of his years in gaol. Thereafter he spent most of the 1930s working as a journalist in London, as his serial from *The Sunday Critic* shows.

Back in Johannesburg from 1940 he contributed variously to *The South African Opinion* and *Trek*, to *The Forum* newspaper and to other less established periodicals, from which the bulk of this selection is drawn. He died in 1951, bringing the curtain down on a multifaceted career which had kept his dedicated South African readers enthralled and entertained like no one else before or after him.

CONTENTS

PREFACE

A TOAST TO HERMAN CHARLES BOSMAN.

The revival of the work of South Africa's leading humorist that has taken place since his death in 1951 is largely the result of the popular success that work has enjoyed on the stage (deftly interpreted by Patrick Mynhardt among others). And the stage success is largely a consequence of the element of humour in its performance. South Africans have not only begun, through Bosman, to laugh at themselves, but have learnt, as so many of his characters do, to enjoy laughing at themselves.

And this enjoyment has kept Bosman's life and times alive for us. Nowadays he is one of our national treasures, beyond all criticism – a resource for us always to call on for refreshment, and parade as our very own genius, if ever we are accused by outsiders of taking ourselves all too seriously. Bosman has made us sophisticated, mature – and yes, able to take a joke.

The impulse of humour, as this book so graphically shows, runs consistently through his work right from the very start. Like conjuring tricks, techniques of humour should perhaps never be explained, for fear of killing the sheer pleasure of the surprise the best of humour relies on. But Bosman's use of humour, even in his most serious work, shows an extraordinary variety. He started with schoolboy japes and gags in that unexpected breeding ground of old, *The Sunday Times* columns of parodies. In the Marico and in prison he picked up, through the banter and sneering of the oral tradition – especially when narrators were in competition – how to chaff and to jibe to hold attention. In England he learnt the weapon of mocking derision, twitting the Brits on their own traditional ground. From Swift he could take up that terrible satirical irony he wields in pieces like "A Visit to

Shanty Town" – beware of its scathing anger over social issues. From the American funny-men he gained the mad exaggeration, drawing from chuckles to cackles – and as he said, thus setting the world back into some saner perspective. Who else is behind the outright farce of "A Bekkersdal Marathon" but genial Mark Twain? From Jerome K. Jerome's classic *Idle Thoughts of an Idle Fellow* he derived the pose of the easy raconteur, so world weary, but actually never missing a trick.

To talk true, Bosman needs no introduction. He best introduces himself, as in his "Humour and Wit" piece here. Generous and good-spirited, he was never slow to acknowledge his debts, either: to the American frontier writers frequently, to the Marico storytellers and the bluecoats, to Shakespeare and more – all sources of inspiration only he knew how to blend and turn around for us to recognise.

The following selection represents a cross-section of his work, for the first time made to stress the bolder examples of his power of humour at work. Fifty years on, like his favourite South African distillate of wild fruits, mampoer, it has lost none of its kick.

Cheers.

Stephen Gray
Johannesburg, 2001

ADVENTURE

I took the hand of a ghost I met in Eloff Street:
I took the ghost's hand
And she led me among ways that were most sweet
As in a strange land.

We went by the post office first
And then past the Y. W. C. A.,
And then into a pub where I quenched my thirst
And after that we lost our way.

But all the time I had my hand in the ghost's hand
And she held her hand in mine,
And we walked down Kerk Street through a faery land
And the faces of the people were bubbled in wine.

And we laughed and we sang and a policeman came
And informed us we were not in faërie;
And we trembled in shame and smirched was our fame
And our dolour was grievous to see.

We parted thereafter
In sorrow and laughter
But what she said then was what grieved me most
When she said she shouldn't have gone out with a ghost.

HUMOUR AND WIT

HOW SHALL WE DEFINE that wayward and mysterious and outcast thing that we term humour – that is for ever a pillar to post fugitive from the stern laws of reality and yet forms so intimate a part of (and even embodies) all truth about which there is an eternal ring?

There isn't as much humour in the world today as there was of yore, I think, and through the realms of culture there do not sweep those gusts of great laughter that blew the lamp-smoke away from thought and left behind an intoxication. The material for splendid mirth is still here, of course; right in our midst. Turn but a stone and the diamonds coruscate. But the men who could make out of this material a supremely godlike brand of jesting we seem not to have with us more.

Lots of people have tried to analyse humour: writers, comedians, clergymen, psychologists, undertakers, political cartoonists, cooks, prison superintendents – in fact, all sorts of men in whose private or professional lives humour plays an important role. But I have never come across any attempt at trying to explain what it is that makes us laugh, that has impressed me very much. You can work out what are the ingredients that go towards the compounding of that rare and very subtle thing that stirs the risible faculties. But that doesn't get you anywhere. You can analyse the elements that embrace laughter, but you can't make anybody laugh with your analysis.

The same thing with those distinctions that people draw between humour and wit. Is there any difference? I don't know. If that rather generally accepted, rough and ready attempt at classification holds water – namely, that humour is born out of the emotions and wit springs from the intellect – then I would naturally be prone to look upon wit as being, to some extent, an intruder, I who am by nature suspicious of the intellect, fancying that in its dark recesses there lurks a specious cunning whose purpose is to gloss over with trickery the soul's deficiencies.

With this deep-seated distrust of the intellect, therefore, I would be inclined to move warily within the domain of wit, if the abovementioned definition were correct. But, funny enough, I don't think there is much truth in it. When something makes me laugh I would have to think twice if I am laughing intellectually or if it's just low, moron joy. And if I had to pause in order to reflect on this problem, I wouldn't want to go on laughing any more.

Humour you find all over the place. But with writers of humour (at least with the kind of humour that appeals to me) it seems to be different. You seem to find them at particular times and in particular places. The Elizabethans had a sense of humour that I can respond to as readily as to a backveld joke about rinderpest and drought. And I regard Shakespeare as the greatest humorist I have ever struck. And the singular thing about it is that he seems to me to have been a humorist primarily in the literary sense (as the Americans of the last century were humorists primarily in the literary sense), for his jests seem to have a spontaneous magic in form of the written word that they lack spoken, dramatised. Because I have always derived much more pleasure from reading Shakespeare's humour than from seeing it on the stage. Perhaps I have never yet seen Shakespeare, when he is being funny, properly acted.

But with the exception of the Elizabethans, there have been no English writers who have risen to such dazzling heights of fantasy or have reached to genius through an utter abandonment of the spirit, that I would be willing to make for them the claim that they should be admitted, without reservation, to the wearing of the true humorist's garland. There is a large number that I would be willing to accept, making allowances for this and for that. But when it comes to my responses to humour, I prefer to be with those for whom I have to make no concessions.

And here I feel that I am in godly company with the American humorists of the last century: Mark Twain and those who preceded him, and those who came after – and quite long after, too, some of them. I feel there has never in the whole history of the world been anything quite so shocking, so sublime and truthful and starlike and inspired, as what those men wrote who contributed to that immortal body of literature that comprises American humour. It began shortly after the American War of Independence, this particular expression of a literary spirit whose goal was the awakening of gigantic laughter. . .

(I had reached to this point, in the writing of the present article, when I was summoned from my desk by a telephone call. A gentleman at the other end of the line informed me that he was the City Fire Department, and that my house was on fire. Naturally I was perturbed, thinking of all my unpublished and uninsured odes and things going up in flame. The gentlemen on the line then informed me that he was not the Fire Department, after all, but that he was one Jumbo, and that he had been informed that I was engaged in writing an article on Humour, and how did I like this false alarm as an example of refined humour? But I felt that the laugh wasn't on me, after all: one day I am going to publish those uninsured odes.)

By the time of the Civil War this new kind of humour (new, not in its essence but in its strength and stark objectivity) had blossomed into quite unimaginable beauty. And it lasted, in the hands of one or two men of genius, right into the early years of the present century. But for as long as a generation before that it had already begun to manifest, deep within its structure, the elements of a dark decay. The writers stopped creating humour for its own sake. They began to apply this powerful weapon to the serving of causes that a creative artist can't believe in. In this respect O. Henry, coming in right at the other end of this epoch, kept his art untainted in a way that Mark Twain, ultimately, didn't.

When the laughter gets forced, the humour dies, and you can see this process beginning its work in the later writings of Artemus Ward, Josh Billings, Bill Nye, Petroleum V. Nasby and several others, including, as I have said, Mark Twain. (Witness the decline in power between Mark Twain's earlier Mississippi sketches and the stuff he turned out a quarter of a century later – his pathetically inept *Joan of Arc*, for instance.) His genius, of course, did not decay. Only, his art suffered immeasurably through his seeking to make it subserve his own (totally mistaken) ideas of himself as a literary figure.

There is nothing that you can detect more easily, or that falls more jarringly on the aesthetic senses, than a false laugh.

But there were also writers of this epoch who remained artistically true to themselves. Among them I can think, off hand, of Max Adler. (He is a gorgeous humorist; free, romantic, superbly imaginative.) And, of course, Bret Harte. There were giants in those days.

American humour today is all right, of course, as far as I am concerned. Only, it has lost its pristine vigour, its startlingly accurate insight into the strengths and frailties of human nature, its divine extravagance. It has lost its human genius; it has run to seed; it has grown tame.

I have devoted so much space to a consideration of American humour because I can understand it better than any humour that has ever come out of Europe, and because I regard it, even in decay, as a mighty and unparalleled manifestation. I can't write humorously about American humour.

There are, of course, lots of kinds of humour that I can't understand at all. I have never yet been able to see anything in *Punch*. (Perhaps *Punch* isn't a funny paper.) And I have never been able to laugh at what have been held out to me as even the most brilliant examples of Cockney wit. (Perhaps Cockney wit, also, is not meant to be amusing. Again I don't know. I can catch about Cockney wit only a devastating quickness. I can sense in it none of that warmth that is the very lifeblood of true humour.)

All the ordinary attempts at evaluating the significance of humour in terms of its social use and its psycho-physiological functioning seem of necessity to have to end in sterility. Humour is something that stands apart from these things. I feel that to get at the true essence of humour it must be approached from the side of the eternities, where it stands as some sort of a battered symbol of man's more direct relationship with God.

In the world's cultural development humour came on the scene very late. And that is the feeling that I have always had about humour, ultimately. That it is one of mankind's most treasured possessions, one of the world's richest cultural jewels. But that humour came amongst us when the flowers were already fading. And that it came too late.

THE DILETTANTE

EVERY MORNING ON MY WAY to the office I found him standing in front of the Library, waiting for the doors to open.

His lofty, intellectual brow increased the general rigidity of his ascetic countenance, while that faraway gaze in his steel-blue eyes showed how distant from mundane matters his thoughts were.

At night, on my return, I noticed that he was always the last to leave the Library, and I observed that occasionally there was a wistful, half regretful look on his face, while at other times his countenance bore an expression of mild complacency – even of benignity and broad philanthropy.

But in the morning there was no mistake about that strenuous eagerness which pervaded his features – which even showed through that look of intense absorption as he stood on the pavement, waiting for the Library doors to open.

Each day when I went to the office he was waiting on the pavement; each day when I returned the Library doors were just being locked behind him, until, having indulged in much speculation to no purpose, I determined to once and for all solve the problem as to which were the books that so irresistibly drew that intellectual giant to the Library.

He was already waiting on the pavement the following morning when I arrived, intent on finding a solution to the puzzle. As soon as the doors swung open he rushed in, while I followed some distance in his wake. Having arrived at the Reference Department, he went up to a shelf, took down a book, and with a sigh of placid contentment plunged into Chapter XXXIV of the seventeenth volume of *The Inner Secrets of Betty's Boudoir*.

Following his example, I likewise took down a volume and commenced reading.

And in the blissful days that followed I was the first to arrive on the pavement, impatiently tapping the kerb with my foot, waiting for the Library doors to open.

The Deserter

Having drawn up the remnants of his forces in battle array, the Red leader harangued his men, exhorting them to fling off their yokes of oppression and reach out after the banner of Liberty, floating on the far horizon. "You've won, boys," the general cried, at the conclusion of his passionate oration, every sentence of which was enthusiastically applauded by the revolutionaries in their trenches. "But, remember, don't kick the capitalist when he's down. Hit him with a pick-handle."

Hardly had the thunder of applause died down when, with a curious sound, like the wailing of a tired wind, a bullet went whistling over their heads and crashed through a plate-glass window, whereupon, wishing he had been a better man and knew more hymns, a Scotsman named Van der Merwe flung away his rifle and raced off madly in the direction of home and safety.

Appalled by such flagrant desertion in the face of the foe, the general made use of language which, no doubt, in calmer moments he would regret. "Fetch him back!" he shouted at length, in a voice like tearing linoleum. Untrustworthy though many members of the commando may have been, there was one man, at all events, whose soul was not dead to all honour – one man who responded to duty's call.

Amid cheers this individual set off in pursuit and, leaping lithely over the obstacles in the road, gradually gained upon his quarry. The general, meanwhile, had hastily climbed a lamp-post, from which point of vantage he shouted out the progress of the race. "He's only half a block behind him," he cried, "and gaining like mad. There's only ten yards separating them now! Three yards! Two feet! He's only about six inches behind the deserter – "

"Damnation!" the general exclaimed as, slipping from the lamp-post, he clasped his brow in anguish, "he's five yards in front of him!"

Prologue to "Mara"

SCENE:	The Johannesburg Town Hall. Enter Mayor, Citizens, Herman Malan, Bishop.
MAYOR:	Ladies and Gentlemen, here this day in the City Hall of Johannesburg, we are assembled to honour Africa's greatest poet. As the Greek of old decked singers with garlands of cypress and myrtle, we in Johannesburg have gathered to bestow on Herman Malan a small token of our esteem and admiration. We lay at his feet the homage of a continent.
HERMAN MALAN:	Lay it down softly, Mr Mayor. Don't let it fall on my sore toe.
BISHOP:	Let us pray.

THE RECOGNISING BLUES

I WAS AMBLING DOWN Eloff Street, barefooted and in my shirt-sleeves, and with the recognising blues.

I had been smoking dagga, good dagga, the real rooibaard, with heads about a foot long, and not just the stuff that most dealers supply you with, and that is not much better than grass. When you smoke good dagga you get blue in quite a number of ways. The most common way is the frightened blues, when you imagine that your heart is palpitating, and that you can't breathe, and that you are going to die. Another form that the effect of dagga takes is that you get the suspicious blues, and then you imagine that all the people around you, your best friends and your parents included, are conspiring against you, so that when your mother asks you, "How are you?" every word she says sounds very sinister, as though she knows that you have been smoking dagga, and that you are blue, and you feel that she is like a witch. The most innocent remark any person makes when you have got the suspicious blues seems to be impregnated with a whole world of underhand meaning and dreadful insinuation.

And perhaps you are right to feel this way about it. Is not the most harmless conversation between several human beings charged with the most diabolical kind of subterranean cunning, each person fortifying himself behind barbed-wire defences? Look at that painting of Daumier's, called "Conversation Piece", and you will see that the two men and the woman concerned in this little friendly chat are all three of them taking part in a cloven-hoofed rite. You can see each one has got the suspicious blues.

There is also the once-over blues and a considerable variety of other kinds of blues. But the recognising blues doesn't come very often, and then it is only after you have been smoking the best kind of rooibaard boom, with ears that long.

When you have got the recognising blues you think you know everybody you meet. And you go up and shake hands with every person that you come across, because you think you recognise him, and you are very glad to have run into him: in this respect the recognising blues is just the opposite of the suspicious blues.

A friend of mine, Charlie, who has smoked dagga for thirty years, says that he once had the recognising blues very bad when he was strolling through the centre of the town. And after he had shaken hands with lots of people who didn't know him at all, and whom he didn't know, either, but whom he *thought* he knew, because he had the recognising blues – then a very singular thing happened to my friend, Rooker Charlie. For he looked in the display window of a men's outfitters, and he saw two dummies standing there, in the window, two dummies dressed in a smart line of gents' suitings, and with the recognising blues strong on him, Charlie thought that he knew those two dummies, and he thought that the one dummy was Max Chaitz, who kept a restaurant in Cape Town, and that the other dummy was a well-known snooker-player called Pat O'Callaghan.

And my friend Rooker Charlie couldn't understand how Max Chaitz and Pat O'Callaghan should come to be standing there holding animated converse in that shop-window. He didn't know, until that moment, that Max Chaitz and Pat O'Callaghan were even acquainted. But the sight of these two men standing there talking like that shook my friend Rooker Charlie up pretty badly. So he went home to bed. But early next morning he dashed round again to that men's outfitters, and then he saw that those two figures weren't Max Chaitz and Pat O'Callaghan at all, but two dummies stuck in the window. And he saw then that they didn't look even a bit like the two men he thought they were – especially the dummy that he thought was Max Chaitz. Because Max Chaitz is very short and fat, with a red, cross-looking sort of face that you can't mistake in a million. Whereas the dummy was tall and slender and good-looking.

That was the worst experience that my friend Rooker Charlie ever had of the recognising blues.

And when I was taking a stroll down Eloff Street, that evening, and I was barefooted and in my shirt-sleeves, then I also had a bad attack of the recognising blues. But it was the recognising blues in a slightly different form. I would first make up a name in my brain, a name that sounded good to me, and that I thought had the right sort of rhythm. And then the first person I would see, I would think that he was the man whose name I had just thought out. And I would go up and address him by this name, and shake hands with him, and tell him how glad I was to see him.

And a name I thought up that sounded very fine to me, and impressive, with just the right kind of ring to it, was the name Sir Lionel Ostrich de Frontignac. It was a very magnificent name.

And so I went up, barefooted and in my shirt-sleeves, to the first man I saw in the street, after I had coined this name, and I took him by the hand, and I said, "Well met, Sir Lionel. It is many years since last we met, Sir Lionel Ostrich de Frontignac."

And the remarkable coincidence was that the man whom I addressed in this way actually *was* Sir Lionel Ostrich de Frontignac. But on account of his taking me for a bum – through my being barefooted and in my shirt-sleeves – he wouldn't acknowledge that he really was Sir Lionel and that I had recognised him dead to rights.

"You are mistaken," Sir Lionel Ostrich de Frontignac said, moving away from me. "You have got the recognising blues."

Royal Processions

One of these days, with the Coronation [of the successor of King George V, expected to be later in 1936], there will be another Royal Procession through the streets of London.

These processions are colourful affairs; they are got up in good style; and in that one moment of scarlet and gold, when your hat is raised, and there is the thunder of hooves on the ground, when the royal carriage is passing, and the air is wild with trumpets and cheering, then you find that your pulse throbs very quickly, and strange thrills are stirring in your heart.

And yet, when it is over, and the crowds surge forward into the roadway, you are left with the feeling that Cecil B. de Mille would have done it differently. Each time I have seen a Royal Procession, I have tried to detect, in its pageantry, the elements of a Roman triumph. But each time my effort has been a failure. The spirit of Imperial Rome – its drama and its flamboyancy – is still in the world, of course, but it is in Hollywood.

On one occasion, at the Marble Arch, when the drums beat, and the rulers of the world went by, I felt something of the majesty of a bygone day. So I tried out a classical allusion. "How's this for panem et circenses?" I asked of a man in the crowd next to me.

"No," he answered, surveying the procession, "no, that one on the left there is Litvinoff."

The best place from which to view a procession is the pavement. And the best time to take up a position is at midnight. This involves a twelve-hour wait in the gutter. But if you don't come early you find that the best stretches of gutter have already been taken up, and you have to content yourself with sitting down on an inferior piece of kerbstone, made of the hardest kind of concrete.

This waiting is very pleasant. And I know what Milton meant when he wrote of those that stand and wait. To me there is always something sublime in the thought of people waiting. Whether it is that they are waiting for a train, or for a king to ride past, or for One Whose coming shall bring peace to the children of men.

Near me was a man who sat reading a library book by the light of a candle.

I think I have had more fun, waiting with the crowd in the gutter, than at most fashionable functions to which, on various occasions, I have been invited. (By mistake, no doubt.) For one thing, at a society wedding, they always engage a number of detectives to breathe down the back of your neck and make you feel jumpy.

By four o'clock in the morning of the Duke of Kent's marriage there was a dense crowd lining the route from Buckingham Palace to Westminster Abbey. A detachment of uniformed men marched past, through the mist, to the accompaniment of some mild cheering from the crowd.

"Who are those men?" I enquired of a neighbour.

"They are blue-jackets," was the answer.

I was very interested to hear that, owing to my having been acquainted with quite a number of blue-jackets in South Africa. I was not surprised, therefore, a few minutes later, when a body of Metropolitan police came marching on behind the blue-jackets. The police force here is justly famed for its quiet efficiency. And when a London policeman arrests a man he gives him the same advice that a South African policeman does: he advises him to plead guilty and make a statement.

Later on there was some more cheering. Again I enquired the cause.

"It is the English dawn," I was informed.

I said that it was very agreeable to hear that. But I wondered how they found out.

This is one of the major difficulties which the English winter presents to a man who is used to blue skies. It is always a problem to distinguish between the kind of darkness that they call night-time, and the other kind that they call day-time. To the uninitiated, all darkness looks about the same.

When he was told that the dawn had come, the man with the library book blew out what was left of his candle, and went on reading in the dark.

It grew later. I got into conversation with the people around me. They told me lots of things about the Royal Family – things I had never heard of before. And I reciprocated by telling them all sorts of things about General Smuts. Things I am sure General Smuts had never heard of, either.

By and by the wedding guests began driving down the Mall on their way to Westminster Abbey. They all looked very distinguished. Maharajahs and Cabinet Ministers and peeresses and foreign ministers and nobilities.

Afterwards a carriage-load of princesses drove slowly past. I stepped off the pavement, in between two policemen, and blew a platonic kiss at the princesses. One of them stuck her hand out of the window and waved back at me. But it was the wrong princess. And before I could explain the mistake – namely, that I didn't mean her, but the one next to her, with the black hair – the carriage had passed on.

C'est la vie.

Came the Big Moment. A spectacular climax of bursting colour and tumultuous cheering and gilded carriages and Horse Guards in dazzling uniforms. . . The King and Queen of England. . . I glanced swiftly at the man with the library book. He was still engrossed in his reading. Not once did he lift his eyes from the printed page. I have often wondered what he came to the procession for.

It was a very successful wedding. There were no assassinations.

That's where England is different from a lot of countries. If this procession had been held in almost any other European capital, I believe there would have been at least one assassination. They would have assassinated the man with the library book.

But I also felt there was something lacking, in respect of medieval conceptions of largesse, in the sight of vendors of sausage rolls hawking their wares among the subdued dusk to 10.30 throngs in Hyde Park and Green Park and St. James's Park. There were no fat oxen turning on spits at Marble Arch, with free chunks of meat for all who came. There were no mighty vats of nut-brown ale set up in Birdcage Walk. Bring your own tankard.

At the Silver Jubilee I was on a Press stand. But the view I got of the procession wasn't up to much. It was not nearly as good as the view from the pavement. And my fellow occupants of the stand were not up to much, either. They consisted of the lowly class of film reviewers who attend the trade shows of 'quota quickies.' (At the Press preview of Charlie Chaplin's *Modern Times*, the Tivoli Theatre was packed to the doors. But what surprised me was the absence of the regular army of newspaper men who write up the films. I saw hardly any of them there. Only afterwards the truth dawned on me: there had been more Dirty Work in Fleet Street. The editors and business managers had collared the press tickets.)

But I obtained a good view of General Hertzog. That was because he held his head up very high. Yet there was a strained look on his face. Perhaps he was trying to remember whether it was the Crown Colonies that J. H. Thomas had promised to hand over to the Union, or whether it was the Crown Jewels.

Perhaps General Hertzog was only homesick.

And I recalled another South African, who drove through London when Victoria was Queen. They still talk about him here. What did he think about, I wonder, when his carriage swung into St. James's Street? About a Bushveld farm, maybe, and the sun lying yellow on whitewashed walls, and the big tree by the dam. And yet I hardly think so. I think it is more reasonable to believe that Paul Kruger was pardonably vain about his triumph. And what he really thought was: "If only the boys in the Rustenburg district could see me now."

It is in their passing that all the world's pageants are the same. The kings have gone, and the clamour has ended, and the sound of marching men is dying in the distance.

LEADER OF GUNMEN

PART OF IT READS LIKE FICTION . . . The mastermind who built up an organisation of gunmen; he inspired them with his own recklessness and his own desperate courage; and then he flung them against society. Crime wave upon crime wave: they terrorised a nation. Members of the police force got scared and resigned; the local judges wavered, so a judge was specially imported from another province to try them – Justice Gregorowski, who had sentenced the Jameson Raiders to death a quarter of a century before. A gang leader who saw his followers go one by one to their doom. They were hanged, they were shot; they passed behind prison-bars with life sentences; their reason gave way and they were flung into asylums; or they died by their own hand. But their leader was not vanquished. Undeterred he set about creating another organisation: a motley assortment of embezzlers, murderers, burglars, sneak-thieves, pimps. He knit them together with a cold purposefulness and a grim energy that was almost Napoleonic in its quality – a wild and inchoate Napoleon, who thought on criminal lines and talked prison-slang. And the first instalment begins now.

To understand the conditions underlying the amazing sequence of events narrated in this true-life story of criminal lawlessness on a super scale, it is necessary to review briefly the state of affairs in South Africa at the end of the Great War.

South Africa had had a stormy past. The major portion of her history has been concerned with conflict – conflict between white man and native, between Boer and Englishman. Up to very recent years this racial antagonism has found expression, regularly and spontaneously, in war.

Indeed the most conspicuous feature of South African history during the past fifty years is the frequency with which its citizens have been in arms:

1880-81:	First Boer War
1896:	Jameson Raid
1899-1902:	Second Boer War
1915:	Rebellion (General De Wet)
1922:	Rand Revolt.

The Revolt on the Rand is almost forgotten now, because it failed. But bombing airplanes, tanks and heavy artillery were employed in its suppression, and more men were killed in it than through the whole of Mussolini's Fascist revolution. There have also been innumerable wars with the natives.

Consequently, the men who have risen to greatness in the history of South Africa have not been men of peace. Shaka and Cetshwayo held their thrones because they were killers. The three prime ministers since the Union – Botha, Smuts and Hertzog – have all owed their prominence, initially, to their conduct of various phases of guerilla warfare: they have all three been generals.

Because they have seen their nation welded together in this fashion, in turbulence, it has become traditional with the people of South Africa to believe that an issue can best be clarified at the muzzle of a rifle; it is part of their bitter heritage, the illusion that right is on the side of him who can shoot quickest and straightest.

In 1914 Claude Satang, who plays the chief part in his story as gunman and gangleader, was a scout on active service in East Africa. It does not appear that Sergeant Satang was in any way different from any of the thousands of young soldiers who had been drafted there. His ambitions were the ambitions of hosts of other normal young men of his age. He certainly had no dreams of becoming a gangster.

He was captured in 1917, near Killosa. He escaped with two other young men. They passed through terrible hardships. Two of them died. The survivor was Claude Satang. He was tougher than his companions. But when the South African troops found him, they had to identify him by his badge. He had lost his memory. So he was sent back to South Africa.

Gradually in the hospital at Roberts Heights, near Pretoria, Claude Satang's memory returned. But with it there came also the frightening knowledge that his outlook on life had altered. He no longer had his casual and easy-going acceptance of things as he found them. In its place was a bitter and unreasoning hatred of society.

He did not understand it at first – this change that had come over him. Later, he understood only too clearly. But by then he was in a prison-cell. . . Before him lay the years of the sentence he had to serve. Behind him was the most stupendous and incredible career of crime that the world had ever known. . .

(*Don't miss next week's instalment of these Amazing Revelations of Gangsterdom from the Inside.*)

A young man who had been discharged as permanently unfit for further war service in East Africa walked through the streets of a Pretoria suburb. He was Claude Satang.

In the near future this young man was going to wake up a nation. And it would be a rough sort of awakening: it would take place to the roar of his gangsters' guns. That was not yet, however. For he had still to collect his gangsters; he had to organise and drill them; but when his task was completed he would have created a band of killer desperadoes whose ruthless efficiency and big-scale slayings were to stagger the African continent.

The following is a list of some of the more prominent members of the Satang Gang. Look out, here they come!

Cloete: actually ate a portion of a live associate; killed, murdered and plundered; many escapes from prison under very difficult circumstances.

Dolly de Klerk (Baby Face): specialised in killing detectives when pursued.

Schwartz: killer; specialised in killing detectives when pursued.

Beauty Bell: recognised as the world's greatest bank robber and safe-blower.

Gardner (alias Gee): killer and dope-friend.

Taffy Long and Lewis: killers, using machine-guns; captured only after being cornered by strong military forces employing heavy artillery, tanks and airplanes.

Dirk Joubert: professor of languages; published volume of verse widely read; first-class killer, noted for numerous sensational escapes; chief lieutenant.

Thus far they are only names. Later we shall deal individually with these gunmen of the Satang Gang, grim and profane swaggerers, uncouth lords of death. We shall explain how they fit into a story that is stained with blood and wreathed in blue gunsmoke.

(The record of their careers is on file at the Pretoria Palace of Justice. It is a complete record, and includes the various dates on which they were hanged or otherwise wiped out.)

It is desirable, at this stage, to draw a distinction between the ordinary American gunman and the genuine African killer.

The American gunman is loudmouthed and flamboyant; he shoots often, but seldom accurately; he hardly ever shoots a policeman; mostly he shoots his pals; he accompanies every killing with a lot of bombast and ballyhoo. For instance, when Dion O'Banion got killed in Chicago, his assassins sent flowers to his funeral.

This is where the African killer is different. Descended from a long line of tight-lipped Puritans and Calvinists, he doesn't understand about things like flourishes. He is a simple soul, not given to gaudy gesture. To the African killer, a killing means shooting a lot of holes into a man. Just that. He is not concerned with making his killings look ornamental. All he is interested in is that they should be fatal.

At the moment, Claude Satang's brain was evolving a scheme. It was an ingenious scheme. It was also comparatively innocuous. But in its method of approach and in the techniques of its execution was the nucleus of many of Claude Satang's subsequent operations.

Incidentally, the project that Claude Satang was busy on bore a strong resemblance to an O. Henry story. In a way, perhaps, this was surprising. Because at this stage Claude Satang had never heard of O. Henry. But then we must remember that O. Henry had also been in prison, and that it was behind the bars of a gaol in a Southern state that the *Gentle Grafter* tales were conceived. A prison cell seems to be a very good place for writing stories.

Claude Satang had heard, casually, that in 1914, owing to the outbreak of the war, less pennies were imported into South Africa from the British mint than in any other year. (That was before the South African mint was established in Pretoria.) There was something about this circumstance that appealed to Claude Satang's imagination. He could see possibilities in it. The question was how to exploit it properly. And he thought he saw a way. It was a big thing to pull off. But, handled properly, there would be big money in it.

Claude Satang spent the next few weeks in studying dates on pennies. And he collected all that were dated 1914. He entered into business relations with an official in the City Treasurer's Department at Pretoria. He offered the official a small premium on as many 1914 pennies as he could supply.

The official took it on. He wasn't actuated so much by the prospect of gain – which was very slight, after all. Rather was it the singular nature of the young man's request that intrigued him. An earnest young man with a crazy idea that he wanted 1914 pennies.

It was with an amused air that the official saw his clerks picking out the 1914 pennies from amongst the thousands of coppers brought in daily by the bus and tram conductors. After a while he got very good at spotting a 1914 penny. He could tell a 1914 penny a long way off.

And all this time the official was taking the whole thing as a joke. But one day he stopped laughing – suddenly.

Claude Satang had collected a huge quantity of 1914 pennies. He believed that, of the pennies in circulation in Pretoria, the proportion bearing the date 1914 had diminished perceptibly (taking into account the small 1914 importation). He was now ready for the next move.

So he sent a number of his agents into the main street of Pretoria. These agents called from shop to shop. Their procedure was the same in each case. The shopkeeper was asked if he had any 1914 pennies. Puzzled by this peculiar request, the shopkeeper enquired as to why the agent wanted them. The agent said that he would pay more for them than their face value. This invariably sent the shopkeeper to the till.

"I'm sorry, I haven't any," the shopkeeper would answer. "What did you want them for?"

"I would pay you a pound each for them," was the agent's reply.

Or: "I've got two," the shopkeeper would say.

"Here's ten shillings for them," was the agent's response, "if you'll let me have them."

That was all.

It was as simple as that. If the shopkeeper had any 1914 pennies the agent offered to purchase them at five shillings a piece. If he hadn't any, the agent offered him a pound. Perhaps two pounds. The result?

Before midday the main occupation of the citizens of Pretoria, the capital of the Union of South Africa, was hunting for 1914 pennies. The news spread like wildfire. As soon as Claude Satang's agent had gone out, the shopkeeper would call on a neighbour, only to discover that the neighbour already knew about the 1914 pennies from another agent, and sometimes he knew a lot more besides.

That they contained gold. That they were worth several pounds apiece. That the shopkeeper was feeling sick; he had sold three pennies to a man who had got only half a crown each for them; he had been swindled. You could see 1914 pennies were different from others, people said. They were more yellow. Or they were heavier. Or they had a clearer ring. Anyway, they were different.

In the meantime Claude Satang thought of the jewellers. A jeweller would be able to say right away that there was no gold in the pennies. Of course, that would not kill the rumours. But it was advisable, nevertheless, to devise a plan that would muzzle the jewellers for a day or two.

Most of the jewellers were concentrated round one square in the city. Claude Satang went into a jeweller's. He produced a number of pennies. "In Johannesburg," he explained, "they are making these 1914 pennies into brooches at ten shillings a time."

He gave the jeweller an order for a couple of brooches. He also dropped a hint to the effect that he believed there was gold in the 1914 pennies, and that that was the reason he had given the order.

The jeweller, anticipating many more lucrative orders for the same sort of thing, was tactfully non-committal. He wouldn't say definitely whether there was gold in the 1914 pennies or there wasn't. He wasn't going to throw away good business.

Claude Satang was satisfied. That was what he wanted. If other people came in to ask if there was gold in the 1914 pennies, the jeweller, thinking of further orders for brooches, would remain tactful and non-committal. This would have the effect of raising the public belief to a pitch of absolute certainty.

That afternoon Claude Satang gave several orders for brooches. And a few days later, when the jewellers tumbled to the position, and announced boldly that the 1914 pennies had no gold content, nobody believed them. People said this was merely a ruse on the part of the jewellers to secure all the 1914 pennies for themselves. The jewellers got themselves into a lot of odium. So did the bankers, for the same reason.

The whole of Pretoria went mad, 1914-pennies-mad. In pubs, on street corners, in restaurants, in business offices, in the homes of the people – they talked of nothing else. The wildest rumours blazed through the city. It was a crazy scramble.

And Claude Satang waited. . .

(*To be continued.*)

(*Don't miss next week's startling inside Record of Crime as it really happened.*)

We regret to inform our readers that we are discontinuing our very popular prison serial, *Leader of Gunmen*, owing to the constant criticism that is being levelled at certain stark features of the story. As we pointed out in previous issues, *The Sunday Critic* was not actuated by any spirit of sensationalism in publishing a description, for instance, of the manner in which a convict ate a portion of his live cell mate.

It was our sincere hope that, by drawing public attention to the debasing effects that prison life has on the strongest mind, we would be able to exercise a powerful influence in the direction of prison reform. We believe that we have attained our purpose.

Consequently we feel justified in withholding from *Sunday Critic* readers the final chapters of this serial which the *World's Press News* has described as "strong meat for strong men", and that has evoked mild shudders in many homes throughout Great Britain.

We therefore leave Claude Satang and his fellow gunmen in the African bush. We leave them still uncaptured. We bid farewell to Cloete and Baby Face de Klerk and Alec the Ponce still inside. We depart from these stern characters, in the evening, when the dusk is falling over the thorn-trees and over the grim walls of the Pretoria Central Prison, and in the cells the cigarettes are being lit, and the hashish smoke is being passed around.

Fratres, valete.

ROSSER

THERE WAS ONE CONVICT in the prison that I saw at intervals on parade. His name was Rosser. He was old and tall and dried-up. He was also morose. He was doing time for murder. I never saw him speak to anybody. On exercise he always walked grim and toothless and alone. Other convicts told me about Rosser. He was doing a very long stretch for murder. Nobody seemed to know exactly how long. And it was doubtful whether even Rosser knew any more. With the years he had grown soft in the head, they said.

It was a peculiar sort of murder, too, that Rosser was doing time for, they explained. It appeared that, suspecting his wife of infidelity, he had murdered her on the Marico farm where they lived. And he had disposed of the body by burying it under the dung floor of the voorkamer of the house. So much was, perhaps, reasonable. He had murdered his wife, and the first place he could think of burying her was under the floor of the living room.

He had filled in the hole again neatly and had smeared the floor with nice fresh cow-dung.

But what made the judge raise his eyebrows, rather, was when it was revealed in court that Rosser had held a dance in the same voorkamer on the evening of the very day on which he had performed those simple sacrificial and funeral rites – whereby his hands got twice stained.

There was a good attendance at the Bushveld party, which went on a long time, and several of the dancers afterwards declared in court that they were very shocked when they learnt that they had been dancing all night on top of the late Mrs Rosser's upturned face. It is true that a number of the guests were able to salve their consciences to a limited degree with the reflection that they had danced only the simple country measures: they had not gone in for jazz. One girl said in court, “Oh, well, I just danced lightly.”

Nevertheless, the Rosser case provided the local dominee, who was a stern Calvinist, with first-class material on which to base a whole string of sermons against the evils of dancing. . .

The above, more or less, were the facts about Rosser’s crime that I was able to glean from fellow convicts. But there were several features that mystified me.

“But why did he do it?” I asked a bluecoat. “I mean, what did he want to go and throw a party for – getting all those people to dance on top of his wife’s dead body?”

“It’s just because he’s got no feelings,” the bluecoat said. “That’s what. Just look at the way his jaw sticks out without teeth in his head. No feelings, that’s what.”

Another convict, again, would reply to the same question. “Well, I suppose it was to get the floor stamped down again. They gives dances in the Bushveld just to stamp the ground down hard.”

A third convict would proffer the explanation, “Well, he was damned glad his wife was dead, see?”

There was a distressing lack of uniformity about the answers I got. And then it suddenly struck me that the convicts were, of course, all going by hearsay. Because, when I questioned them on that point, individually, each agreed that he had never spoken to Rosser. Not as much as passed him the time of day, ever. Rosser just wasn’t the sort of person you would ever take it into your head to talk to, anyway.

If Rosser’s case was as horrifying as all that, I wondered, then why did the Governor-General in Council reprieve him? Why wasn’t he hanged? That question, too, I once put to a fellow convict. And the answer I got surprised me not a little.

“I suppose,” the convict said, “why Rosser was reprieved was because the judge put in a recommendation for mercy – because it was such a good party.”

In the end, there was nothing else for me to do about it. I had to get the facts from Rosser himself, at first hand. I had to approach him and talk to him, and put my question straight out. That wasn't an easy thing to do. I had to screw up every nerve in my body to get so far as to address him. It took me a little while to work up enough guts to go up to Rosser and say, "Hello. How do you do?" In fact, it took me about two years.

And when I did get so far as to talk to Rosser, I realised that he was quite harmless. Only, because nobody had spoken to him for so many years, it was with a considerable effort on his part that he was able to enunciate any words at all. And then, when he spoke, I had to turn my face aside. The way his jaw came up and the way his toothless gums got exposed when he struggled with the unfamiliar thing of speech – the sight of it gave me an acute sense of disgust. But, God knows, his story was simple enough.

"I done my wife in with a chopper because she was sweet on another man," Rosser explained. "And I buried her under the floor and all. And then what happens, but when I got everything clean again, a lot of people come in with concertinas and bottles of wine and brandy. It was a surprise party. And I couldn't say, 'Look here, you can't hold a surprise party in my dining room. I just buried my wife here.' So I just said, 'Welcome, friends. Come in and sing and dance.'"

So there was not more to the whole thing than just that.

"And the man," Rosser went on, in his lewd-gummed wrestling with the strangeness of words, "the man that I thought my wife was sweet on – he was the one that got the neighbours together and said, 'Let us go and have a surprise party at Rosser's place.' And all that night he was looking for my wife. But I dunno – "

"Dunno what?" I asked with feigned interest, for I was anxious to be off. One conversation with Rosser in a lifetime was enough.

"I dunno if my wife ever really was sweet on him," Rosser said. "I mean, now I been in prison fifteen years, I dunno. Because I have always been a much better-looking man than what that man is."

THE BLUECOAT'S STORY

COLOURFUL CONVERSATION. The way these old lags talked, the bluecoats and the near bluecoats. Their vivid phraseology sounded like poetry to me. It was incredible that here, in South Africa, there was actually a class of person who spoke an argot that was known only to his kind. Boob-slang, they called it. Boob, and not jug, being the Swartklei Prison word for a prison. The name for a warder was a screw. You never heard any other name for him. Shoes they called daisies; trousers, rammies. A cell was a peter. "I forgot it up in my peter." For "the going is difficult" they would say "the game is hook." Or crook. Or onkus. They would have clichés, like "The boys in the game are still the same." And the queer thing was that nobody outside of ex-convicts knew these expressions, while the criminal class habitually spoke no other language. And all this was going on here, in South Africa, and I had lived to the age of twenty years, and I had never known that there really was a world such as this, here in our midst, with its own criminal parlance, and its own terribly different, terribly mysterious way of life.

And the inside stories of burglaries... In house- and store-breaking one man stays outside to keep watch – the longstall, they call him. And when the johns come he tips his pals off. "I was longstall when Snowy Fisher and Pap done that job in Jeppes. And I piped what looks like two johns coming round the johnny horner. And I gives them the office to edge it. But something had gone hook with the soup (dynamite). The soup spills before they got it in the hole in the safe (the dynamite exploded prematurely). And so Snowy Fisher comes out of the window, all right, with half his rammies burnt off him, right into the arms of them two johns. But it's shutters for Pap. All of him that come out of the bank then was his foot, that got blowed through the fanlight. Pap never was no good with the soup. He always had his own ideas. And one of the johns pipes me and I starts ducking for a fence, and I gets over it, with the john after me – and who do you think I nearly falls on to, on the other side of the fence?"

"The Governor-General?" I guessed, facetiously, "Doing a spot of illicit liquor-selling?"

"No, it wasn't the Governor-General. It wasn't the Prime Minister, neither. Nor even the Minister for Posts and Telegrafts. It was none other than the One-Eyed Bombardier."

"You mean the Bombardier?" I asked, "The one that works in the carpenter shop?"

"Him," was the reply, "And he was all steamed up with dagga and he was as calm as you please, relieving himself standing up against the fence, not knowing that there was a job going on in that same block, and that Pap had been blowed to hell and that Snowy Fisher was pinched and that there was a john trailing me all out that very moment. 'So long, Bomb,' I shouts out, 'I got to run.' 'Wait till I finish, and I'll run with you,' he says, 'What's the gevolt?' But I got no time to tell him, what with the john's footsteps coming nearer all the time, other side the fence. So we beats it through a dark passage the Bombardier and me, and a few minutes later we hears bang-bang from the gun of the john that has just seen us ducking into the opening of another passage. And we runs a bit faster. But we know also that we'll get away. The john wouldn't let fly with his shooter if he didn't know he couldn't catch up with us no more. By that time it's about three o'clock in the morning.

"'Got anywhere to sleep?' the Bombardier asks me when we goes along the railway track on the way to Doornfontein, keeping all we can to the dark places. So I says to him, no, I can't go back to the pozzy I'm sharing with Snowy Fisher and the late Pap. Like as not the johns is already laying for me there. Looks like I'll have to go in smoke. 'Well,' the Bombardier says, 'I know a good place where you can go in smoke. Where they won't never think of looking for you, neither.'

So I says I hope he don't mean the Rietfontein Lazaretto. Because the Rietfontein Lazaretto is out. One time, yes, it was a good pozzy. You just go along and report your dose and the quack examines you and he says, Okay, you're a danger to the public with that dose. You better come as a in-patient for treatment until we cures you. That was all right in the old days. The Rietfontein Lazaretto was the best pozzy for going into smoke in. The johns would never nose round there. All the time you're having a easy rest, lying on the flat of your back and getting treatment for venereal disease that you've had ever since you slept with Big Polly, what has already been dead for ten years, all this time the johns is wasting petrol and getting blisters on their feet looking for you in Fordsburg or Vrededorp. But the Lazaretto is crook, now. Since a detective head constable was took there for his dose. This john gets took there for treatment and what does he see but half a dozen boys what has been in smoke a long time doing a flit out the dormitory the moment he walks in.

"So I says to the Bombardier that if he knows of a place where I can go in smoke it better be a good place. And it also better not be the Rietfontein Lazaretto, or any kind of lazaretto, where a john with syph can come walking in and me flat on my back with no chance to scale out of the window. But the Bombardier says, no, the place what he knows is a good pozzy to go to smoke in. It's on a farm, the Bombardier says. 'You know what a farm is, I expect?' the Bombardier says to me, looking suspicious, as though I had never heard of a farm. So I told him that I had growed up on a farm. And that I never came to Johannesburg before I was fifteen. And that I was already turned seventeen before the first time I got pinched. I told him I wasn't like one of the Joburg reformatory rats that can't stay out of reform school after they passed the age of fourteen. 'Look how many young blokes go to reformatory before they is fifteen,' I says to the Bombardier. 'That shows you what it is to be brung up in a city, dragged up in the gutter, you might say. But with me. No, chum, with me it was different. I was brung up on a farm. So I was a long way past seventeen before the johns nabbed me. And then they wouldn't have got me, neither, if one of my pals hadn't gone and squealed on me. No, what I says is, bring up a child in the city, and he'll go wrong. Look at me. I been brought up on a farm. And I smoke dagga. And I been twice warned for the coat. And if I was brought up in a city, where would I be today, I'd like to know?' And the Bombardier says I would be a criminal, most likely, seeing as how a child brought up in the city had got no chances at all to learn honesty and a respect for the law.

"By this time we come to the top end of Siemert Road, just by the side of the railway cutting, and we sits down on a piece of brown rock, feeling safe, now, with the johns the other end of town, taking Snowy Fisher to Marshall Square and Pap to the mortuary. And the Bombardier takes a piece of paper out of his pocket and tears it into the right size and then he pulls out some of the old queer and mixes some cigarette tobacco with it, and in a few minutes we are sitting as happy as you please on that rock, pulling away at the dagga-stoppie. It was good dagga. We both feels very honest. Because in between the Bombardier had let on to me that he was also brought up on a farm. And so we each tries to let the other see how much good it does one to be brought up on a farm, and we each try to sound more honest and good than the other one.

"I starts off by telling the Bombardier about all the times I done tried to look for a job of work. There was twice that I could remember for sure. But there was another time, also, that I seemed to think I had applied for a job, but I couldn't quite just remember, because I had got that time mixed up with another time when I asked Alec the Ponce if I could help him to live on the earnings of prostitution of some of the trollops he was trailing around with. But the Bombardier said that that showed you. I had walked myself black and blue, trudging the whole country, looking for a job of honest work. And that was because I had had the good fortune to have been brung up on a farm. Then we starts talking about all the times we had tried to reform. We found we had each of us tried a whole lot of times. Me, at least twice, again. And the Bombardier more than three times.

"There was a time, too, when the Bombardier had gone about making a clean breast of things. A Salvation Army captain had spoke to the Bombardier once, just before he was coming out of boob after his fourth stretch, and the Salvation Army captain had said to the Bombardier to go out that time and make a clean breast of it. 'Go out of the boob, my man,' the Salvation Army captain says to the Bombardier, 'and own up as you done wrong, and look the world in the face.' But before the Bombardier can go on with his story, when he passes me the dagga-smoke again, I remembers when a parson said the same thing to me. So I also decides right on the turn to go round and make a clean breast of it. That was one of the times in my life what I told you about when I went to look for a job of work. Not when I seen Alec the Ponce about doing a spot of poncing, but the real first time in my life when I went to look for a job. I was forty-two years old then. And this parson bloke had said to me, 'Don't try and conceal your past,' he says, 'for your past will catch up with you, and just when you think you've pulled the wool over your employer's eyes, you'll find yourself dropped in the muck.' I could see that this parson had got the game pretty well measured up. I never laugh at a parson. I've found as there is lots of things as a parson knows that you don't give him credit for at the time and then afterwards you find if you had done what he worked out for you you would have clicked. I have even thought perhaps when I get out of boob this time I can go to a parson and get him to work out the lay of a crib for me. Perhaps I can even go and crack my next safe dressed as a parson. Only, if I get pinched, Gawd, how won't the boys in the awaiting trial yard rib me, me turning up charged with safe-blowing, and in a parson's suit and with a round collar and a hymn-book. I can just picture a parson sitting in the corner of a cell on his hymn-book, smoking dagga.

"But I followed that parson's advice. I decided to go straight and to work honest-like, and if the johns come and try to put my pot on with the boss, what a laugh they'll get when he knows my rep as good as the johns does. So I looks in *The Star* situations vacant and I pipe a advertisement, wanted, a caretaker for a ladies social club premises, must be sober, light duties. A skinny moll with specs opens the door and gives me a dekko. 'I suppose you'll do,' she says, 'You been drinking a lot, I suppose, on your last job, and that's how they fired you?' But I says, no, all I had to drink in five years was prison-soup. Soup with carrots in, I says. 'Ho, so you are a ex-convict?' she says, 'Do come in.' She makes me sit down and gives me a cup of tea. 'Is it really as dreadful in prison as what reports of it is?' she asks, very inquisitive. And I says, no, it's all right if you can get a bit, now and again. And a dagga stompie sometimes. And on Christmas Eves there is a concert, I says. And on Sunday every month you gets pepper in your stew.

"The skinny moll with the specs and the high collar gets real interested. 'Tell me,' she says, 'is it really as bad about the – about the – I mean, you didn't say a bit of *bun*, did you?' Then I twigs, 'Oh, *that*,' I says, 'missus, don't let that upset you, missus. What you expect a man to do, locked up night after night, and no women? And that going on for years. Not even a kaffir-woman. Or a coolie-woman pushing a vegetable cart. Not a smell of a woman. For years and years. Well, a man is only human, ain't he? You can't expect a man to be more than what flesh and blood can stand, can you?' And she said, no, she thought not, and she said she was real worried, and she had been for a long time, and the other molls in her club, also, about unnatural sex acts as men gets up to, when they is locked away by themselves. And I says there is nothing unnatural about it, and I couldn't feel there was anything unnatural about me, even though I am sure I have had more men as what she has had women. And she just shakes her head and says as I can start right away, and have I told her everything. So I remembers the advice the parson bloke give me, and I come my whole guts, clean, and I thinks, now if a john comes and blabs to my employer about my previouses, won't that john get a earful.

"So I pulls my whole rep to the skinny moll. 'I been in boob seven times,' I says, putting in a extra one for good measure, in case the johns come round and tells her I done six stretches. 'And I smokes dagga,' I says. 'And I am rotten with syphilis,' I says. 'And I also wants to tell you – '"

But at that moment the bell rang, and the exercise period was over, and so I had to fall in, without hearing the rest of this bluecoat's story. So I never knew what the upshot was of his attempt at reformation, or whether he did go into smoke on that farm. The whole story ended just like that, in mid-air, leaving him sitting on that stone near the Siemert cutting, smoking dagga with the One-Eyed Bombardier. But I knew I could go back to him any time, and he would continue with that story from the point where he had left off, if I had asked him to. Or else he would have told me a brand new story, starting just from anywhere and ending up nowhere – exactly like his own life was. And what was wonderful to me was the fact that any bluecoat, or any convict who had served five or six fairly long sentences in prison, could tell stories in exactly the same strain. You don't go to prison, over and over again, just for nothing.

TEX FRASER'S STORY

ONE DAY, WHILE WE WERE still sitting peacefully with our stone hammers, in calm convict rows, before we had started extending the wall, a bluecoat, Texas Fraser, told me a little story about a woman he loved. I was really moved by this tale.

Tex Fraser was doing his second bluecoat. He was a tall, thin man, very emaciated looking. His face was seamed with deep wrinkles. And he was toothless. When he smiled he displayed two rows of empty gums. And yet, when he spoke, there were times when I could picture Tex Fraser as he had been in the old days, before he had done his first coat. He must have looked quite the lad, then, I should imagine, with his shoulders set up very straight and tall, and a devil may care look in his eyes. (It is singular how in books novelists romanticise this devil may care look, and how in real life girls fall for it. But it is only a criminal look. Every criminal has got it, until he starts off on his first bluecoat.)

The story Bluecoat Tex Fraser told me, one afternoon when we were seated side by side in front of a pile of stones, and the warder was yawning in the sunlight, affected me a good deal during the telling. But afterwards I started getting doubts about it.

"That was Maggie Jones," Tex Fraser said, talking sideways so that the warder couldn't see too clearly that he was talking, "I dunno how I come to fall for her. She was a damn nice bit of skirt. The best-looking moll I'd set eyes on in years. She was dark and her face was long and thin, but smiley, if you know what I means, and her hips was broad. Well, I was working the hug in them days, and I was doing good."

"What is the hug, Tex?" I asked, also trying to talk sideways, so the screw wouldn't jerry to me talking.

I felt, somehow, that when Tex Fraser said he was 'doing good', it didn't mean that he was going about doing good in the Christian charitable organisation sense. I guessed that he was doing only himself good.

"The hug?" Tex Fraser repeated, "Well, there's something, now. I don't know as how I can explain it. And I can't show you unless I'm standing up, and you standing up, too, sort of half in front of me – "

"Now, now, Tex," I said, facetiously, "None of your homosexual business."

Bluecoat Tex Fraser laughed.

"No," Tex Fraser said, "It's not like what you think. The hug is very heasy after you been showed a few times. It ain't what you think. What I means is as I can't show you here, where we is sitting down. But I'll show you just before fall in. You got to be standing up, and me, too."

He demonstrated the trick to me, just before we got back into line, and I could see it was very effective. So much so that a warder, witnessing the demonstration from a distance, and not knowing that it was a friendly matter, blew his whistle and wanted to have Tex Fraser charged before the Governor for 'attempting to rob a fellow-convict.' But there was no such charge on the book of regulations, it was discovered. For the reason that a convict has got nothing to be robbed of.

Anyway, I learnt, then, that the hug consists of another man getting hold of you from behind, when you are walking down a dark street – and preferably a bit drunk, too, although this is not altogether essential. The man who puts the hug on you sneaks up from behind. He throws his right arm around your neck, from behind, and he rests his fingers on your left shoulder, quite lightly. At the same moment he sticks a knee into the back of your left leg. Then he's got you where he wants you. If you start struggling he just rests the fingers of his right hand a little less lightly on your left shoulder, thereby shooting his forearm heavily in under your chin, making it go back higher than the stars and making you feel you're getting strangled. And all the time he's got his left hand free, enabling him to go through your pockets more or less like he wants to. That, according to the way Tex Fraser demonstrated it to me on the stone-pile, was the hug.

"So I done my dash with the sandbag," Tex Fraser was explaining, "I made up me mind, there and then, that I wasn't going to do no more sandbagging. That was just before – or was it just after? – I met Maggie Jones. Yes, there was a moll for you. She was all moll, if you knows what I mean. Nothing off the shelf or the police informant about her. And so I decides to go straight, of course. I won't go in for any game except the hug, I decides. All the crook stunts they can keep, I say."

"But why did you give up sandbagging?" I asked, "I thought you were doing quite well hitting people over the head with a sandbag?"

"It was because of that red-faced miner," Bluecoat Tex Fraser pursued. "I was following him all the way down End Street. I walked after him out of the Glossop. I had a nice little sock on me, all neatly filled with sand from a minedump. We used to say, in the slogging game, that for miners minesand was the best, and that was in the days when miners was getting over two hundred pounds in their pay cheques, end of each month. And this was the end of the month and I was follering this miner down to the bottom end of End Street. And all this time I don't get a chance to slog him. Every time I got the old sandbag raised, a coloured person or a policeman or a liquor-seller comes past me in the dark. So I knows what it is going to be, and that it is going to finish up as a roomer. Afterwards the miner, who has had a lot to drink and is staggering plenty, comes to a long row of rooms. And all this time I don't get a chance to slog without some goat showing up. Then the miner turns in at a little gate and in at the door of a room. I toddles in after him. One time I was just going to cosh, but the top of the doorframe gets in the way. The game looks crook. What you want to pull a roomer for, when you can cosh a man in the street? And this miner goes and he lies right down on his bed, and I can see as how he is single and lives in that room by himself. I douses the glim and I goes up to the bed. The moon is shining through the window, partly, and on to the bed, just where this miner's head is. This time I got him. I hoists the old sandbag, and I brings it down, bash, right on that miner's clock. And what do you think happens? The sandbag splits. Yes, it does a bust wide open, and the soft minesand starts trickling out of that bust sock, and flows all over the miner's face. And he got a red face. Even in the moonlight you can see how red-faced that miner is. And the sand starts flowing over his cheek and his moustache, and he gets tickled. And there, with me bending over him, still holding on to a broken sandbag and the sand running over his clock, tickling him, that red-faced miner bursts out laughing in his sleep.

"So I ducks out of that room quick, without waiting to collect anything, not even the sand out of the sandbag. But I'll never forget that feeling what I got. Coshing that red-faced miner over the clock with the sandbag, and all he does is burst out laughing. All the way down the street, as I ducked, I still hears that miner laughing.

"So I does me dash with the sandbag. I goes in for the hug, instead. And I am still doing the hug when I meets Maggie Jones. Maggie thinks at first as I works on the trams as a greaser. But afterwards she finds out through a john what comes up and pulls my rep to her, that I works the hotels looking for miners with pay cheques that I puts the hug on – "

It was a long story that Tex Fraser told me, the story of his love for Maggie Jones, and I am trying to find some way of condensing it. Perhaps I should explain that it was an Enoch Ardenish sort of theme.

Anyway, Maggie Jones tried to reform Tex Fraser (that was before he had got even his first bluecoat) and he had responded reasonably well, and they were madly in love with each other, and she used to work in a clothing factory down City and Suburban way, and she had a room where he came to visit her, and she said she would always love him, and that even if he found that he couldn't go straight, it wouldn't make any difference to her (although her dream was to see him become an honest man) and that whatever happened, she would always be his, if he went to prison, even. (How on earth, I wondered, could Maggie Jones have thought of so remote, so utterly unlikely a contingency?) However long he got, he would find her waiting for him, patiently and in chastity. Whenever he came out he had merely to find her: wherever she was, she would be his.

One day the johns got him.

"It was a miner what had over a hundred leaves on him. But the johns jumped on me the minute I hands him the hug. And it's seven years. And I done most of them seven years. I cracked a screw, that time I was doing my stretch, and I didn't get mush remission. But I knew Maggie Jones would be waiting for me. So I goes down to City and Suburban, and they tells me Maggie is married more than five years, and she has several kids, and her husband is a blacksmith, and she stays in Jeppes. They gives me the address. I finds my way there. I know I only got to say, 'It's Tex,' and she'll leave her husband and kids and house: all just like that. Just on the turn. I knows Maggie. I knows she would of married that blacksmith just because she was sorry for him, and the both of them lonely. But just let her pipe little old Tex Fraser. Just once. She's my moll. My moll and no one else's moll.

"I finds the house. It's half brick and half iron. There's a little path up to the front door. And on both sides of the path is flowers. And there's two little green curtains before the windows. And in the back I hear kids' voices. And I says to myself that Maggie Jones is my moll, all the same. I just got to whistle, and she'll come running. I just got to say, 'Maggie, this is Tex back,' and she'll forget her husband and kids right on the turn. But as I goes up to the door I starts thinking. Maybe this man she married is only a blacksmith. But he's given her this nice little home. And I knows as I can't ever give Maggie anything. With me she'll be on the lam all the time. She'll have to be telling the police all sorts of tales as to where I was night before last. I can't pull her out of this, I says. And I gets to the veranda, and right up to the front door. But I don't knock. I make up my mind right away.

"And just as I am turning back the front door opens. It's Maggie. She says she heard the gate creak. She says that for months, now, each time she hears the gate creak she thinks it's me. And she comes up to me with her arms out, and she says, 'I've been waiting for you for seven years. I knew you would come.' But I pushes her away, oh, very soft, and I don't say a word, but I walks out down the garden path, and out of the little gate painted green, and I never looks back. . . And to think as I never even kissed her."

I was moved by Bluecoat Tex Fraser's story, hearing it from his own lips, there in the stone-yard, seated beside him with a pile of stones in front of us. Tex Fraser could see that I was touched by the narrative, and what made me feel somewhat suspicious of the author's sincerity was the fact that at the same time that he was keeping his hammer going up and down, grasping it in his right hand, his left hand was beginning to feel along the back of my legs: for I was sitting close to Tex Fraser.

"Yes," the bluecoat added. "And I didn't never even kiss her."

His hand kept on travelling. I got uneasy. "Edge that, Tex," I said, shifting away.

Jim Fish

He was an African from a kraal in the Waterberg, and he had not been in Johannesburg very long. His name was Mletshwa Kusane. That was his name in the kraal in the Waterberg. In Johannesburg he was known as Jim Fish. That name stood on his pass, too. Since it is Christmas, the season of goodwill, Mletshwa Kusana, alias Jim Fish, comes into the story skulking a little.

In those days a black man didn't mind what sort of 'working name' he adopted. He had not come to Johannesburg to stay, anyway. At least that was what he hoped. And while he stayed in the city, saving up money as fast as he could to take back to the farm with him, he didn't particularly care what name his employer chose to bestow on him, provided that his employer handed over his wages with due regularity on pay day.

Jim Fish had found work in a baker's shop in a part of the town known as the Mai-Mai. He lived in a shack behind the bakery, the proprietor of which in this way received back as rent a not inconsiderable part of his employees' emoluments. Since his employees were also his tenants, the owner of the bakehouse did not have to employ a rent-collector. Afterwards, when Johannesburg took on more of the external characteristics of a city, the owner of the bakery was to find that this arrangement did not pay him quite so well, any more. For the City council began introducing all sorts of finicky by-laws relating to hygiene. In no time they brought in a regulation making it illegal for the owner of a bakery to accommodate his native services on the bakery premises. The result was that, at a time when business wasn't too good, the owner of the bakery found himself with a municipal health inspector on his pay-roll. Afterwards it was two health inspectors. And they came round every month for their rake-off like clockwork.

Because of this increase in his overheads the bakery proprietor had been reluctantly compelled to cancel an advertisement that he had been running in a religious magazine for a long time. It was purely a goodwill advertisement, bread being a staple commodity that didn't require advertising. But on the following Sunday the baker – who was also a sidesman – had to listen to a sermon on the evils of avarice. He knew the parson meant him, of course. But he had cancelled the ad that for years had been the church magazine's mainstay. But there were moments, in the course of the sermon, when the baker could not, in his sinful mind, help associating words like 'cupidity', 'selfishness' and 'money-grubbing' with those two municipal health inspectors.

Jim Fish's main work at the bakery consisted of helping his black colleages – there were quite a number of them – to carry in the sacks of meal and to clean the mixers of yesterday's dough. (The mixers *were* cleaned, quite often, in spite of what quite a lot of bread-consuming citizens might have thought, going by the taste.) He had also to carry the pans to the oven, and to help stoke the fires, and to help pull out the baked loaves with long wooden scoops. Because Jim Fish was black, that was about as far as his duties went. The white men on the night shift were there in a supervisory capacity.

There had been one or two nights, however, when Jim Fish and his black-skinned colleagues had, through the machinery breaking down, to perform certain additional duties that brought them into somewhat more intimate contact with the ancient rites of bread-baking. On those occasions that particular bakery's proud boast that its products were, from start to finish, untouched by human hand, was only literally correct, in the sense that it excluded human feet. Strict adherents of the school of thought that places the coloured races outside the pale of humanity as such would in this situation find themselves in something of a dilemma. For it would not be human hands or feet, but just the feet of niggers that kneaded the dough, in long wooden troughs, at those times when the electric power at the bakery failed.

The white supervisors would be in a state of nerves, all right, on a night when there was mechanical trouble. They would be all strung up – hysterical and panicky, almost, like ballet-dancers.

"Hey, you, go and wash that coal off your feet before you get into that — trough," the night foreman would shout at a nigger. And at another nigger the night foreman would shout, "Hey, you black sausage – don't you bloody well sweat so much, right into the kneading trough and all."

For it is a characteristic of any person whose ancestors have lived in Africa for any length of time that he does sweat a lot. Whether he's a nigger, or a white Dutch-speaking Afrikaner, or a white English-speaking Jingo from Natal, if his forebears have resided in Africa for a couple of generations he sweats at the least provocation. Readers of Herodotus will recall that that great historian and geographer said the same thing about the Nubians of his time.

Because he was a simple soul, Jim Fish was, taken all in all, happy in his work. If he were asked by an American newspaper correspondent, or by an earnest inquirer delegated to the task by a UNO committee (UNO being in those days as much of an anachronism as nylons), Jim Fish would probably have confessed that he was deserving of one shilling and sixpence extra on a night when the bread-making machinery did not function as it should. The one shilling and sixpence would be to cover all that extra work he had in treading, Jim Fish would explain, marking time, left right, left right, to explain. And also to recompense him for all that trouble he took in cleaning himself, washing his legs and feet and toes in hot water. No, not when he got into the kneading trough. He never worried much about *that*, Jim Fish would declare, truthfully. It was when he had to get the sticky white dough off him afterwards. There was a job for you, now.

The real trouble about his job at the bakery, Jim Fish, alias Mletshwa Kusane, would confide to the correspondent of an American newspaper was the fact that it was nearly all night work. He didn't mind the pay so much. That was all right. Even after he had paid his rent and he had bought mealie-meal and goat's meat and such odds and ends of clothing as he needed, he was still able to save quite a bit, each month. This was a lot more than most white wage or salary earners were able to do, incidentally. All that happened to white people who worked for a boss was that they got deeper into debt, every month. Jim Fish would admit that he was saving, here in the city of Johannesburg. But he needed every penny he could scrape together. All the money he saved in Johannesburg had to go in lobola, when he got back to the kraal. Lobola was the money he had to pay some girl's father, so that he could get that girl as his wife. It wasn't any particular girl that Jim Fish was thinking about, of course. Practically any girl belonging to his tribe would do. As long as she could bear him children, and work for him, planting mealies and hoeing in the bean-fields, and bringing him a clay pot full of beer when he called – him lying in the sun in front of the hut, and following the sun around. And maybe afterwards, if he came to Johannesburg again, and worked for the bakery for another season, he would even be able to buy a second wife, having enough money for another lobola. And then his children would be able to work for him, too, the children of the first and his second wife – and the children of this third wife, too, if he went to Johannesburg that often to make money to save up for lobola. And who he would also have to work for him would be quite incidental children, that weren't his own, even, but that one or other of his wives begot by some other nigger man while he himself was in Johannesburg, working in the bakery.

That was a laugh on that other nigger man, all right.

It couldn't be too pleasant for that other nigger man, carrying on with Mletshwa's wives, and all that, in Mletshwa's absence, when what would happen out of it would be that that nigger man's children, by Mletshwa's wife, would end up by working for Mletshwa: tending his cattle for him, if they were boys; planting beans and kaffir-corn for him, if they were girls.

And if it turned out that the child of Mletshwa's wife conceived while Mletshwa was working in Johannesburg wasn't the child of another nigger man at all, but was the child of the white missionary at the Leboma mission station, then it would be a laugh on the white missionary, right enough. For that child would be lighter of skin than its brothers and sisters. Instead of its having a complexion like boot-polish, the missionary's child by Mletshwa's wife would be dark lemon in colour, with its hair less peperkorrel than the average negro's and in the cast of its features there would be a couple of European traits. Consequently, that child would receive special privileges at the mission school and would be educated to be a school-teacher, or maybe even higher than a school-teacher, so that Mletshwa would be good for at least a pound a month from that child, whose education had cost him nothing. No wonder, therefore, that many a missionary walks about with an embittered look.

Late one night Mletshwa Kusane, alias Jim Fish, came away from the bakery with a deep sense of inner satisfaction. He felt he was somebody, and no mistake. For the mixing machine had broken down again. And this time he had been set to tread the dough in a confectionery trough. Not the dough for plebeian quartern loaves and twist loaves and standard brown loaves. But he had walked up and down, left right, left right, in a trough that had chilled eggs, even, mixed with the flour and water and yeast. Left right, left right, he was kneading, with his feet – brown on top and pinkish between the toes – the dough for slab cake and cream cakes and (with a few sultanas thrown in) for wedding cakes. The night foreman had noticed that, last time there was trouble with the mechanised equipment, Jim Fish had seemed to sweat somewhat less than the other niggers. And that was how Mletshwa got promoted to the confectionery trough. What the night foreman didn't notice was the effect that this unexpected promotion had on Mletshwa. Because he had been picked out for the unique honour of treading the dough in the confectionery container, Mletshwa suddenly started thinking that he was a king. A great king, he thought he was. And he started chanting in the Sechuana tongue a song that he had made up about himself, in the same way that any primitive African makes up a song about himself when he finds that, by chance, he is standing first in a line of pick-and-shovel labourers digging a ditch, or, if it's a gang of railway labourers moving a piece of track and he happens to be walking in front.

And so that night, having been selected to tread the dough in the confectionery trough because he sweated less than other niggers, Mletshwa really let himself go. He felt no end proud of himself.

"Who is he, who is he, who is he?" Mletshwa chanted, going left right, left right, in double quick time,

Who is he chosen by the Great White Man
To walk fast in the fine meal with the broken eggs in it?
Who is he but Mletshwa? –
Who is he but Mletshwa Kusane whose kraal is by the Molopo?

Who is he, the Mighty Trampling Elephant, elephant among elephants,
He with his feet washed clean in carbolic soap?
Who is the Mighty Elephant with his feet washed clean
With the thick white bubbles coming out of
The red carbolic soap – the White Man's red carbolic soap?
Who is he but Mletshwa Kusane whose kraal is by the Molopo?

Who is he that treads heavier than the rhinoceros –
The rhinoceros with his feet washed in the water from the White Man's faucet?
Who is he that treads with his feet washed cleaner than the White Man's feet?
Treading out white flour and yellow, stinking eggs and yeast
That is the beautiful food of the White Man?
Who is he but Mletshwa –
Who is he but Mletshwa Kusane whose kraal is by the Molopo?

Inspired to unwonted exertions by his singing, Mletshwa was making a first-class job of treading that dough. When the night foreman looked again, Mletshwa was leaping up and down in the tub. One hand was raised up to the level of his shoulder, balancing an imaginary assegai. His other arm supported an equally imaginary raw-hide shield. What were not fictitious were the pieces of dough clinging to his working pants and shirt and even to one side of his neck. The night foreman was not a little surprised to see a nigger performing a Zulu war dance in a kneading trough at that time of the night. Especially when those white splashes of dough could have passed as war paint.

"None of that, Jim Fish," the night foreman called out – impressed, in spite of himself. "Get on with your work."

One of the other Natives guffawed. But it *was* his work, this Native thought. In prancing up and down like that, in the dough, Mletshwa was only doing his work. And here was the boss angry with Mletshwa about it. Surely, the ways of the White man were strange.

It was only a little later that the night foreman noticed what other effect the violent exercise had had on Jim Fish: he was sweating like a dozen niggers; the sweat was pouring off Mletshwa as though from a shower bath. Which was something that Mletshwa had never had in his life – a showerbath or any other kind of a bath.

This time the night foreman swore.

"Get out of that tub, you black son of a bitch," he shouted. "That's for cake for White people to eat, you bloody — Look at all the sweat running off your — backside into White people's cake."

Mletshwa's was a temperament that was easily cowed. In a moment the sound of the night foreman's voice had changed him from a bloodthirsty warrior to a timid Bushveld thing trying to escape from a trampling rhinoceros among rhinoceroses. In a split second he was out of the tub and halfway across the bakery floor towards his kaya in the back yard.

He had to return to the tub, however. The night foreman saw to that. The night foreman also saw to it that Mletshwa scraped all the dough off his feet and other parts of his person, and stuck it back where it belonged.

"Trying to make off with half the confectionery dough sticking to him," the night foreman said to the mechanic who was working at the motor, working to get it started again. Then the night foreman addressed Mletshwa once more.

"Cha-cha," he shouted. "Inindaba wena want to steal wet meal, huh? Come on, put it all back. That lump between your toes, too. It's for the cake for White people to eat. You meningi skelm, you."

A Visit to Shanty Town

Situated on the slope of a hill ten miles outside the City of Johannesburg is a township whose expanding dimensions should soon entitle it to the prestige of being termed a city, also. At present it is known as Shanty Town.

Shanty Town today contains several thousand shacks, each consisting of a rough framework of poles covered with sacking and each housing a native family. Here let it be explained that our visit took place in bright sunshine. It was a pleasant morning and as far as the writer was concerned the visit was not made in any spirit of sociological crusading, which seems to demand of the individual a preconceived righteous indignation against the existing economic order – so that whatever is experienced and observed gets fitted into appropriate and readymade emotions.

Consequently, where this picture of actual conditions in Shanty Town may appear to fall short will be in respect of its deliberate avoidance of the obvious. Stories of squalor, told with a consistent drabness, in grey shadows unrelieved by the light of imagination, tend, in their ultimates, to pall. The heart gets tired of the same old note struck over and over again. It is not in human nature for one's feelings to be kept at the same pitch of human intensity – whether the feelings are of pity or of righteous wrath – all the time. There is such a thing as tedium. And if it is not polite to yawn at a platitude, it is, at all events, natural.

For this reason this article will be confined to an objective description of an interesting little town, healthfully situated on a hillside, and it will be left to the reader to make his own comments, such as "Dastardly" or "Delightful", depending alike on his own subjective reactions and his capacity for reading between the lines.

What first struck the writer, who has considerable practical knowledge of constructive engineering, was that two distinct types of building material are employed in the erection of the shanties. Most of the residential abodes are covered with mealie sacks. A few – and these belonging obviously to the more aristocratic section – have their walls and roofs constructed of sugar pockets bearing the trademark of Messrs. Hulett. Close examination shows that the hessian in a sugar pocket is of finer texture and better woven than that in a mealie bag and is consequently a superior building material. It keeps out the elements better.

Each shack is numbered in some dark-coloured paint. These numbers run into thousands, thereby affording a rough and ready means of computing the population of the place. It also makes it easier for the postman on his rounds to deliver correspondence and newspapers. One does not imagine that the residents of Shanty Town get troubled much with tradesmen's circulars, however. Although an enterprising house agent can, if he so desires, strike an incongruous note by circularising the area with printed literature about "Why Pay Rent? Let Us Show You How to Build Your Own House."

There is little about these hessian covered shacks that is in conflict with the fundamental laws of architecture, which are that a building should be planned in accordance with the purpose for which it is required, that it should carry no ornamentation that is outside of this purpose and that its design should be guided by the type of material that is employed. From an aesthetic point of view the architecture of Shanty Town can therefore be described as not undignified. About none of these shacks is there that false attempt at drama that makes Park Station an eyesore.

And when a native woman told us that she was suffering from chest pains as a result of her hut having been drenched during the recent rains, and that most of the people there were suffering from various illnesses contracted through sleeping under soaked blankets, her complaints were not based on artistic grounds but on the simple scientific fact that sacking is porous and lets in the water in the rainy season.

But from the point of view of pure architecture there is not much wrong with these dwellings. The washed-out yellows of the hessian roofs and walls blend prettily with the grass of the South African veld in mid-winter. Washed-out yellow against bleached fawn. Pretty. And veld-coloured huts built close to the soil seem much more appropriate for South African conditions than skyscrapers and blocks of flats. The shacks in the main street of Shanty Town seem to express the true spirit of Africa in a way that the buildings of Eloff Street do not.

But all these things are merely by the way. For that matter one feels that if a number of Kalahari Bushmen were brought to Johannesburg on a visit to a fashionable block of city flats they would go back to the desert with strong feelings about the white man's degradation. "Like living in an ant-hill," they would say. "Squalor," "Unhygienic." "Like pigs." "And you ought to see some of those pictures they hang on their walls. . . just too awful."

What was most interesting about Shanty Town was the human side. One felt in the place the warmth of a strong and raw life. Deplorable though their economic circumstances were, there was about these men and women and children a sense of life that had no frustration in it. A dark vitality of the soil. An organic power for living that one imagined nothing in this world could take away. Was there anything about us, about this party of white visitors, that the residents of Shanty Town could genuinely envy? In our hearts the answer was, no.

The replies that the natives returned to our questions were prideful. Their attitude was a lesson in breeding. They resented our presence, in the way that any proud person resents the intrusion into his affairs of curiosity or patronage. And they received us with that politeness that shames. We wanted to know what had happened to Mapanza, the headman who had fought against the humiliating introduction of soup kitchens, and they informed us, with grave dignity, that "he was not there." Although everybody knew, what we subsequently learnt from a police boy, that Mapanza was in gaol.

Whatever information we got we received from the police boy: from the side of the authorities and not from the side of the residents. And when we left, a native woman asked us if we were going to send blankets. It was a perfect snub, whose imputation could not be lost even on the most obtuse. A duchess could not have administered it better.

Whatever ill effects detribalisation may have had on the natives, it has done nothing, judging from what is happening in Shanty Town, to the stateliness of their aristocracy. Living under what are nothing less than ghastly conditions, deprived apparently of even the barest necessities of human existence, the inhabitants of Shanty Town are displaying, in the face of adversity, a sublime courage that goes far beyond questions of economics and sociology.

If life is spirit, what the natives of Shanty Town bear about them is not poverty but destiny.

OLD CAPE SLAVE RELICS

THE OTHER DAY, in an antique shop, I saw an article of furniture that was obviously a museum piece. It was an old Cape chair with dowel-pins less than an eighth of an inch in diameter, and the mortise and tenon joints as solid as when the chair was constructed over a century ago. I was much impressed. Then I read, on the dealer's tag attached to the chair by a comparatively new piece of string, these words, 'Old Cape Slave Chair.'

Well, well, I thought. Old Cape Slave Chair. Fitted with a neck rest and side supports for the elbows, it was an ideal piece of furniture for the Old Cape Slave to relax in every morning after breakfast. This chair just showed you, all over again, that there was a certain spaciousness, a measure of refinement pleasing to good taste, about the way they lived in the Western Province about the turn of the eighteenth century. That way of life has departed for ever. And that Old Cape Slave Chair seems to epitomise, somehow, that spirit of vanished elegance, that old world charm that has passed away.

And while musing thus on the bygone splendours of an age that enriched us with thick-walled gabled dwellings and gracious legends and hippopotamus hide sjamboks, I felt that it would be very nice indeed if some Africana enthusiast were to retrieve from the loft of some Old Cape House a few more eighteenth-century relics that would serve to remind us of our cultured past.

An Old Cape Slave Embroidered Waistcoat, for instance. There you would have something, now. The lace and gold facing would be sewn on to the brocade with long stitches: you would be able to see from the insultingly inferior quality of needlework that those were indeed the bad old days when just about any sort of embroidered waistcoat was considered good enough for the Old Cape Slave.

And how about an Old Cape Slave Sedan Chair? That would find a place of honour in any museum. We don't use that type of conveyance any more. But I can readily conceive of what an Old Cape Slave Sedan Chair would look like. The handles would be all right, encrusted with jewels, and all that sort of thing: and they would be sumptuously padded, making it easy for the owner of the estate to carry the Old Cape Slave down to the plantation to work every day. But from the interior furnishings of the Old Cape Slave Sedan Chair you would be able to recognise the fact that those were indeed the days of slavery. There would be just a coarse horsehair cushion to sit on, and in place of a curtain a strip of undyed hessian would flutter from the window opening. All this would serve to make it clear to you as to how unenlightened that past age was really. Nothing was too good for the boss: the handles had to be jewelled and padded because they made contact with his aristocratic neck and illustrious shoulders. The Old Cape Slave had to put up with a horsehair cushion and a piece of sacking for a curtain. He simply had no status. Why, they wouldn't carry a mine native to work today, seated on a horsehair cushion.

It is hard to keep one's temper when one reflects on some of the more disagreeable features that skulked behind the imposing facades of gentility and refinement that appeared to constitute the order of things in the Old Days at the Cape.

I have made mention in a previous article of the keen competition in the curio and antique trade today for Old Cape prints and Old Cape fittings. We make those things no more. The factories of the post-Industrial Revolution have put an end to the highly skilled craftsmen turning out the products of his trade by hand. The machine has swept all that away. And I am pleased that Old Cape relics are today held in such high esteem.

But the Old Cape Slave has so far been somewhat neglected. And it is nice to think that he is at last coming into his own. I feel that the Old Cape Slave Chair I saw in an antique shop the other day is opening up a number of splendid and hitherto unexplored possibilities. We all know about an Old Cape Slave Bell. There are lots of them about. More rare is the Old Cape Slave Chain. This is a formidable affair, and rather frightening. The links are solidly fashioned out of a yellowish metal, and the Old Cape Slave was even proud to wear his Chain on Sundays: it dangled cumbrously from the lower part of his Old Cape Slave Embroidered Waistcoat, the links flashing in the sun.

I am sure that there are still lots of Old Cape Slave souvenirs waiting to be discovered by collectors in Old Cape lofts. An Old Cape Slave Dinner Service, for instance, should command more than passing interest. And what about an Old Cape Slave Suitcase?

I feel that a very romantic story could be woven around the Old Cape Slave Suitcase. "I have borne your arrogance and your meanness and your pretty larcenies long enough," the Old Cape Slave would say to Hendrik Terreblanche, the Old Cape Slave-owner. "I have packed my suitcase and I am off."

"But you can't do that," the eighteenth-century Cape Slave-owner would answer. "Or if you must go, won't you at least stay on until the end of the month?"

"A slave does not work on a month to month basis," the Old Cape Slave would reply with icy dignity. "I have packed my suitcase and I am going. Fare you well, Simon Legree."

"But you got me all wrong," the Old Cape Slave-owner would reply. "You got me mixed up with the Southern cotton plantations. You're talking nineteenth-century liberation propaganda. If you walk off like that, carrying your suitcase and all, you'll be betraying a whole epoch. Be your age, man."

Thus appealed to, in the historical realisation of the fact that the honour of an entire era was at stake, the Old Cape Slave would put down his suitcase in the shade of an Old Cape Slave Oak-tree and, seizing the hand of Hendrik Terreblanche in a manly grasp, he would proclaim, "Never will I desert you. I shall never go down in history in obloquy. I would rather go in a ricksha. I refuse to walk out of the eighteenth century, carrying a suitcase. Toujours, l'esprit de corps!"

"Noblesse oblige," Hendrik Terreblanche would answer simply, the tears starting to his eyes as he crushed the Old Cape Slave's fingers in a vice-like grip. After that he would trip up the Old Cape Slave and kick him a number of times in the stomach and ribs. And for quite a long while after that he would be jumping up and down on the Old Cape Slave's face.

Done on the stage, this should be a very moving finale, with the curtain falling to slow music. A stage play on these lines, with the title *Saving a Century* or *The Honour of the Eighteenth*, should prove very successful, especially if some tie-up could be effected with Bradman's eighteenth century in first-class cricket or with one of Gordon Richard's more outstanding turf triumphs.

It is possible that present day taste may recoil somewhat from the realism of the climactic scene, on the score that while it is certainly very lifelike, it errs in respect of being too robust. But I think that the necessary adjustments could be made quite readily. Thus, if a company were touring the smaller towns of the Free State highveld, the more virile ending to the play, *'n Eeu van Ondergang Gered*, could be safely retained.

On the other hand, if the play is produced in amateur circles – by Form Four convent girls, for instance – at the moment when Hendrik Terreblanche and the Old Cape Slave shake hands the slave-owner's little daughter could walk on to the stage with a pretty, mincing gait and bearing, clutched in her arms, a copper eighteenth-century coal-scuttle filled with assorted fruits. Tableau.

Another light touch that could also be introduced in the last scene, and should go down well with the audience, would be to arrange, the instant the Old Cape Slave puts down the suitcase, for a couple of silver spoons, bearing Hendrik Terreblanche's monogram, to drop out.

The stage props should consist of genuine period furniture and fittings that may be had on loan from the antique dealers. All the Old Cape Slave stuff may then be trotted out. Everything from an Old Cape Slave Dinner Wagon to an Old Cape Slave Antique Cabinet.

WITPOORTJIE FALLS

ABOUT FIFTEEN MILES FROM Johannesburg, on the way to Krugersdorp, is Witpoortjie, the railway halt for a natural beauty spot which for over half a century has been the regular resort of picnickers from Johannesburg and the West Rand.

Among my earliest childhood recollections is an outing to Witpoortjie in the company of my parents and some relatives and a number of friends. I remember that the party included two gentlemen with prominent cheekbones who carried bagpipes. I thought of, and referred to, these gentlemen as Scotchmen. It was only years later that I learnt that they were, in reality, Scots.

I was also impressed very vividly by the waterfall, which for a long time afterwards I tried to make drawings of in coloured crayons. Those were better crayons than one can get today. And I believe that those drawings, too, were better than anything I can do now.

And I remembered also for a long time afterwards how a bottle of whisky got broken on a boulder. One of the Scotsmen broke it when he was busy pulling out the cork, and the whisky flowed away along the side of the boulder and into the grass. My youthful mind was not able to distinguish readily, in action in which an adult was involved, between accident and design. And so I thought that the gentleman with the bagpipes had broken the bottle on purpose. What lent colour to this belief was the way in which the other gentleman with the bagpipes spoke about it, enquiring of his fellow musician as to what the hell he wanted to go and do that for now.

He said many other words, also, and he spoke for a considerable while, and it was only after everybody had had several turns at explaining to him that there were ladies present, and also children above the age of two, that he grew quieter and contented himself with kicking the crockery about that had been stacked on a white cloth spread on the grass. The cups and saucers and plates had all been piled on one spot, so that it was easy for him to kick the whole lot around without having to walk much.

I have often thought, since that picnic at Witpoortjie, that Scotsmen could also swear better in those days than they can now. In the important ways the world is not what it used to be.

The other day, in a party of three, I revisited Witpoortjie.

From the railway station a footpath leads over rough ground to the foot of two tall koppies, separated from each other by a narrow ravine that winds away through rocky vastnesses to a waterfall of not unimposing dimensions. A stream of water flows through Witpoortjie all the year round. And through the slow millenniums this stream, assisted by the elements and seasonal flood times, has eroded its course down to its present level, so that the person who treads the footpath in the deep valley between the koppies walks in the shadows of precipitous crags that have been eaten out by the quiet waters that he scoops up to make tea with.

From the station to the entrance to the poort is a walk of about thirty-five minutes. That is, it takes the holiday-maker thirty-five minutes to traverse the distance from the station to where the more exuberant scenery starts. But the return journey is different. Refreshed from a day in the open air, invigorated with the play of the wind on his body and the sun on his brow, when he strides back from the mouth of the gorge to the station the visitor to Witpoortjie rarely does the distance in under three hours.

For the geologist Witpoortjie is a source of unending interest. Students from the Witwatersrand University go there every year to make notes about the rock formations. Now and again the professor in charge of the students loses his way there, and when evening comes the students make their way back to the station, alone, singing their college songs, and the professor gets rescued, a year later, by the next geological expedition from Wits.

There is one place in the poort where a colossal pile of rocks looms ominously overhead, and where the footpath leads over a mountain of debris which the eye of even the untrained geologist can identify as being the result of a recent fall. Recent, that is, geologically speaking. At all events, the debris did not seem to bear signs of more than ten thousand years of weathering. And it looked doubtful whether the overhanging crags would stay in position, like that, very long. I gave those overhanging crags another fifteen thousand years, at the outside. I went through that part of the poort quickly, geologically speaking.

It was about here, where the ravine was at its narrowest, and the road seemed all but impassable even to the pedestrian – if being a pedestrian includes wading through mud at ankle deep and clambering on all fours over boulders – it was at this stage that one of us mentioned the fact that a party of Voortrekkers had taken their wagons through Witpoortjie on their way to the Northern Transvaal. Whatever admiration I had entertained for the Voortrekkers until that moment was nothing compared with the feeling that overwhelmed me when the full import of my friend's statement sank into my consciousness. Was there nothing they did not dare, these sturdy pioneers, intrepid in their perseverance, dauntless in their faith?

No doubt they felt that the strength of their trek-chains that had not failed them over a thousand miles of veld, from the Western Province of the Cape to the Witwatersrand, would stand them in stead through Witpoortjie, also. But it must have taken each wagon about a week to get through. Whereas if they had gone a couple of miles east or west they could have travelled over level veld. Indeed, they must have gone considerably out of their way to have found Witpoortjie at all.

I came to the conclusion that the Voortrekkers must have been just a shade too consciously rugged in carrying out their pioneering mission.

I could not help but feel that they realised they were creating history and that it was expected of them to do it the hard way.

And viewed from the perspective of history, there is no doubt that the Voortrekker was right. There was not much prestige about taking the short cut to the Limpopo across flat and open country. Anybody could do that. The trail of the Voortrekker had to lead through the gorges of Witpoortjie, even if it meant a detour of several hundred miles to get there.

We can imagine the look of exultation on the face of the leader of that pioneer band when the last ox-wagon, battered from its toilsome journeying over giant boulder and through muddy stream, rolled heavily on to level ground.

"That was a good piece of work, kêrels," we can hear the leader of that party of Voortrekkers saying. And it was, of course. It was a feat of pioneering courage and determination, and as such it was unforgettable. There was only one way in which they could have improved on it. They could have taken off the wheels and carried their wagons over the top of the koppie. Over the high one with the slippery sides.

Today, when you want to get to Witpoortjie Falls from the station, you have to pay sixpence toll to a private landowner. This seems wrong, somehow.

But I believe there is an alternative route over the top of a kop-pie. . . Yes, over the high one.

Politics and Love

On the blackboard that you could see every time the speaker moved his head to one side was a multiplication sum: 973 x 8 = . There had been a number there, after the equals, but the schoolmaster had rubbed it out quickly, before the first members of the audience filed into the classroom for the meeting.

It was just possible that the answer wasn't quite correct, the schoolmaster reflected, and he didn't want any nonsense about it from some busybody, afterwards.

The schoolmaster did not feel called upon to erase, from the blackboard, a brief statement to do with the geographical regions traversed by the Vaal River.

Thus it came about that every time Lennep van Ploert, the representative for Bekkersdal, moved his head to one side or the other, or bent forward to think – which he did not appear to do very deeply – there was revealed behind him, on the blackboard, in addition to the arithmetic, this sentence whose truth few would question, or, rather (this being a political meeting) would cavil at: "The Vaal River is in Africa."

Lennep van Ploert wore a black suit and a high, stick-up collar. And his voice was just as impressive as his looks. Many of the farmers and their wives present at the meeting had received their education in that same classroom and sitting on those same benches. Consequently, more than one member of the audience identified Lennep van Ploert in his mind with the Hollander school inspector who had come round annually to tell the pupils whether they had passed or failed.

There was a good attendance of farmers and their wives and children from the Rooibokspruit area to hear Lennep van Ploert report, in that schoolroom that served for a night as a political party venue, on the way he had furthered his constituents' interests during the past year in a building of more imposing dimensions than the schoolhouse, and with statelier portals.

Another point of difference between the two buildings was that in the Marico schoolroom the older pupils seldom threw chalk, any more. Most of them had also learnt to reject the cruder formularies of comedy built up around the placing of drawing pins on the schoolmaster's chair.

"And so in your interests I went and had tea with the Marquis de Monfiche," the voice of Lennep van Ploert boomed. "And while I was drinking tea with that distinguished French aristocrat and insurance representative – "

"Are you sure it was tea?" a man in a khaki shirt sitting at the back of the classroom interjected.

A couple of people in the audience giggled. Others said "Sh— " Among the latter was the wife of a wealthy local cattle-smuggler. She was hoping that Lennep van Ploert would go on to say how the wife of the distinguished French marquis was dressed.

The only person who was in no way embarrassed was the speaker himself. The remark made by the man in the khaki shirt was of a pattern accepted as wit in that other building (the one with the proud traditions and the coat of arms over the front stoep). Lennep van Ploert felt at home, then.

"No, it wasn't tea," the speaker said. "It was a milkshake."

In that noble edifice in which Lennep van Ploert shone as a debater, such a brilliant piece of repartee would have received due appreciation. Grim features would have relaxed in smiles. A policeman wearing white gloves would have gone to the assistance of an elderly legislator who was in stitches through laughing.

There would have been jovial shouts of "Withdraw!" There would have been a row of stipples in Hansard, the short-hand reporter not being able to get down the next couple of sentences on account of his emotions being so mixed. And afterwards, in the lobby, even some of

Lennep van Ploert's opponents would have come and grasped Lennep van Ploert by the hand.

But, singularly enough, in that Marico schoolroom with the whitewashed walls and the thatched roof and with no inspiring statuary on the premises – unless a child's clay model on a window-sill of Adam with a pipe and braces could fit into that category (one of Adam's braces having slipped off his shoulder on to a level with his knee) – in that Marico classroom there was no immediate response of the sort that Lennep van Ploert had looked for.

Instead, the audience started wondering if there was something that they had missed, perhaps, in what Lennep van Ploert had just said. Or was he taking them to be just a lot of simpletons, because they were living out in the most northern part of the Bushveld that you could live in and still be allowed to vote?

The only positive reaction, however, came from the man in the khaki shirt. He vacated his place at the back of the schoolroom and moved up to a seat nearer the front.

"After I had signed the insurance papers for an endowment policy," Lennep van Ploert proceeded, "the French marquis said he would be honoured if my wife and I would visit him at his chateau next time we were in France. He did not know exactly when he would be going back to France, though. The marquis told me straight out that there was something about South Africa that he *liked*. Anyway, I told him that, speaking on behalf of my constituents, I would accept his invitation." (Applause.)

The man in the khaki shirt had been sitting between a young fellow with a blue and orange tie and a young girl with a selon's rose in her hair.

The young man looked sideways at the girl and even in the uncertain light of the paraffin lamps the flush on his face was evident. The redness extended to the top part of his ears.

"I can't hear too well from there," the young fellow explained, moving into the seat vacated by the man with the khaki shirt.

The girl did not answer.

"Is he – is he your father?" the young man enquired in a faltering voice, at the same time indicating the man in the khaki shirt, who was then engaged in feeling through his trousers pockets, thereby occasioning noticeable discomfort to the farmer sitting next to him, by reason of the confinement imposed by the school bench.

"He's my uncle," the girl answered. "I stay with him. I lost my parents when I was young."

"I have before today tried to speak to you," the young fellow with the blue and orange tie went on. "But he was always with you."

"I know," the girl answered, unconsciously putting her hand up to the selon's rose in her hair.

"At Zeerust with the last Nagmaal, now," the young man went on. "By the side of the kerkplein."

"Yes," the girl responded, simply.

"Only, your uncle kicked out, then, at – " the young man proceeded.

"He kicked just at a wild berry," the girl explained. "He's been like that since he came back from the mines."

"Well, I just didn't understand, then," the young man said. "My name is Dawie Louw. What's yours?"

"Lettie," the girl answered.

"Well, it was because your uncle kicked out, like that," Dawie Louw went on, "that I didn't – "

"Didn't come up and speak to us," Lettie helped him out.

"Yes, and I think Lettie is a lovely name," the young fellow said.

"And I like the name Dawie, also," the girl said in a soft voice.

"And there was another time when I nearly came up and spoke to you," Dawie Louw went on. "It was right in front of – "

"Solly's hardware store," Lettie said. "Next to the four-disc harrows."

From her voice it sounded like it was the rose garden of the Capulets under a Veronese moon.

"That's right," Dawie Louw said. "Only your uncle was again with you, and just when I was coming up, after pulling my tie straight – it was a purple tie with – "

"Green spots," Lettie announced, looking slightly pained.

"Well," Dawie Louw said, "just as I was coming up, your uncle – "

"Kicked out at a four-disc harrow's disc," Lettie said. "That's another habit my uncle has brought back from the mines. He also carries a bicycle chain, through having lived in Fordsburg."

Meanwhile, on the platform, Lennep van Ploert was continuing with his report to his constituents of his legislative activities.

" – wlawlawski," Lennep van Ploert was saying. "And it was coffee I had with him, that time, I mean with that distinguished Polish prince, who happened to have a few shares in a washing machine company to dispose of, at the moment, and that I purchased. He invited me, on behalf of my constituents, to drop in at his palace in Poland whenever I was passing that way. But he didn't think he would go back there himself quite soon, the prince said. For one thing, he *liked* South Africa, he said. And he also mentioned something about their just *waiting* for him to come back, in his native country of Poland."

The man in the khaki shirt, Lettie's uncle, spoke up for himself, then.

"Could they give my trousers a bit of a press?" he asked. "That Polish washing machine company of yours, that is?"

At the same time the man in the khaki shirt got up and moved to a seat that was still nearer the front.

"Has your uncle had – " Dawie Louw asked of Lettie.

"A few too many? Yes, I think so. It's since," Lettie said, once more, "he's come back from the mines."

Dawie Louw asked the girl with the selon's rose in her hair if she didn't think it was a queer thing that, after all that, they should at last have the chance of meeting and of talking to each other, sitting right next to each other on a school bench, even.

He was young and sanguine, then, and he didn't know that a school bench actually was the right place where two young lovers should meet. For who would yet have more to learn of the ways of the world than a boy and girl in love?

"Praat politiek," somebody shouted out to Lennep van Ploert. It was not the man in the khaki shirt (Lettie's uncle) that shouted. It was some other farmer, who had come to hear about policy and about election promises, and who couldn't understand that Lennep van Ploert, who had been such a firebrand a few years before, should now be content to hand out milksop stuff. For Lennep van Ploert was now talking about when he had cocoa with a Spanish nobleman who did a spot of real estate agency work in his spare time.

Lennep van Ploert leant forward to think, for a few moments, then.

And so Dawie Louw and Lettie were able to see what was written on the blackboard. And they spelt out, between them, the statement that the Vaal River was in Africa. And they laughed – just for no reason at all. They did not know that they would have been far better occupied in working out that arithmetic sum, instead. But young people in love don't know that at the time, of course. They think they know better.

"The first time I saw you was at the fat stock sale at Schooneesdrif," Dawie Louw said to Lettie. "You were with your uncle and you wouldn't look at me."

"The first time I saw you," Lettie said, "was before Schooneesdrif."

"At Schooneesdrif you had on a frock with – " Dawie Louw started again.

But it was as much at Lettie's suggestion as his own that they slipped out of the door of the classroom, then, the two of them together, hand in hand. And they stood like that, a long time, hand in hand, in silence, under the unclothed stars.

That was how they came to miss the unhappy incidents that took place inside the schoolroom a little later. For the man in the khaki shirt (Lettie's uncle) had eventually found what he was looking for, in his trousers pocket. But he was pulled off Lennep van Ploert before he could assault him to any serious purpose with his bicycle chain. But before that Lettie's uncle had borne the legislator back against the blackboard.

And that was how the meeting ended. And, strangely enough, although Lennep van Ploert represented, for many members of the audience, the school inspector of their youth, they were not unwilling to forgive the man in the khaki shirt for having dealt with him in that fashion.

Because of the way he had been pressed backwards against the blackboard by Lettie's uncle, you were able to read afterwards, on Lennep van Ploert's suit – the figures being the wrong way around – part of the sum in arithmetic. What was also legible on Lennep van Ploert's jacket – reading from right to left – was a chalked statement to the effect that the Vaal River flows in Africa.

But of neither of these circumstances did Dawie Louw and Lettie know anything. They stood at the side of the schoolhouse, holding hands under the stars. And they were young. And they were in love. And they were foolish. And they would not have cared about what vital sort of decision any statesman would have arrived at, then.

And they would have laughed about any Parallel that any general might have decided to cross.

New Elder

"This is Elder Haasbroek," Wynand Geel said, and we shook hands all round.

"He is the new elder from – " Wynand Geel began again, when Hans Combrinck broke into a laugh. The rest of us laughed, also. It sounded funny, "*new elder*." The only one that didn't laugh was the new elder himself. He drew himself up straight and you could see from his manner that he thought people from our part of the Groot Marico were somewhat easily amused. Childishly easy, sort of.

Wynand Geel started trying to explain to Elder Haasbroek.

"Why they are laughing," he said, "is because it sounded, well, something to laugh at, you know – saying, '*nuwe ouderling*'."

"Yes," Elder Haasbroek answered, "oh, yes, I see. Quite."

Even without Wynand Geel having introduced him, however, we would have known that he was an elder. And we would still have known it if he had had on ordinary farm clothes, instead of the black manel suit with the white tie that he was wearing.

We got in each other's way, finding seats on Wynand Geel's stoep. For Elder Haasbroek had taken the armchair that Oom Doors Perskes usually occupied, and so we had all of us to shift into different places, and we sat upright.

We heard Wynand Geel's daughter moving about in the front bedroom. Wynand called her.

"I suppose you'll have the usual little old Bushveld refreshment, Elder?" Wynand Geel asked Elder Haasbroek.

When Drieka came out on to the stoep we understood what she had been doing in the bedroom. Her hair was now fastened back with a pink ribbon. Before Wynand Geel could ask her if she had coffee on the stove, Elder Haasbroek spoke.

"Well, I was thinking that it was perhaps a bit early in the morning," Elder Haasbroek said to Wynand Geel. "But I have heard that it is a custom you have here in this part of the Groot Marico. So I won't offend you. Make mine just three inches of peach mampoer."

"*Mamp–* " Hans Combrinck started to blurt out in surprise, stopping himself halfway, however.

By that time it was too late for Wynand Geel to explain that he had meant coffee, and that we weren't used to taking anything stronger at that time of the day. Wynand went into the voorhuis himself and fetched out glasses and a bottle. There have probably never been any more astonished Groot Marico farmers than that little group that sat on the front stoep, in the forenoon, drinking mampoer, with an elder of the church in their midst.

A little later, Wynand Geel fetched out another bottle.

After Elder Haasbroek had gone, we said that when Wynand Geel had spoken of him as a new elder, he hadn't been so far wrong. He was at all events a new *sort* of elder.

We learnt that, some time later, Elder Haasbroek again called at Wynand Geel's home, with a couple of tracts. And Wynand was away in Zeerust, as Drieka told him when she answered the door. And Elder Haasbroek stayed quite a long time.

We realised, then, that Elder Haasbroek was not such a new sort of elder, after all.

SHY YOUNG MAN

HANS COMBRINCK NUDGED CHRIS VAN BLERK.

"Why don't you ask Wynand now – like you said you would?" Hans wanted to know.

Because he was young, and diffident, Chris van Blerk mumbled something about there being so many people sitting here on the stoep smoking their pipes and drinking coffee and about it perhaps being better if he spoke to Oom Wynand Geel about it afterwards, when there weren't so many people sitting here on the stoep drinking their pipes and smoking – at least, what he meant to say was – His mumble got lost in the sound of coffee being poured into saucers and the rattle of crockery.

Hans Combrinck laughed.

"What do you think of that, Wynand?" he asked. "I told Chris van Blerk last week that he would come right as far as your house, and he would sit here on your stoep, with his one veldskoen on the support of a chair, just like he's doing now, and he still wouldn't ask you."

Immediately Oom Doors Perskes started talking about the old days, when you were fully grown up, with adult responsibilities, by the age of fifteen, and you could distil your own moepel brandy by the time you were twelve. So there wasn't such a thing as a shy young man in the old days, Oom Doors said. Indeed, there wasn't such a thing as a young man at all. Not when you had to cure your own chewing tobacco before you were ten and grind up your own snuff before you were two, Oom Doors said. He forgot now at what a ridiculously early age you would have to shoot your own Mshangaan.

"What I can remember, though, is the time they needed an assistant magistrate for the Pilanesberg," Oom Doors Perskes went on. "The old landdrost couldn't cope with all the work himself anymore, as he was getting on in years. He was close on to thirty, I think. Well, somebody had to step in, and we felt it was up to the Perskes family. My father was too old, of course. In fact, he was, if anything, even older than the old landdrost. Moreover, my father couldn't spell long words. Still, in that respect he wasn't much different from the old landdrost, who, I believe, couldn't spell at all. My elder brothers were busy deepening the Molopo River and throwing a barrage across it. So I had to go."

"I suppose you were about eleven, then, when you became a magistrate?" Hans Combrinck asked, sarcastically.

"Eleven and a half," Oom Doors Perskes replied. "My younger brother couldn't take on the job because the part he was playing in politics at that time made him an unsuitable candidate for the judiciary. But, anyway, that's how we were in those days. Men. No want of confidence. Sure of ourselves."

Drieka Geel came on to the stoep with the tray to collect the cups and saucers.

"You've been doing it *again*," she said when she came to where Oom Doors Perskes was sitting. "Knocking out your pipe on the arm of this chair that I've got to polish with olieblaar."

Oom Doors looked abject. Then he stammered out some lie by way of excuse, saying that it was maybe somebody else that had knocked out his pipe on the arm of the chair.

When we were leaving, Wynand Geel took Chris van Blerk slightly aside and replied to the question that Chris had not put to him. "Better ask her yourself," Wynand Geel said.

In the Withaak's Shade

Leopards? – Oom Schalk Lourens said – Oh, yes, there are two varieties on this side of the Limpopo. The chief difference between them is that the one kind of leopard has got a few more spots on it than the other kind. But when you meet a leopard in the veld, unexpectedly, you seldom trouble to count his spots to find out what kind he belongs to. That is unnecessary. Because, whatever kind of leopard it is that you come across in this way, you only do one kind of running. And that is the fastest kind.

I remember the occasion that I came across a leopard unexpectedly, and to this day I couldn't tell you how many spots he had, even though I had all the time I needed for studying him. It happened about midday, when I was out on the far end of my farm, behind a koppie, looking for some strayed cattle. I thought the cattle might be there because it is shady under those withaak trees, and there is soft grass that is very pleasant to sit on. After I had looked for the cattle for about an hour in this manner, sitting up against a tree-trunk, it occurred to me that I could look for them just as well, or perhaps even better, if I lay down flat. For even a child knows that cattle aren't so small that you have got to get on to stilts and things to see them properly.

So I lay on my back, with my hat tilted over my face, and my legs crossed, and when I closed my eyes slightly the tip of my boot, sticking up into the air, looked just like the peak of Abjaterskop.

Overhead a lone aasvoël wheeled, circling slowly round and round without flapping his wings, and I knew that not even a calf could pass in any part of the sky between the tip of my toe and that aasvoël without my observing it immediately. What was more, I could go on lying there under the withaak and looking for the cattle like that all day, if necessary. As you know, I am not the sort of farmer to loaf about the house when there is man's work to be done.

The more I screwed up my eyes and gazed at the toe of my boot, the more it looked like Abjaterskop. By and by it seemed that it actually was Abjaterskop, and I could see the stones on top of it, and the bush trying to grow up its sides, and in my ears there was a far-off, humming sound, like bees in an orchard on a still day. As I have said, it was very pleasant.

Then a strange thing happened. It was as though a huge cloud, shaped like an animal's head and with spots on it, had settled on top of Abjaterskop. It seemed so funny that I wanted to laugh. But I didn't. Instead, I opened my eyes a little more and felt glad to think that I was only dreaming. Because otherwise I would have to believe that the spotted cloud on Abjaterskop was actually a leopard, and that he was gazing at my boot. Again I wanted to laugh. But then, suddenly, I knew.

And I didn't feel so glad. For it was a leopard, all right – a large-sized, hungry-looking leopard, and he was sniffing suspiciously at my feet. I was uncomfortable. I knew that nothing I could do would ever convince that leopard that my toe was Abjaterskop. He was not that sort of leopard: I knew that without even counting the number of his spots. Instead, having finished with my feet, he started sniffing higher up. It was the most terrifying moment of my life. I wanted to get up and run for it. But I couldn't. My legs wouldn't work.

Every big-game hunter I have come across has told me the same story about how, at one time or another, he has owed his escape from lions and other wild animals to his cunning in lying down and pretending to be dead, so that the beast of prey loses interest in him and walks off. Now, as I lay there on the grass, with the leopard trying to make up his mind about me, I understood why, in such a situation, the hunter doesn't move. It's simply that he can't move. That's all. It's not his cunning that keeps him down. It's his legs.

In the meantime, the leopard had got up as far as my knees. He was studying my trousers very carefully, and I started getting embarrassed. My trousers were old and rather unfashionable. Also, at the knee, there was a torn place, from where I had climbed through a barbed-wire fence, into the thick bush, the time I saw the Government tax-collector coming over the bult before he saw me. The leopard stared at that rent in my trousers for quite a while, and my embarrassment grew. I felt I wanted to explain about the Government tax-collector and the barbed wire. I didn't want the leopard to get the impression that Schalk Lourens was the sort of man who didn't care about his personal appearance.

When the leopard got as far as my shirt, however, I felt better. It was a good blue flannel shirt that I had bought only a few weeks ago from the Indian store at Ramoutsa, and I didn't care how many strange leopards saw it. Nevertheless, I made up my mind that next time I went to lie on the grass under the withaak, looking for strayed cattle, I would first polish up my veldskoens with sheep's fat, and I would put on my black hat that I only wear to Nagmaal. I could not permit the wild animals of the neighbourhood to sneer at me.

But when the leopard reached my face I got frightened again. I knew he couldn't take exception to my shirt. But I wasn't so sure about my face. Those were terrible moments. I lay very still, afraid to open my eyes and afraid to breathe. Sniff-sniff, the huge creature went, and his breath swept over my face in hot gasps. You hear of many frightening experiences that a man has in a lifetime. I have also been in quite a few perilous situations. But if you want something to make you suddenly old and to turn your hair white in a few moments, there is nothing to beat a leopard – especially when he is standing over you, with his jaws at your throat, trying to find a good place to bite.

The leopard gave a deep growl, stepped right over my body, knocking off my hat, and growled again. I opened my eyes and saw the animal moving away clumsily. But my relief didn't last long. The leopard didn't move far. Instead, he turned over and lay down next to me.

Yes, there on the grass, in the shade of the withaak, the leopard and I lay down together. The leopard lay half-curled up, on his side, with his forelegs crossed, like a dog, and whenever I tried to move away he grunted. I am sure that in the whole history of the Groot Marico there have never been two stranger companions engaged in the thankless task of looking for strayed cattle.

Next day, in Fanie Snyman's voorkamer, which was used as a post office, I told my story to the farmers of the neighbourhood, while they were drinking coffee and waiting for the motor-lorry from Zeerust.

"And how did you get away from that leopard in the end?" Koos van Tonder asked, trying to be funny. "I suppose you crawled through the grass and frightened the leopard off by pretending to be a python."

"No, I just got up and walked home," I said. "I remembered that the cattle I was looking for might have gone the other way and strayed into your kraal. I thought they would be safer with the leopard."

"Did the leopard tell you what he thought of General Pienaar's last speech in the Volksraad?" Frans Welman asked, and they all laughed.

I told my story over several times before the lorry came with our letters, and although the dozen odd men present didn't say much while I was talking, I could see that they listened to me in the same way that they listened when Krisjan Lemmer talked. And everybody knew that Krisjan Lemmer was the biggest liar in the Bushveld.

To make matters worse, Krisjan Lemmer was there, too, and when I got to the part of my story where the leopard lay down beside me, Krisjan Lemmer winked at me. You know that kind of wink. It was to let me know that there was now a new understanding between us, and that we could speak in future as one Marico liar to another.

I didn't like that.

"Kêrels," I said in the end, "I know just what you are thinking. You don't believe me, and you don't want to say so."

"But we do believe you," Krisjan Lemmer interrupted me, "very wonderful things happen in the Bushveld. I once had a twenty-foot mamba that I named Hans. This snake was so attached to me that

I couldn't go anywhere without him. He would even follow me to church on a Sunday, and because he didn't care much for some of the sermons, he would wait for me outside under a tree. Not that Hans was irreligious. But he had a sensitive nature, and the strong line that the predikant took against the serpent in the Garden of Eden always made Hans feel awkward. Yet he didn't go and look for a withaak to lie under, like your leopard. He wasn't stand-offish in that way. An ordinary thorn-tree's shade was good enough for Hans. He knew he was only a mamba, and didn't try to give himself airs."

I didn't take any notice of Krisjan Lemmer's stupid lies, but the upshot of this whole affair was that I also began to have doubts about the existence of that leopard. I recalled queer stories I had heard of human beings that could turn themselves into animals, and although I am not a superstitious man I could not shake off the feeling that it was a spook thing that had happened. But when, a few days later, a huge leopard had been seen from the roadside near the poort, and then again by Mtosas on the way to Nietverdiend, and again in the turf-lands near the Molopo, matters took a different turn.

At first people jested about this leopard. They said it wasn't a real leopard, but a spotted animal that had walked away out of Schalk Lourens's dream. They also said that the leopard had come to the Dwarsberge to have a look at Krisjan Lemmer's twenty-foot mamba. But afterwards, when they had found his spoor at several waterholes, they had no more doubt about the leopard.

It was dangerous to walk about in the veld, they said. Exciting times followed. There was a great deal of shooting at the leopard and a great deal of running away from him. The amount of Martini and Mauser fire I heard in the krantzes reminded me of nothing so much as the First Boer War. And the amount of running away reminded me of nothing so much as the Second Boer War.

But always the leopard escaped unharmed. Somehow, I felt sorry for him. The way he had first sniffed at me and then lain down beside me that day under the withaak was a strange thing that I couldn't understand. I thought of the Bible, where it is written that the lion shall lie down with the lamb.

But I also wondered if I hadn't dreamt it all. The manner in which those things had befallen me was all so unearthly. The leopard began to take up a lot of my thoughts. And there was no man to whom I could talk about it who would be able to help me in any way. Even now, as I am telling you this story, I am expecting you to wink at me, like Krisjan Lemmer did.

Still, I can only tell you the things that happened as I saw them, and what the rest was about only Africa knows.

It was some time before I again walked along the path that leads through the bush to where the withaaks are. But I didn't lie down on the grass again. Because when I reached the place, I found that the leopard had got there before me. He was lying on the same spot, half-curled up in the withaak's shade, and his forepaws were folded as a dog's are, sometimes. But he lay very still. And even from the distance where I stood I could see the red splash on his breast where a Mauser bullet had gone.

Marico Moon

I BUTTONED UP MY JACKET because of the night wind that came whistling through the thorn-trees (Oom Schalk Lourens said); my fingers on the reins were stiff with the cold.

There were four of us in the mule-cart, driving along the Government Road on our way back from the dance at Withaak. I sat in front with Dirk Prinsloo, a young school-teacher. In the back were Petrus Lemmer and his sister's step-daughter, Annie.

Petrus Lemmer was an elder in the Dutch Reformed Church. He told us that he was very strongly opposed to parties, because people got drunk at parties, and all sorts of improper things happened. He had only gone to the dance at Withaak, he said, because of Annie. He explained that he had to be present to make quite sure that nothing unseemly took place at a dance that his sister's step-daughter went to.

We all thought that it was very fine of Petrus Lemmer to sacrifice his own comfort in that way. And we were very glad when he said that this was one of the most respectable dances he had ever attended.

He said that at two o'clock in the morning. But before that he had said a few other things of so unusual a character that all the women walked out. And they only came back a little later on, after a number of young men had helped Petrus Lemmer out through the front door. One of the young men was Dirk Prinsloo, the school-teacher, and I noticed that there was quite a lot of peach brandy on his clothes. The peach brandy had come out of a big glass that Petrus Lemmer had in his hand, and when he went out of the door he was still saying how glad he was that this was not an improper party, like others he had seen.

Shortly afterwards Petrus Lemmer fell into the dam, backwards. And when they pulled him out he was still holding on to the big glass, very tightly. But when he put the glass to his mouth he said that what was in it tasted to him a lot like water. He threw the glass away, then.

So it came about that, in the early hours of the morning, there were four of us driving along the road back from Withaak. Petrus Lemmer had wanted to stay longer at the dance, after they had pulled him out of the dam and given him a dry pair of trousers and a shirt. But they said, no, it wasn't right that he should go on sacrificing himself like that. Petrus Lemmer said that was nothing. He was willing to sacrifice himself a lot more. He said he would go on sacrificing himself until the morning, if necessary, to make quite sure that nothing disgraceful took place at the dance. But the people said there was no need for him to stay any longer. Nothing more disgraceful could happen than what had already happened, they said.

At first, Petrus Lemmer seemed pleased at what they said. But afterwards he grew a bit more thoughtful. He still appeared to be thinking about it when a number of young men, including Dirk Prinsloo, helped him on to my mule-cart, heavily. His sister's step-daughter, Annie, got into the back seat beside him. Dirk Prinsloo came and sat next to me.

It was a cold night, and the road through the bush was very long. The house where Dirk Prinsloo boarded was the first that we would come to. It was a long way ahead. Then came Petrus Lemmer's farm, several miles further on. I had the longest distance to go of us all.

In between shivering, Petrus Lemmer said how pleased he was that nobody at the dance had used really bad language.

"Nobody except you, Uncle," Annie said then.

Petrus Lemmer explained that anybody was entitled to forget himself a little, after having been thrown into the dam, like he was.

"You weren't thrown, Uncle," Annie said. "You fell in."

"Thrown," Petrus persisted.

"Fell," Annie repeated firmly.

Petrus said that she could have it her way, if she liked. It was no use arguing with a woman, he explained. Women couldn't understand reason, anyway. But what he maintained strongly was that, if you were wet right through, and standing in the cold, you might perhaps say a few things that you wouldn't say ordinarily.

"But even before you fell in the dam, Uncle," Annie went on, "you used bad language. The time all the women walked out. It was awful language. And you said it just for nothing, too. You ought to be ashamed of yourself, Uncle. And you an elder in the Reformed Church."

But Petrus Lemmer said that was different. He said that if he hadn't been at the dance he would like to know what would have happened. That was all he wanted to know. Young girls of today had no sense of gratitude. It was only for Annie's sake that he had come to the dance in the first place. And then they went and threw him into the water.

The moon was big and full above the Dwarsberge; and the wind grew colder; and the stars shone dimly through the thorn-trees that overhung the road.

Then Petrus Lemmer started telling us about other dances he had attended in the Bushveld, long ago. He was a young man, then, he said. And whenever he went to a dance there was a certain amount of trouble. "Just like tonight," he said. He went to lots of dances, and it was always the same thing. They were the scandal of the Marico, those dances he went to. And he said it was no use his exercising his influence, either; people just wouldn't listen to him.

"Influence," Annie said, and I could hear her laughter above the rattling of the mule-cart.

"But there was one dance I went to," Petrus Lemmer continued, "on a farm near Abjaterskop. That was very different. It was a quiet sort of dance. And it was different in every way."

Annie said that perhaps it was different because they didn't have a dam on that farm. But Petrus Lemmer replied, in a cold kind of voice, that he didn't know what Annie was hinting at, and that, anyway, she was old enough to have more sense.

"It was mainly because of Grieta," Petrus Lemmer said, "that I went to that dance at Abjaterskop. And I believed that it was because she hoped to see me there that Grieta went."

Annie said something about this, also. I couldn't hear what it was. But this time Petrus Lemmer ignored her.

"There were not very many people at this dance," he went on. "A large number who had been invited stayed away."

"It seems that other people besides Grieta knew you were going to that dance, Uncle," Annie remarked then.

"It was because of the cold," Petrus Lemmer said shortly. "It was a cold night, just like it is tonight. I wore a new shirt with stripes and I rubbed sheep-fat on my veldskoens, to make them shine. At first I thought it was rather foolish, my taking all this trouble over my appearance, for the sake of a girl whom I had seen only a couple of times. But when I got to the farmhouse at Abjaterskop, where the dance was, and I saw Grieta in the voorkamer, I no longer thought it was foolish of me to get all dressed up like that."

Petrus Lemmer fell silent for a few moments, as though waiting for one of us to say what an interesting story it was, and would he tell us what happened next. But none of us said anything. So Petrus just coughed and went on with his story without being asked. That was the sort of man Petrus Lemmer was.

"I saw Grieta in the voorkamer," Petrus Lemmer repeated, "and she had on a pink frock. She was very pretty. Even now, after all these years, when I look back on it, I can still picture to myself how pretty she was. For a long time I stood at the far end of the room and just watched her. Another young man was wasting her time, talking to her. Afterwards he wasted still more of her time by dancing with her. If it wasn't that I knew that I was the only one in that voorkamer that Grieta cared for, I would have got jealous of the way in which that young fellow carried on. And he kept getting more and more foolish. But afterwards I got tired of standing up against that wall and watching

Grieta from a distance. So I sat down on a chair, next to the two men with the guitar and the concertina. For some time I sat and watched Grieta from the chair. By then that fellow was actually wasting her time to the extent of tickling her under the chin with a piece of grass."

Petrus Lemmer stopped talking again, and we listened to the bumping of the mule-cart and the wind in the thorn-trees. The moon was large and full above the Dwarsberge.

"But how did you know that this girl liked you, Oom Petrus?" Dirk Prinsloo asked. It seemed as though the young school-teacher was getting interested in the story.

"Oh, I just knew," Petrus Lemmer replied. "She never said anything to me about it, but with these things you can always tell."

"Yes, I expect you can," Annie said softly, in a far-away sort of voice. And she asked Petrus Lemmer to tell us what happened next.

"It was just like I said it was," Petrus Lemmer continued. "And shortly afterwards Grieta left that foolish young man, with his piece of grass and all, and came past the chair where I was sitting, next to the musicians. She walked past me quickly, and what she said wasn't much above a whisper. But I heard all right. And I didn't even bother to look up and see whether that other fellow had observed anything. I felt so superior to him, at that moment."

Once again Petrus Lemmer paused. But it was obvious that Annie wanted him to get to the end of the story quickly.

"Then did you go and meet Grieta, Oom Petrus?" she asked.

"Oh, yes," Petrus answered. "I was there at the time she said."

"By the third withaak?" Annie asked again. "Under the moon?"

"By the third withaak," Petrus Lemmer replied. "Under the moon."

I wondered how Annie knew all that. In some ways there seemed little that a woman didn't know.

"There's not much more to tell," Petrus Lemmer said. "And I could never understand how it happened, either. It was just that, when I met Grieta there, under the thorn-tree, it suddenly seemed that there was nothing I wanted to say to her. And I could see that she felt the same way about it. She seemed just an ordinary woman, like lots of other women. And I felt rather foolish, standing there beside her, wearing a new striped shirt, and with sheep-fat on my veldskoens. And I knew just how she felt, also. At first I tried to pretend to myself that it was the fault of the moon. Then I blamed that fellow with the piece of grass. But I knew all the time that it was nobody's fault. It just happened like that.

"As I have said," Petrus Lemmer concluded sombrely, "I don't know how it came about. And I don't think Grieta knew, either. We stood there wondering – each of us – what it was that had been, a little while before, so attractive about the other. But whatever it was, it had gone. And we both knew that it had gone for good. Then I said that it was getting cold. And Grieta said that perhaps we had better go inside. So we went back to the voorkamer. It seemed an awfully quiet party, and I didn't stay much longer. And I remember how, on my way home, I looked at the moon under which Grieta and I had stood by the thorn-tree. I watched the moon until it went down behind the Dwarsberge."

Petrus Lemmer finished his story, and none of us spoke.

Some distance further on we arrived at the place where Dirk Prinsloo stayed. Dirk got off the mule-cart and said good night. Then he turned to Annie.

"It's funny," he said, "this story of your uncle's. It's queer how things like that happen."

"He's not my uncle," Annie replied. "He's only my stepmother's brother. And I never listen to his stories, anyway."

So we drove on again, the three of us, down the road, through the thorn-trees, with the night wind blowing into our faces. And a little later, when the moon was going down behind the Dwarsberge, it sounded to me as though Annie was crying.

THE STORY OF HESTER VAN WYK

WHEN I THINK OF THE STORY OF Hester van Wyk I often wonder what it is about some stories that I have wanted to tell (Oom Schalk Lourens said). About things that have happened and about people that I have known – and that I still know, some of them; if you can call it knowing a person when your mule-carts pass each other on the Government Road, and you wave your hat cheerfully and call out that it will be a good season for the crops, if only the stalk-borers and other pests keep away, and the other person just nods at you, with a distant sort of a look in his eyes, and says, yes, the Marico Bushveld has unfortunately got more than one kind of pest.

That was what Gawie Steyn said to me one afternoon on the Government Road, when I was on my way to the Drogedal post office for letters and he was on his way home. And it was because of the sorrowful sort of way in which he uttered the word 'unfortunately' that I knew that Gawie Steyn had heard what I had said about him to Frik Prinsloo three weeks before, after the meeting of the Dwarsberg debating society in the schoolroom next to the poort.

In any case, I never finished that story that I told Frik Prinsloo about Gawie Steyn, although I began telling it colourfully enough that night after the meeting of the debating society was over and the farmers and their wives and children had all gone home, and Frik Prinsloo and I were sitting alone on two desks in the middle of the schoolroom, with our feet up, and our pipes pleasantly filled with strong plug-cut tobacco whose thick blue fumes made the school-teacher cough violently at intervals.

The schoolmaster was seated at the table, with his head in his hands, and his face looking very pale in the light of the one paraffin lamp. And he was waiting for us to leave so that he could blow out his lamp and lock up the schoolroom and go home.

The schoolmaster did not interrupt us only with his coughing but also in other ways. For instance, he told us on several occasions that he had a weak chest, and if we had made up our minds to stay on like this in the classroom, talking, after the meeting was over, would we mind very much, he asked, if he opened one of the windows to let out some of the blue clouds of tobacco smoke.

But Frik Prinsloo said that we would mind very much. Not for our sakes, Frik said, but for the schoolmaster's sake. There was nothing worse, Frik explained, than for a man with a weak chest to sit in a room with a window open.

"It is nothing for us," Frik Prinsloo said, "for Schalk Lourens and myself to sit in a room with an open window. We are two Bushveld farmers with sturdy physiques who have been through the Boer War and through the anthrax pestilence. We have survived not only human hardships, but also cattle and sheep and pig diseases. At Magersfontein I even slept in an aardvark hole that was half-full of water with a piece of newspaper tied around my left ankle for the rheumatism. And even so neither Schalk Lourens nor I will be so foolish as to be in a room that has got a window open."

"No," I agreed. "Never."

"And you have to take greater care of your health than any of us," Frik Prinsloo said to the school-teacher. "With your weak chest it would be dangerous for you to have a window open in here. Why, you can't even stand our tobacco smoke. Look at the way you are coughing right now."

After he had knocked the ash out of his pipe into an inkwell that was let into a little round hole in one of the desks, an action which he had performed just in order to show how familiar, for an uneducated man, he was with the ways of a schoolroom, Frik started telling the school-teacher about other places he had slept in, both during the Boer War and at another time when he was doing transport driving.

Frik Prinsloo embarked on a description of the hardships of a transport driver's life in the old days. It was a story that seemed longer than the most ambitious journey ever undertaken by ox-wagon, and much heavier, and more roundabout. And there was one place where Frik Prinsloo's story got stuck much more hopelessly than any of his ox-wagons had ever got stuck in a drift.

Then the schoolmaster said, please, gentlemen, he could not stand it anymore. His health was bad, and while he could perhaps arrange to let us have the use of the schoolroom on some other night, so that I could finish the story that I appeared to be telling to Mr Prinsloo, and he would even provide the paraffin for the lamp himself, he really had to go home and get some sleep.

But Frik Prinsloo said the schoolmaster did not need to worry about the paraffin. We could sit just as comfortably in the dark and talk, he said. For that matter, the schoolmaster could go to sleep in the classroom, if he liked. Just like that, sitting at the table.

"You already look half asleep," Frik told him, winking at me, "and sleeping in a schoolroom is a lot better than what happened to me during the English advance on Bloemfontein, when I slept in a donga with a lot of slime and mud and slippery tadpoles at the bottom. . . "

"In a donga half-full of water with a piece of mealie-sacking fastened around your stomach because of the colic," the school-teacher said, speaking with his head still between his hands. "And for heaven's sake, if you have got to sleep out on the veld, why don't you sleep on top of it? Why must you go and lie inside a hole full of water or inside a slimy donga? If you farmers have had hard lives, it seems to me that you yourselves did quite a lot to make them like that."

We ignored this remark of the schoolmaster's, which we both realised was based on his lack of worldly experience, and I went on to relate to Frik Prinsloo those incidents from the life of Gawie Steyn that were responsible for Gawie's talking about Marico pests, some weeks later, in gloomy tones, on the road winding between the thorn-trees to the post office.

And this was one of those stories that I never finished. Because the schoolmaster fell asleep at his table, with the result that he didn't cough anymore, and I could see that because of this Frik Prinsloo could not derive the same amount of amusement from my story. And what is even more strange is that I also found that the funny parts in the story did not sound so funny anymore, now that the schoolmaster was no longer in discomfort. The story seemed to have had much more life in it, somehow, in the earlier stages, when the schoolmaster was anxiously waiting for us to go home, and coughing at intervals through the blue haze of our tobacco smoke.

"And so that man came round again the next night and sang some more songs to Gawie Steyn's wife," I said, "and they were old songs that he sang."

"It sounds to me as though he is even snoring," Frik Prinsloo said. "Imagine that for ill-bred. Here are you telling a story that teaches one all about the true and deep things of life and the schoolmaster is lying with his head on the table, snoring."

"And when Gawie Steyn started objecting after a while," I continued, with a certain amount of difficulty, "the man said the excuse he had to offer was that they were all old songs, anyway, and they didn't mean very much. Old songs had no meaning. They were only dead things from the past. They were yellowed and dust-laden, the man said."

"I've got a good mind to wake him," Frik Prinsloo went on. "First he disturbs us with his coughing and now I can't hear what you're saying because of his snoring. It will be a good thing if we just go home now and leave him. He seems so attached to his old schoolroom. Even staying behind at night to sleep in it. What would people say if I liked ploughing so much that I didn't go home at night, but just lay down and slept on a strip of grass next to a furrow?"

"Then Gawie Steyn said to this man," I continued, with greater difficulty than ever before, "he said that it wasn't so much the old songs he objected to. The old songs might be well enough. But the way his wife listened to the songs, he said, seemed to him to be not so much like an old song as like an old story."

“Not that I don’t sleep out on the lands sometimes,” Frik Prinsloo explained, “and even in the ploughing season. But then it is the early afternoon of a hot day. And the kaffirs go on with the ploughing all the same. And it is very refreshing, then, to sleep under a withaak tree knowing that the kaffirs are at work in the sun. Sleeping on a strip of green grass next to a furrow . . . ”

“Or inside the furrow,” the schoolmaster said, and we only noticed then that he was no longer snoring. “Inside a furrow half filled with wet fertiliser and with a turnip fastened on your head because of the blue tongue.”

As I have said, this story about Gawie Steyn and his wife is one of those stories that I never finished telling. And I would never have known, either, that Frik Prinsloo had listened to as much of it as I had told him, if it wasn’t for Gawie Steyn’s manner of greeting me on the Government Road, three weeks later, with sorrowful politeness, like an Englishman.

There is always something unusual about a story that does not come to an end on its own. It is as though that story keeps going on, getting told in a different way each time, as though the story itself is trying to find out what happened next.

It was like the way life came to Hester van Wyk.

Hester was a very pretty girl, with black hair and a way of smiling that seemed very childlike, until you were close enough to her to see what was in her eyes, and then you realised, in that same moment, that no child had ever smiled like that. And whether it was for her black hair or whether it was because of her smile, it so happened that Hester van Wyk was hardly ever without a lover. They came to her, the young men from the neighbourhood. But they also went away again. They tarried for a while, like birds in their passage, and they paid court to her, and sometimes the period in which they wooed her was quite long, and at other times again she would have a lover whose ardour seemed to last for no longer than a few brief weeks before he also went his way.

And it seemed that the story of Hester van Wyk and her lovers was also one of those stories that I have mentioned to you, whose end never gets told.

And Gert van Wyk, Hester's father, would talk to me about these young men that came into his daughter's life. He talked to me both as a neighbour and as a relative on his wife's side, and while what he said to me about Hester and her lovers were mostly words spoken lightly, in the way that you flick a pebble into a dam, and watch the yellow ripples widening, there were also times when he spoke differently. And then what he said was like the way a footsore wanderer flings his pack on to the ground.

"She's a pretty girl," Gert said to me. "Yes, she is pretty enough. But her trouble is that she is too soft-hearted. These young men come to her, and they tell her stories. Sad stories about their lives. And she listens to their stories. And she feels sorry for them. And she says that they must be very nice young men for life to have treated them so badly. She even tries to tell me some of these stories, so that I should also feel sorry for them. But, of course, I have got too much sense to listen. I simply tell her – "

"Yes," I answered, nodding, "you tell her that what the young man says is a lot of lies. And by the time you have convinced her about one lover's lies you find that he has already departed, and that some other young man has got into the habit of coming to your house three times a week, and that he is busy telling her a totally new and different story."

"That's what he imagines," Gert van Wyk replied, "that it's new. But it's always the same old story. Only, instead of telling of his unhappy childhood the new young man will talk about his aged mother, or about how life has been cruel to him, so that he has got to help on the farm, for which he isn't suited at all, because it makes him dizzy to have to pump water out of the borehole for the cattle – up and down, up and down, like that, with the pump-handle – when all the time his real ambition is to have the job of wearing a blue and gold uniform outside of a bioscope in Johannesburg. And my daughter Hester is so soft-hearted that she goes on listening to these same stupid stories day after day, year in and year out."

"Yes," I said, "they are the same old stories."

And I thought of what Gawie Steyn said about the man who sang old songs to his wife. And it seemed that Hester van Wyk's was also an old story, and that for that reason it would never end.

"Did she also have a young man who said that he was not worthy of her because he was not educated?" I asked Gert. "And did she take pity on him because he said people looked down on him because of his table manners?"

"Yes," Gert answered with alacrity, "he said he was badly brought up and always forgot to take the teaspoon out of the cup before drinking his coffee."

"Did she also have a young man who got her sympathy by telling her that he had fallen in love years ago, and that he had lost that girl, because her parents had objected to him, and that he could never fall in love again?"

"Quite right," Gert said. "This young man said that his first girl's parents refused to let her marry him because his forehead was too low. Even though he tried to make it look higher by training his eyebrows down and shaving the hair off most of the top of his head. But how do you know all these things?"

"There are only a few stories that young men tell girls in order to get their sympathy," I said to Gert. "There are only a handful of stories like that. But it seems to me that your daughter Hester has been told them all. And more than once, too, sometimes, by the look of it."

"And you can imagine how awful that young man with the low forehead looked," Gert continued. "He must have been unattractive enough before. But with his eyebrows trained down and the top of his head shaved clean off, he looked more like a – "

"And for that very reason, of course," I explained, "your daughter Hester fell in love with him. After she had heard his story."

And it seemed to me that the oldest story of all must be the story of a woman's heart.

It was some years after this, when Gert van Wyk and his family had moved out of the Marico into the Waterberg, that I heard that Hester van Wyk had married. And I knew then what had happened, of course. And I knew it even without Gert having had to tell me.

I knew then that some young man must have come to Hester van Wyk from out of some far-lying part of the Waterberg. He came to her and found her. And in finding her he had no story to tell.

But what I have no means of telling, now that I have related to you all that I know, is whether this is the end of the story about Hester van Wyk.

THE SELON'S ROSE

ANY STORY (Oom Schalk Lourens said) about that half-red flower, the selon's rose, must be an old story. It is the flower that a Marico girl most often pins in her hair to attract a lover. The selon's rose is also the flower that here, in the Marico, we customarily plant upon a grave.

One thing that certain thoughtless people sometimes hint at about my stories is that nothing ever seems to happen in them. Then there is another kind of person who goes even further, and *he* says that the stories I tell are all stories that he has heard before, somewhere, long ago – he can't remember when, exactly, but somewhere at the back of his mind he knows that it is not a new story.

I have heard that remark passed quite often – which is not surprising, seeing that I really don't know any new stories. But the funny part of it is that these very people will come around, say, ten years later, and ask me to tell them another story. And they will say, then, because of what they have learnt of life in between, that the older the better.

Anyway, I have come to the conclusion that with an old story it is like with an old song. People tire of a new song readily. I remember how it was when Marie Dupreez came back to the Bushveld after her parents had sent her overseas to learn singing, because they had found diamonds on their farm, and because Marie's teacher said she had a nice singing voice. Then, when Marie came back from Europe – through the diamonds on the Dupreez farm having given out suddenly – we on this side of the Dwarsberge were keen to have Marie sing for us.

There was a large attendance, that night, when Marie Dupreez gave a concert in the Drogedal schoolroom. She sang what she called arias from Italian opera. And at first things didn't go at all well. We didn't care much for those new songs in Italian. One song was about the dawn being near, goodbye beloved and about being under somebody's window – that was what Marie's mother told us it was.

Marie Dupreez's mother came from the Cape and had studied at the Wellington seminary. Another song was about mother see these tears. The Hollander schoolmaster told me the meaning of that one. But I didn't know if it was Marie's mother that was meant.

We didn't actually dislike those songs that Marie Dupreez sang. It was only that we weren't moved by them.

Accordingly, after the interval, when Marie was again stepping up on the low platform before the blackboard on which the teacher wrote sums on school days, Philippus Bonthuys, a farmer who had come all the way from Nietverdiend to attend the concert, got up and stood beside Marie Dupreez. And because he was so tall and broad it seemed almost as though he stood half in front of her, elbowing her a little, even.

Philippus Bonthuys said that he was just a plain Dopper. And we all cheered. Then Philippus Bonthuys said that his grandfather was also just a plain Dopper, who wore his pipe and his tobacco-bag on a piece of string fastened at the side of his trousers. We cheered a lot more, then. Philippus Bonthuys went on to say that he liked the old songs best. They could keep those new songs about laugh because somebody has stolen your clown. We gathered from this that Marie's mother had been explaining to Philippus Bonthuys, also, in quick whispers, the meanings of some of Marie's songs.

And before we knew where we were, the whole crowd in the schoolroom was singing, with Philippus Bonthuys beating time, "My Oupa was 'n Dopper, en 'n Dopper was Hy." You've got no idea how stirring that old song sounded, with Philippus Bonthuys beating time, in the night, under the thatch of that Marico schoolroom, and with Marie Dupreez looking slightly bewildered but joining in all the same – since it was her concert, after all – and not singing in Italian, either.

We sang many songs, after that, and they were all old songs. We sang "Die Vaal Hare en die Blou Oge" and "Daar Waar die Son en die Maan Ondergaan" and "Vat Jou Goed en Trek, Ferreira" and "Met My Rooi Rok Voor Jou Deur." It was very beautiful.

We sang until late into the night. Afterwards, when we congratulated Marie Dupreez's mother, who had arranged it all, on the success of her daughter's concert, Mevrou Dupreez said it was nothing, and she smiled. But it was a peculiar sort of smile.

I felt that she must have smiled very much the same way when she was informed that the diamond mine on the Dupreez farm was only an alluvial gravel-bed, and not a pipe, like in Kimberley.

Now, Marie Dupreez had not been out of the Marico very long. All told, I don't suppose she had been in Europe for more than six months before the last shovelful of diamondiferous gravel went through Dupreez's sieve. By the time she got back, her father was so desperate that he was even trying to sift ordinary Transvaal red clay. But Marie's visit overseas had made her restive.

That, of course, is something that I can't understand. I have also been to foreign parts. During the Boer War I was a prisoner on St. Helena. And I was twice in Johannesburg. And one thing about St. Helena is that there are no Uitlanders on it. There were just Boers and English and Coloureds and Indians, like you come across here in the Marico. There were none of those all-sorts that you've got to push past on Johannesburg pavements. And each time I got back to my own farm, and I could sit on my stoep and fill my pipe with honest Magaliesberg tobacco, I was pleased to think I was away from all that sin that you read about in the Bible.

But with Marie Dupreez it was different.

Marie Dupreez, after she came back from Europe, spoke a great deal about how unhappy a person with a sensitive nature could be over certain aspects of life in the Marico.

We were not unwilling to agree with her.

"When I woke up that morning at Nietverdiend," Willie Prinsloo said to Marie during a party at the Dupreez homestead, "and I found that I couldn't inspan my oxen because during the night the Mlapi kaffirs had stolen my trek-chain – well, to a person with a sensitive nature, I can't tell you how unhappy I felt about the Marico."

Marie said that was the sort of thing that made her ill, almost.

"It's always the same kind of conversation that you have to listen to, day in and day out," Marie Dupreez said. "A farmer outspans his oxen for the night. And next morning, when he has to move on, the kaffirs have stolen his trek-chain. I don't know how often I have heard that same story. Why can't something different ever happen? Why can't a kaffir think of stealing something else, for a change?"

"Yes," Jurie Bekker interjected, quickly, "why can't they steal a clown, say?"

Thereupon Marie explained that it was not a clown that had got stolen in that Italian song that she sang in the schoolroom, but a girl who had belonged to a clown. And so several of us said, speaking at the same time, that she couldn't have been much of a girl, anyway, belonging to a clown. We said we might be behind the times and so forth, here in the Bushveld, but we had seen clowns in the circus in Zeerust, and we could imagine what a clown's girl must be like, with her nose painted all red.

I must admit, however, that we men enjoyed Marie's wild talk. We preferred it to her singing, anyway. And the women also listened quite indulgently.

Shortly afterwards Marie Dupreez made a remark that hurt me, a little.

"People here in the Marico say all the same things over and over again," Marie announced. "Nobody ever says anything new. You all talk just like the people in Oom Schalk Lourens's stories. Whenever we have visitors it's always the same thing. If it's a husband and wife, it will be the man who first starts talking. And he'll say that Afrikaner cattle are in a bad way with the heart-water. Even though he drives his cattle straight out on to the veld with the first frost, and he keeps to regular seven-day dipping, he just can't get rid of the heart-water ticks."

Marie Dupreez paused. None of us said anything, at first. I only know that for myself I thought this much: I thought that, even though I dip my cattle only when the Government inspector from Onderstepoort is in the neighbourhood, I still lose just as many Afrikaner beasts from the heart-water as any of the farmers hereabouts who go in for the seven-day dipping.

"They should dip the Onderstepoort inspector every seven days," Jurie Bekker called out suddenly, expressing all our feelings.

"And they should drive the Onderstepoort inspector straight out on to the veld first with the first frost," Willie Prinsloo added.

We got pretty worked up, I can tell you.

"And it's the same with the women," Marie Dupreez went on. "Do they ever discuss books or fashion or music? No. They also talk just like those simple Boer women that Oom Schalk Lourens's head is so full of. They talk about the amount of Kalahari sand that the Indian in the store at Ramoutsa mixed with the last bag of yellow sugar they bought off him. You know, I have heard that same thing so often, I am surprised that there is any sand at all left in the Kalahari desert, the way that Indian uses it all up."

Those of us who were in the Dupreez voorkamer that evening, in spite of our amusement also felt sad at the thought of how Marie Dupreez had altered from her natural self, like a seedling that has been transplanted too often in different kinds of soil.

But we felt that Marie should not be blamed too much. For one thing, her mother had been taught at that woman's college at the Cape. And her father had also got his native knowledge of the soil pretty mixed up, in his own way. It was said that he was by now even trying to find diamonds in the turfgrond on his farm. I could just imagine how *that* must be clogging up his sieves.

"One thing I am glad about, though," Marie said after a pause, "is that since my return from Europe I have not yet come across a

Marico girl who wears a selon's rose in her hair to make herself look more attractive to a young man – as happens time after time in Oom Schalk's stories."

This remark of Marie's gave a new turn to the conversation, and I felt relieved. For a moment I had feared that Marie Dupreez was also becoming addicted to the kind of Bushveld conversation that she complained about, and that she, too, was beginning to say the same thing over and over again.

Several women started talking, after that, about how hard it was to get flowers to grow in the Marico, on account of the prolonged droughts. The most they could hope for was to keep a bush of selon's roses alive near the kitchen door. It was a flower that seemed, if anything, to thrive on harsh sunlight and soapy dishwater and Marico earth, the women said.

Some time later we learnt that Theunis Dupreez, Marie's father, was giving up active farming, because of his rheumatics. We said, of course, that we knew how he had got his rheumatics. Through having spent so much time in all kinds of weather, we said, walking about the vlei in search of a new kind of sticky soil to put through his sieves.

Consequently, Theunis Dupreez engaged a young fellow, Joachem Bonthuys, to come and work on his farm as a bywoner. Joachem was a nephew of Philippus Bonthuys, and I was at the post office when he arrived at Drogedal, on the lorry from Zeerust, with Theunis Dupreez and his daughter, Marie, there to meet him.

Joachem Bonthuys's appearance was not very prepossessing, I thought. He shook hands somewhat awkwardly with the farmers who had come to meet the lorry to collect their milk-cans. Joachem did not seem to have much to say for himself, either, until Theunis Dupreez, his new employer, asked him what his journey up from Zeerust had been like.

"The veld is dry all the way," he replied. "And I've never seen so much heart-water in Afrikaner herds. They should dip their cattle every seven days."

Joachem Bonthuys spoke at great length, then, and I could not help smiling to myself when I saw Marie Dupreez turn away. In that moment my feelings also grew warmer towards Joachem. I felt that, at all events, he was not the kind of young man who would go and sing foreign songs under a respectable Boer girl's window.

All this brings me back to what I was saying about an old song and an old story. For it was quite a while before I again had occasion to visit the Dupreez farm. And when I sat smoking on the stoep with Theunis Dupreez it was just like an old story to hear him talk about his rheumatics.

Marie came out on to the stoep with a tray to bring us our coffee. – Yes, you've heard all that before, the same sort of thing. The same stoep. The same tray. – And for that reason, when she held the glass bowl out towards me, Marie Dupreez apologised for the yellow sugar.

"It's full of Kalahari sand, Oom Schalk," she said. "It's that Indian at Ramoutsa."

And when she turned to go back into the kitchen, leaving the two old men to their stories, it was not difficult for me to guess who the young man was for whom she was wearing a selon's rose pinned in her dark hair.

A Bekkersdal Marathon

At Naudé, who had a wireless set, came into Jurie Steyn's voorkamer, where we were sitting waiting for the railway lorry from Bekkersdal, and gave us the latest news. He said that the newest thing in Europe was that young people there were going in for non-stop dancing. It was called marathon dancing, At Naudé told us, and those young people were trying to break the record for who could remain on their feet longest, dancing.

We listened for a while to what At Naudé had to say, and then we suddenly remembered a marathon event that had taken place in the little dorp of Bekkersdal – almost in our midst, you could say. What was more, there were quite a number of us sitting in Jurie Steyn's post office, who had actually taken part in that non-stop affair, and without knowing that we were breaking records, and without expecting any sort of a prize for it, either.

We discussed that affair at considerable length and from all angles, and we were still talking about it when the lorry came. And we agreed that it had been in several respects an unusual occurrence. We also agreed that it was questionable if we could have carried off things so successfully that day, if it had not been for Billy Robertse.

You see, our organist at Bekkersdal was Billy Robertse. He had once been a sailor and had come to the Bushveld some years before, travelling on foot. His belongings, fastened in a red handkerchief, were slung over his shoulder on a stick. Billy Robertse was journeying in that fashion for the sake of his health. He suffered from an unfortunate complaint for which he had at regular intervals to drink something out of a black bottle that he always carried handy in his jacket pocket.

Billy Robertse would even keep that bottle beside him in the organist's gallery in case of a sudden attack. And if the hymn the predikant gave out had many verses, you could be sure that about halfway through Billy Robertse would bring the bottle up to his mouth, leaning sideways towards what was in it. And he would put several extra twirls into the second part of the hymn.

When he first applied for the position of organist in the Bekkersdal church, Billy Robertse told the meeting of deacons that he had learnt to play the organ in a cathedral in Northern Europe. Several deacons felt, then, that they could not favour his application. They said that the cathedral sounded too Papist, the way Billy Robertse described it, with a dome 300 feet high and with marble apostles. But it was lucky for Billy Robertse that he was able to mention, at the following combined meeting of elders and deacons, that he had also played the piano in a South American dance hall, of which the manager was a Presbyterian. He asked the meeting to overlook his unfortunate past, saying that he had had a hard life, and anybody could make mistakes. In any case, he had never cared much for the Romish atmosphere of the cathedral, he said, and had been happier in the dance hall.

In the end, Billy Robertse got the appointment. But in his sermons for several Sundays after that the predikant, Dominee Welthagen, spoke very strongly against the evils of dance halls. He described those places of awful sin in such burning words that at least one young man went to see Billy Robertse, privately, with a view to taking lessons in playing the piano.

But Billy Robertse was a good musician. And he took a deep interest in his work. And he said that when he sat down on the organist's stool behind the pulpit, and his fingers were flying over the keyboards, and he was pulling out the stops, and his feet were pressing down the notes that sent the deep bass notes through the pipes – then he felt that he could play all day, he said.

I don't suppose he guessed that he would one day be put to the test, however.

It all happened through Dominee Welthagen one Sunday morning going into a trance in the pulpit. And we did not realise that he was in a trance. It was an illness that overtook him in a strange and sudden fashion.

At each service the predikant, after reading a passage from the Bible, would lean forward with his hand on the pulpit rail and give out the number of the hymn we had to sing. For years his manner of conducting the service had been exactly the same. He would say, for instance: "We will now sing Psalm 82, verses 1 to 4." Then he would allow his head to sink forward on to his chest and he would remain rigid, as though in prayer, until the last notes of the hymn died away in the church.

Now, on that particular morning, just after he had announced the number of the psalm, without mentioning what verses, Dominee Welthagen again took a firm grip on the pulpit rail and allowed his head to sink forward on to his breast. We did not realise that he had fallen into a trance of a peculiar character that kept his body standing upright while his mind was a blank. We learnt that only later.

In the meantime, while the organ was playing the opening bars, we began to realise that Dominee Welthagen had not indicated how many verses we had to sing. But he would discover his mistake, we thought, after we had been singing for a few minutes.

All the same, one or two of the younger members of the congregation did titter, slightly, when they took up their hymn-books. For Dominee Welthagen had given out Psalm 119. And everybody knows that Psalm 119 has 176 verses.

This was a church service that will never be forgotten in Bekkersdal.

We sang the first verse and then the second and then the third. When we got to about the sixth verse and the minister still gave no sign that it would be the last, we assumed that he wished us to sing the first eight verses. For, if you open your hymn-book, you'll see that Psalm 119 is divided into sets of eight verses, each ending with the word "Pouse."

We ended the last notes of verse eight with more than an ordinary number of turns and twirls, confident that at any moment Dominee Welthagen would raise his head and let us know that we could sing "Amen."

It was when the organ started up very slowly and solemnly with the music for verse nine that a real feeling of disquiet overcame the congregation. But, of course, we gave no sign of what went on in our minds. We held Dominee Welthagen in too much veneration.

Nevertheless, I would rather not say too much about our feelings, when verse followed verse and Pouse succeeded Pouse, and still Dominee Welthagen made no sign that we had sung long enough, or that there was anything unusual in what he was demanding of us.

After they had recovered from their first surprise, the members of the church council conducted themselves in a most exemplary manner. Elders and deacons tiptoed up and down the aisles, whispering words of reassurance to such members of the congregation, men as well as women, who gave signs of wanting to panic.

At one stage it looked as though we were going to have trouble from the organist. That was when Billy Robertse, at the end of the 34th verse, held up his black bottle and signalled quietly to the elders to indicate that his medicine was finished. At the end of the 35th verse he made signals of a less quiet character, and again at the end of the 36th verse. That was when Elder Landsman tiptoed out of the church and went round to the konsistorie, where the Nagmaal wine was kept. When Elder Landsman came back into the church he had a long black bottle half hidden under his manel. He took the bottle up to the organist's gallery, still walking on tiptoe.

At verse 61 there was almost a breakdown. That was when a message came from the back of the organ, where Koster Claassen and the assistant verger, whose task it was to turn the handle that kept the organ supplied with wind, were in a state near to exhaustion. So it was Deacon Cronjé's turn to go tiptoeing out of the church. Deacon Cronjé was head-warder at the local gaol. When he came back it was with three burly native convicts in striped jerseys, who also went through the church on tiptoe. They arrived just in time to take over the handle from Koster Claassen and the assistant verger.

At verse 98 the organist again started making signals about his medicine. Once more Elder Landsman went round to the konsistorie. This time he was accompanied by another elder and a deacon, and they stayed away somewhat longer than the time when Elder Landsman had gone on his own. On their return the deacon bumped into a small hymn-book table at the back of the church. Perhaps it was because the deacon was a fat, red-faced man, and not used to tiptoeing.

At verse 124 the organist signalled again, and the same three members of the church council filed out to the konsistorie, the deacon walking in front this time.

It was about then that the pastor of the Full Gospel Apostolic Faith Church, about whom Dominee Welthagen had in the past used almost as strong language as about the Pope, came up to the front gate of the church to see what was afoot. He lived near our church and, having heard the same hymn tune being played over and over for about eight hours, he was a very amazed man. Then he saw the door of the konsistorie open, and two elders and a deacon coming out, walking on tiptoe – they having apparently forgotten that they were not in church, then. When the pastor saw one of the elders hiding a black bottle under his manel, a look of understanding came over his features. The pastor walked off, shaking his head.

At verse 152 the organist signalled again. This time Elder Landsman and the other elder went out alone. The deacon stayed behind on the deacon's bench, apparently in deep thought. The organist signalled again, for the last time, at verse 169. So you can imagine how many visits the two elders made to the konsistorie altogether.

The last verse came, and the last line of the last verse. This time it had to be "Amen." Nothing could stop it. I would rather not describe the state that the congregation was in. And by then the three native convicts, red stripes and all, were, in the Bakhatla tongue, threatening mutiny. "Aa-m-e-e-n" came from what sounded like less than a score of voices, hoarse with singing.

The organ music ceased.

Maybe it was the sudden silence that at last brought Dominee Welthagen out of his long trance. He raised his head and looked slowly about him. His gaze travelled over his congregation and then, looking at the windows, he saw that it was night. We understood right away what was going on in Dominee Welthagen's mind. He thought he had just come into the pulpit, and that this was the beginning of the evening service. We realised that, during all the time we had been singing, the predikant had been in a state of unconsciousness.

Once again Dominee Welthagen took a firm grip of the pulpit rail. His head again started drooping forward on to his breast. But before he went into a trance for the second time, he gave out the hymn for the evening service. "We will," Dominee Welthagen announced, "sing Psalm 119."

Local Colour

We were talking about the book-writing man, Gabriel Penzhorn, who was in the Marico on a visit, wearing a white helmet above his spectacles and with a notebook and a fountain pen below his spectacles. He had come to the Marico to get local colour and atmosphere, he said, for his new South African novel. What was wrong with his last novel, it would seem, was that it did not have enough local colour and atmosphere in it.

So we told Penzhorn that the best place for him to get atmosphere in these parts was in that kloof other side Lobatse, where that gas came out from. Only last term the school-teacher had taken the children there, and he had explained to them about the wonders of Nature. We said to Gabriel Penzhorn that there was atmosphere for him, all right. In fact, the schoolmaster had told the children that there was a whole gaseous envelope of it. Penzhorn could even collect some of it in a glass jar, with a piece of rubber tubing on it, like the schoolmaster had done.

And as for local colour, well, we said, there was that stretch of blue bush on this side of Abjaterskop, which we called the bloubos. It wasn't really blue, we said, but it only looked blue. All the same, it was the best piece of blue bush we had seen anywhere in the Northern Transvaal. The schoolmaster had brought a piece of that home with him also, we explained.

Gabriel Penzhorn made it clear, however, that that stretch of blue bush was not the sort of local colour he wanted at all. Nor was he much interested in the kind of atmosphere that he could go and collect in a bottle with a piece of rubber tubing, just from other side Lobatse.

From that we could see that Gabriel Penzhorn was particular. We did not blame him for it, of course. We realised that if it was things that a writer had to put into a book, then only the best could be good enough. Nevertheless, since most of us had been born in the Marico, and we took pride in our district, we could not help feeling just a little hurt.

"As far as I can see," Johnny Coen said to us one day in Jurie Steyn's post office, "what this book-writing man wants is not atmosphere, but stinks. Perhaps that's the sort of books he writes. I wonder. Have they got pictures in, does anybody know?"

But nobody knew.

"Well, if it's stinks that Penzhorn wants," Johnny Coen proceeded, "just let him go and stand on the siding at Ottoshoop when they open a truck of Bird Island guano. Phew! He won't even need a glass jar to collect that sort of atmosphere in. He can just hold his white helmet in his hand and let a few whiffs of guano atmosphere *float* into it. But if he puts a white helmetful of that kind of atmosphere into his next book, I think the police will have something to say."

Oupa Bekker looked reflective. At first we thought that he hadn't been following much of our conversation, since it was intellectual, having to do with books. We knew that Oupa Bekker had led more of an open-air sort of life, having lived in the Transvaal in the old days, when the Transvaal did not set much store on book learning. But to our surprise we found that Oupa Bekker could take part in a talk about culture as well as any of us. What was more, he did not give himself any airs on account of his having this accomplishment, either.

"Stinks?" Oupa Bekker enquired. "Stinks? Well, let me tell you. There never have been any stinks like the kind we had when we were running that tannery on the Molopo River in the rainy season, in the old days. We thought that the water of the Molopo that the flour-mill on the erf next to us didn't use for their water-wheel would be all right for us with our tannery. We didn't need running water. Just ordinary standing water was good enough for us. And when I say standing water, I mean standing. You have got no idea how it stood. And we didn't tan just plain ox-hides and sheepskins, but every kind of skin we could get. Tanning was our business, you understand. We tanned lion and zebra skins along with the elephant and rhinoceros hides. After a while the man who owned the flour-mill couldn't stand it any longer. So he moved higher up the river. And if I tell you that he was a Bulgarian and he couldn't stand it, that will possibly give you an idea of what that tannery smelt like. Then, one day, a farmer came from the Dwarsberge. . . Yes, they are still the same Dwarsberge, and they haven't changed much with the years. Only, today I can't see as far from the top of the Dwarsberge as I could when I was young. And they look different, also, somehow, with that little whitewashed house no longer in the poort, and with Lettie Gouws no longer standing at the front gate, in an apron with blue squares."

Oupa Bekker paused and sighed. But it was quite a light sigh, that was not so much regret for the past as a tribute to the sweetness of vanished youth.

"Anyway," Oupa Bekker continued, "this farmer from the Dwarsberge brought us a wagon-load of polecat skins. You can imagine what that stink was like. Even before we started tanning them, I mean. Above the smell of the tannery we could smell that load of muishond when the wagon was still fording the drift at Steekgrasvlei. Bill Knoetze – that was my partner – and I felt that this was going slightly too far, even though we were in the tanning business. At first we tried to laugh it off, in the way that we have in the Marico. We tried to pretend to the farmer from the Dwarsberge when he came into the office that we thought it was he that stank like that. And we asked him if he couldn't do something about it. Like getting himself buried, say. But the farmer said no, it wasn't him. It was just his wagon. He made that statement after he had held out his hand for us to shake and Bill Knoetze, before taking the farmer's hand, had play-acted that he was going to faint. And it wasn't just all play-acting either. How he knew that there was something about his wagon, the farmer said, that was peculiar, was through his having passed mule-carts along the road. And he noticed that the mules shied.

"All the same, that was how we came to give up the first tanning business that had ever been set up along the Molopo. Bill Knoetze left after that wagon-load of polecat skins had been in the tanning fluid for about a fortnight. I left a week later. But just before that the Chief of the Mahalapis had come from T'lakieng to find out if we had koedoe leather that he wanted for veldskoens. And when he walked with us through the tannery the Chief of the Mahalapis sniffed the breeze several times, as though trying to make up his mind about something. In the end, the Chief said it would appear to him as though we had a flower garden somewhere near. And he asked could he take a bunch of asters back to his kraal with him for his youngest wife, who had been to mission school and liked such things. It was too dry at T'lakieng for geraniums, the Chief said."

Oupa Bekker was still talking when Gabriel Penzhorn walked into Jurie Steyn's voorkamer. He intended taking the lorry back to civilisation, Penzhorn explained to us. His stay in the Marico had been quite interesting, he said. He didn't say it with enthusiasm, however. And he added that he had not been able to write as many things in his notebook as he had hoped to.

"They all say the same thing," Gabriel Penzhorn proceeded. "I no sooner tell a farmer or his wife that I am a novelist and that I am looking for material to put into my next book, than he or she tells me – sometimes both of them together tell me – about the kind of book that *they* would write if they only had time; or if only they remembered to order some ink, next time they went to the Indian store at Ramoutsa."

He consulted his notes in a dispirited sort of way.

"Yes," Penzhorn went on, "the Indian store at Ramoutsa. Most of the farmers use also another word, I've noticed, in place of Indian. Now, what can one do with material like that? What I want to know are things about the veld. About the ways of the bush and the way the farmers think here. . . I've come to the conclusion that they don't think here."

At Naudé pulled Penzhorn up sharp, then. And he asked him, what with the white ants and galblaas, if he thought a farmer ever got time to think. And he asked him, with the controlled price of mealies 24s. a bag, instead of 24s 9d., as we had all expected, what he thought the Marico farmer had left to think *with*? By that time Fritz Pretorius was telling us, with a wild sort of laugh, about the last cheque he got from the creamery, and Hans van Tonder was saying things about those contour walls that the Agriculture Department man had suggested to stop soil erosion.

"The Agriculture Department man looks like a contour wall himself," Hans van Tonder said, "with those sticking up eyebrows."

Meanwhile, Jurie Steyn was stating, not in any spirit of bitterness, but just as a fact, the exact difference that the new increase in railway tariffs meant to the price of seven-and-a-half-inch piping.

Gabriel Penzhorn closed his notebook.

"I don't mean that sort of talk," he said. "Buying and selling. The low language of barter and the market-place. I can get that sort of talk from any produce merchant in Newtown. Or from any stockbroker I care to drop in on. But I don't care to. What I came here for was – "

That was the moment when Jurie Steyn's wife, having overheard part of our conversation, flounced in from the kitchen.

"And what about eggs?" she demanded. "If I showed you what I pay for bone-meal then you would have something to write in your little notebook. Why should there be all that difference between the retail price of eggs and the price I get? I tell you it's the middlem – "

"Veld lore," Gabriel Penzhorn interrupted, sounding quite savage, now. "That's what I came here for. But I can see you don't know what it is, or anything about it. I want to know about things like the red sky in the morning is the shepherd's warning. Morgen rood, plomp in die sloot. I want to know about how you can tell from the yellowing grass on the edge of a veld footpath that it is going to be an early winter. I want to know about when the tinktinkies fly low over the dam is it going to be a heavy downpour or a slow motreën. I want to know when the wren-warbler – "

"I know if the tinktinkies fly low over my dam, the next thing they'll be doing is sitting high up eating my cling-peaches in the orchard," At Naudé said. "And if that canning factory at Welgevonden ever thinks I'm going to deal with them again . . . "

In the meantime, Jurie Steyn's wife was talking about the time she changed her Leghorns from mealies and skim milk to a standard ration. They went into a six-month moult, Jurie Steyn's wife said.

When the lorry from Groblersdal arrived Hans van Tonder was feeling in his pockets to show us an account he had got only the other day for cement. And Gabriel Penzhorn, in a voice that was almost pathetic, was saying something, over and over again, about the red sky at night.

The driver told us afterwards that on the way back in the lorry Gabriel Penzhorn made a certain remark to him. If we did not know otherwise, we might perhaps have thought that Gabriel Penzhorn had overheard some of the earlier part of our conversation in the voorkamer that morning.

"The Marico," Gabriel Penzhorn said to the lorry-driver, "stinks."

SECRET AGENT

THE STRANGER WHO ARRIVED on the Government lorry from Bekkersdal told us that his name was Losper. He was having a look round that part of the Marico, he said, and he did not expect to stay more than a few days. He was dressed in city clothes and carried a leather briefcase. But because he did not wear pointed black shoes and did not say how sad it was that Flip Prinsloo should have died so suddenly at the age of sixty-eight, of snakebite, we knew that he was not a life insurance agent. Furthermore, because he did not once seek to steer the conversation round to the sinful practices of some people who offered a man a quite substantial bribe when he was just carrying out his duty, we also knew that the stranger was not a plain-clothes man who had been sent round to investigate the increase in cattle-smuggling over the Conventie-lyn. Quite a number of us breathed more easily, then.

Nevertheless, we were naturally intrigued to know what Meneer Losper had come there for. But with the exception of Gysbert van Tonder – who did not have much manners since the time he had accompanied a couple of Americans on safari to the lower reaches of the Limpopo – we were all too polite to ask a man straight out what his business was, and then explain to him how he could do it better.

That trip with the two Americans influenced Gysbert van Tonder's mind, all right. For he came back talking very loudly. And he bought a waistcoat at the Indian store especially so that he could carry a cigar in it. And he spoke of himself as Gysbert O. van Tonder. And he once also slapped Dominee Welthagen on the back to express his appreciation of the Nagmaal sermon Dominee Welthagen had delivered on the Holy Patriarchs and the Prophets.

When Gysbert van Tonder came back from that journey, we understood how right the Voortrekker, Hendrik Potgieter, had been over a hundred years ago, when he said that the parts around the lower end of the Limpopo were no fit place for a white man.

We asked Gysbert van Tonder how that part of the country affected the two Americans. And he said he did not think it affected them much. But it was a queer sort of area, all round, Gysbert explained. And there was a lot of that back-slapping business, too. He said he could still remember how one of the Americans slapped Chief Umfutusu on the back and how Chief Umfutusu, in his turn, slapped the American on the ear with a clay pot full of greenish drink that the chief was holding in his hand at the time.

The American was very pleased about it, Gysbert van Tonder said, and he devoted a lot of space to it in his diary. The American classed Chief Umfutusu's action as among the less understood tribal customs that had to do with welcoming distinguished white travellers. Later on, when Gysbert van Tonder and the Americans came to a Mshangaan village that was having some trouble with hut tax, the American who kept the diary was able to write a lot more about what he called an obscure African ritual that that tribe observed in welcoming a superior order of stranger. For that whole Mshangaan village, men, women and children, had rushed out and pelted Gysbert and the two Americans with wet cow-dung.

In his diary the American compared this incident with the ceremonial greeting that a tribe of Bavendas once accorded the explorer Stanley, when they threw him backwards into a dam – to show respect, as Stanley explained, afterwards.

Well anyway, here was this stranger, Losper, a middle-aged man with a suitcase, sitting in the post office and asking Jurie Steyn if he could put him up in a spare room for a few days, while he had a look round.

"I'll pay the same rates as I paid in the boarding-house in Zeerust," Meneer Losper said. "Not that I think you might overcharge me, of course, but I am only allowed a fixed sum by the department for accommodation and travelling expenses."

“Look here, Neef Losper,” Jurie Steyn said, “you didn’t tell me your first name, so I can only call you Neef Losper – ”

“My first name is Org,” the stranger said.

“Well, then, Neef Org,” Jurie Steyn went on. “From the way you talk I can see that you are unacquainted with the customs of the Groot Marico. In the first place, I am a postmaster and a farmer. I don’t know which is the worst job, what with money orders and the blue-tongue. I have got to put axle-grease on my mule-cart and sealing wax on the mailbag. And sometimes I get mixed up. Any man in my position would. One day I’ll paste a revenue stamp on my off-mule and I’ll brand a half-moon and a bar on the Bekkersdal mailbag. Then there will be trouble. There will be trouble with my off-mule, I mean. The post office won’t notice any difference. But my off-mule is funny, that way. He’ll pull the mule-cart, all right. But then everything has got to be the way *he* wants it. He won’t have people laughing at him because he’s got a revenue stamp stuck on his behind. I sometimes think that my off-mule *knows* that a shilling revenue stamp is what you put on a piece of paper after you’ve told a justice of the peace a lot of lies – ”

“Not lies,” Gysbert van Tonder interjected.

“A lot of lies,” Jurie Steyn went on, “about another man’s cattle straying into a person’s lucerne lands while that person was taking his sick child to Zeerust – ”

Gysbert van Tonder, who was Jurie Steyn’s neighbour, half rose out of his riempies chair, then, and made some sneering remarks about Jurie Steyn and his off-mule. He said he never had much time for either of them. And he said he would not like to describe the way his lucerne lands looked after Jurie Steyn’s cattle had finished straying over them. He said he would not like to use that expression, because there was a stranger present.

Meneer Losper seemed interested, then, and sat well forward to listen. And it looked as though Gysbert van Tonder would have said the words, too. Only, At Naudé, who has a wireless to which he listens in regularly, put a stop to the argument. He said that this was a respectable voorkamer, with family portraits on the wall.

"And there's Jurie Steyn's wife in the kitchen, too," At Naudé said. "You can't use the same sort of language here as in the Volksraad, where there are all men."

Actually, Jurie Steyn's wife had gone out of the kitchen, about then. Ever since that young schoolmaster with the black hair parted in the middle had come to Bekkersdal, Jurie Steyn's wife had taken a good deal of interest in education matters. Consequently, when the stranger, Org Losper, said he was from the department, Jurie Steyn's wife thought right away – judging from his shifty appearance – that he might be a school inspector. And so sent a message to the young schoolmaster to warn him in time, so that he could put away the saws and hammers that he used for the private fretwork that he did in front of the class while the children were writing compositions.

In the meantime, Jurie Steyn was getting to the point.

"So you can't expect me to be running a boarding-house as well as everything else, Neef Org," he was saying. "But all the same, you are welcome to stay. And you can stay as long as you like. Only, you must not offer again to pay. If you had known more about these parts, you would also have known that the Groot Marico has got a very fine reputation for hospitality. When you come and stay with a man he gets insulted if you offer him money. But I shall be glad to invite you into my home as a member of my own family."

Then Org Losper said that that was exactly what he didn't want, any more. And he was firm about it, too.

"When you're a member of the family, you can't say no to anything," he explained. "In the Pilanesberg I tore my best trousers on the wire. I was helping, as a member of the family, to round up the donkeys for the water-cart. At Nietverdiend a Large White bit a piece out of my second-best trousers and my leg. That was when I was a member of the family and was helping to carry buckets of swill to the pig troughs. The farmer said the Large White was just being playful that day. Well, maybe the Large White thought I was also a member of the family – *his* family, I mean. At Abjaterskop I nearly fell into a disused mineshaft on a farm there. Then I was a member of the family, assisting to throw a dead bull down the shaft. The bull had died of anthrax and I was helping to pull him by one haunch and I was walking backwards and when I jumped away from the opening of the mineshaft it was almost too late.

"I can also tell you what happened to me in the Dwarsberge when I was also a member of the family. And also about what happened when I was a member of the family at Derdepoort. I did not know that that family was having a misunderstanding with the family next door about water rights. And it was when I was opening a water furrow with a shovel that a load of buckshot went through my hat. As a member of the family, I was standing ankle-deep in the mud at the time, and so I couldn't run very fast. So you see, when I say I would rather pay, it is not that I am ignorant of the very fine tradition that the Marico has for the friendly and bountiful entertainment that it accords the stranger. But I do not wish to presume further on your kindness. If I have much more Bushveld hospitality I might never see my wife and children again. It's all very well being a member of somebody else's family. But I have a duty to my *own* family. I want to get back to them alive."

Johnny Coen remarked that next time Gysbert van Tonder had an American tourist on his hands, he need not take him to the Limpopo, but could just show him around the Marico farms.

It was then that Gysbert van Tonder asked Org Losper straight out what his business was. And, to our surprise, the stranger was very frank about it.

"It is a new job that has been made for me by the Department of Defence," Org Losper said. "There wasn't that post before. You see, I worked very hard at the last elections, getting people's names taken off the electoral roll. You have no idea how many names I got taken off. I even got some of our candidate's supporters crossed off. But you know how it is, we all make mistakes. It is a very secret post. It is a top Defence secret. I am under oath not to disclose anything about it. But I am free to tell you that I am making certain investigations on behalf of the Department of Defence. I am trying to find out *whether something has been seen here*. But, of course, the post has been made for me, if you understand what I mean."

We said we understood, all right. And we also knew that, since he was under oath about it, the nature of Org Losper's investigations in the Groot Marico would leak out sooner or later.

As it happened, we found out within the next couple of days. A Mahalapi who worked for Adriaan Geel told us. And then we realised how difficult Org Losper's work was. And we no longer envied him his Government job – even though it had been especially created for him.

If you know the Mtosas, you'll understand why Org Losper's job was so hard. For instance, there was only one member of the whole Mtosa tribe who had ever had any close contact with white men. And he had unfortunately grown up among Trekboers, whose last piece of crockery that they had brought with them from the Cape had got broken almost a generation earlier.

We felt that the Department of Defence could have made an easier job for Org Losper than to send him round asking those questions of the Mtosas, they who did not even know what ordinary kitchen saucers were, leave alone flying ones.

White Ant

Jurie Steyn was rubbing vigorously along the side of his counter with a rag soaked in paraffin. He was also saying things which, afterwards, in calmer moments, he would no doubt regret. When his wife came into the voorkamer with a tin of Cooper's dip, Jurie Steyn stopped using that sort of language and contented himself with observations of a general nature about the hardships of life in the Marico.

"All the same, they are very wonderful creatures, those little white ants," the schoolmaster remarked. "Among the books I brought here into the Marico, to read in my spare time, is a book called *The Life of the White Ant*. Actually, of course, the white ant is not a true ant at all. The right name for the white ant is isoptera – "

Jurie Steyn had another, and shorter, name for the white ant right on the tip of his tongue. And he started saying it, too. Only, he remembered his wife's presence, in time, and so he changed the word to something else.

"This isn't the first time the white ants got in behind your counter," At Naudé announced. "The last lot of stamps you sold me had little holes eaten all round the edges."

"That's just perforations," Jurie Steyn replied. "All postage stamps are that way. Next time you have got a postage stamp in your hand, just look at it carefully, and you'll see. There's a law about it, or something. In the department we talk of those little holes as perforations. It is what makes it possible for us, in the department, to tear stamps off easily, without having to use a scissors. Of course, it's not everybody that knows that."

At Naudé looked as much hurt as surprised.

"You mustn't think I am so ignorant, Jurie," he said severely. "Mind you, I am not saying that, perhaps, when this post office was first opened, and you were still new to affairs, and you couldn't be expected to *know* about perforations and things, coming to this job raw, from behind the plough – I'm not saying that you mightn't have cut the stamps loose with a scissors or a No. 3 pruning shears, even. At the start, mind you. And nobody would have blamed you for it, either. I mean, nobody ever has blamed you. We've all, in fact, admired the way you took to this work. I spoke to Gysbert van Tonder about it, too, more than once. Indeed, we both admired you. We spoke about how you stood behind that counter, with kraal manure in your hair, and all, just like you were Postmaster-General. Bold as brass, we said, too."

The subtle flattery in At Naudé's speech served to mollify Jurie Steyn.

"You said all that about me?" he asked. "You did?"

"Yes," At Naudé proceeded smoothly. "And we also admired the neat way you learnt to handle the post office rubber stamp, Gysbert and I. We said you held on to it like it was a branding iron. And we noticed how you would whistle, too, just before bringing the rubber stamp down on a parcel, and how you would step aside afterwards, quickly, just as though you half-expected the parcel to jump up and poke you in the short ribs. To tell you the truth, Jurie, we were *proud* of you."

Jurie Steyn was visibly touched. And so he said that he admitted he had been a bit arrogant in the way he had spoken to At Naudé about the perforations. The white ants had got amongst his postage stamps, Jurie Steyn acknowledged – once. But what they ate you could hardly notice, he said. They just chewed a little around the edges.

But Gysbert van Tonder said that, all the same, that was enough. His youngest daughter was a member of the Sunshine Children's Club of the church magazine in Cape Town, Gysbert said. And his youngest daughter wrote to Aunt Susann, who was the woman editor, to say that it was her birthday. And when Aunt Susann mentioned his youngest daughter's birthday in the Sunshine Club corner of the church magazine, Aunt Susann wrote that she was a little girl staying in the lonely African wilds. *Gramadoelas* was the word that Aunt Susann used, Gysbert van Tonder said. And all just because Aunt Susann had noticed the way that part of the springbok on the stamp on his youngest daughter's letter had been eaten off by white ants, Gysbert van Tonder said.

He added that his daughter had lost all interest in the Sunshine Children's Club, since then. It sounded so uncivilised, the way Aunt Susann wrote about her.

"As though we're living in a grass hut and a string of crocodiles around it, with their teeth showing," Gysbert van Tonder said. "As though it's all still konsessie farms and we haven't made improvements. And it's no use trying to explain to her, either, that she must just feel sorry for Aunt Susann for not knowing any better. You can't explain things like that to a child."

Nevertheless, while we all sympathised with Gysbert van Tonder, we had to concede that it was not in any way Jurie Steyn's fault. We had all had experience of white ants, and we knew that, mostly, when you came along with the paraffin and Cooper's dip, it was too late. By the time you saw those little tunnels, which the white ants made by sticking grains of sand together with spit, all the damage had already been done.

The schoolmaster started talking some more about his book dealing with the life of the white ant, then, and he said that it was well known that the termite was the greatest plague of tropic lands. Several of us were able to help the schoolmaster right. As Chris Welman made it clear to him, the Marico was not in the tropics at all. The tropics were quite a long way up. The tropics started beyond Mochudi, even. A land-surveyor had established that much for us, a few years ago, on a coloured map. It was loose talk about wilds and gramadoelas and tropics that gave the Marico a bad name, we said. Like with that Aunt Susann of the Sunshine Children's Club. Maybe we did have white ants here – lots of them, too – but we certainly weren't in the tropics, like some countries we knew, and that we could mention, also, if we wanted to. Maybe what had happened was that the white ants had come down here *from* the tropics, we said. From way down beyond Mochudi and other side Frik Bonthuys's farm, even. *There* was tropics for you, now, we said to the schoolmaster. Why, he should just see Frik Bonthuys's shirt. Frik Bonthuys wore his shirt outside of his trousers, and the back part of it hung down almost on to the ground.

The schoolmaster said that he thought we were being perhaps just a little too sensitive about this sort of thing. He was interested himself in the white ant, he explained, mainly from the scientific point of view. The white ant belonged to the insect world, that was very highly civilised, he said. All the insect world didn't have was haemoglobin. The insect had the same blood in his veins as a white man, the schoolmaster said, except for haemoglobin.

Gysbert van Tonder said that whatever that thing was, it was enough. Gysbert said it quite hastily, too. He said that when once you started making allowances for the white ant, that way, the next thing the white ant would want would be to vote. And *he* wouldn't go into a polling booth alongside of an ant, to vote, Gysbert van Tonder said, even if that ant was white.

This conversation was getting us out of our depths. The talk had taken a wrong turning, but we couldn't make out where, exactly. Consequently, we were all pleased when Oupa Bekker spoke, and made things seem sensible again.

"The worst piace I ever knew for white ants, in the old days," Oupa Bekker said, "was along the Molopo, just below where it joins the Crocodile River. *There* was white ants for you. I was a transport rider in those days, when all the transport was still by ox-wagon. My partner was Jan Theron. We called him Jan Mankie because of his wooden leg, a back wheel of the ox-wagon having gone over his knee-cap one day when he had been drinking mampoer. Anyway, we had camped out beside the Molopo. And next morning, when we inspanned, Jan Mankie was saying how gay and *light* he felt. He couldn't understand it. He even started thinking that it must be the drink again, that was this time affecting him in quite a new way. We didn't know, of course, that it was because the white ants had hollowed out all of his wooden leg while he had lain asleep.

"And what was still more queer was that the wagon, when he inspanned it, also seemed surprisingly light. It didn't strike us what the reason for that was, either, just then. Maybe we were not in a guessing frame of mind, that morning. But when our trek got through the Paradys Poort, into a stiff wind that was blowing across the vlakte, it all became very clear to us. For the sudden cloud of dust that went up was not just dust from the road. Our wagon and its load of planed Oregon pine were carried away in the finest kind of powder you can imagine, and all our oxen were left pulling was the trek-chain. And Jan Mankie Theron was standing on one leg. His other trouser leg, that was of a greyish coloured moleskin, was flapping empty in the wind."

Thus, Oupa Bekker's factual account of a straightforward Marico incident of long ago, presenting the ways and characteristics of the termite in a positive light, restored us to a sense of current realities.

"But what are you supposed to do about white ants, anyway?" Johnny Coen asked after a while. "Cooper's dip helps, of course. But there should be a more permanent way of getting rid of them, I'd imagine."

It was then that we all turned to the schoolmaster, again. What did it say in that book of his about the white ant, we asked him.

Well, there was a chapter in his book on the destruction of termites, the schoolmaster said. At least, there had been a chapter. It was the last chapter in the book. But he had unfortunately left the book lying on his desk in the schoolroom over one weekend. And when he had got back on Monday morning there was a little tunnel running up his desk. And the pages dealing with how to exterminate the white ant had been eaten away.

Laugh, Clown, Laugh

"It's the clown," Johnny Coen said, starting to laugh all over again. "The tall clown in the fancy dress – yellow and blue and the smart way of walking. I could go to the circus and see it all through again, just to laugh at that clown. He kept a straight face even when they chucked the bucket of water over him. It was a real scream to see his new clothes getting all soaked . . . oh, *soaked*. And he went on standing there in the middle of the ring as solemn as you like, not being able to make out where the water came from, even."

Johnny Coen laughed as though he was seeing all that happening again, right in front of his eyes, and for the first time.

But Oupa Bekker said that what he liked best at the circus were the elephants. The way they stood on their hind-legs and the way they walked on bottles, Oupa Bekker said, balancing themselves to music. "It's years ago since I was last able to balance *myself* to music," Oupa Bekker continued, "leave alone walk on bottles."

"Or stand on your hind-legs," Jurie Steyn commented – not loud enough for Oupa Bekker to hear, though.

In the old days, there wasn't any such thing in the Transvaal, Oupa Bekker went on, as walking on bottles. Even though the whole of the Marico up to the Limpopo was elephant country in those days, Oupa Bekker said – and, in consequence, he prided himself on knowing something of the habits of elephants – he would never have imagined their walking on bottles.

If an elephant had seen a bottle in his path he would simply have walked over it. To him an elephant in those days was just an elephant, Oupa Bekker said.

And the same thing applied to lions, when the Groot Marico was lion country, Oupa Bekker added. To him a lion was just a *lion*, and not a bookish person that – that, well, we all saw what those lions *did* at the circus, didn't we, now? There was more than one white man in this part of the Marico that wasn't nearly as well educated as some of those circus lions, Oupa Bekker said.

Of course, he acknowledged that not every white person in this part of the Marico had had those same opportunities of schooling as the lions had.

Then At Naudé said that what he just couldn't get over, at the circus at Bekkersdal, were the trained zebras.

"And to think that this was also zebra country," At Naudé remarked. "But I would never have imagined a zebra wearing a red ostrich feather on his head, just like he's a Koranna Bushman. Or a zebra, while galloping down to the waterhole, first stopping to write something on a blackboard with chalk."

We spoke also about other animals that we had seen at the circus, and we said that the Groot Marico had at one time been that kind of animal's country, too. And all the time we had never known what those animals were really like. That sort of thing made you think, we said.

When Jurie Steyn was talking about the mule we had seen at the circus, that could jump six feet, and Jurie was saying that the Groot Marico was also mule country, Gysbert van Tonder suddenly gave a short laugh.

"And the clowns, that Johnny Coen was mentioning," Gysbert van Tonder said. "Well, it seems to me that for a pretty long while the Marico has been good clown country. And still is."

That was something that made you think, too, didn't it? – Gysbert van Tonder asked.

We were more than a little surprised, at a remark like that coming from Gysbert van Tonder. And several of us told him that we thought he should be the last person to talk. We proceeded to give Gysbert van Tonder some sound reasons, too, as to why we believed he should be the last person to talk. And some of the reasons we gave him had to do with things that hadn't happened so long ago, either.

This discussion would probably have gone on for quite a while, with each of us being able to think up a fresh reason every few minutes, when Chris Welman started talking about the fine insouciance with which the red-coated ringmaster cracked his whip.

The ringmaster didn't look very particular as to whether it was the gaily caparisoned horse he hit, or the blonde equestrienne hanging head downwards from the saddle, her golden locks trailing in the sawdust – so it seemed to Chris Welman, anyway.

"She didn't once stop smiling, either," Chris Welman said, "all the time the music played."

From the way Chris Welman spoke, it was apparent that, in the sounds discoursed by the circus band, his ear detected no harsh dissonances. Nor to his eye did the set smile of the equestrienne convey any suggestion of artifice. It was, however, significant that in his unconscious mind he had, indeed, established a link between two circus reciprocals – the music's blare and the set smile.

"After the circus was over and I had got back home, I was still thinking of her a long time," Chris Welman said. "I thought of her a good way into the night. I thought of her with the electric light on her hair, hanging down on the ground, and her spitting out the sawdust every time that it came into her mouth from the way she was riding, hanging down."

It was obvious that Chris Welman had occupied a ringside seat.

"But mostly I thought of her, about what she was doing after the show was over," Chris Welman said. "I pictured her there under that tent, locked up alone in her cage. It must be an unnatural sort of life, I thought, for a girl." And he winked.

We were able to put Chris Welman right on that point, however.

It wasn't that we had any sort of inside knowledge of circus life, of course, but we just went by common sense. It was only the more wild kind of performers in a circus that got locked in cages, we said. The tamer ones just got knee-haltered, we said, or tied with stakes with riems. So he was quite wrong in thinking of the blonde equestrienne as having to be locked in a cage after the show was over, we told Chris Welman. Likely as not they even let her go loose, we said. And we also winked.

Thereupon At Naudé said that that was the trouble.

And after we had pondered At Naudé's remark carefully, we realised that there was much truth in it.

A pretty girl, we said, if she was wild enough, was a lot more dangerous than any kind of lion. And no matter how fiercely the lion might roar, either, we said. Because all a pretty girl needed to do was to lower her eyelashes in a particular way, we said. And for that she did not have to be an equestrienne or anything else, we added.

It was only natural, after that, that the talk should turn on the subject of pretty girls in general. And it was still more natural that, before we knew where we were, we should be discussing Pauline Gerber.

What made it somewhat difficult for us to talk as freely as we would have liked about what we had been hearing of Pauline Gerber lately, was the fact that Johnny Coen was there, sitting in Jurie Steyn's voorkamer. And we knew full well how Johnny Coen had felt about Pauline Gerber, both before she went to the finishing school in the Cape, and after she came back from finishing school.

As it happened, however, Johnny Coen helped us out, to some extent, and perhaps without knowing it, even.

Gysbert van Tonder had just made the admission that, insofar as he was able to judge, Pauline Gerber was not only just the prettiest girl in this part of the Marico Bushveld, but also the most attractive. "If you know what I mean by *attractive*," Gysbert van Tonder added. "Otherwise I could tell you – "

That was when Johnny Coen had interrupted Gysbert van Tonder.

"No, no, you don't need to tell us," Johnny Coen said hastily, "not in words, and all that. And not when it's – when it's Pauline Gerber, I should say. You've told us things like that before today. About what you find attractive in girls, that is. And so if you perhaps don't say it all over again, we won't feel that we have missed anything. Because you've said it all *before*, that is."

After a few moments' reflection, Gysbert van Tonder conceded Johnny Coen's point. He had spoken on that subject quite a good bit, he acknowledged, but there was still just this one thing he wanted to say –

"Not now, please," Johnny Coen interjected. And he spoke so sharply, and with such unwonted heat, that Gysbert van Tonder shut up, looking slightly puzzled, all the same.

"I was only going to say – " Gysbert van Tonder concluded in an aggrieved tone, and left it at that. For if Johnny Coen was going to act funny, and so on, well, it was not a matter for him, Gysbert van Tonder, to have to go out of his way to help Johnny right.

"Well, I've only seen Pauline Gerber a few times since she's been back from finishing school," Johnny Coen said. And from the way he said "few" we knew that he wanted us to think it meant more than, say, exactly twice.

But, of course, we weren't really interested in the number of times that Johnny Coen had seen Pauline Gerber of late. What we were anxious to learn was how often the young schoolmaster, Vermaak, had been seeing her. For it was in relation to young Vermaak, and not to Johnny Coen, that a certain amount of talk was going on about Pauline Gerber.

"Well, the few times that I have seen her," Johnny Coen went on, "it was a bit difficult for me to know what to think, exactly. The first time I saw her the schoolmaster had just left. And the second time – I mean, *on another occasion* when I saw her at her house, she was sort of expecting Meneer Vermaak to come round. But what I want to say is that what Chris Welman said about the circus girl – why, that is exactly what I *feel* about Pauline Gerber. About how pretty she is, and all that. And what makes it still more queer is that she talks about herself like Chris Welman talks about the girl that rides in the circus.

"She feels she's shut up in a *cage*, Pauline Gerber says. To have to live here in the Bushveld, with everybody so narrowminded, Pauline Gerber says, is like being shut up in a cage."

Johnny Coen went on at considerable length, after that, acquainting us with the true nature of the sentiments he entertained for Pauline Gerber. But we were not interested. We did not in any way doubt the purity or sincerity of his feelings. Only, we were not concerned with all that. What we really wanted to know was what was going on between Pauline Gerber and the young schoolmaster. And it was apparent that Johnny Coen couldn't tell us more than what we already knew. It was a pity that Johnny Coen should be struck with such blindness, we thought. It would be better if the scales were to drop from Johnny Coen's eyes, we felt.

It was Oupa Bekker who brought the talk back to a discussion of the circus – which was, after all, where we had started from.

"Walking on, bottles," Oupa Bekker was saying. "Well, that's a new one for me. And I've known the Marico when it was elephant country. Unless, maybe, it was giraffe country. And what a giraffe would look like, standing on his hind-legs, I just can't think of, right away."

That was what gave Johnny Coen his chance to get back to the clowns, once more.

"The one clown poured water from the step-ladder out of a bucket on to that other clown that I was telling you about," Johnny Coen said. "And I just about laughed my head off, each time, to see how that other clown got soaked. And they have Natives to come running in from the back entrance with more buckets of water. And it all went over that clown. I enjoyed it more than I enjoyed the Chinese acrobat, even, who jumped through two wheels with knives in them. And all the time that clown didn't know what was happening. Every time I saw a Native come running in with another bucket of water, why I just about *died* laughing."

We gazed at Johnny Coen pretty steadily as he spoke. And we thought of what was going on between Pauline Gerber and young Vermaak, the schoolmaster. And all the time Johnny Coen went on feeling the way he did about Pauline. And we wondered if Gysbert van Tonder had been so far wrong, when he said that this was clown country.

The tears started coming into Johnny Coen's eyes, eventually, the way he was laughing about that clown.

Divinity Student

"For the way you're feeling now," Jurie Steyn said to At Naudé, "if you want my advice, I'd say you should go somewhere where you can get away from civilisation, for a bit. Nerves, that's what you've got. Why don't you go on a fishing trip to the Molopo for a week? You know – get right away from things."

Chris Welman had another suggestion to make.

"If you want my advice," Chris Welman said to At Naudé, "you'd go and camp for a while at the Bechuanaland end of the Dwarsberge. That's almost on the edge of the Kalahari. You've got no idea how desolate that part is. It's a howling wilderness, all right.

"You've got to be there only a day or two, and you'll forget that there ever was such a thing as civilisation. You could even take Gysbert van Tonder along with you. That should help your state of mind a lot. With Gysbert van Tonder around, the lower end of the Dwarsberge would look absolutely barbaric. Gysbert has got that effect even on a city, I mean."

Somehow, Gysbert van Tonder did not seem quite as pleased as he might have been at the subtle flattery conveyed in Chris Welman's speech.

"You go and –," Gysbert van Tonder started ungraciously. Then he bethought himself.

"Ah, well," Gysbert van Tonder ended up, "I suppose one can have too much of civilisation. And I am quite willing to believe that that is At Naudé's trouble – his listening in to the wireless and reading the newspapers every day. His brain has got too active. But you can be glad that that is a kind of sickness that you will never suffer from, Chris Welman."

Gysbert van Tonder seemed very pleased with himself, the way he made that remark.

Strangely enough, the friendly controversy in which Gysbert van Tonder and Chris Welman saw fit to indulge did not tend to allay any of the restlessness with which At Naudé's spirit was charged.

For At Naudé acted in what we could not help feeling was a quite singular fashion. First he half-rose to his feet, emitting a long moan. Then he suddenly slumped back again into his riempies chair, at the same time smacking the open palm of his right hand in a despairing manner against his forehead. His visage was noticeably contorted.

"All the same old childishness," At Naudé exclaimed, "that's supposed to be clever or that's supposed to be funny. I can't stand it any more, this heavy what's assumed to be Marico *fun*. If it's not Jurie Steyn doing it, it's Chris Welman. Or it's Gysbert van Tonder. And if it's not Jurie Steyn's wife, it's Oupa Bekker or it's *me*. And if it's not me, it's – oh, I tell you it's driving me mad. And when I switch on the wireless it's the same thing. It's either the Free State Monday Jokers or it's the Tuesday Choir of Comical Ouderlings or it's the Wednesday Half Laughs with the Upington District and Schweizer-Reneke/Kaokoveld Trek Boers.

"And then, when I try to escape from all that, and I come here to Jurie Steyn's post office to fetch my letters, what do I hear but somebody saying, 'That's a good one, ha, ha, ha'?"

It was clear to us that At Naudé was in a bad way. Gysbert van Tonder opened his mouth to say something, but Oupa Bekker nudged him to silence. We all felt that an unreasoned remark, at that moment, could have a very adverse effect on At Naudé. And we also knew that it would be no unique thing for Gysbert van Tonder to *make* an unreasoned remark. It was best that At Naudé should be allowed to talk himself out, we felt.

Some time in the future, making use of diplomatic skill, we would be able to point out to him, talking as man to man, the dangers to which he exposed himself, sitting day after day in his voorhuis alone, reading the newspapers and listening in to wireless programmes. If At Naudé went on like that much longer, he would become somebody learned before he knew where he was.

And where would At Naudé be then, in this part of the Groot Marico, if he had learning? Just nowhere, we felt.

"Another idea," Gysbert van Tonder suggested, "would be for you to go and pitch a tent alongside the Crocodile River. It's quiet enough there. At least, one of the banks is quiet, the one where there isn't much grass on. No, on second thoughts, I don't think you should go there. Because you might just by mistake pick the wrong bank – the one that the Crocodile River gets its name from. You'd be surprised how busy things can be on that side, in the season."

So Oupa Bekker said that if it was civilisation that At Naudé wanted to get away from, well, there was Durban. He had been to Durban only once, Oupa Bekker said, but it was enough. It was quite a story, too, how he got to Durban, in the first place, Oupa Bekker added. But Durban was quite a good place to go to, if you were sick of civilisation.

"The same old thing," At Naudé remarked to Oupa Bekker. "And I know exactly what you're going to say, too. It was in the old days. And you went there by mule-cart. Or you were a transport driver, and you went there by ox-wagon. And on the way back you gave a young student of divinity a lift as far as Kimberley.

"And years later you saw the young student of divinity's photograph in a newspaper. And he was a bit older then, but not much, for the years had treated him kindly. And then you realised, for the first time, that the young divinity student with the handsome sidewhiskers that you had given a lift to from Durban was Solly Joel. I don't know how often I haven't heard that kind of story."

When we spoke about it afterwards, we said among ourselves that the expression on At Naudé's face was quite fiendish.

"And if it wasn't Solly Joel," At Naudé continued, "it was some other Rand millionaire. And if it wasn't a student of theology or a Sunday school superintendent – but, no, it *had* to be. It couldn't be anything else. Without that, you oldtimers wouldn't think there was any point to your stories.

"I mean, I've never heard of any of you transport drivers giving a lift as far as Johannesburg to an Australian doing the three-card trick. But you must have, otherwise how could they have got there? No, it's either Solly Joel, or Wolf Joel, or Lionel Phillips or Sammy Marks – and they were doing nothing all the time but thumbing lifts on ox-wagons between Durban and the Rand.

"When did the Rand magnates find time to float their companies, then? Or time to have a bath in champagne – like we know they did? I tell you, it's more than a year, now, that I've been listening in to every wireless programme that's got somebody talking about life in South Africa in the old days. And you'd be surprised how many of them are transport drivers.

"It must have been a very healthy life, I should think, driving a heavily loaded ox-wagon from the coast to the Transvaal, before there was a railway. And sometimes, when one of these old transport drivers says that what he was bringing up from Durban was a big consignment of dynamite – and the announcer starts asking him questions over the wireless – I begin to hope.

"But it turns out, in the end, that it really was a healthy life. They had no trouble with the heavy load of dynamite to speak of.

"But there was a religious looking young man with handsome sidewhiskers that the transport driver gave a lift to. And that young man became the chairman of a mine that ends with the word *Deep*. And a Johannesburg suburb is today called after him. And that whole load of dynamite, from the coast to the Rand, didn't as much as singe the young theologian's sidewhiskers. You see, it's not that I don't like Oupa Bekker. My trouble is just that I've heard him and so often.

"There isn't a day passes but I hear something like 'Uit die Ou

Dae' over the wireless. Or 'Toeka se Tyd.' Or 'So het die Ou Mense Gelewe.' Or 'Ja, Nee.'

"And I get sick of it. I just can't help it, but I do. And then, when I come here and sit down in Jurie Steyn's post office, and I hear Oupa Bekker talk of the old days, and I realise that he didn't have any trouble with cases and *cases* of dynamite, either (I mean, otherwise he wouldn't be here), well, it isn't that I wish Oupa Bekker any harm, you understand.

"But I've heard everything he's got to say. Every time Oupa Bekker speaks it sounds to me as though he is being introduced by a wireless announcer, and as though there is somebody playing the piano for background effects. I mean, Oupa Bekker, isn't real to me, any more.

"Even the way he spits behind his chair – well, it looks to me like a *put on* sort of spit, if you know what I mean. I don't feel that Oupa Bekker is spitting just because he's got to."

We looked at At Naudé in amazement. It was clear that he was in a pretty bad way. There was no telling how far this sort of thing could go. We felt that we wanted to help him, if we could. The next thing he would do, he would start crying, and right there in front of us. And all because of his nerves. We had seen just the same thing happen before, with a stranger from the city.

The stranger had been with us for quite a while, and was really trying to understand us, and the things going on in our minds. And he was taking notes, even. And then one day – just like that – he started crying. We felt that At Naudé was going the same way, through too much civilisation that he was getting over the wireless and from reading newspapers.

It came as a relief to us – for At Naudé sake – to hear Oupa Bekker's voice once more.

"The last time I went to Durban wasn't in the old days, but two years ago," Oupa Bekker said. "And why I said that it was like a story was because I went there by train. I had never before in my life travelled so far by train. And that was a wonderful thing for me. Because I never would have believed, otherwise, that you could journey so far by train. We didn't once have to get out and walk. Or change to a post-cart. Or mount a horse ready saddled that would take us along a bridle path over the worst part of the rante – "

"Then it couldn't have been in the Union," Chris Welman shouted out, trying to be *really* funny. "You couldn't have been travelling over the S. A. R."

We were pleased that Oupa Bekker ignored Chris Welman.

"No trouble over the whole journey," Oupa Bekker continued. "It was only when I got off at the station and a Zulu came and pulled my portmanteau out of my hands. But I had never in my life seen a Zulu like that. He had bull's horns on his head and seashells on his feet. That was just how my grandfather had told me that the Zulus were dressed at Vechtkop."

We laughed at that, of course. After all, those of us who had been to Durban knew that about the Durban ricksha pullers. The way they dressed up to look ferocious. But all they did was to transport you and your luggage to an hotel.

"That sort of talk," At Naudé began, his lip curling, "and I suppose when you got to the hotel – "

"That's why I say that Durban is so uncivilised," Oupa Bekker explained. "Because it was only when we got to the hotel that the ricksha puller started apologising for all the boot-polish brown that was coming off his chin. He was working his way through college, he told me. He said it was more steady work than looking after babies or mowing lawns, the seashells on him rattling as he spoke. He was a divinity student, the ricksha puller said."

FINDING THE SUBJECT

WHEN LEON FELDBERG ASKED ME to write, as usual, for the Rosh Hashanah issue of *The South African Jewish Times*, it seemed that it was going to be straight forward enough. All that was needed – so it seemed – was for me to get a subject, something with a kind of angle on the relations between Jew and Gentile – the rest to be left to the typewriter and chance. In the end I was to find that the only part of the article that was simple was to be the writing of it.

Getting hold of a subject proved to be an almost insurmountable problem.

"Jew and Boer on the Platteland," Feldberg suggested. Done to death, I thought.

Then, "How about *The Merchant of Venice*? A new interpretation of Shylock?"

But I remembered many long essays that I had read on Shylock. Humbly, I felt that, if I were some day, perhaps, to throw a small amount of new light on the character of Shakespeare's Jew, it wouldn't be in the course of a thousand words turned out on the spur of the moment. I had just seen an advance notice of Edith Sitwell's *A Notebook on William Shakespeare*, to be published in England next month. "A phrase is studied and will be found to hold the whole meaning of the play. . . a work which serves to illumine Shakespeare's mighty and many-sided genius" – so the blurb to Edith Sitwell's book read.

Where would I be, among these writers of scholarly treatises, with my 1 000 word dissertation on Shylock, dashed off at speed?

A little later Edgar Bernstein suggested that I wrote on the subject, "The Jewish Contribution to South African Literature." Well, I would try, I reflected – especially as he lent me a little publication dealing with the Jewish Book Festival and containing a considerable number of informative articles from which I could crib. I paged through the booklet. Somehow the thought of rehashing the contents and dishing them up in a different form did not make a strong appeal to me. In any case, everybody would know that an article on these lines would not be the result of original research: they would all know where I cribbed it from.

I paged through the list of contributors. Ehrhardt Planjé, I read. Uys Krige. That seemed an idea. They found subjects to write about. I would learn from them how they did it. I might get a lead that way.

I tried Ehrhardt Planjé first. He was out.

But Uys Krige understood my problem right away. I said, "If I have got to start now going into the genealogies of South African writers, to find out which are Jews and which aren't – "

"That's exactly what the Jews complain about the Nazis having done," Krige said. "In any case, to discuss a specifically Jewish contribution to South African culture could become something like special pleading. It's an insulting thing to do to a people."

He explained that he wrote the article on Olga Kirsch because latterly she had improved very considerably, and he felt that after the way Greshoff had dealt with her, considerations of fair play demanded a more balanced assessment of her work, which had great and obvious merit.

"What about David Fram?" Krige asked. "Write about him. There's a good subject for you. Fram has got a far bigger reputation in America than he has in this country."

That seemed to open up possibilities. Meanwhile, I again tried to get hold of Planjé. That article he had written, "The Jew as Depicted in the Afrikaans Novel", was highly intriguing. Some years before he had written an essay, "The Elephant on the Monkey." He seemed good at titles. Perhaps he would be able to think out something equally good for me. I learnt, however, that Planjé had not yet come home.

Accordingly I tackled David Fram, whose great drawback in the field of literature is his excessive modesty. And this time Fram was not only modest. He was also sick. He could hardly talk. But he was able to supply me with a number of statistics. His temperature was

104. Of his poems, 60 per cent had a South African setting. He would not be able to move around for another fourteen days. His longest poem, "In Dorem Afrika", ran to 83 pages. He was taking medicine every three hours. His poem, "The Boers", was 3 200 lines in length. He had just taken three tablets, each containing 0.5 grains of Beta-phenyllisopropylamine sulphate.

There was not much doing there, it seemed to me. So I tried Planjé again. He had still not come home.

Thereupon I went for a stroll down Fox Street. I interviewed one or two Jewish businessmen I knew, explaining my difficulty. Couldn't they perhaps help me to get a lead? "What is the average Jewish businessman's attitude towards culture?" I asked the proprietor of a furniture shop. "Oh, just about the same as the attitude of the average non-Jewish businessman," the furniture dealer's clerk answered pointedly.

That gave me something to think about.

I mentioned the other alternative – an article on Shylock.

"Well, why not say that *The Merchant of Venice* is true to life?" the aforementioned clerk replied, his tone seeking to convey a light irony. "Look for how many years now writers have been apologising for Shakespeare or for the Jews, and have been trying to explain Shylock away. Why not just say, well, the pound of flesh and all that – is life not life? That's an original approach, isn't it?"

"It's original enough," I conceded, "but, I mean to say, isn't there enough anti what-you-m-call-it in the world as it is? No, I'm afraid your suggestion is out. Perhaps Planjé could put me on to something."

But Planjé, too, was out. He had still not found his way home.

Shortly after that I saw S. A. Rochlin. "Can you help me to get a subject to write on?" I asked him. "You know, I want to turn out something worthwhile, thought provoking and so on. Not just another goodwill potboiler."

"Do you know what I have got to write about for the Rosh Hashanah issue?" Rochlin asked me.

"No," I said, "I don't. What?"

"A survey of the history of the relations between the Jews and the Nationalist Party. That means I'll have to go back to 1912. Think how much research there is in that."

I shuddered. "You'll have to mention the 1932 Germiston by-election," I said. "A Jew, Schlosberg, was the Nationalist candidate. I wrote a number of articles, at the time, supporting him. He didn't get in."

But I wasn't getting any nearer to writing this article for *The South African Jewish Times*. And there was my photo going in, and all.

Suddenly I thought of Ignatius Mocke. I contacted him. And I regretted the fact, then, that I had not thought of him earlier. His conversation suggested not one article to me, but ten. Effortlessly and unconsciously, in practically every sentence he spoke, he produced a theme for something nice and chatty to write about.

"I had often thought that of the various races immigrating into this country," Mocke said, "the Jew would be able – and willing – to do most for Afrikaans literature." There was an article for you, I thought, readymade. "The Jews have the greatest capacity of any people," Mocke went on, "to appreciate and identify themselves with an indigenous culture." Again, something I could elaborate on, and expand into a couple of columns.

Mocke went on to say that he had been aware for a long time of how similar the Jew's background was to the Afrikaner's. "The struggle of these two small peoples for national survival and independence have many parallel features," he said. He added that, some years ago, when anti-Semitic propaganda began to be disseminated among the Afrikaners on an organised scale, he was in a position to know to what extent it formed part of a deliberate divide and rule policy employed by interests antagonistic to both Jew and Afrikaner. He said that he was able to throw a good deal of light on various aspects of what he called 'politieke kattakwaad.'

I realised that I should have got in touch with Mocke earlier. . . Perhaps I would remember about him before next Rosh Hashanah.

Up to the time of going to press, Ehrhardt Planjé had not yet got back home.

WRITING

THE OLDER I GROW, the more puzzled I get as to what life is for and how to live it.

Since my early adolescence I have had one fervent longing: to have twelve months of leisure in which I should be able to devote myself in exclusiveness and abandonment to the task of writing the things that have surged blindly inside me for expression. Just a quiet room somewhere and a piece of floor space to lie down on, and pen and ink, and a ream of 48-lb. cream-laid paper cut into quarto size. That is the one thing I have wanted all my life, and always it has evaded me. There have been times when I have seemed on the verge of achieving this ambition, and then on each occasion what has seemed to be the beginning of this period of leisure has in actual fact been but the prelude to fresh turmoil, the calm before the storm.

I can always get the ream of cream-laid easily enough, and my connections with the printing industry make it a simple matter for me to get a quad-cap ream cut up into the right sized sheets, and ink is cheap. A piece of quiet floor-space and a strip of hessian to lie on, though more difficult to procure, are not completely beyond the range of my organisational capacity. But it is then, when I have got all these things together, and I am well set on Act I, Scene 1 of a sublime high tragedy, and I have got to "Enter Bernardus van Aswegen" – it is then that the outside world enters with shouting and banners, and I proceed to roll up my strip of hessian and I sighfully set alight to the 48-lb. cream-laid, and I take the nib out of the pen-holder and break off the points and fasten a strip of folded paper to the back of it, and shoot it into the ceiling.

I don't remember, just off hand, how many times in my life I have got as far as "Enter Bernardus van Aswegen" – and at that point the world has entered, swearing and flat-footedly trampling. Sometimes it has been creditors. On one occasion it was the bailiffs. Once it was a demolition gang come to tear down the building. Once, also, it was the police. And always I have had to get up from the floor, with Bernardus's momentous opening speech unwritten.

I have got so, now, that I accept it as inevitable that there is a curse on Bernardus van Aswegen; he is bad luck; he will never be allowed to walk on to the centre of the stage, his brow furrowed in thought, his right arm raised dramatically to say: ". . . " But it is okay. I won't write down the opening words of his speech, which I know off by heart just as well as he does. I don't want this article to be interrupted, also. I have learnt cunning with the years.

And with the years I have begun, in some strange fashion, to identify myself with Bernardus van Aswegen. I feel that the world won't allow me to have my say. It gives me a queer sense of intimacy with Bernardus. What he feels, I feel. His hopes are my hopes. And we have both learnt this same truth from life, Bernardus and I – and it is knowledge as ineluctable as death – and that is that we are both doomed to eternal frustration every time we really want to open our mouths.

And I regret to say that with the years Bernardus van Aswegen has begun to grow embittered. There is today a cynical twist to the left part of his upper lip that I don't like. It doesn't help him to win and keep friends. And it is no use my trying to reason with him, either. "Aren't I as good as Lear?" he asked of me. "What has Othello got that I haven't got? And you know I can make rings round Hamlet, can't I?"

"Well, Bernardus," I reply, "I wouldn't say rings. But as good, yes. And there is that soliloquy I got for you on the death of your little daughter. But I started it all so long ago, and we have both grown so old in the meantime that I am afraid it will now have to be your little grand-daughter. And there is that opening speech, right in the beginning, in the first scene, when you say. . . "

"Oh, cut it out," Bernardus replies petulantly, "I never get so far. If it isn't creditors it's men with picks and shovels. Or it's a couple of johns from Marshall Square."

"Don't use such dreadful solecisms, Bernardus," I answer soothingly. "Remember you are a character in a great tragedy. Don't say 'johns.'"

And so it goes on.

But I am trying to write of life and its meaning, if any, and I have reluctantly come to accept a conclusion that has been persistently forced on me by external circumstances. And I can't evade this conclusion. Within my experience the same situation has repeated itself over and over again so often. I believe that, speaking strictly for myself personally, the practising of the creative art of letters is contrary to the laws and demands of life. It is always when I have turned out my best work, and I have got the right sort of recognition for it, too, in terms of people dubiously enquiring as to whether I think that I should go on writing at all – it is at these times, when my creative powers, such as they are, have been at their peak, that the worst kinds of disasters have invariably overtaken me.

And this is something I can't understand. I have become afraid to pick up the pen. Or, when I do pick it up, to dip it in too deep.

And this is something that, I have noticed, applies to other writers as well. Recently I read another biography of Edgar Allan Poe, in which the story of his life is related with a strict regard to chronology. I got to 1845. This year, states the biographer, was a year of great literary creativeness for Edgar Allan Poe. "Next year, 1846," I thought, "Edgar Allan Poe will have dropped in the. . . " I read on and found that, by 1846, he had.

Taking it by and large, it is far better not to write.

But I think I have solved the problem of Bernardus van Aswegen. I shall keep him out of the play until right at the end. He will enter only in the last scene of Act V. He comes on at the opposite prompt side. He knows his lines. He walks on to the centre of the stage and raises his right hand and just as he opens his mouth the curtain falls. Title: *Bernardus van Aswegen*, a Tragedy in Five Acts.